ENEMY OF THE PEOPLE

A KYLE DAWSON NOVEL

PETER EICHSTAEDT

WILDBLUE
PRESS

WildBluePress.com

ENEMY OF THE PEOPLE published by:
WILDBLUE PRESS
P.O. Box 102440
Denver, Colorado 80250

WILDBLUE PRESS is registered at the U.S. Patent and Trademark Offices.

ISBN 978-1-948239-21-9   Trade Paperback
ISBN 978-1-948239-20-2   eBook

Interior Formatting by Elijah Toten
www.totencreative.com

ENEMY OF
THE PEOPLE

Political extremism involves two prime ingredients: an excessively simple diagnosis of the world's ills, and a conviction that there are identifiable villains back of it all.

—**John W. Gardner**, 1912-2002, American educator, former US Secretary of Health, Education and Welfare, founder of Common Cause and the Corporation for Public Broadcasting.

CHAPTER 1

Tariq stared at the camera. *I will do this.*

Hot wind swept across the desert, pushing against him, rippling his black cotton shirt and blousy pants. A black scarf encircled his head, exposing only his dark eyes.

Two nine-millimeter automatic pistols hung loosely at his sides, each in a brown leather holster dangling from shoulder straps. A knife in his left hand, he felt invincible.

I was born to jihad. I have known that since I was very young.

Tariq put his right hand on the shaved head of the American journalist who knelt at his feet, a knee against the bound man's back. The journalist wore orange prison garb, mimicking the men in Guantanamo who Tariq considered his brothers in global *jihad.*

They stopped me from going to Somalia to join al-Shabaab. They stopped me from marrying the woman of my dreams. They wanted me to betray my Muslim brothers. They will suffer and pay for their arrogance.

Tariq glanced pitifully down at the journalist's pale skin and scruffy beard, the hands bound behind his back.

The prisoners call us the Beatles because we are British. But, we are not British. We were born on sacred Arab soil, then raised among the infidels. It was not of our choosing. The others say we are not true jihadis. But they lie. I will show them what a true jihadi does. They will tremble in awe.

Tariq lifted his eyes to the camera, drew a breath, and began to talk, his voice deep and resolute, muffled by the scarf. "I'm back, President Harris, and I'm back because of your arrogant foreign policy towards the Islamic state."

Tariq pointed the blade at the camera.

"You continue to bomb our people despite our serious warnings. You, President Harris, have nothing to gain from your actions but the death of another American. Just as your missiles continue to strike our people, our knives will continue to strike the necks of your people. You, President Harris, with your actions, have killed another American citizen."

Tariq waved his knife.

"This is also a warning to those governments that enter an evil alliance with America against the Islamic State to back off and leave our people alone."

Bracing his knee against the journalist's back, he grabbed the man's chin with his right hand and pulled up, exposing and stretching the throat. Tariq's stomach knotted. His heart pounded.

Do it! Do it!

With a furious burst, Tariq drew the thick blade across the American's neck, the blade biting , unleashing a torrent of blood spilling over the man's chest.

Moments later, Tariq's hands shook, his body pulsating with the pounding of his heart.

Calm yourself. This is for the glory of Allah.

The eyes of the American were empty, lifeless. He bent over the body to finish the job. He rolled the American's body onto its back and placed the severed head on the chest. He stood back to inspect his work. He exhaled, the task complete, his hands still shaking.

"How does it look?" Tariq asked the *jihadi* behind the video camera.

"Excellent," the *jihadi* said. "God is great."

"That will show the American infidels that we are serious," Tariq said. "God willing, they will all die if they try to defeat us."

Another *jihadi* handed Tariq a bucket of water and a rag. "Tariq, you are destined to be the face and the voice of all *jihad*."

"*In'shallah*," Tariq said. He dipped the knife and his hands into the water and washed, turning the water a deep pink.

CHAPTER 2

At the fitness club south of Santa Fe, New Mexico, Kyle Dawson hovered, his hands poised just above the wide, chromed bar that held 265 pounds in iron weights. On the bench below him was Raoul Garcia, whose face was taut and red. Raoul lowered the bar to his chest, held it a moment, then groaned as he pushed it back up, fully extending his arms.

Doubting he could hold the bar if Raoul's arms gave out, Kyle gripped it and guided it to the rack. The bar clunked into place.

Raoul exhaled noisily through puffed cheeks and stared up at Kyle.

"One more? Just one more?" Kyle coaxed, envious of Raoul's build and bulk.

"Remember," Raoul said, "you're next."

His face beaded with sweat, Raoul sucked in a couple of quick breaths as Kyle helped him ease the bar up and off the rack. Exhaling slowly, Raoul lowered the bar to within an inch of his chest, then struggled to push it back up. His elbows bent, his muscled arms quivering, the bar stopped moving upward.

Kyle grabbed it and strained, providing just enough lift for Raoul to get it back onto the rack. His armed splayed, Raoul panted and growled, "Holy mother of God." He sat up and massaged his triceps.

"They've got a gym up there at Vista Verde, don't they?" Kyle asked.

"They got every damned thing," Raoul said. "That's how we keep the trainees occupied. They're working out every day, twice a day."

"Must get boring."

"It's a lot of things, but it's never boring," Raoul said. "Most days, I feel like a drill sergeant. But it's a damned paycheck, so I can't complain."

"A damned good paycheck, from what I understand," Kyle said.

"They want me to work overseas again," Raoul said, his words hanging in the air.

"Let me guess. You told them you'd had enough of Iraq and Afghanistan."

"I've been lucky, Kyle." Raoul tapped each arm and leg. "I've still got my limbs. I know too many guys who don't. After a while, you wonder how many lives you have left."

"So, what do they want you to do? Or can't you talk about it?"

"Green zone security. Baghdad."

"At least it's not night raids hunting for *hajjis*."

"Been there, done that," Raoul said with a shake of his head. "I've got Miguel and Viviana to think about." He gazed at Kyle. "But family never stopped you, did it?"

That stung. Kyle swallowed hard, but Raoul was right. He'd spend the past dozen years moving from one war zone to another as a correspondent for the *Washington Herald*. A year each in Afghanistan and Iraq, mixed with stops in the Congo, Kenya, and Somalia.

But now he was back in Santa Fe where he'd started. His son Brandon was in the Santa Fe Little League and his daughter Erica was a standout on her high school freshman soccer team. He was seeing his kids regularly, no longer the absentee father who occasionally talked to them on Skype from parts unknown.

"How's Miguel doing, anyway?" Kyle asked.

"He's finishing his freshman year at UNM," Raoul said. "Came through with a 2.7 grade average first semester. Not bad, but I know he could do better."

"The first year is always tough," Kyle said.

Raoul shook his head. "He's got a girlfriend, already. I think he spends too much time with her."

"That can be a good thing," Kyle said. "Keeps him out of the bars."

Raoul stood and massaged his shoulders. "She's Iranian. Drop dead beautiful."

"What's her name?"

"Aliyah Muhadi."

"How did that happen?"

"Like it always does. Boy meets girl."

Kyle nodded. "Hmmm."

"Her father's a scientist," Raoul continued. "Fled the Ayatollah Khamenei. Now works at Sandia Laboratories in Albuquerque."

"Probably his reward for telling the CIA all he knows about the Iranian nukes."

"Probably."

"Physicist?"

Raoul shrugged.

"Does Miguel have a roommate?" Kyle asked.

Raoul nodded, drying his hands with a small towel. "A kid from the north."

"The north? As in northern New Mexico?"

"Yeah. Smart kid. Carlito."

Kyle nodded. "That's good."

"Yes and no," Raoul said.

"What does that mean?"

"The kid's a Muslim."

"What? Carlito? A Muslim? Everyone in northern New Mexico is Roman Catholic. Santuario de Chimayo and all that. Easter pilgrimage. People walking all the way up there from Albuquerque."

"I know," Raoul said. "The way Miguel explains it, Carlito hooked up with some people at a mosque over there in Abiquiu."

"There's a Benedictine monastery in the north. Christ in the Desert, it called. So, what's with the mosque?"

"That's all I know Kyle."

Kyle stared across the weight and workout room and out through the windows, remembering his first big story in northern New Mexico. He'd worked for the Santa Fe daily newspaper back then. It seemed like ages ago. "I knew a kid named Carlito from the north," Kyle said slowly. "I wonder if it's the same one. His father was shot and killed by the state police. I was there. The kid saw the whole thing."

"Shot and killed?" Raoul asked. "What the hell was going on?"

His mind swimming in a sea of memories, Kyle shook his head and focused on Raoul. "It was a land grant protest. It got real ugly."

"I guess so." Raoul pointed to the bench. "Your turn, buddy."

Kyle drew a deep breath, then glanced at one of several flat-screen televisions hanging on the wall. He lifted a hand. "Hold on."

The face of CNN's Anderson Cooper, cropped white hair and black rimmed glasses, filled the screen. "CNN has just learned that the Islamic state has released a video depicting the beheading of what appears to be American photo journalist Nathan Kennard," Cooper said. A grab shot of a man wearing an orange prison jump suit filled the screen. The man was on his knees, his arms tied behind his back, in front of a figure clad in black.

"The executioner in the video," Cooper continued, "who intelligence officials are calling Jihadi John, says that the killing of the journalist is in retaliation for US air strikes against Muslim extremists of the Islamic state, a territory carved out of portions of Syria and Iraq."

Cooper's face was replaced by another slightly blurred shot of the black-clad executioner pointing his knife at the camera, his voice barely audible in the blowing wind. "Intelligence officials in the UK and the US are analyzing the voice on the video in hopes of positively identifying the killer."

Kyle stared, his mouth agape, his stomach knotted. "That's Nate," he groaned, clenching his jaw as he stared at Raoul. "We worked together in Afghanistan."

His arms folded across his chest, Raoul shook his head in disgust. "Fuckin' animals."

"Nate went to Syria because no one was buying photos about the war in Afghanistan anymore," Kyle said.

"He jumped from the frying pan into the fire," Raoul said.

"They killed him, Raoul!" Kyle said, his throat tight, his voice rising. "They cut his head off!" He looked at Raoul with wide, angry eyes. His mind roiling, Kyle shook his head slowly, and still clenching his jaw, settled onto the bench. "Take a couple fifties off the bar," Kyle said. "I can't lift like you." As Raoul removed some of the plates, Kyle stared at the overhead lighting, his head filled with images of Nate's moments before his death. Kyle shook his arms to warm them.

"One seventy five," Raoul said. "You can handle that."

Kyle gripped the bar, and with a grunt, lifted it off the rack, his arms straining against the weight, his mind swirling with thoughts of Nate Kennard. He slowly lowered the bar to his chest, drew a deep breath, and groaning loudly, pushed the bar upwards, once, twice, then a third and fourth time before his arms began to burn.

"C'mon," Raoul said, staring down at Kyle's face. "One more."

Kyle lowered the bar to his chest, then sucked in a breath and emitted a loud "ahhhhgggh," as he pushed the bar upwards, his arms fully extended. He let the bar drop into the rack and stared at the overhead lights, his chest tight with anger.

CHAPTER 3

That evening, his face lighted by the glow of laptop screen, Kyle sat at the heavy wooden dining table that doubled as his writing desk. He scoured the internet for stories of how and why his friend and photo journalist Nate Kennard had been captured, despite the gnawing suspicion he already knew the answers. Information was coming to light from other journalists who were in and around the area at the time.

Kennard had been with a British freelance reporter named Eric McCovey, on assignment for the *London Telegraph*. McCovey had been writing about the weapons flowing to the Kurds and other Syrian rebels fighting the forces of Syrian President Bashir al-Assad.

Kennard and McCovey had stopped to file stories and photos at an internet café at a small town inside northern Syria and near the border with Turkey. They apparently figured it was safe since they were in rebel-held territory—certainly safer than the areas held by the Assad regime, whose police and army arrested and imprisoned journalists.

Kyle knew the Syrian rebels were a mixed bag. He'd been in Syria briefly and now tracked the war there from afar. The civil war had begun as a popular uprising in the spring of 2011 with short-lived, pro-democracy demonstrations. Assad responded brutally, as he had in the past, using his secret police and their ruthless military tactics. Civilian militias had formed for self-protection and within months morphed into the Free Syrian Army. Most western powers, especially the US, weary of the wars in Iraq and Afghanistan, had hoped Assad would fall quickly and cleanly. But Russia stepped in to prop up Assad, one dictatorship helping another, and as Syria's civil war dragged on, the popular uprising degenerated into chaos.

Kyle knew most news organizations kept their staff out of the mayhem and relied on Syrian reporters. Only a handful of foreign freelancers ventured into the fray, praying they'd make it out alive, but knowing their exclusive stories and photos commanded top dollar.

What made Syria more deadly than most war zones were the fundamentalist *jihadis* who had coalesced around a man named Abu al-Bakar. The man was an Iraqi religious scholar, a part-time Islamic fighter, and had served time in a US prison in Iraq. When the US pulled out of Iraq, al-Bakar and his followers became the Islamic State in Iraq and Syria, or ISIS.

Al-Bakar took advantage of the chaos and sent his fanatics into rebel-held towns and provinces, hanging people, mutilating women and children, and cutting off heads. ISIS grew exponentially, seizing Syrian oil fields and selling oil on the black market, much of it to Turkey. Flush with cash and weapons, ISIS demanded absolute obedience to its brand of oppressive Islam. They weren't alone. Other competing Islamic fundamentalist groups like the al-Nusra Front, an al-Qaeda affiliate, joined the fray, turning the territory in hell on earth.

Kyle's felt sick as the accounts of Kennard's and McCovey's capture raised more questions than they answered. One said after Kennard and McCovey had filed their stories and photos and had left the internet café near the Syrian border that day, their translator flagged down a taxi driver to take them to the small guest room where they'd stayed the night before to retrieve their bags.

Kyle wondered why then, with their gear and gags in hand, the two journalists had not crossed the border into

Turkey, but had driven deeper into Syria, southwest toward Aleppo and into the heart of rebel territory. He guessed they'd gotten a tip. *But about what?*

Along the way, McCovey and Kennard were forced off the road by a small white van, according to one account. The people in the van must have known who was in the taxi. *But how?* The taxi driver was a possible source, but more likely it was their translator, their "fixer."

Fixers were vital to foreign journalists working in war zones and were often local journalists who spoke passable English. In Muslim countries, fixers walked a fine line. Neighbors often viewed them as collaborators with western infidels—traitors to Islam, and as such deserved to die. Most fixers took the risk, however, hoping their work would get them a visa to the US. The lives of foreign journalists were in the hands of their fixers, so good ones were like gold. Bad ones were deadly.

Kyle drew a deep breath as his stomach soured. He remembered talking with Kennard about a story that had puzzled him ever since he'd been in Libya and written about the attack on the US consulate in Benghazi. Kyle's story had been about weapons, tons of them, that had disappeared from Libya after the fall of Muammar Gaddafi.

Kyle shook his head to refocus on McCovey's and Kennard's demise. After the van forced their taxi to the side of the road, three armed had men leapt from it, and at gunpoint, took Kennard and McCovey, the driver, and their fixer. The armed men were not Syrians because they apparently spoke Arabic with foreign accents. This meant the men in the van were probably Arab members of ISIS or al-Qaeda.

When he read that the taxi driver was set free, Kyle figured the Syrian fixer had been bribed, possibly threatened, into giving up the two western journalists. Kennard and McCovey then disappeared. Now, six months later, Kennard had been executed on camera by Jihadi John. Kyle felt sick, knowing the hell Kennard and McCovey had endured.

As he stared at the laptop screen, Kyle's mind drifted to a day a couple of years earlier when he and Kennard had worked together in Helmand Province, Afghanistan. It was spring and the poppies were in bloom and the Afghan opium harvest was peaking as the fat green bulbs laced with delicate pink petals bobbed atop tall stalks and oozed their precious milky sap, having been lacerated with razor blades. Kyle and Kennard rode with the Afghan police to do a story about the country's token poppy eradication program. They'd eaten a breakfast of eggs and *nan*, the chewy Afghan flat bread, and savored several cups of black tea inside the provincial governor's heavily secured compound in the provincial capital of Lashkar Gah. They'd climbed into the back seat of a dark green Ford Ranger pickup truck fitted with a double roll bar mounted with a .30 caliber machine gun. The back seat was cramped, but Kennard and Kyle sandwiched themselves inside, letting Daoud, their Afghan translator, a young man in his 20s, sit in the front seat beside the Afghan police driver. The truck was one of six in the convoy that included Afghan soldiers armed with AK-47s.

The convoy rolled through the capital on gritty roads of concrete and asphalt, slowing through the crowded commercial center, clogged with people milling about the streets, seemingly oblivious to the motor traffic, intent on what they were doing.

After horn honks and shouts from the soldiers, they were soon rolling along the wide graveled roads that networked the country, raising a thick plume of choking, chalky dust.

Kyle and Kennard kept the windows open, preferring the breeze despite the swirling dust and heat. About twenty miles outside the city, they encountered a convoy of behemoth MRAPs, the US army's mine-resistant, ambush-protected vehicles draped with camo netting and trailed by a cloud of fine dust that hung over the road like tunnel of fog.

They arrived at a sprawling mud brick farm house set amid a patchwork of fields of flowering poppies on the banks of the Helmand River, a shallow, meandering ribbon of brown water snaking southward from the distant Hindu Kush mountains, now just dark humps on the northern horizon.

Kyle recalled the historic irony of the region's lush and irrigated fields flanking the river. In the 1950s, in an effort to curtail the spread of communism by the Soviet Union, the US began a decade-long project to establish viable farming along the Helmand River. The river was dammed and an extensive network of canals was dug to direct water to the fields. But the Afghan soil was bereft of nutrients and nothing grew. Except poppies.

After a decade of failure, the farming project ended. The American engineers and agricultural specialists packed up and went home. But the water and canals left behind quickly became valuable. In the years that followed, Afghanistan became the world's largest supplier of opium, the raw ingredient to heroin, providing ninety percent of the world's market.

Kyle and Kennard had climbed out of their truck and surveyed the scene. A half-dozen gray-uniformed Afghan police took positions at the corners of the sprawling poppy field, their AK-47s at their sides. Several more heavily armed policemen surrounded the Afghan farmer and his two sons, who were backed against the mud-plastered walls of their farmhouse. The women remained, for the moment, inside and out-of-sight.

The farmer and his sons watched helplessly as the diesel engine of a sturdy gray tractor roared to life, belching black smoke in the still morning air, and backed off a low, flatbed trailer. The farmer was in his fifties, Kyle guessed, with a deeply creased, brown leathery face and a smudged gray skull cap on the back of his balding head. His soiled white *shalwar chamise* hung loosely from thin shoulders, the shirt tails dangling to his knees and covering blousy pants. Badly scuffed leather shoes, the heels broken down and laces missing, covered his feet like makeshift slippers. His two boys, young teenagers, were similarly dressed, their eyes wet with tears dribbling down their brown cheeks.

Speaking through Daoud, Kyle asked the farmer what the poppy harvest was worth. The farmer looked at him with glistening dark eyes and barked out a number. About $5,000, Daoud said, the family's annual income.

"Why do you grow the poppies?" Kyle asked.

The farmer shrugged. "Why does anyone grow anything?"

"Why don't you grow wheat?" Kyle asked, which was what the Afghan government said it wanted the poppy farmers to do, mostly at the insistence of the US and other foreign militaries occupying Afghanistan.

"Wheat takes too much water," the farmer said, shaking his head slowly. "And, there is no money in it."

They turned back to the tractor, which had lowered a steel frame fitted with multiple plow heads onto the ground at the edge of the field. The engine revved and the knobby back tires of the tractor rolled forward, the plows biting deep into the damp soil, uprooting the green and flowering poppies, turning them under.

Kennard had trotted ahead of the tractor to photograph it, capturing shots of the oncoming tractor with from within the midst of the poppy stalks. He'd then held up his hand for the tractor driver to stop. Kennard climbed behind the driver and motioned for him to continue as he grabbed his Nikon D-5 for video. The tractor driver shifted gears, the engine revved, and the tractor resumed its slow grind through the field.

Sounding like rocks striking the hard mud plaster, bullets smacked the farmhouse walls, followed by a staccato crackle of automatic gunfire. Kyle instinctively ducked and turned to find the source of the shots: an irrigation ditch skirting this and other poppy fields.

The Afghan farmer flinched, and with his sons disappeared through the blue painted doorway and into the mudbrick house. The lethargic Afghan soldiers and remaining police leapt from their trucks and knelt near the house, returning fire.

Kyle shouted at Kennard, who'd not heard the shots over the growling tractor engine, his eyes mashed against the viewfinder, his left hand gripping the lens. Kyle and Daoud scrambled to take cover behind a green pickup.

Moments later, a half dozen of the Afghan police humped along the edge of the field toward the source of the shooting, clutching their weapons. At the edge of the field, some paused to shoot, laying down a barrage of protective fire, and were followed by a cluster of other policemen, who advanced keeping low, then crouched and fired, holding the attackers at bay.

The movement had drawn Kennard's attention. He flicked off his video camera, stuffed it into his camera bag, and leapt from the tractor to the freshly plowed earth, tumbling to the ground. Kennard scrambled to his feet and stumbled from the field to join Kyle behind the pickup truck.

Kennard was panting. "What the fuck?"

"Someone doesn't like the government tearing up poppy fields," Kyle said.

"Taliban," Daoud said, then pointed over the bed of the truck to where figures with dark turbans near the river were shooting at the on-coming police and soldiers.

"I'm going after them," Kennard said, his eyes wide.

"You got what you need," Kyle said. "This story isn't worth taking a bullet, Nate."

But Kennard was already gone, sprinting after the assaulting force, bent low, his camera in hand, the strap wrapped around his forearm. "Shit," Kyle muttered, and drew a deep breath. He turned to Daoud, nodded, and said, "let's go." They humped along the edge of the field, following Kennard.

Flashes sparked from the barrels of AK-47s at the far edge of the poppy field, forcing Kyle, Daoud, and Kennard to dive to the dirt. Breathing heavily, sweat dripping down Kyle's forehead, he waited until the firing paused. Then nodding to each other, the three scrambled to their feet and joined the police, who'd taken cover behind the remains of a washed away mudbrick wall that paralleled the irrigation ditch.

The shooting stopped. After a few moments, Kyle lifted his head. What looked to be Taliban fighters, men dressed much like the farmer and wearing turbans, were beating a retreat, the Afghan police firing after them. But the attackers weren't done yet. They scrambled into the weathered ruins of another old farmhouse, nothing more than a square of low and weathered mudbrick walls, and returned fire, forcing Kyle, Daoud, and Kennard again behind the wall.

The air popped and snapped with automatic fire from the police AKs, then stopped again, leaving Kyle's ears ringing. He was tempted to glimpse over the wall again, but didn't, knowing his skull would be a target.

An Afghan policeman trotted up from behind carrying an old Russian-style rocket propelled grenade launcher, generating a burst of excitement among the Afghans, who shouted and pointed to the mudbrick walls about fifty yards away where the Taliban fighters hid. Kneeling behind the protective wall, the policeman lifted the RPG to his shoulder, took aim, and with a ferocious whoosh, the missile-shaped grenade shot out, trailed by a spiral of white smoke, then exploded into the low mud wall protecting the Taliban, reducing it to dust and dirt.

The policemen cheered, thinking it was a direct hit. For a long moment, silence. Kyle waited as a warm breeze blew and looked at what remained of the waving, chest-high stalks of flowering poppies in the adjacent fields. Poppies were tough and resilient, he mused, like the people who cultivated and harvested them. Gunfire suddenly erupted from the

Taliban position, the air popping once more, forcing the Afghan police and army to hunker down.

After a couple of minutes of silence, Kyle peeked over the wall. The Taliban shooters were fleeing, having made their statement against the Afghan national forces.

As Kennard followed the Afghan forces firing at the fleeing Taliban, Kyle looked back at the poppy field. The tractor had continued to plow the field, undeterred by the shooting, where the dark, freshly turned soil contrasted with the pale dirt and dust of the sun-dried land surrounding it. With just a few stalks still standing, waving defiantly in the breeze, destruction of the poppies was over. Ten minutes later the soldiers and police returned and stated the obvious: Taliban had fled.

Back at the house, the farmer wrung his hands, his eyes wet with tears as he viewed his mangled poppy crop, his livelihood and life destroyed. The plows now raised, the tractor chugged out of the field and back onto the low trailer.

Kyle tugged on Daoud's sleeve and nodded toward the police chief, a man with stripped epaulettes on his shoulders. Daoud called out to the chief, a thick-bodied man with no neck, shaved and rounded cheeks, and a thick, black mustache. Hands on hips, the chief narrowed his dark eyes.

"Why was this field targeted and not the others we passed?" Kyle asked.

The chief lifted his gray cap from his head and ran a meaty hand over his thick black hair. "I am not the one who makes that decision. You need to talk to the governor's office."

Eradication was supposed to push the farmers away from the poppies. Instead, it drove them into the arms of the Taliban, who controlled much of the opium trade. Farmers like the one whose field had been destroyed, Daoud explained on the return trip, got loans from the Taliban to grow the poppies and were obligated to sell the raw opium paste to the Taliban. In return, the Taliban protected them. Opium was their financial lifeblood.

"What will happen to this farmer if he's obligated to sell his opium to the Taliban?" Kyle asked. "Won't they kill him?"

The chief shrugged. "It is a risk that farmers must take if they make deals with the Taliban."

Later, back at the hotel inside the governor's compound, Kyle, Kennard, and Daoud sat on the stone steps in the cool of the evening. Daoud said the farmer's field had been selected because he was being punished. He was probably a relative of the local Taliban commander. Plowing the poppies sent a message to the Taliban: we know who you are and where you and your relatives live.

"The police know who's growing and buying the opium?" Kyle asked.

Daoud smiled and nodded, embarrassed at the truth. "Everyone makes money from the opium. The government, the police, the army. And, of course, the Taliban."

"So everyone is in on the opium trade?"

Daoud nodded. "It's the only export Afghanistan has." He took a pack of cigarettes from the folds of his *shalwar chamise*, tapped out a cigarette, and lit it with a gas lighter. "A few years ago, the former governor was removed because he had three hundred pounds of raw opium in the basement of his office, right over there." He pointed to a plastered and painted office building in the middle of the compound.

"The whole eradication program is joke," Kyle said.

Daoud nodded again. "Poppies can never be eliminated."

"A field here and a field there are destroyed each year," Kyle said, "but only to appease the foreigners?"

Daoud drew on his cigarette and stared silently.

A few days later, Kyle's story was on front page of the *Washington Herald* along with Kennard's color photo of the tractor ripping through the field of pink and green poppies.

Kennard had lived a full life, but it had been cut short. Kyle swallowed hard and sucked in a halting breath.

CHAPTER 4

Tariq loved the noisy snap of the large black flag of the Islamic State flapping above the cab of his tan Toyota HiLux pickup truck as it tore down the street. It reminded him of the crackle of gunfire that put the fear of Allah in the hearts of men. The truck slowed at one of the large and open plazas of the ancient Syrian city of Raqqa, where men and women lined the periphery, eyes averted, heads bent. Some of the women were on their knees, dressed in black as they wailed and pleaded, their arms outstretched, fingers interlocked in supplication.

At the base of what was left of a toppled statue, now chunks of stone scattered on the patched concrete and asphalt, a dozen men were also on their knees and blindfolded, their hands bound with wire behind their backs. A single *jihadi* fighter stood behind each kneeling man, the fighters wearing camouflage pants, tunics draped around their shoulders, heads wrapped with black scarves, revealing only the flash of their dark eyes. Each pointed the barrel of an automatic pistol or an AK-47 at the back of the kneeling men's heads. A *jihadi* screamed and raised his hand high, then shouted a command. Shots echoed. Bodies fell forward to the pavement. More gunshots popped as the executioners riddled the dead, insuring their fate.

Tariq watched with satisfaction, then glanced to the wooden platform built for public hangings. The population was being purged of *kafirs*, the non-believers, the deceivers, the disrespectful. It was a necessity if the goals of *jihad* and the Islamic State were to be achieved.

Bloated and discolored bodies hung from the metal racks atop the platform, arms still bound and sliced to the bone with wires, skulls crushed and broken, eye sockets empty and black with dried blood. Tariq nodded to the driver, who slammed the truck into gear and revved the engine, the truck tires screeching, spewing white smoke as the HiLux lurched from the plaza.

After pausing at a checkpoint, the truck was waved through by the coterie of armed men, their heads swathed in black cloth, then soon rolled to a stop at the front of a stone building. Tall Arabic-styled windows with pointed arches flanked the entry door. Tariq stepped from the truck cab and hurried to the entrance where two more well-armed men, their heads also wrapped with turbans, their eyes defiant and fearless, blocked his path. Tariq stepped back, then let his pistols and holster straps slip from his shoulders, along with his knife and sheath. He stood with his arms outstretched as the guards patted him down, nodded, and waved him inside.

The foyer was cool and Tariq hurried down a darkened hallway, his blood-stained desert boots sounding softly along the tiled corridor as he followed his escort to a large door. The escort lifted a hand, bowed his head, then pointed to Tariq's boots, which Tariq unlaced and put beside the other shoes and sandals lining the hallway.

The door opened, revealing a man in gray robes and black turban. The man looked Tariq up and down, as if he were an apparition, then raised a hand for Tariq to wait outside a moment. The door clicked closed. Tariq heard muffled voices behind it, then the door reopened. He was motioned in.

Stepping inside, Tariq leaned against the wall and paused beside the door, which closed quietly. Hands clasped in front of him, he scanned the room. Abu al-Bakar, the caliph and leader of the ISIS, sat against the far wall on thick, red silk cushions, his arms resting in his lap. Tariq's stomach knotted as he became increasingly nervous, more nervous than he'd ever been. His throat was tight and his mouth dry, his head pounding as his forehead beaded with a thin layer of cold sweat. He had no idea why he had been called or what he should say and do. Despite his jumbled emotions, Tariq was thrilled to be visiting the man he had revered. Abu al-Bakar was his true father, he believed—not his birth father, a man he despised, a weakling, an apostate who had succumbed to the world of the Christian crusaders.

Abu al-Bakar, his dark eyes set in a round face, his beard long and full, lifted his manicured hand and signaled for Tariq to wait.

As he stood absolutely still, Tariq looked upon the man as a kindly cleric, convinced al-Bakar was not, as the Christian Crusaders claimed, the leader of the world's most vicious and successful jihadist movement since the death of Osama bin Laden. Al-Bakar spoke softly to the half dozen men seated in a circle facing him, then dismissed them, saying they'd gather again after their midday meal. The men quickly rose, murmuring to each other, then bowed and filed past Tariq and out the door.

Al-Bakar motioned for Tariq to sit beside him, waiting as Tariq settled onto a nearby cushion. They sat in silence as the barefoot aide disappeared and moments later returned to place between them a silver platter with an ornately engraved and polished silver teapot and two clear glass teacups in gleaming metal holders. The aide poured green tea into each glass cup, then turned and left. Al-Bakar lifted the lid to the ceramic sugar bowl and emptied two teaspoons of sugar into the steaming, pale liquid, stirring slowly with a small silver spoon.

Tariq did the same, his hands cool and twitching with anxiety, despite the heat.

Al-Bakar gently cleared his throat. "You have accomplished many things for the glory of Islam," he said, stroking his beard slowly as he let his tea cool.

"God is great," Tariq replied, raising the steaming liquid to his lips for a sip. It burned.

"We have brought the infidel scum to their knees," al-Bakar said. "Soon all of Syria will be ours. Then, God willing, we will have Baghdad and all of Iraq."

"The rise of the Islamic State is the will of Allah. It cannot be stopped," Tariq said. "I pray that I can continue to serve God in this way."

"Your execution of the foreign journalists and the other *kafirs* sends a message to the cowardly crusaders. We are proud of your work."

"I am most grateful."

"Now, you must listen carefully."

Tariq swallowed, his throat thick with expectation, and nodded.

"I have another, even more important mission for you."

"I am prepared to do whatever you ask."

"God willing, we will be able to sever the head of the Great Satan."

CHAPTER 5

Tariq's feet ached. He and his men had been walking in the Sonoran Desert for two days now. The soft shuffle and tramp of their feet was monotonous, mind-numbing. Yet, the anger burning inside propelled him forward. *If they have lied to me, they will surely die.* Tariq clenched his teeth, mashing his lips tightly. *And if they have told the truth, they will also die.*

Tariq worried they'd been walking in circles. Yet, he and the other *jihadis* trudged through desert scrub, following their two Mexican guides, their coyotes. He liked the term coyotes because it meant the Mexicans were animals, a species of dogs. It would be easy to kill them. Tariq chuckled silently to himself. They were not *like* dogs, they *were* dogs. *I will take care of them as I would any dog, but only when the time comes.*

It was late in the day and the air was warm and dry, the wind and the gritty soil of this northern Mexican desert reminding him of eastern Syria. *I am a Kuwaiti. I am of the desert. The desert is my home. My home? What is home? I am a jihadi now. Now and forever. I have no home on this earth. My home is in heaven with Allah.*

He and his men had traveled far, first crossing the border from Syria into Turkey, then riding in panel vans to Istanbul. There, they'd shed their *jihadi* garb and bought jeans and western shirts in the sprawling, open air markets where no one gave them a second glance and gladly took their cash.

They had arranged for airline tickets, and using forged passports, had flown from Istanbul to Mexico City, a nerve-wracking, circuitous route with connections in Madrid, then Caracas, and on to Mexico City. But it had worked. They had purchased round-trip tickets to avoid suspicion, though they had no intention of returning. They were met at the Mexico City's Benito Juarez airport by their cartel handlers and taken to a hotel near the airport. The next day they'd flown north Hermosillo, where two vans had taken them to the town of Altar. It had all gone smoothly. *In'shallah.*

Once at Altar, their coyote, José, had balked when Tariq said he needed to buy weapons. It was not part of his agreement, José said. He was only going to take them across the border. He was not going to get involved in any other business.

José was a solid man, with thick salt-and-pepper hair, curly sideburns widening as they descended his cheeks. He wore a straw cowboy hat and had the beginnings of a belly. José's thick thighs filled his jeans from the years of walking. His scuffed hiking shoes seemed molded to his feet. José had a partner, a slighter, thinner version of himself, a man named Fernando, who said little but seemed to know José's every thought and move.

At the clothing store in Altar, Tariq and his men bought the clothes and backpacks to make them look like Mexican migrants. Each now wore a baseball cap, desert camouflaged cargo pants and a hooded camouflaged sweatshirt. In each backpack was a gallon jug of water, a package of tortillas, and plenty of dried beef. *What did they call it? Jerky? A stupid name.*

José had no choice, Tariq had said. He and his men needed weapons and José would get them. Otherwise, Tariq said, he would find someone else to take them across the border. After calls back to Syria and calls to José's cartel bosses, a dozen AK-47 pistols were secured, each light, short-barreled, and reliable. Tariq preferred them, having used them in Syria. Each had a pistol grip and wooden front grip, making it easy to control as the barrel spewed death and destruction. Best of all, the weapons came with a 30-round magazine and each man carried a dozen magazines. Tariq touched his nine-millimeter Beretta, the one he carried in the waistband of his pants. He had another in his backpack.

Tariq trailed José along the barely discernable path around the spindly bushes and squat trees dotting the landscape, keeping back a short distance. Tariq didn't like José, whose face remained hidden under a baseball cap and behind sunglasses. José also carried a 9 mm pistol in a black nylon holster attached to his belt at his right hip. Tariq knew José would put up a good fight, given the chance. He'd take José by surprise.

But not now. He needed José—at least until they crossed the border. He didn't trust José and knew José didn't trust him either. José was arrogant, a mental condition that affected most western infidels, and the Mexicans were the worst. They had treated Tariq and his men like dogs. *But,* Tariq thought, *they are the dogs and I know what to do with dogs.*

José stopped suddenly, turned and stared at Tariq, then motioned to a cluster of small bushes that offered mottled shade. "We rest here for a couple of hours," he said.

Tariq shook his head in disgust, wanting to continue the trek. But a pang of hunger pierced his stomach. Maybe José was right. He drew a breath, looked to the others, and speaking in Arabic, said, "Time to rest. Drink water. Eat something." Tariq dropped his backpack in the thin shade of a desert bush. Once settled on the dirt, Tariq twisted the top from his nearly empty water jug and gulped thirstily.

The water was warm and tasted of plastic. Tariq longed for the crisp, cold water that came from the deep desert wells. It refreshed the lips, the mouth, and the soul, he thought. *God's water.* He had an impulse to spit out the warm water, but thought better of it, knowing that he needed every drop for the rest of the journey. He replaced the lid and pushed the jug into his pack. Tariq scrambled over to José, settled beside him, and asked, "How much further?"

"Be patient, my friend," José said. "It is hot now and necessary for us to rest."

Tariq had a mission and did not want to waste time. *I won't take orders from you much longer.* He then growled, "Answer my question! How much further?"

José winced, irritated at the tone in Tariq's voice. José pulled the sunglasses from his face, then glanced at the sky as if asking God for relief. He dropped his gaze to the horizon, squinted as he scanned the desert terrain, then said, "Two hours. Maybe three."

"That's what you said three hours ago, Mexican!" Tariq barked. "You guaranteed that we would cross in two days. It has been two days. Your time is finished."

José glared, his dark eyes glistening. "We wait until dark," he said with finality. "Otherwise *la migra* will see us." He paused, knowing Tariq understood he was referring to the US Border Patrol. "Is that what you want?"

Tariq clenched his jaw, exhaled slowly, and forced himself to be calm. "If they find us, you're a dead man," he said, then looked at Fernando. "Him, too."

José narrowed his eyes, struggling to contain his anger. He slowly moved his hand to his sidearm.

Tariq yanked his own pistol from his waistband and thrust it inches from José's face.

José slowly raised his right hand and smiled as he showed Tariq his empty palm. "Get some rest," he said. "Then we will go."

Tariq glared for a long moment, lowered his pistol, and returned to the shade of his bush. Again, he turned to his men, and raising his hands, said, "It is time for us to pray."

There was no dissent. His men had been carefully picked for their dedication and devotion to Islam, to ISIS, and to Abu al-Bakar. Tariq pulled his thin prayer rug from his backpack, unfurled it with a shake, and spread it on the dirt toward what he guessed was the direction of Mecca. Satisfied, he stood at one end of the rug, hands clasped in front, and with eyes closed, silently recited his prayers. He dropped to his knees, and with his eyes still closed, bent forward to press his forehead to the rug.

His prayers finished, Tariq spread the rug beside his backpack. Despite his exhaustion and his distrust of José, Tariq lay on the rug, resting his head against his backpack. He was reluctant to close his eyes, but fatigue overcame him. As the warm desert breeze brushed his cheeks, he dreamt of walking on the desert sands of his native Kuwait. He dreamt he was alone and felt the desert wind against his robes as he trekked across crusted dirt and rocks. He heard the voice of his father calling him, and even as he felt the tug of that ancient longing, his anger smoldered. Dressed in western clothes, his father reached out for him. As Tariq watched unmoved by his father's appeal, the man's image faded.

Then in his dream, Tariq heard a soft voice calling his name, like a whisper, yet laden with yearning and sadness. Tariq strained, and seeing the face of his fiancé, his desire for her burned hot. But he couldn't move. He was frozen in place, and as much as he strained, he couldn't reach her. She was a shimmering apparition, her silky scarfs caressing her face, revealing only her eyes, dark and mysterious. He called out, "Fiona, Fiona."

Tariq jerked awake to the sound of his own voice. He blinked and looked around. The dream gone, but the image of Fiona lingered. But his anger soon returned, stronger than ever, as he remembered he'd been banned from traveling to see her. The British government had refused to let him travel from England to Kuwait so he could marry Fiona due to his known affiliations with Islamic fundamentalists. Fiona's family then decided Tariq was too much of a risk for her. Their daughter could not marry him, despite the protests lodged by Tariq's father that his son's problems with immigration authorities were only a misunderstanding.

Tariq sat up and looked around to get his bearings in the waning light of the day. The sun had set and the ache and tiredness had melted from Tariq's feet and legs.

José looked at Tariq and nodded. "We can go now, since you are in such a hurry."

Tariq stood and called to his men, "We must go."

CHAPTER 6

The sun had dropped below the western horizon, painting the sky orange and red. The air was cooler, almost comfortable. They'd been walking for two days and a night, falling easily into the rhythm of the slow, steady trek across the desert. Tariq lifted his eyes to the fading sky and thanked *Allah* that so far, nothing had gone wrong. *"Allah akhbar,"* he whispered.

Soon the shadows were gone, along with the light. Tariq felt like he was drowning in a sea of numbness and monotony, unsure of where he was or where he was going. *We must be in the US by now.* He had studied the maps and knew that once they had entered the low, rugged mountains with the stunted and twisted pine trees, they were at the border. *How long have we been in this terrain? Why has José said nothing about it to me?*

Tariq pressed the button at the side of his wrist watch and the dial glowed green for a moment, then faded. 9:43 p.m. They'd been walking for nearly three hours since their last break. Of course they were in the US now, because they'd walked up and down the sides of low mountains, snaking between the hills, now humps in the darkness. Tariq turned to his comrades, all shadowy figures shuffling behind him.

Tariq froze at the ominous sound of a helicopter thudding through the night sky. His heart pounded, his throat tightened.

José waved his hands and shouted, *"Corréis! Escondéis!* Run! Hide!"

Tariq mimicked José, waving to the others to disperse and hide. His men knew what to do and dove under the stubby trees and bushes, huddling against rocks—anything they could find. Tariq crouched under a bush, closed his eyes, and covered his ears as a Black Hawk chopper swooped low, dust and grit swirling and pelting his face. The chopper disappeared into the distance, then turned for another pass. Tariq pulled out his pistol and scrambled over to José who crouched under a small tree. Tariq pointed his gun at José's head. "They've found us!" Tariq growled.

José stared, his eyes wide with fear. His left hand extended, José's right hand hovered above his holstered pistol.

"Don't!" Tariq growled with a shake of his head.

José's hand quivered an inch above the grip, his breath short.

Tariq jammed the gun barrel against José's chest.

José slowly raised his right hand. "Don't … kill … me," he said in his halting English. "I beg of you. I have a family." José glanced anxiously to the dark sky as the helicopter thudded closer, its bright spotlight sweeping the ground with stark white light.

Tariq squinted as the chopper moved closer, like an airborne demon thundering through the night.

Tariq caught movement in the corner of his eye as José grabbed for the pistol at his side. Tariq reflexively pumped two rounds into José's chest, the *crack-crack* of the shots muffled by sounds of the approaching Black Hawk.

The chopper arched upwards, the spotlight having found its prey, then turned in a tight circle and hovered for a moment over Tariq and his men, floating and churning the air with dust and grit. The chopper's spotlight cast a cone of intense white light on the men cowering beneath trees and bushes, their heads down and covered with camouflaged hoodies.

Dust swirled as Fernando, the second Mexican coyote, crawled on his hands and knees to the dying José. He stopped and looked in horror at José's bloody chest. He raised one hand in surrender, and using the other to shade his eyes from the bright spotlight, squinted and blinked in the swirling air.

Tariq pointed the Beretta at Fernando and shouted, "How far away to the pickup point?"

Fernando gestured to the distance, waving and pointing. *"No lejo.* Not far! *Alla! Alla!* There! There! *Por favor, señor.* Please,"* he said, begging Tariq not to kill him.

Tariq fired. Fernando's head snapped backwards, his body twisting and falling to the dirt.

At the sound of the gunshots, the Black Hawk lifted and turned sharply away. After retreating about one hundred yards, it swiveled back toward them, hovering at a safer distance and angling the spotlight again at Tariq and his men.

Tariq ducked behind a bush, and sinking a hand inside his backpack, extracted his AK-47 pistol. His back to the light, he fished a banana clip from his pack and snapped it tight into the weapon. Shading his eyes with one hand, he shouted for his men to grab their weapons. The chopper again floated toward them as the spotlight washed the ground.

Tariq caught movement as five or six Border Patrol agents emerged from the shadows, weapons drawn.

"Alto! Alto! Manos arriba!" the first agent shouted.

"Stop. Put your hands up," another shouted.

Tariq wheeled, and holding his AK-47 at his side, shouted to the others in Arabic. "Kill them!"

Shots erupted, Tariq's men firing and killing three of the green-clad agents. The remaining agents returned fire, sending one of Tariq's men to the ground, clutching his chest.

Holding his AK-47 pistol at his side, his left hand grabbing the barrel guard, Tariq squeezed off a burst of three shots, the bullets pinging as they penetrated the metal skin covering the nose of the chopper. The spotlight still shined. He fired another burst and the chopper's spotlight went dark.

The Black Hawk pulled up like a surprised and wounded animal, exposing its belly. Tariq squeezed the trigger and raked the bottom of the Black Hawk, bullets banging into the riveted steel of the wounded chopper, which rose and swooped away, disappearing into the darkness.

The chopper gone, the hillside fell eerily silent, the air thick and black as coal. Any remaining border agents had fled, Tariq guessed, or were hiding nearby, having seen they were outnumbered and outgunned. Tariq dropped to his knees, his chest heaving, the taste of dirt in his mouth, dust floating in the air. Clutching his weapon, he stood unsteadily, his breath heavy and short.

In the darkness Tariq found José's backpack. Searching it, he found the flashlight José carried. He flicked it on, and pointing it to the ground, let his eyes adjust to the shaft of light, even though the light might draw a shot. It didn't. A moment later, he moved toward the moans of his wounded *jihadi* fighter and shined the light onto the man's face. The dying man's eyes glistened, his chest soaked with blood, his breath labored and gasping. The man licked his lips and whispered, *maá*, begging for water.

Tariq held his Beretta to the fighter's head, but hesitated to pull the trigger. He could not afford to lose a single man because it might compromise the mission. But a badly wounded *jihadi* was useless and would only slow them down. And if they left him behind and still alive, he could be captured and tortured into talking. That possibility was intolerable. "*Allah akhbar*," Tariq said softly, then pulled the trigger. The fighter's head jerked, blood spurting from the man's temple. Tariq's stomach clenched. Though he had killed many men with his own hands, shooting a friend was different. Tariq wretched and gagged, the bile burning his throat and nose, then spit and wiped his mouth with his sleeve.

Tariq stood again and swung the flashlight to shadowy movement in the distance. Two green-clad US border agents scrambled up the hillside and away from them, attempting to flee.

Stop!" Tariq yelled at the agents, then fired several shots over their heads. He flicked off the flashlight, then paused and listened, but heard nothing but the agents' frantic footsteps.

"Capture them!" Tariq barked to his men in Arabic, waving his gun and pointing, as the agents' backs disappeared among the bushes. "But don't kill them."

Tariq's men fanned out and clambered after the agents, following them in the faint light now provided by a slice of the recently risen moon. The scrambling footsteps of his men faded. Then he heard nothing, as if the world had stopped.

Shots broke the silence, flashing sparks piercing the darkness, coming from up the slope. The border agents were less than fifty yards away and firing at their pursuers. His men returned fire, prompting sporadic shots from the agents, who Tariq guessed would soon be out of ammunition. Tariq trotted up the slope toward his men, who were spread throughout the trees and bushes. The firing stopped. After a pause, he broke the silence and shouted, "Drop your weapons, and you will live."

The border agents fired in his direction, the bullets ripping through the branches of the nearby trees.

"We don't want to kill you," Tariq shouted. "Drop your weapons and you will live. Or, you can die here and now. It's up to you."

The agents replied with another burst of gunfire.

Tariq wondered how much ammunition each agent carried, guessing it was minimal. They could not have anticipated an extended fire fight, but didn't want to be captured alive. Tariq continued up the slope, despite an occasional shot, pausing to listen as his men closed in, stepping clumsily through the darkness. Neither he nor his men could afford the expenditure of more ammunition, but they had no choice.

A few moments later, one of his men shouted gleefully in Arabic: "We have them! Come now, Tariq! We have them!"

Tariq' heart leapt and his lungs ached as he hustled up the slope until he faced the two agents standing back-to-back, their fearful eyes glinting in the dim moonlight. The two agents pointed their weapons at their captors.

"Drop your weapons," Tariq ordered in his accented British English.

"Fuck you," one agent growled.

Sizing up their situation, the other said, "It's our only chance." The agent lowered his pistol, and after a moment, so did the other.

"Drop them," Tariq ordered.

The agent's weapons clunked to the dirt and each slowly lifted his hands. "Out of ammo," the second one said.

"Grab them!" Tariq barked.

His men leapt forward and seized the two agents.

"Take us to your trucks," Tariq said. Motioning to his men, he spoke in Arabic. "Go back to where the other agents were. Collect all the weapons you can find. Strip the dead of their clothes. Hurry. We have very little time."

With their weapons at the agent's backs, Tariq and his men ambled down the sparsely vegetated slope and soon were at three white-and-green Border Patrol pickup trucks, each with a large container unit mounted in the truck bed and designed to carry eight captive migrants. Tariq pulled off his shirt and pants and stuffed his clothes into his backpack, telling his men to do the same.

He put on a green Border Patrol shirt and pulled on a pair of pants they'd stripped from one of the dead agents. He fitted a border patrol cap onto his head, as three of his men did the same. Tariq stepped away, and taking a satellite phone from his backpack, tapped in a number. "*Sal'am alekum,*" he said, speaking rapidly in Arabic. "We must change the pickup point. I will call you in one hour and tell you where."

Tariq turned to his men, motioned them close, and explained the plan. Without a word, they split up, several climbing into one of the mounted container units, the rest in the other, then pulled the doors shut.

Inside the cab of the first truck, Tariq held his gun to the head of one of the captured border agents, who now sat behind the driver's wheel. "You're going to drive us to freedom, my friend. At the checkpoint, you tell them you have the Mexicans in the back and you need to get us to Tucson, fast. Any problems and I'll kill you. Understand?"

The agent nodded, clenching his jaw.

Tariq turned to the cab of the second truck. Another of his men, also dressed as an agent, had climbed into the passenger side of the cab, and like Tariq, held a pistol to the head of the second border agent, who also was driving. He signaled he was ready. The truck engines revved and the two trucks nosed into the darkness.

***

Twenty minutes later, the Border Patrol trucks turned from a dirt road in the Pajarita Wilderness Area of the Coronado National Forest. It was a lightly protected border region and the trucks rolled along the paved, two-lane highway in the darkness of the desert night. Tariq tensed as a cluster of pole-mounted floodlights glowed in the distance, bathing a remote Border Patrol checkpoint in harsh, white light. Tariq motioned for the agent to slow. "Do as I say and you won't get hurt."

Tariq pulled a simple, palm-sized walkie-talkie from his pocket and clicked it on. "We're coming to a check point," he said in Arabic to his fellow *jihadi* in the second truck. "Be calm. Don't say anything. Tell the driver to do the talking. Keep your weapon out of sight. *Allah akhbar.*"

The two Border Patrol trucks slowed as the truck lights shined on rows of orange traffic cones, flanked by more Border Patrol vehicles parked at the roadside, guiding traffic into a single lane where a lone Border Patrol agent waited in the glare, watching warily as the trucks approached.

Tariq withdrew his gun from the ribs of the driver, who gripped the steering wheel casually with his right hand, keeping his jacketed left arm resting in the opened window. The truck came to a stop. The checkpoint agent bent to the window and peered inside. He nodded to the driver, then glanced at Tariq, his eyes falling on Tariq's uniform. He stared at Tariq's face, not recognizing Tariq as an agent, or even an American. The agent's face told Tariq he suspected something wasn't right as the man's eyes clouded with confusion. Tariq lifted a couple of fingers to the bill of his cap and with a mock salute, said, "Evenin', boss," using a forced western accent.

The checkpoint agent blinked, then nodded slowly. "Did you hear about the shoot-out?"

The agent at the wheel grimaced. "We got the bastards," he said, and pointed his thumb over his shoulder to the back of the truck.

The checkpoint agent nodded to the driver then glanced again at Tariq. "Get'em behind bars where they belong," he said, then stood back and motioned for the trucks to pass.

As the trucks pulled away, Tariq exhaled and leaned back, then looked into the rearview mirror at his right as the second the Border Patrol truck rolled through the checkpoint unimpeded and quickly drew close behind. Tariq watched the lights of the checkpoint fade from view.

CHAPTER 7

Kyle gazed distractedly at the passing scrub of the Arizona desert landscape as he rode south out of Tucson on Interstate 19 in a green and white Border Patrol pickup truck. He couldn't shake the feeling that he was headed back to a war zone. As much as he hated to admit it, that was what the borderlands had become.

He'd gotten a call two days earlier from his old boss, Ed Frankel at the *Washington Herald*, who, as he eased his way toward retirement, now managed the newspaper's network of freelance reporters. Some were former staff writers, who like Kyle, were off writing books, but still kept a finger in the news business.

Frankel had called as soon as news broke about the Border Patrol agents who'd been killed while apprehending Mexican migrants crossing the border. Kyle had grown up in El Paso and considered the borderlands his home turf. Of course he'd take the assignment.

Some 40,000 Border Patrol agents worked the 2,000-mile dividing line between Mexico and the US, along with the federal Drug Enforcement Administration, the Alcohol, Tobacco and Firearms agents, the FBI, branches of the US military, and thousands of state and local lawmen and women. People were killed and died every day as armed men surged back and forth across the border, ferrying people, drugs, and weapons into and out of the US. Now three border agents had been murdered, the single worst loss of life in Border

Patrol history and the deadliest border incident since Pancho Villa crossed the border in 1916 and attacked the town of Columbus, New Mexico.

Kyle glanced at the driver, Agent Ricardo "Rico" Chavez, whose muscled arms strained the sleeves of his uniform. His cap sat over his iridescent sunglasses, making his eyes look reptilian. He occasionally scratched at the thick mustache that covered his upper lip and spread down the sides of his chin, Fu Manchu style.

"Me and Raoul served together in Iraq," Chavez said. "He said you're an okay guy."

"We're cousins, actually," Kyle said.

"*El primo! Que bueno!*" Chavez said. "That's good. Raoul said you wanted to do a story, so I said, sure. The more people know about the situation on the border, the better. But, I had to clear this trip with the boss. They were cool with it once I told them you were with *Washington Herald.*"

Kyle nodded uncomfortably. He disliked notoriety, despite more than a decade with the newspaper, but was thankful for the insider access. Chavez explained he had left the US Special Forces and signed on with the Border Patrol. But he was not your average agent. He was part of the elite border tactical unit, or BORTAC, lethal night fighters who tangled with the *vajadores*, the Mexican bandits who prowled the borderlands like packs of wolves, robbing and occasionally killing their fellow Mexican migrants or any US border agents who got in their way.

"*Vajadores!*" Chavez said with a snort. "*Animáles* is more like it. They go after the ones who carry the weed across the border for the cartels. They steal it and sell it themselves."

"Maybe they work for competing cartels," Kyle said.

"Most of them are small time operators," Chavez said. "We call them rip crews. Short for rip offs. They pick on the people forced to carry the weed. The cartels tell them they don't have to pay to cross the border if they carry the drugs. That's how they turn the migrants into drug mules."

Kyle jotted in his notebook, then looked up as they approached the border crossing at Nogales. Chavez veered off the main road and into the parking lot of the patrol's station on the US side of the border. "I want to show you something."

Kyle followed Chavez around to the back of the station and into a cavernous warehouse. The charred hulks of what were once two Border Patrol trucks sat on the bare concrete, lighted by a dozen overhead florescent lamps. The air reeked of burned plastic and paint. Chavez parked his sunglasses on his forehead and stood with balled fists on his hips, his jaw muscle flexing slowly. "This is what's left of the vehicles that were taken," he said.

"Nothing," Kyle said.

Chavez cleared his throat. "Even their damned badges melted."

"You think the cartels did it?"

Chavez shook his head. "No way."

"Why not?"

"The cartels know better than to go head-to-head with the Border Patrol," Chavez said. "It's bad for business. They have too much to lose. Besides, there's no need."

"No need?" Kyle asked.

"Think about it. There are tens of thousands of Mexicans who will pay $3,000 to $4,000 per person to the drug cartels to get them across the border and into the US. So what if you lose a few?"

"Lose a few migrants or coyotes?"

Chavez shrugged. "Either. It don't matter. The coyotes, the men who bring the migrants across, run when we show up. They go back across the border, find another group, and come again. They work for the cartels. Killing the Border Patrol is not in the coyote playbook."

"Maybe it was the *vajadores*?"

"Maybe. But they're the rip crews. *Banditos*. The agents who died had nothing to steal. There was nothing to be gained by killing them."

"So, who killed them?"

"Someone who didn't care who they killed or why," Chavez said. "They didn't want to leave any traces, either."

"That doesn't sound good."

"It's not."

"Where did they go?"

"We don't know," Chavez said. "They were met and picked up by someone, though."

"How do you know they didn't walk away?"

"They would have been spotted."

"How is it possible for a group of people to cross into the country, kill three border agents, and then disappear?" Kyle asked.

"C'mon," Chavez said. "I'll show you."

Kyle followed him up a steel and concrete stairway to the second floor then down a dim hall and pointed to the patrol's armory. "We can check out most kinds of weapons here, night vision goggles, that kind of thing. But we're still over powered by the cartels and the *vajadores*. They can buy the latest on the market and most of it comes directly from the US."

"So American arms dealers are selling guns that are used against the Border Patrol agents?"

"Yep." Chavez grimaced as he leaned against a heavy metal door and turned the handle.

They entered a large dark room where several agents sat at keyboards with what looked like computer game joysticks. Large video screens covered the nearby wall, each depicting a stretch of desert. Chavez waved to screens. "The cameras are mounted on towers along the border. We monitor a limited number of sections 24/7."

"The virtual fence?"

Chavez nodded. "We've got video for daylight and infrared for night. They can be rotated and zoomed in and out. If the monitors pick up any movement, we track it and send our agents."

Kyle nodded. "Looks incredibly efficient."

"Yeah, well," Chavez shrugged. "It only covers about forty miles of the border and it cost millions of dollars."

"Forty miles? The border is two thousand miles long."

"Yeah. I know. It makes me long for the old days when agents rode horses and carried Winchesters. One agent could cover twenty miles in a day."

"So, that means a hundred agents could patrol the border in a day."

"There's nothing like eyes and boots on the ground."

"But not if they're targets," Kyle said.

Chavez nodded grimly.

CHAPTER 8

Alan Morris stood on the graveled parking lot of the Al-Salam mosque in the parched hills a few miles from the small village of Abiquiu in northern New Mexico. He faced his daughter Jennifer, waiting for her to respond. The sun was high and heavy on his shoulders. He'd never felt so helpless and alone. He squinted as he scanned the raked gravel paths lined with rocks connecting the cluster of plastered adobe buildings of the Islamic studies center. The grounds were landscaped with blossoming yellow blade cactus, angular *cholla* cactus festooned with white flowers, and the pale gray-green of the *chamisa* bushes.

Morris's eyes returned to Jennifer. She wore a loose, ankle-length skirt, a long-sleeved blouse, and a scarf covering her head and tied under her chin. He hardly recognized her any more. *What the hell happened to her?* But he knew. When his wife Anne had died of a rapidly metastasizing form of skin cancer, he had buried his grief and himself in his work. He contemplated an early retirement and she was all he had left.

It had been particularly hard for Jennifer. Losing her mother at the age of sixteen had set Jennifer adrift. Morris knew she had needed the comfort of her father as much as he had needed the comfort of a daughter, but had turned inward rather than reaching out. It was a huge mistake, he now realized, and wanted to make things right, refusing to admit it was too little, too late. He'd been a man who was all but gone from her life and now was paying the price.

He had convinced himself it didn't matter. Jennifer immersed herself in her classes and clubs at Los Alamos High School and graduated with honors, earning a full-ride academic scholarship to the University of New Mexico in Albuquerque. Morris was immensely proud—until the day she announced she was converting to Islam. *What the hell is she doing at this mosque, anyway?*

"Come home with me," Morris said, exasperated. "Forget this Islamic stuff. If I didn't know better, I'd say you were brain washed."

Jennifer scowled and shook her head. "You just don't understand. This is what I want. This is me now."

Morris blamed it all on Jennifer's roommate, Aliyah Muhadi, the bright young woman from that Iranian family. Aliyah's father was a scientist at Sandia National Laboratory. Morris had met the man and liked him.

Jennifer's embrace of Islam began innocently enough. When Aliyah became involved in the university's Muslim Student Association, Jennifer had tagged along. The two girls had protested the bombing of children by the al-Assad regime in Syria. Then Aliyah and Jennifer had joined the Students for Justice in Palestine and they'd clashed with some aggressive members of Hillel, the Jewish student group. Chants were met by taunts and shoves. The campus police were called. When bystanders began throwing bottles at the campus cops, students were detained, including Aliyah and Jennifer.

Morris had written it off as springtime on campus.

But it wasn't just Jennifer and Aliyah. Their boyfriends were involved, a couple of boys named Carlito Mondragon and Miguel Garcia. Morris had learned this after he made the trip to Albuquerque to secure Jennifer's release from jail. Like Jennifer and Aliyah, Carlito and Miguel were roommates.

Aliyah had flawless olive skin and large dark eyes, made even larger with eye-liner, and Morris understood why Miguel Garcia had been enthralled with her. It verged on devotion. Jennifer and Carlito had introduced Aliyah to Miguel and they quickly became a foursome.

Jennifer had known Carlito from years earlier, although the two had never dated until they met again at UNM. That, too, had begun innocently. It was shortly after his wife had died and Morris and Jennifer were returning from a hiking trip to Wheeler Peak near Taos. They stopped for something to eat just south of Abiquiu, and on a whim, Morris took her to a store that featured handwoven wool products made from locally grown wool.

Jennifer had selected a serape from a young man who worked in the store and introduced himself as Carlito. He had flirted as he helped slip the serape over her shoulders and she had smiled and spun like the ballet dancer for him, the serape flying out to her side. She enthused about homespun wool and later had returned for weaving workshops taught by Carlito's mother. But that had been the extent of it. Jennifer had forgotten the store and Carlito-- or so Morris thought.

Palestine had been the trigger. One evening over dinner at the Frontier restaurant on Central Avenue, as she devoured a Duke City burger and Morris dug into red chili enchiladas, Jennifer explained how the Palestinians had suffered at the hands of the Israelis, going back to the loss of their lands during the 1967 six-day Arab-Israeli war.

Morris tried to convince her there was much more to the problem and that some Islamic nations had vowed to destroy Israel. It was only natural that the Israelis would aggressively defend themselves. Didn't the Israelis have a right to an historic homeland and to live free from the threat of imminent destruction?

"That's not what this is about!" Jennifer said, as if he was clueless.

The conversation had gone nowhere, with Jennifer refusing to admit she was wrong. Morris let the issue drop, hoping she'd soon come to her senses. He did not press her further, fearing he'd lose her. Instead of fading, however, Jennifer's interest in Islam had deepened as she and Aliyah became ever closer. His attempts to draw her away from Islam only drove her deeper into it. She grew irate when he criticized Islam as a religion that advocated and condoned violence against non-Muslims. She shouted about the hundreds of thousands of Iraqi men, women and children who had died during America's war and on-going presence in Iraq, a war based on the lie Saddam Hussein had possessed weapons of mass destruction.

Now she was living in this mosque in in the hills outside of Abiquiu. Morris clenched his jaw and drew a nasally breath. All four of them, Aliyah, Jennifer, Carlito and Miguel, had been attending weekend retreats at the mosque to learn the truth about Islam, she said. . And now, she was spending the summer there. Morris' stomach churned as he silently waited for her response.

Jennifer stood still, immobile, as if weighting her options. After what seemed to him like an eternity, the only sound being the wind moving through the stubby piñon pines, he reached out to take her hand. "Please, Jennifer," he said. "Come home."

Jennifer yanked her hand away and stepped back. "My name is Halima."

Morris's heart sank. He swallowed hard, struggling to make sense of it all as he fought to restrain his anger. The mosque billed itself as a center for Islamic studies. A place of peace, she had said. But Morris wondered. Northern New Mexico has been home to various cults in the past. High, dry, and remote, it was home for more than a few fringe characters, a place where a person or group could be easily ignored and largely forgotten.

"Your mother, God rest her soul, gave you a beautiful name," he said, narrowing his eyes. "Honor her by using it."

"Honor me by using my new name," she replied.

Morris glared. "Please come home, Jennifer. You're all that I have left."

"Why can't you accept that I've become a Muslim?"

"You're not a Muslim, that's why."

Jennifer's face darkened, her mouth dropping into a frown, and she shook her head slowly in disgust. She turned and walked away. Pausing at the double wooden doors of the entrance, she spun around to confront her father from a distance. Her face contorted with anger, her fists balled, and she shouted, "Go away and leave me alone! Just leave ... me ... alone!"

Morris sprang forward and grabbed her by the arms. "Enough of this stupid nonsense! You're not a Muslim! Don't try to tell me you are!"

Jennifer twisted free of her father's grasp, yanked the door open, and darted inside, slamming the door shut behind her.

Morris stared at the closed door, his heart pounding, his breath heavy. He shook his head in disgust, his shoulders slumped in defeat, and strode back to his car. *It's Aliyah's fault, and that boy Carlito,* he told himself. *How could this have happened?*

***

The air inside the al-Salam mosque was still and cool. Tariq sat on a rug with several of his *jihadis*, all facing the elderly mullah, a man with a gray beard, his mustache shaved clean and head topped with white skull cap. "Who was that man?" Tariq asked.

"Didn't you see?" the elderly mullah asked. "He is the father of Halima."

"The American convert?"

"She's very devout. Not like her friend, Aliyah."

"Tell me about her father."

"He's a scientist at the Los Alamos laboratory."

"A nuclear scientist?"

"Aren't they all? They design and make bombs there."

Tariq smiled and gently scratched his thin beard, lost in thought.

CHAPTER 9

The marked-up manuscript, its pages looking like they'd been lacerated with a red pen, sat beside Kyle's laptop. Months earlier, he'd settled into a guesthouse in Santa Fe's upscale Acequia Madre neighborhood, just steps from Canyon Road's celebrated cafés, shops, and restaurants. A fifteen minute walk put him on the Santa Fe Plaza.

Portions of the sprawling adobe house dated from the late 1600s, long before the American colonies declared themselves an independent country. At the time, Santa Fe had been a lonely outpost in the northern territories of Spain's new world colonies.

Kyle's presence there was due to Seamus McGregor, the publisher of his first and only book, who lived in the property's sprawling main house. The scion of a wealthy east coast family, he was a fine-art photographer of some repute, specializing in dramatic and large format black-and-white desert landscapes. McGregor had formed a publishing company so he could sell his photographic work in the form of coffee-table books. He'd been successful.

McGregor was soon publishing books on various Southwestern topics that intrigued him. At the time, Kyle had been writing news stories about the federal government's controversial nuclear waste dump in southern New Mexico. McGregor called Kyle and asked if he'd like to write a book about a related topic, something much more dire: the death and environmental devastation caused by uranium mining on and around the Navajo Reservation. Kyle had readily agreed.

That was years earlier, but Kyle remembered it well as he massaged his aching left knee, bashed by a cartel boss during the chaotic and violent end of the extended true crime exposé he was now writing. Kyle contemplated the stack of paper on the desk in front of him, each page detailing the sordid events that had taken his father's life and nearly cost him his own. He thought about the day he had stood in the cold and dismal rain on the sidewalk in the Georgetown neighbor of Washington, DC. He hadn't felt the satisfaction he expected as he faced the large, brick home of former US Senator Micah Madsen, who walked out the front door and through a gauntlet of journalists, his hands cuffed, accompanied by stoic FBI agents, who stuffed Madsen into the backseat of gray sedan and drove away.

Madsen and his closest aides had lorded over a secret drug-running operation with rogue agents working under the protection of the Drug Enforcement Administration. Infiltrating the Mexican drug cartels was why the DEA black ops team had been formed, but as the committee chair that oversaw the so-called War on Drugs, Madsen realized there was money to be made. He went into business with one of the largest and most vicious of Mexico's drug cartels.

When his father was shot and killed in the desert west of El Paso, Kyle had followed a trail that led him to Madsen's doorstep. Kyle had lived to write about it, despite being nearly beaten to death by Marco Borrego, the next generation leader of the Borrego Cartel, who was smarter and more vicious than his father had been. Kyle had the scars to prove it. Madsen was serving a five-year sentence in La Tuna, the minimum security federal prison north of El Paso, Texas. Not a bad place to spend prison time, Kyle thought. It was a Spanish mission styled prison on the banks of the Rio Grande and topped with a gleaming white stucco bell tower. Madsen was one of about a thousand inmates who had committed nonviolent crimes. They included people like the man convicted of producing the anti-Islamic film that the US State Department wrongly said triggered the attack on the US consulate offices in Benghazi, Libya. Another was a former Navy SEAL who tried to get rich by smuggling US weapons from Iraq and Afghanistan back to the US and into Mexico where he sold them to the Mexican drug cartels.

Feeling exhausted, Kyle gazed at the manuscript pages, but lacking the energy to make any further edits, he put off further work until the next morning when he'd hopefully be fresh. He pushed the manuscript aside, rose, and stepped across the polished brick floor to his kitchen. He gurgled three fingers' worth of his favorite *añejo* mescal into a glass just as he heard the melodic sound of an incoming Skype phone call on his laptop.

Drink in hand, Kyle clicked on the flashing icon to accept the call. The face of his former boss, Ed Frankel, filled the screen. It was nearly 9 p.m. in Washington, and Kyle wondered why Frankel was still at the office. The man looked tired and drawn, more tired than Kyle had ever seen him. Stocky, with a white moustache that matched his thinning hair, Frankel was past retirement age. The thought occurred to him that Frankel might die at his desk.

"When are you going to retire?" Kyle asked.

Frankel gazed at him guiltily, as if he'd been thinking the same thing. He nodded. "Good idea in theory. I ought to write a memoir, I suppose."

Frankel had plenty of stories to tell from his days as a reporter. He'd humped the boonies in Vietnam, tromped through the Central American jungles with the Sandinista rebels in Nicaragua, and had helped expose the details of President Ronald Reagan's Iran-Contra scandal. Kyle and Frankel were of like minds, separated by a generation.

"Why don't you?" Kyle asked.

"I'd drive Dorothy nuts."

Kyle smiled. "You do have a way of doing that."

"If I'm not facing down a daily deadline, I don't know what to do with myself."

"Give Dorothy my regards," Kyle said. "You need to learn to relax."

"It's too late for that."

"What happened to the beach house you bought in Belize all those years ago?"

Frankel shook his head in disgust. "Still there. Only go there for a couple of weeks each year."

"Change of scenery might do you good," Kyle said. "Help you transition into retirement."

Frankel grunted a reply, then asked, "How's your book coming?"

"Almost finished with the hard copy edits. With the freelance assignments you keep handing me, it's a wonder I have time to work on it."

"That was a good story you wrote on the border agents being murdered," Frankel said. "It's a no man's land down there."

"The Border Patrol is still reeling."

"Have they found the killers?"

"No, and I don't think they will. But they did find that suspicious body. Not a Mexican, but they couldn't identify it, however."

"How could they not know where the killers went?"

Kyle shrugged. "They vanished."

"People don't vanish, Kyle. There must be some clues. What about fingerprints? DNA?"

Kyle sipped his mescal. "They torched the vehicles, like I wrote. When I saw them, the charred metal still reeked of burned rubber and plastic."

Frankel rubbed his face to wake himself up, then groaned. "So the killers could be anywhere?"

"Yep," Kyle said. "Speaking of killers, whatever happened to Jihadi John, the ISIS executioner of Nate Kennard and those others? Anyone found him?"

Frankel shuffled papers on his desk. "We have people working on a series of stories about the kidnapping and killing of foreigners, especially journalists."

"Nate and I went through some shit together."

Frankel dropped his gaze, then looked out his darkened office window. "Yeah, I know you did. Why don't you write a column about Kennard? About the need for journalists who are willing to risk their lives to find and deliver the truth."

"Especially since we're now being called the enemies of the people?" Kyle said.

"Yes, especially because of that." Frankel paused, then cleared his throat. "But that's not why I called."

"I didn't think this was a social call." Kyle drew a breath and waited.

"I have another assignment for you, closer to home," Frankel said. "I think you'll like it."

"This better be good because I have a book deadline."

"It is," Frankel said. "We've gotten word that President Harris and the conservative leadership in Congress have arranged a hush-hush meeting away from Washington DC."

"They've been at each other's throats for the past three years," Kyle said. "Now they want to get chummy?"

"It's a huge turnaround," Frankel said. "Historic, actually. That's why I need you there."

"What's behind it?" Kyle asked. "It's not because anyone has had a change of heart."

"The conservatives control Congress," Frankel said. "They want to take the White House in the coming election."

"Of course they do," Kyle said.

"The conservatives are desperate to show they have a viable political agenda," Frankel said.

"You mean other than voting down each and every Harris proposal without debate?"

"But to do that, they need President Harris to sign some of their bills."

"Which he refuses to do."

"Exactly," Frankel said, rubbing his eyes. He yawned noisily. "They want to work out a compromise."

"Shocking, actually," Kyle said. "Where are they meeting?"

"In your backyard," Frankel said.

"Santa Fe?"

"Nope. A private ranch resort there in the mountains of northern New Mexico."

"The Vista Verde Ranch?" Kyle asked.

"You know it?"

"Yeah, I do," Kyle said. "It's got a long and tangled history. Currently it's owned by the billionaire media mogul, David Benedict, the man who owns Wolfe News Network."

"Yep. That's him," Frankel said. "Benedict owns high-end properties all over the world. He's hosting the event."

"The ranch is set in the middle of one of the most pristine pieces of wilderness in the West," Kyle said. "From what I understand, Benedict uses it to wine and dine congressmen, his friends and their girlfriends, and even a Supreme Court judge or two. They brag about the ranch's trophy elk, bear, and trout fishing. It's all on Benedict's tab. But of course he denies he's trying to influence government decisions."

Frankel laughed. "Gee, that would be politics-as-usual, wouldn't it? And Benedict complains about the need to drain the Washington swamp. Go figure."

"Remember Supreme Court Justice Scarlotti, the one who died recently?" Kyle asked.

"Of course," Frankel said. "The Senate has refused to consider a replacement until after the next election."

"Yeah, well, Scarlotti was at Benedict's mountain ranch when he had his heart attack."

"I'd forgotten that," Frankel said.

"It was not widely reported," Kyle said. "He was at the ranch because a couple of cases were coming before the court that affected Benedict's companies."

"We all know the judicial branch is supposed to be above that kind of thing," Frankel said with a cynical chuckle.

"But a few of them aren't above accepting an all-expenses paid visit to a fancy mountain ranch retreat," Kyle said. "Especially a ranch owned by people who share their political views."

"Sad but true," Frankel said.

"Benedict has his fingers in every political pie imaginable," Kyle continued. "His money flows from political action committees into the campaign treasuries of dozens of candidates. He almost single handedly supports the right wing of the party."

"Even the conservatives can't get anything passed without them," Frankel said. "The right wing is a tight-knit voting block."

"So, then meeting tells me the conservatives have two choices," Kyle said. "Make a deal with the liberals or give into the demands of far right."

"I think it's how the Congress works … or doesn't work," Frankel said. "So what do you say? Can you do the story?"

Kyle's mind was on fire. "I first wrote about David Benedict twenty years ago."

"You did? What was that about?"

"It was back when Benedict had just purchased the Vista Verde Ranch," Kyle said. "Back then a shepherd, a well-loved old man, was found murdered up in the mountains. The old man had been accused of trespassing and cutting fences to let his sheep graze on the Benedict's ranch land. So, when the old man was found dead, it triggered a protest by the heirs of the big Mexican land grant up there that dated back to the 1820s. The heirs claimed the Vista Verde Ranch was theirs. They armed themselves and set up camp on a corner of Benedict's ranch."

"How did that turn out?" Frankel asked, again with a chuckle.

"The leader of the protest was shot and killed by a state police sniper."

"That's a hell of a story," Frankel said. "Why didn't I ever hear about it?"

"It was outside of the beltway, that's why."

"Maybe you can work that into a background piece for us," Frankel said.

"There's something else you should know. The Vista Verde Ranch is also the headquarters of Atlas Global, the big private security company. It's run by Benedict's son, Hank."

"Atlas Global? That company is all over the world."

"I know. They provide contract security for US embassies and private companies operating overseas," Kyle said.

"I didn't know it was based at the ranch."

"Hank is one of David Benedict's five children. They all attended Ivy League schools, but Hank dropped out. At the age of 20, he joined the Navy and become a SEAL. Ten years later, with daddy's help, he formed Atlas Global Security."

"You know all about the Benedicts, I see," Frankel said.

"I've run into Atlas Global personnel everywhere I've worked."

"Well, of course you would have," Frankel said, "if they provide security to US government personnel."

"They've even got a marine division," Kyle said. "They provide security for ocean freighters cruising the Gulf of Aden. They like to shoot Somalia pirates."

"What does any of this have to do with the meeting at Vista Verde?" Frankel asked.

"Not much, I suppose. But, I know someone who works for Atlas," Kyle said. "He's tight with Hank Benedict. They served together in Iraq and Afghanistan."

"You have an inside source! That's great," Frankel said. "So, we need an advance story on the meeting. Throw in all that background."

"And you're sure President Harris has agreed to the Vista Verde Ranch meeting?" Kyle asked.

"Yes," Frankel said. "Why? Is that surprising?"

Kyle took a deep breath, and exhaled slowly. "I've got a bad feeling about this, Ed."

"What's the matter?" Frankel asked, sounding irritated. "It's a plum assignment. Our chief political reporter and a columnist, both want to go out there, but can't. The press corps will be very limited. Just one reporter each from the TV majors, and Wolfe news of course, a couple of the news services, the New York Times, us, and the LA Times."

"Hmmm. Not a lot," Kyle said.

"President Harris, along with the House Speaker and the Senate majority leader are flying out there tomorrow, Thursday afternoon. The plan is for them to meet Friday, Saturday, and Sunday morning, then return to Washington DC on Sunday afternoon. They supposedly will have something to announce at noon on Sunday before they return. It'll be easy."

Kyle sighed. "Okay. I can handle a weekend assignment."

"Thanks. I knew you could."

Kyle signed off with Frankel, closed his eyes, and exhaled. He swallowed the last of his mescal and stared across the living room to the handmade polished tin cross on the wall. It was going to be a longer week than he'd expected.

CHAPTER 10

Kyle returned the kitchen, poured himself another glass of mescal, and pried the top off a bottle of Modelo beer. He'd known of Hank Benedict and his Atlas Global Security company from his time in Iraq and Afghanistan, where Benedict's heavily armed, heavily muscled, and highly-paid army of ex-Special Forces prowled streets and skies over Baghdad and Kabul.

Benedict's contract security forces were everywhere, it seemed, and Kyle knew he shouldn't have been surprised to encounter Benedict and his men in Libya. Kyle had arrived in September 2012, just days after the attack on the US consulate in Benghazi, which had left the ambassador, a consulate colleague, and two guards dead.

Kyle's nose and throat had burned from the stench of the consulate's burned-out interior, the shards of glass crackling under his feet as he took slow, deliberate steps, the sound echoing off the scorched walls. He gagged on the harsh, thick air. Outside, the sun's white light was framed by broken windows, lighting the charred debris. Anything worth taking was gone. The rest destroyed. He felt like a voyeur in a chamber of horrors.

"This is where they found him," Jamal had said, breaking the silence and motioning to the blackened walls of what had been the safe room. Jamal was Kyle's fixer, a slender man with a clean shaven face, dark wavy hair, and eyes like polished black agates. He was a freelance journalist and photographer with a small, on-line news agency, Libya Today, and he'd rushed to the Al-Hawari neighborhood that night when word spread that the US consulate was under attack.

"They said there was a foreigner inside," Jamal explained. "They said he was alive. Praise God, they shouted." Jamal fell silent, lost in the memory as his eyes darted around the blackened room. "That's when I and the others rushed in. We didn't know who it was!" His voice trailed off. "Only later that we heard it was the ambassador."

Kyle had worked with Jamal a year earlier, flying into Tripoli from Istanbul to write about the death of Libyan dictator Muammar Gaddafi. At the time, Libya was in turmoil. Tripoli had fallen to Libyan rebels, backed by bomb-dropping US drones, and British and French fighter jets. Gaddafi had disappeared, then surfaced in Sirte, where he had loyal supporters, and had tried to flee deep into Libya's southern desert. Gaddafi's convoy, said to be nearly 75 vehicles, was decimated by air and ground strikes, forcing the dictator, his son, and his former army chief to flee on foot. They were found cowering in a culvert. Gaddafi was sodomized by either a bayonet or broom stick—the stories differed—then shot in the head.

Kyle had made the six-hour drive from Tripoli to Sirte in Jamal's car, the air conditioning unable to beat off the searing heat. He and Jamal found the blood-stained culvert and the men who'd killed Gaddafi. Kyle remembered their energetic shouting, how they'd talked proudly of killing Gaddafi, as if they were the vengeful fist of Allah, rending swift and brutal justice.

Back in Tripoli, Kyle and Jamal talked with the interim government officials, men who claimed they were eager to transform Libya. Later he viewed Gaddafi's refrigerated corpse, put on public display in the seaside city of Misrata so all of Libya could see the man was truly dead. It had been easy to work in Libya back then. Kyle was an American and the Americans had helped bring Gaddafi down.

But it was different when he'd returned for the Benghazi story. Libya's transitional government struggled to contain the resurgent Islamic jihadists, led by Al-Qaeda splinter groups and their militias spawned by the civil war and bent on imposing Sharia law throughout the country. They'd been part of the attack on the Benghazi consulate that had killed Ambassador Gregory Arnold and two of Hank Benedict's Atlas Global security contractors.

The US State Department initially had said the consulate attack was in reaction to an anti-Islamic video. Even then the explanation for the attack didn't make sense. After demolishing the US consulate, the attackers had moved to the CIA's annex building just a mile away, which they'd pounded with mortars. Kyle knew most protesters didn't carry that kind of weaponry. They simply showed up, shouted and chanted, then threw rocks. But not this time. Kyle remembered wandering the demolished US consulate and thinking that nothing made sense: neither the shooting, nor the fire, nor all the anti-American graffiti sprayed on the walls. In the consulate's kitchen, he'd found a box of meals ready to eat, MREs. Military food. Had the consulate been a cover for a military operation? He had no way of knowing, not then anyway. "So, what happened when they found the ambassador?" Kyle had asked Jamal.

"They found him in the room over there," Jamal said. "They carried him out and put him on the patio." Jamal pointed to the compound entrance. "Someone called for a medic." He shook his head. "But there was no one around. So, I said, take him to my car."

"He was still alive?" Kyle had asked.

"You saw the video taken by my friend," Jamal replied. "The ambassador was near death. But he was moving his lips, trying to talk. And his eyes moved."

Kyle nodded. He'd seen the video. Ambassador Arnold had looked alive, but barely, his eyes unfocused, his face, jeans and white t-shirt smudged with smoke and soot.

"He couldn't move," Jamal said. "They carried him to my car and put him in the back seat."

"And you took him to the hospital?"

Jamal shrugged. "What else could I do?"

"You did the right thing," Kyle had said. "Can we find the doctor who treated the ambassador? I want to talk with him."

"No problem," Jamal had said, as puzzled look clouded his face. "Why did the security guards leave the ambassador alone? He was the most important person."

"I don't know," Kyle said. It was another piece of the puzzle that didn't fit. Kyle tried to imagine the chaos, the shooting the fire. It had been bad, real bad, he thought, then shook his head in disgust. Nothing had made sense. "C'mon, let's go."

The Benghazi Medical Center consisted of three tall tan brick buildings. Kyle and Jamal easily found Dr. Ahmed Zia, the man who had treated the ambassador and who agreed to meet them in his office. The hospital was clean and well-equipped, as good as Kyle had seen anywhere in north Africa, certainly far better than most third-world countries he'd been. But then this was Libya and Libya had oil.

Dr. Zia was a compact man, with closely cropped black hair speckled with gray and beard to match. He wore a white lab coat over a white t-shirt and spoke calmly and methodically, with Jamal translating and explaining that Ambassador Arnold had been unresponsive when he had arrived at the hospital.

"He was already dead?" Kyle asked.

Zia shrugged. "He had no vital signs."

"But you tried to revive him anyway?"

"Of course," Zia said. "I've seen this before. It is possible to bring people back to life when they seem dead. I gave him oxygen. I tried to stimulate the heart."

"But nothing worked?" Kyle asked.

Zia shook his head and stared at the floor.

"How long did this go on?"

Zia squinted in thought. "About forty-five minutes."

"Then you gave up?"

Zia nodded. "When the brain goes without oxygen that long, the damage is severe, even if the body is alive."

Kyle jotted notes. "So, he died in route to the hospital?"

Zia nodded again. "His lungs were damaged badly from smoke inhalation. The body lacked oxygen. He died of asphyxiation. I did what I could."

Kyle scribbled the quote into his notebook, then looked the doctor. "What happened to the body?"

Zia shrugged. "Someone took it away."

"Do you know who?"

Zia shook his head. "The Americans have it now. That's what I've been told."

Kyle had returned to his hotel room to write the story, yet another one that left him with more questions than answers. The US ambassador had been killed. The first in decades. Something had gone wrong, very wrong. But what? Why, he had wondered, were so many people at the CIA annex?

The next day, Kyle and Jamal had flown to Tripoli, landing at the Mitiga International Airport. The airport interior looked like any other in the world, with its molded benches, long check-in counters, and rumbling baggage claim conveyor belts. But Kyle had no baggage to claim. He always traveled light, carrying only an oversized day pack that held his laptop, a tooth brush and razor, a couple of lightweight fishing shirts with plenty of pockets, an extra pair of pants, and fresh underwear. He was good to go.

He and Jamal had climbed into their rented silver, four-door Peugeot with tinted windows and a serviceable air conditioner, with Jamal at the wheel. The airport was close to the Mediterranean Sea and Jamal swerved out of the airport and sped along the Al-Shat Road between the city and water.

"Any luck with the interviews?" Kyle had asked, as he gazed at the azure sea, marveling at how clear and blue it was. He'd asked Jamal to find top officials with the interim government in Tripoli who might know something about what had actually happened that night in Benghazi.

Jamal nodded and grunted, weaving through the chaotic traffic. Fifteen minutes later, they'd checked into the Al Waddan Hotel in the heart of the city. They had just enough time for a quick lunch, Jamal said, because he'd arranged an interview with a man named Abdel Hakim Malik.

"Who is he?"

"One of our leaders of the Libyan rebellion," Jamal said proudly. "He's in charge of our military council."

"Okay. Does he have a title?"

Jamal shrugged. "Supreme commander or something," he said, throwing his head back with a laugh.

They found a shaded table on the restaurant's deck overlooking the lower patios and pool, offering a commanding view of the Tripoli harbor and the sea. They ordered water, an espresso for Jamal, and a *caffé macchiato* for Kyle, and two pasta dishes, the menu reflecting the strong Italian influence on Libya dating from the days of the Roman Empire.

"So, tell me about this man, Abdel Hakim Malik."

"The new military council is trying to impose order on the country," Jamal had said. "Malik is the cousin of my father."

"That's how you got the interview?" Kyle asked, smiling.

Jamal nodded. "He knows a lot. Malik worked with CIA and the ambassador."

Kyle's heart skipped a beat. He gave Jamal a puzzled look. "The CIA and the ambassador? You're serious?"

"Of course," Jamal said.

"Doing what?"

Jamal shrugged. "He can tell you."

An hour later they were in Malik's office. The man was of average height, with thin dark hair that he combed over a shiny head. He had a round, full face and thick lips topped by a bushy black mustache. He wore a desert camouflaged shirt, cargo pants, and desert boots, but had no insignia or obvious rank.

He shook Kyle's hand and looked sad, saying in low and mournful tones he was sorry for what had happened to Ambassador Arnold. "It was a terrible thing," Malik had said.

Kyle had nodded, thanking the man for meeting with him, and settled into wooden chair facing Malik's broad and polished desk. Malik leaned on his elbows and interlaced his fingers in front of his chin. The man seemed genuine, and for a moment, Kyle thought the man might be forthcoming.

"The death of the ambassador raises a lot of questions," Kyle said. "Why did it take nearly nine hours for the local Libyan forces to show up at the CIA annex?"

Malik's eyes clouded and his forehead furrowed, as if formulating a reasonable explanation. "It was not of Libya's doing. These people are outsiders, not Libyans."

Kyle's eyes had widened at Malik's remark.

"It caught everyone by surprise," Malik continued. "We were not sure what was happening."

Malik's brief explanation sounded reasonable, but unlikely, Kyle thought. "The US State Department in Washington knew what was going on not long after it started," he said. "If people several thousand miles away knew about the attack, how is it that the police and army in Benghazi didn't know? The burning compound lit up the night sky in Benghazi."

Malik shook his head slowly and had offered Kyle a sympathetic smile. "We didn't get a call from them until the early morning. By then, it was almost over."

"No call?" Kyle asked, incredulous at the answer.

Malik shook his head again. "The embassy and the CIA take care of their own business. They told us not to interfere with them. Ever! So, we did as they wished. We left them alone."

Kyle stared, processing the answer.

"The truth is, we were busy cooperating with the Americans with something else," Malik said.

"Something else? What was it?"

"The weapons," Malik said.

"The weapons? What weapons?"

Malik cleared his throat and sighed. "Gaddafi was in power more than forty years. During that time, he had amassed stockpiles of small weapons, from pistols and machine guns to shoulder-fired rockets capable of downing aircraft. Some of these weapons had been captured by the rebels and were used against Gaddafi."

Kyle scribbled notes.

"But with Islamic militants and *jihadis* on the rise, our interim government knew these weapons could and would be used against them as well," Malik had said.

"Let me guess," Kyle said, holding up a hand. "The US helped you round up the weapons and get them out of the country?"

Malik smiled and nodded. "Exactly! It was good for everybody! Don't you see? It helped us control the *jihadi* militias. We did what we could to help the US, which had a use for them."

"A use for them?"

Malik shrugged.

"Where are the weapons now?" Kyle had asked.

"On the ship," Malik said. "In the harbor."

"Now?" Kyle had said, stunned at Malik's revelation.

Forty minutes later, Kyle, Jamal, and Malik climbed out of Malik's official vehicle at the Tripoli harbor. It was not a large port, just several concrete and asphalt docks where rusted and aging cargo ships were tied beside stacks of rusting cargo containers.

Three armed men, two with automatic rifles, appeared from the ship's shadowy interior wearing dark polo shirts embroidered with the distinctive yellow Atlas Global logo, sun glasses covering their eyes, full beards covering their faces. They bristled when they saw Kyle.

"What's he doing here?" one of the Atlas Global agents asked Malik. The agent was shorter than the others, but looked and acted very much in charge. He had closely cropped, sandy brown hair, and looked extremely fit, as did the others.

Malik explained he was showing Kyle about how the new Libyan government was cooperating with the US and how important it was that people did not think Libya was against the US.

Kyle handed his business card to the Atlas Global agent.

"Jesus H. Christ," the agent said, turning the card over in his hands. Glaring at Malik, he barked, "You brought a fucking reporter here?"

Malik looked surprised, then confused, realizing he'd done something wrong.

"Who are you?" Kyle asked.

"None of your fucking business," the Atlas agent barked, and turning to Malik, growled, "Get him the hell out of here."

Malik had grabbed Kyle by the elbow and led him away, but by then bells were clanging in Kyle's head like he'd hit the jackpot at a slot machine. On the way back to Malik's office, Kyle pummeled the general with more questions. But Malik remained tight-lipped, staring out the window at the passing cityscape as if it was the most interesting thing he'd ever seen.

Kyle thanked Malik as they parted in the parking lot. Back at his hotel, Kyle went straight for the bar, found a quiet corner, opened his lap top, and began flipping through his notes as he pounded out an extensive memo to Frankel. Kyle realized he'd stumbled into a secret operation to funnel weapons to Syrian rebels, something that President Harris had said publically he was not going to do. But in fact, he was. Kyle had just enough facts to write an analysis, a speculative article about what had really happened at the consulate and why.

As he wrote, the US's claim the attack on the consulate was about an anti-Islam video was laughable. The consulate was attacked because that is where the *jihadis* had thought the massive weapons stockpile was being kept. The weapons had already helped depose Gaddafi and the Islamists wanted the weapons now to help them install fundamentalist rule. But the weapons weren't there. They had been at the CIA's annex before being loaded onto a cargo ship. And, the US had other uses for the weapons. Sitting in the cool darkness of the hotel bark, Kyle had ordered a beer, and when it arrived, he took a long drink and began to write.

CHAPTER 11

Kyle wiped a bead of sweat from his right temple. He shifted his weight to relieve the nagging ache in his left knee. He wore low cut hiking shoes, not his usual cowboy boots, and swiped his palms on his jeans, feeling the heat under his light cotton shirt. He adjusted his sunglasses and lifted a notebook to shade his eyes. An oversized American flag rippled noisily atop a tall flagpole behind him.

Kyle scanned the valley once again. Sloping, tree-covered hills rose gently to distant, snow-capped peaks, clear and sharp against a deep blue sky. A fleet of hulking black SUVs, jeeps, and military Humvees lined the curved driveway nearby. The SUVs were part of the motorized convoy that had delivered him and the other reporters, along with a platoon of political aides, to the lodge in advance of the arrival of President Harris and the congressional leaders. Kyle turned back to the grassy expanse where the President's helicopter was about to land.

The ranch retreat was certainly remote enough, Kyle thought. President Harris and his political adversaries wanted to get away from the fishbowl of Washington, D.C., the White House had said. The geography alone seemed to provide ample protection for this elite gathering. Beyond the landing site, broad and well-stocked trout ponds extended to the piñon and ponderosa pine forests that covered the surrounding hills. And beyond the nearby slopes was some of the most remote and pristine high country in North

America. The Vista Verde Ranch was a playground for the rich and the super-rich and had been for more than a century. Kyle shifted from foot to foot, growing anxious. He and the others had waited dutifully for an hour now, behind a half-circle of yellow plastic rope where they'd been herded by the White House staff like corralled animals and kept clustered outside the massive stone and wood main lodge of the Vista Verde Ranch. This was the so-called "lame-stream" news media, a phrase that turned his stomach. Lately the derisive tones had become worse. Reporters and correspondents were labeled as "enemies of the people." It was understandable because most residents of the far right were presented as nut jobs, blinded by their allegiance to a political ideology often contrary to simple and obvious facts. It was championed by a small group in the US Congress who called themselves the Liberty League. Ironically, they opposed government in general and any new laws in particular. They exerted undue influence because the conservatives needed them to keep their razor-thin majority on both houses of Congress. The Liberty League claimed to be the true voice of the people. But they weren't. They were the voice of their own misguided groupies, yet if anyone pointed it out, they were called enemies of the people.

It was the oldest game in the book. Rather than refute the facts, it's easier to discredit the source. It was how lawyers got the guilty to go free. Argue that the accuser is the problem, not the crime. Trust in the traditional news media was at an all-time low, way down there with politicians. Garbage collectors had more respect.

Some said the news media only had itself to blame, because objective journalism required that each side have its say. But what if both sides were lying? Political spin was countered with more spin, until it all spun out of control. Journalists knew it was all nonsense and so did most readers and viewers.

Because of the perceived new media bias, David Benedict's Wolfe News had mushroomed into the most popular source of news and information in the nation. The Wolfe News message was that what you see and hear anywhere else was a twisted version of the truth. Only on Wolfe News could one get the facts. It didn't matter that Wolfe News was effectively the mouthpiece of the Liberty League and got its facts wrong as often as right.

Kyle shook his head to clear his musings as the gleaming green and white Marine Corps One presidential helicopter circled high over the pine-covered slopes that defined the valley. He lifted his notebook to shade his eyes as the presidential helicopter descended, the flag casting a wavering shadow over the news media scrum.

The Marine One downdraft raised a swirling cloud of dust and grit as it settled onto the expanse of sparse grass where a white "X" has been spray-painted inside a large white circle. The chopper's engine wound down and the spinning blades slowed as the side door opened and stairs flopped out and onto the ground.

President Harris appeared in the doorway, glanced from side to side, smiled broadly, waved, then stepped to the ground. America's first black man to be elected president, he wore an open collar white shirt, his shirtsleeves rolled up on his sinewy forearms. The cuffs of his dark pants rested on polished shoes. Harris stepped aside and waited for the others to emerge.

Next came Martin Blount, the senior senator from Tennessee and the Senate majority leader, an elderly, frail looking man with a receding chin and sunken chest. Thick-lens glasses enlarged his eyes, lending him a wide-eyed look of permanent astonishment. He glanced around furtively, as if he didn't want to be there, and carefully descended the steps.

Blount was followed by Troy Divine of Texas, the Speaker of the House. Known as "The Ram" for his ability to cram legislation through Congress, Divine wore alligator hide cowboy boots, jeans, and a bright red western-style shirt with pearl snaps and white piping, along with a bolo tie made of a large piece of turquoise. He adjusted his wide, white cowboy hat and took a deep breath of the mountain air, puffing out his barrel chest, then flashed a wide, toothy smile.

Harris walked to a small lectern with two foam-covered microphones and turned to wait until he was joined by Blount and Divine. The three men stood side-by-side as Harris squinted in the sunlight to collect his thoughts.

"The Congress and my administration have been at odds for much of my two terms in office," Harris began. "At the invitation of the leaders in the House and Senate, I have agreed to meet this weekend in hopes we can move this country forward."

One of the regular White House correspondents raised a hand.

"Let me finish," Harris said with a wave. "I know there are many skeptics who are critical of my decision to meet here in this particular way. But, that kind of criticism is nothing new. I've been hearing it for the past few years. It's an unfortunate fact of political life that Congress has done nothing but stonewall any and all efforts to solve America's toughest problems, here at home and abroad. That being said, we're committed breaking this impasse, knowing that it can only help the American people in the near and far term."

Harris turned to the men at his side and nodded, then looked back at the press. "We've agreed to keep remarks at a minimum so we can get down to business immediately. There is no time to waste. I'll take just a few questions." Harris pointed to one of the television network reporters. "Yes, Jim."

"Why do you think you'll be able to reach compromise now after years of political gridlock?" the correspondent asked.

"It's simple," Harris said. "Where there's a will, there's a way."

Kyle raised his hand and Harris pointed to him.

"Members of your own party have criticized this meeting," Kyle said, "saying that not only is it useless, that the location is, well, questionable because of its remoteness."

Harris scowled and shook his head. "As I've said many times before, I will meet with anyone, anywhere to do what's right for America. I can think of no other place more conducive to our work than this. I don't believe that the deer and elk around here, or the eagles, or the trout in the pond pose will cause any disruptions."

A few of the correspondents chuckled.

"Seriously," Harris continued, "in addition to my normal security contingent, this ranch is the headquarters of Atlas Global Security, one of the world's most highly respected private security companies. As you know, Atlas Global provides security for many of our diplomatic missions. Highly trained, dedicated, and experienced men and women staff all of these agencies. I have no worries that this location is ideal for the work we have to do."

Harris pointed to another reporter.

"Let's hear from Senator Blount and Speaker Divine," the correspondent said.

Harris nodded, stepped back from the small lectern, and motioned both men forward.

Blount leaned close to the microphone, and glancing around with his enlarged eyes, said, "Well, there's not a lot I can add to the president's remarks. I think it's pretty clear why we're here."

"Why do you think you can accomplish something at this meeting when you haven't in the past?" the correspondent asked.

"As members of the opposition party," Blount said, "we have certain specific goals we would like to discuss with President Harris. Among them are badly needed changes to the health care act, what has become known as Harris Care. That's one. We also want to re-examine the Wall Street reforms because we believe they are severely restricting investment and economic growth. Another is border security. This country is being flooded with illegal immigrants. Those are just a few of the issues, but they're the big ones. If we can make progress on any those fronts, then I'll count this meeting as a success."

A couple of the other correspondents raised their hands, but Blount waved them off, and instead turned to Divine, who stepped to the lectern, smiled and nodded, and gripped it with both hands.

"Tell ya what," Divine said. "I'm happy as hell to be here and, well…." He paused and looked around the ranch, his eyes settling on the trout ponds. "I can't wait to throw a line into that water over there. I hear tell they got some trophy trout in there." Divine grinned widely, nodded, and waved as he stepped away. "Thanks for coming. We'll be talking to y'all later."

As Divine, Blount, and Harris walked toward the lodge, other reporters shouted out questions, but Harris only waved. The press conference was over.

The trio was greeted by the staff of the Vista Verde Ranch who had lined the steps, including the lodge's chef who wore a tall chef's hat, and the house maids, all dressed in black with white tops and crowns. Television cameras tracked the men's progress up the steps and through the lodge's open doors.

Kyle turned to one of the other correspondents. "That was worthless."

The man, who had swapped his suit for jeans and a safari shirt, grimaced behind sunglasses. "Welcome to the White House press corps," he said.

"I never joined," Kyle said softly as he turned, and like the other correspondents, began to drift away, each tapping numbers into their phones. Kyle dialed, listened to the ring, and after a moment, Frankel answered.

"Harris didn't say much. The leadership didn't say much either. They'll have a statement later when they have something to say."

Frankel exhaled noisily. "We need a story, Kyle, something strong for tomorrow's paper. We just can't go with only Harris' lame remarks and happy talk."

"Let's just forget the usual he-said, she-said stuff," Kyle said. "I'm going to write an analysis that this is Harris's last ditch effort to salvage the last year of his term, and well, the legacy of his administration."

"Kinda states the obvious, doesn't it?" Frankel said.

"Maybe, but that's the point of this exercise," Kyle said. "I can work in a variety of issues and write about Harris's opposition. The conservatives need to get something big out of this meeting as well. Because of the Liberty League, they're labeled as the party of no. This could change their image."

"Okay," Frankel said. "But 'just say no' has been working for them. When can you have it to me?"

"Give me a couple of hours." Kyle hung up and headed to one of the many outlying bungalows scattered around the main lodge and half hidden in the surrounding forest. The rest of the White House press corps and the congressional and presidential staffers were also housed in bungalows, while President Harris, Speaker Divine, and Senator Blount were in the main lodge's upper rooms. Kyle would not be alone. He'd be bunking with his cousin Raoul, who was a key part of the Atlas Global security detail at the lodge, the right-hand man for his boss, Hank Benedict.

***

An hour and a half later, Kyle looked up from his laptop to the knock on his cabin door. "Come in," he said.

Raoul's face popped through the open doorway. "Howdy, primo," he said, closing the door quietly behind him. "Am I disturbing the genius at work?"

Kyle motioned to the bungalow's leather couch. "Have a seat."

Raoul wore tan cargo pants, a dark black polo shirt emblazoned with the Atlas Global logo, desert boots, and his camouflaged boonie hat. "You finished? Or what?"

"Almost." Kyle scanned the last few sentences of his story, and satisfied, closed out the story, attached it to an email, and clicked the mouse to send it to Frankel. The tension in his neck and shoulders extended down his back. "God. I haven't written on deadline for a long time." He rolled his shoulders several times, then leaned back and stretched his arms high above his head, twisting his head one way and then another, the cartilage crackling.

"It could be worse," Raoul said.

"How's that?"

"Not writing at all."

"Good point," Kyle said. "I have a request."

"Just one?"

Kyle groaned. "I want to check out the accommodations and security detail."

"Are you a terrorist?"

"It depends on who you ask," Kyle said. "I've been called the enemy of the people."

"The security is as good as it gets," Raoul said. "Trust me."

"I'd still like to see it."

"Why are you so fixated on security up here? Who in the hell could get up here, anyway? There's nothing easy about it. And even if they did, they'd encounter the largest collection of protective services this country can muster."

Kyle shrugged. "Let's see, okay?"

CHAPTER 12

A dozen Secret Service agents and an equal number of Atlas Global personnel surrounded the lodge, but at a distance, some in the shadowy pines at the edge of the valley, most wearing sun glasses and bulky holsters under their loose-fitting clothes. Raoul touched the brim of his hat and nodded to the two Atlas Global men posted at the entry to the lodge as he and Kyle scaled the steps and pushed through the large, double wood doors.

Kyle and Raoul stood in a large, rustic foyer with its polished slate floor and varnished overhead log beams. Mounted heads of bear, deer, antelope, and buffalo stared glassy-eyed from the walls.

"A lot of animals gave their life for the cause," Kyle said.

An array of chairs and couches fronted a wide fireplace of river rock that rose to the cathedral ceiling. Raoul pointed to the wide and curving stairs rising to the second story. "The President, Speaker Divine, and Senator Blount are staying in the upstairs rooms."

"Do they share a bathroom?"

"What?" Raoul asked.

"I'm joking."

Raoul shook his head in disgust, then pointed to the far end of the spacious foyer. "The library is over there. Looks like something from an old English castle. Leather bound books. It's where they're meeting starting tomorrow. The dining hall and kitchen are there. The massage and spa are there."

"Massage and spa? I thought this was a no-frills meeting."

Raoul shrugged. "It's a full service lodge. During the summer, they swim in the big trout pond out front. It's got a small floating dock. "

Kyle stepped to the door with a small engraved sign: "MASSAGE." Over it was a photo of a woman with curly brown hair, crystalline blue eyes, and a welcoming smile. The name read: Ariel Brady, masseuse. "Damn, but she looks familiar," Kyle said. "I dated a woman once who looked just like her. Years ago. She went by the name of Aurora Borealis."

"Isn't that the northern lights?"

"The name was appropriate," Kyle said. "She was about as spacey as they come." He flashed a mischievous smile.

"Like those people who say they can live on light?"

"And a few carrots," Kyle said.

They'd met when he was a young reporter covering the land grant protest that had erupted in one of the northern mountain villages. It was the most fun he'd ever had in his short career. He spent a few days at the camp with the protestors and nights at a room at the ancient hot springs hotel ten miles away. Ariel had worked there as a masseuse, then with the name of Aurora. It was her vegetarian-earth mother-goddess-of-healing phase. It had been a good time for both of them.

"I have to find out," Kyle said. Knocking on the massage room door, he leaned in close to hear a response.

"One moment, please," said a clear and strong feminine voice from behind the door. The door opened, revealing a fit and tanned woman wearing a light blue polo shirt under the short white smock. She stood in the doorway, smiling quizzically. "You ordered a massage?"

Kyle grinned as he recognized her. "Aurora?"

She looked at him, confusion clouding her face. "Kyle? Kyle Dawson?"

Kyle couldn't restrain his grin and nodded. "So, it's Ariel now?"

"Oh, my God! It's been...."

"About twenty years."

"It can't be."

Kyle shrugged. "It can."

"Yes, ah, Ariel Brady now." Her excited eyes searched his. "So much has happened...."

"You're right," Kyle said, unable to stop smiling. "How did you end up here?"

Ariel shrugged. "I...ah ... have a son, Jason. He's eleven now."

"I have two kids," Kyle said. "A boy and a girl."

"Do they have names?" she asked.

"Erica and Brandon, who's about the same age as your son."

They lapsed into silence, unable to take their eyes off each other.

"So.... you want a massage?" Ariel asked.

Kyle turned to Raoul. "We have time?"

Raoul raised his hands. "I'll leave you two to ... ah, get reacquainted."

***

Twenty minutes later, Kyle was stretched out on the massage table, his face in the padded donut hole, his backside covered with just a towel. Ariel had worked her way down from his neck and shoulders and squirted aromatic massage oil on his calves as she began kneading the muscle. "You have scars on the side of your knee. What happened?" she asked.

"Someone didn't want me to write a story that needed to be written."

"Maybe you should find another line of work."

"That's what my ex-wife said."

"Divorced?"

"A few years now."

"Never remarried?"

"I work overseas a lot. It's hell on relationships."

"Tell me about it. My husband worked overseas. That's where he died."

"Sorry to hear that."

"In Iraq."

"I was there," Kyle said.

"I figured so."

"What city?" he asked.

"Don't know," Ariel said. "Karbala. Fallujah. One of those. He was with Atlas Global. Protecting Americans, he said."

"Atlas?" Kyle asked. "The people who own this ranch?"

"Yep. Hank Benedict. He's my boss."

"Atlas is his baby," Kyle said. "Big government contracts to protect embassy personnel."

"My husband worked closely with Hank."

"What was his name?"

"Jerome. Jerome Brady. He came home in a casket. A closed casket."

"And now you're here?" Kyle asked.

"Turn over."

Kyle turned slowly as Ariel carefully kept the towel in place. Kyle sighed as he settled onto his back. He hadn't felt so relaxed in months. He looked up at Ariel, who caught his gaze and held it for a long, silent moment. Kyle felt a stirring of desire, but did his best to ignore it. He couldn't stop thinking of those nights long ago when they'd been together.

Ariel stopped for a moment, her eyes locked on his. Kyle reached out and slipped a hand around her waist and pulled her hips close. His hand moved inside her shirt and to her lower back. She slowly leaned close and kissed him, the warmth of her soft lips flooding him.

***

The lodge's main dining room was crowded and noisy, the talk loud and excited, the silverware clinking on plates as a handful of waiters bustled, removing and replacing plates, pouring pitchers of ice water, and uncorking bottles of wine. President Harris, Senator Blount, and Speaker Divine, along with their top aides, sat at a large, round corner table. Massive chandeliers made of elk antlers hung over the dining room.

Kyle, Raoul, and Ariel sat at one of the dozen smaller round tables with Hank Benedict. Kyle had dreaded the dinner, Raoul having warned him that they'd be dining with his boss. Kyle remembered Benedict now from their short encounter at the shipping dock in Tripoli and knew this dinner could be a golden opportunity. He had a thousand questions for Benedict, most of which would never be answered. Ironically, it was Benedict who started to talk.

"Raoul tells me you guys go way back," Benedict said, staring quizzically at Kyle.

"We're cousins," Kyle said. "We played high school football together. In El Paso."

"I feel lucky that Raoul has joined our organization," Benedict said. "A man with his talent and experience is hard to find."

"Don't you think it's risky to have the President and the congressional leaders under one roof and in such a remote location like this?" Kyle asked. "Think what it would mean to this country if something happened here to these men."

Benedict shook his head, no. "We have the finest security service in the world. If these men are not secure here, they're not secure anywhere." He paused for a moment and refilled his wine glass. Taking a sip, he continued. "It's important to get these men together. We need to get this country back on track."

"I didn't know it was off track," Kyle said.

Benedict stared at Kyle for a moment, leaned back in his chair. "I guess we have a difference of opinion."

Benedict was about to continue when Ariel interrupted. "Do we have to talk politics?" she asked. "Why can't we just enjoy this dinner?"

Benedict, Kyle, and Raoul look at each other sheepishly.

"Good point, Ariel," Kyle said.

Benedict grabbed the bottle of French wine and topped off each of their glasses, then examined the label. "There're only about a hundred cases of this Grand-Puy-Lacoste Bordeaux left. We're lucky to have some of it here."

Kyle turned to Ariel, who was seated beside him, and watched her use one of the antler-handled steak knives to slice a lean filet. "I thought you were, ah ... vegan! Now you're eating buffalo?"

Ariel popped the meat into her mouth and chewed. She nodded and swallowed, dabbing her lips with a cloth napkin. "When I met Jerome, a lot of things changed."

"I'd like to propose a toast drink to Jerome," Benedict said, raising his glass. "He was one of the best."

They nodded in unison, lifted their glasses, and drank.

"What exactly happened to Jerome?" Kyle asked Benedict.

Benedict looked at his plate a moment, as if he struggled to answer, then lifted his eyes, filled with intensity. "Let's just say he died a hero."

CHAPTER 13

Kyle's head ached. He adjusted his sunglasses, waiting for the two ibuprofens to take effect, and regretted some of the previous evening. They'd polished off another two bottles of the wine, which Kyle knew sold for several hundred dollars a bottle, and finished the evening sipping rare bourbon. It was more than he usually drank, but by that time of night, it was going down too smoothly. As much as he enjoyed the food and drink, he was dismayed how people like Benedict acted as if they deserved to live like that, day in and day out.

People in the valleys and mountain villages surrounding the Vista Verde ranch had been there for generations and struggled to get by, raising sheep, grazing a few head of cattle, and growing large gardens irrigated by mountain streams. They lived a lifestyle that dated back centuries. The deadly land grant protest he'd covered more than twenty years earlier had taken place about ten miles as the crow flies from where was now. Was this location for the meeting an ironic coincidence? As he pondered, he realized the source of his anxiety about this political event.

Little or nothing that the men in the Vista Verde Ranch dining hall would decide over the next couple of days, months, or even years would have any discernable effect on the lives of those who lived in the surrounding mountains. Yet, these power brokers talked and laughed, and without a moment's hesitation, devoured the best the world had to offer.

Kyle pushed the thoughts to the back of his mind as he gazed at Hank Benedict, who had his arms crossed over his chest as he leaned against a gleaming black Atlas Global Humvee, its doors painted with the yellow globe logo. Benedict squinted in the early morning sunlight, then nodded as Kyle and Raoul approached. Benedict was in his Atlas Global garb: a tight black polo shirt embroidered with the Atlas Global logo, tan cargo pants, and a black boonie cap, also with the Atlas logo. He shook Kyle's hand and nodded to Raoul.

"I hope you enjoyed last night's dinner," Benedict said.

"Yes, I did," Kyle said. "I didn't expect it to be so... gourmet."

"When you can get the best, well, you take it."

Kyle winced at the remark, and was about to respond, when Benedict added, "So, Raoul says you want a tour of the Atlas training center?"

Kyle nodded. "Well, yes. For the next couple of days, you're hosting the President of the United States, along with the two top elected officials in the country. But nobody knows what the Vista Verde Ranch is all about."

"That's right," Benedict said, adjusting his hat. "We like it like that. It's why we wanted to use this place for this political summit. The less people know about Vista Verde, the safer it is. It makes our job easier."

"Perhaps," Kyle said. "But if something happens...well, the whole world is going to want to know."

Benedict squinted in the morning light and adjusted his sun glasses. "Let's go. If you want to be back for the noon press conference, we need to move," he said, and pulled open the driver's door to his Humvee. "Get in the other side. You sit up front with me. We can talk on the way." The vehicle surged from the graveled parking lot onto the graded road, trailed by a plume of dust.

Kyle gazed out the window, seemingly made of standard window glass, unlike the thick, bullet-proof and tinted glass of the combat-equipped Hummers he ridden in Afghanistan. This Hummer felt familiar, the engine quieter, however, than the Hummer that day when he'd rolled and bounced across the bone-dry moonscape wastelands of Afghanistan's southern Ghazni Province, some of the most bleak and barren terrain he'd ever seen.

He'd been embedded with a US Army mechanized patrol rolling out of the ancient fortress town of Ghazni, a few hours south of Kabul, in a convoy of three armored Humvees. It was a National Guard unit from Fort Riley, Kansas, and the soldiers were raw-boned, pink-faced farm boys. Fort Riley had been the home of Gen. George Custer and his 7th Cavalry, but Kyle didn't bring mention it, hoping Custer's fate would not be what the patrol would meet that day.

Half a dozen Afghan soldiers were part the patrol and were dressed like army irregulars, wearing smudged green berets and carrying beat-up AK-47s. Another couple wrapped their heads in black scarves, bandoliers draped from their shoulders and crisscrossing their chests over camouflaged clothing, their thigh pockets stuffed with banana clips. They rode in the back of an aging and open troop carrier with wooden bench seats, double rear axels, and topped with a 30-caliber machine gun bolted to the top of the truck cab.

The convoy had stopped in a village of mud brick houses. The low-slung homes cascaded down a hillside that emitted a swarm of boys who appeared, cheering and waving as the US soldiers arrived. The village mullah had a clean, white turban, sported a trimmed black goatee, and wore a gray vest over his light blue, *shalwar chamise*, his feet clad in scuffed leather sandals. The mullah had an oriental cast to his face, telling Kyle the villagers were Hazara, descendants of the Mongolian invaders who had overrun Afghanistan 800 years earlier. The Hazara were despised by some because they were Shia Muslims, unlike the Sunni Taliban.

The Kansas unit's lieutenant, a tall and lanky man with cropped light brown hair and sunburned cheeks, greeted the mullah. Using a translator, he'd asked if the villagers had any recent contact with the Taliban. No, the mullah had said, there were no Taliban in the area. The lieutenant, nodded, accepting the mullah's word, then turned to Kyle. "C'mon," he said, "I want to show you what we've done for these people."

Kyle followed the lieutenant to a mudbrick school built on a nearby knoll where the village's young school girls lined the path to it, each wearing a coarse black dress and white head scarf. The school was cool inside, smelling of earth and dust, the floors covered with threadbare carpets. The small school's narrow hallway was decorated with warning posters depicting unexploded ordnance and illustrations of the mortars, grenades, and cluster bombs littering the landscape and routinely shredding limbs and lives.

Kyle remembered the chalk marks on a piece of black-painted plywood hanging from a peg that served as a blackboard. Above it were letters of the Arabic alphabet. A solitary young girl knelt on the carpet, her head bowed in silence as dust floated and sparkled in the sunlight streaming through the open window. The girl had looked at him quickly, then returned her gaze to the pink cloth bag on the floor in front of her.

The convoy had rolled out of the village on a dirt road, then dropped into a wide and rocky dry stream bed, slowing as the Humvees shifted into low gear and four-wheel drive so they could churn through the course gravel and over the boulders. The lieutenant said the streambed was safer because the Taliban wouldn't plant land mines in it.

After the Afghans complained the streambed was ruining their truck's rear axel, the convoy climbed back onto the dirt road, angling up and across the face of a long and barren slope where the knobby tires of the Humvees churned through the powdery dirt and under the sun hanging in an opaque sky like a hazy burning orb. The convoy stopped at the summit where the lieutenant, his first sergeant, and the interpreter consulted a map they spread on hood of the Humvee. A dark and indistinct ridge of shadowy mountains sat along the northern horizon, and at its base a ribbon of green extended far to the east, a small river lined with leafy trees.

When the convoy reached the valley floor, the lead vehicle stopped so the lieutenant could question two young boys who stood at the side of the road, one with a crude shovel made from a piece of flat, hand-pounded metal, the other with a rake. The lieutenant accused the boys of planting road bombs. The interpreter told the lieutenant the boys were harmless and stood by the road pretending to fill holes and hoping for a handout from passing motorists. Only the Taliban, not these boys, would plant road bombs. Quivering with fear, sweat beading their stricken faces, the boys ran off when the lieutenant told them leave.

The convoy continued, rolling across the sun-baked landscape, dark rocks scattered across the terrain as if placed by a Zen garden master gone mad, lost and wandering the Afghan wastelands. In the monotonous drone of the engines, Kyle had nodded off.

His eyes blinked open when the earth erupted. The lead truck with the Afghans lifted skyward and the air was sucked out of Kyle's lungs. He jerked forward against the straps of his seatbelt as the Humvee rose up and back, turning on its rear end, then fell onto its side.

Kyle gasped for air, dust coating his mouth and throat, and coughed hard, his eyes burning. He hung by the shoulder straps as dirt and rocks rained from the sky. The hiss and blast of a rocket propelled grenade came first, followed by a second deafening blast as an RPG hit one of the damaged Humvees. Then came the jack-hammer staccato of automatic gunfire and the *whack-whack-whack* of bullets slamming into the metal skin of the Humvee's underside, now exposed. They'd driven into an ambush.

Then the shooting suddenly stopped, followed by only sporadic bursts of fire. Kyle extracted himself from the tangle of his restraints, and climbed out when the armor hardened side door lifted open and the first sergeant's face appeared. His nerves jangled, his movements jerky after the jumped to the ground and gained his feet, Kyle surveyed the aftermath.

He remembered the medevacs and gunships sweeping low overhead as he wandered the kill zone. The attackers had fled on motorcycles moments after the attack. A large pit, wide and deep enough to bury a small car, marked where the mine had been buried, the air stinking of scorched earth, burned rubber, and twisted metal.

Kyle circled the site, taking photos with his pocket camera. Body parts from the Afghan army soldiers littered the ground, scattered among the metal pieces of what was once their truck. A broken axel pointed skyward like a monument. Sunlight glinted from a fragment of a headlight. Beside it was a man's head, the skin of his cheek detached. A boot with a foot still inside. The shred of a pant leg. A bloody hand missing a couple of fingers. Ten yards away was another dead Afghan soldier, the eyes blank.

The image of the Afghan's truck rising skyward, as if spring loaded, tumbling, twisting, then crashing nose first and falling upside down, replayed in Kyle's mind. The spinning had tossed the Afghans like rag dolls, leaving bodies scattered across the grit. Five dead. A couple of the US soldiers had minor injuries and one was dead, the machine gunner who'd been the most exposed. The lieutenant said the Taliban had stacked two or three land mines like pancakes. It could have been worse, he said. But Kyle wondered.

The war in Afghanistan was like that. No front lines, no back lines. War was where you found it. American and

Afghan units patrolled the country side, prodding the enemy, drawing attacks that sometimes came, sometimes didn't.

Kyle shook his head to clear the memories. He was again riding in a Humvee, but this one was slick, not the dusty dun-colored machinery that crawled the deserts of southern Afghanistan. This one had plush leather seats. Wood interior trim. GPS screens. Radios. The works. "Nice ride," Kyle said.

Benedict smiled weakly and nodded, as if it didn't need to be said.

"It's interesting that you and your father are hosting President Harris."

"Why's that?" Benedict asked.

"I didn't know you were fans."

"We're not." Benedict gazed at Kyle, pausing to draw a breath. "Harris is a God-damned Communist. He'd strip all of the wealth out of the country if he could and hand it all over to those who don't deserve it."

Kyle squinted at Benedict and clenched his jaw, mulling a response. "The ones who don't deserve it? You mean the ones who can't get it and will never be able to get it?"

Benedict looked out his side window, then softly said, "You know I'm right."

"I do?" Kyle asked.

Benedict nodded. "You people in the media won't admit the truth."

"Maybe you don't know as much about the news media as you think."

"I read the papers, watch TV, and follow social media," Benedict said. "It's obvious."

"The one percenters own and control the news media," Kyle said. "It's corporate. It's not controlled by a bunch of wild-eyed liberals."

"The owners don't report the news, do they? It's the liberals. They spin it."

"Not if the bosses say no. Your father, for example, and his Wolfe News. Wolfe is not exactly liberal in the way it reports the news."

Benedict smiled. "The news was getting so twisted that my father was forced to do something about it. That's why he created Wolfe News. The real voices of the people were being ignored. Now they're front and center."

"Real? As opposed to what?"

"You know what I'm talking about," Benedict said.

"Maybe the facts don't match what some people, *real* people as you say, want to believe."

"Maybe the facts are distorted to match what the news media believes?"

Kyle shook his head. "That's ridiculous. Facts are facts. If people don't understand that, well, they have problem with reality."

"At least there's a choice now," Benedict said.

"Do you believe there is such a thing as objective truth?" Kyle asked.

Benedict thought for a moment. "It's hard to say."

"I thought so."

Benedict considered his words. "Everyone sees the world differently."

"Yeah, they do," Kyle said. "But two plus two equals four. Not three, not five. Your point of view doesn't matter."

"The best part is that people said it couldn't be done," Benedict continued. "They said there was no room for a new television network. My father showed they were wrong. Now Wolfe News is the most popular, most successful news and entertainment network in world." Benedict paused, flexing his jaw muscle, then forced a weak smile. "I don't trust the news media, but I'm giving you a tour of Atlas Global only because of Raoul. He's one of best in the business. That's why we have him on our team."

Benedict looked over his shoulder at Raoul and nodded.

Kyle fell silent, deciding to stay focused on the story. Benedict was taking him inside the heart of one of the largest, and most secretive private security organizations in the world. The story would be an exclusive for the *Washington Herald* and he didn't want to blow it by getting into an argument with Benedict. No one else in the national news media had been allowed inside Atlas Global. Until now.

***

The Humvee swerved from the gravel, bumped onto asphalt paving, and slid to a stop. They were in the middle of complex of Quonset huts and a couple of large yellow prefabricated metal buildings that functioned as air hangars, along with several concrete block structures sprouting antennas and mounted with satellite dishes. Kyle climbed out and surveyed the scene, adjusted his sun glasses, and tugged his baseball cap down tight.

A wide runway stretched into the distance. Three sleek turbo-prop airplanes sat in front of the hangars, each with retractable doors open, revealing a selection of small aircraft. Six Black Hawk gunships painted with the Atlas Global logo sat at the opposite side of the runway, silent, and lethal, like giant wasps waiting to rise and sting.

"We keep a selection of aircraft here, mostly for training purposes."

Benedict pulled open the door to the closest large building and they stepped into a large gymnasium where mats covered the floor and about two dozen men and women practiced mixed martial arts. Bodies slammed onto the mats with thuds, shouts caroming off the cavernous walls, as legs bent and kicks flew high. Some were engaged in hand-to-hand weapons combat.

"Our personnel are highly trained in martial arts," Benedict said with a smile. Kyle dutifully nodded and held his digital camera to his face and took a series of shots. Benedict led them from the gym and down the hall where he opened the door to another large room filled with desks and dividers, each with a student sitting attentively and wearing head phones.

"We have our own language specialists, all native speakers, who teach the world's major languages. Arabic is in high demand."

They moved further down the corridor to a large amphitheater style lecture hall where an instructor stood in front of large pull-down map of the world. The instructor wriggled a laser pointer at the Middle East.

"This is where we educate our personnel on geo-political dynamics," Benedict said. "We don't want to send anyone into a region where they don't know the players or the history."

"What a concept," Kyle said. "The US does it all the time."

Closing the door quietly, Benedict continued down the corridor and pushed through a set of double doors to the outside. They walked along a wide graveled path as the sound of gunfire grew louder. They rounded a bunker and faced an extensive gun range.

"And of course no training center would be complete without a state-of-the-art gun range," Benedict said. "All of our personnel graduate with a thorough familiarity with all weapons on the market today."

Kyle and Raoul trailed Benedict down concrete steps to the dozen shooting positions, stopping at one. A shooting instructor handed Kyle a pair of safety glasses and protective earphones. He fitted them on. The instructor handed him an AR-15 tactical rifle. Kyle hesitated, looked at Raoul, and then Benedict, who nodded and said, "Try it."

Kyle spread his legs, braced himself, raised the rifle to his shoulder, and drawing a breath, squeezed the trigger. He was surprised at the mild kick, expecting it would be stronger.

He fired another burst, and then another, until the magazine clicked empty. Kyle lowered the rifle and squinted at the target. It was peppered with holes, but few within the tight black circles.

Kyle shook his head in disgust. He pressed the magazine release button with his index finger and the magazine dropped to the carpet-covered stand. Kyle accepted a loaded magazine from the shooting instructor, who wore dark-tinted eye shields and nodded encouragingly. Kyle snapped the magazine into the slot. He lifted the rifle to his shoulder, aimed, and again squeezed the trigger. He lowered the gun and squinted at the target. Most of the shots were within the black circles. He smiled and nodded to Raoul.

CHAPTER 14

At five minutes before noon, along with the other clustered members of the press corps, Kyle faced President Harris, Senate Leader Blount, and House Speaker Divine posing on the front steps of the Vista Verde Ranch lodge, each wearing jeans and casual, western-style shirts.

"I'm happy to tell you that in this short amount of time," Harris proclaimed, "we've already made progress."

"Can you give us some specifics?" a reporter shouted.

"I'd prefer not to do that at this point," Harris said, frowning as if the gravity of their work was a private matter. "Just getting us in the same room is progress," he said, a grin lighting his face.

"What do the others have to say?" Kyle shouted.

President Harris shrugged, stepped back, and turned to Blount, who leaned forward to the microphones.

"The news media and the rest of the country need to know that our fundamental positions have not changed," Blount said in his soft southern accent. "However, we are looking for areas of compromise." He gazed at the group from behind his thick-lensed glasses, nodded, and smiled.

"That doesn't sound optimistic," another reporter barked.

Rather than responding, Blount stepped back and looked to Divine, who stepped forward, lifted his cowboy hat from his head, and smoothed his thinning dark hair. "I'm just glad for the opportunity to get to know President Harris a little better," Divine said. "As was just mentioned, our fundamental positions have not changed. But that does not mean we can't find areas of agreement."

"What areas would those be?" a reporter shouted.

Divine smiled and pointed. "Well, one thing we can find agreement on is that trout pond over there. I say we get to it. There's not a moment to waste. I can't wait to throw a line in it."

Ignoring more reporters' questions, the three men descended the steps and headed across the open field to the large trout pond, trailing a fishing guide who wore chest-high waders, a fishing vest, and carried three fly fishing rods.

Several television cameras on tripods waited at the pond's edge. As President Harris donned a fishing vest and pulled rubber boots up to his thighs, the fishing guide handed Blount and Divine each a rod. Harris followed the guide, wading knee-deep into the pond where the guide waved the fly rod like a wand, demonstrating how to cast a fly.

The thick orange fly fishing line floated on the air, the line growing longer and longer with each flick of the wrist, then silently settled onto the smooth surface of the water. The guide reeled in the line and handed the rod to Harris, who hefted it in his right hand, then pulled a section of line from the reel with his let, and gathered it , just as the guide had shown.

Harris fed line out as he slowly worked the rod back and forth, the line floating through the air, further and further with each swing until it settled on the surface of the pond. Harris stared at the pond as the collected press, staff, and security watched, transfixed.

Kyle felt foolish. About thirty sets of eyes watched Harris fish, focused on the rippled surface of the pond. Kyle fly-fished as often as he could, more lately since he was on leave from the *Herald*. Fly fishing demanded the fisherman get in sync with the surroundings, the stream, and the feeding habits of the trout. It was a solitary activity, a time to exhale, find peace and tranquility, abandon oneself to the natural world. Yet now he gawked as if fly fishing were a spectator sport.

A large trout broke the surface with a sudden and noisy splash, having struck at the fly, as if on cue. Groans arose from the onlookers, followed by a small applause as Harris excitedly reeled in the fish, which broke the surface several times, doing a tail dance before splashing back into the water. Harris whooped excitedly as the pole bent and wriggled

The fishing guide assisted as Harris haltingly reeled in the sizeable trout, slipping a net under the thrashing fish. The guide plunged his hand into the water to withdraw the trout, and holding it behind the head, easily extracted the barbless hook. He then helped Harris hold it up for the cameras.

"The man's a natural," the guide shouted.

Not quite, Kyle thought, but, it made for excellent video.

***

Thirty minutes later, Kyle sat in his stuffy outbuilding feeling burdened. The trout fishing event lacked substance, tempting him to give it a tongue-in-cheek treatment. He envisioned a headline: President Survives Trout Encounter. Clustering the press at the pond's edge was media management at its finest. Kyle hated it. Harris, his advisors, and the other politicians worked hard to control how they appeared in the press. Bad press cost votes. Lost votes meant lost power. Lost power meant lost contributions. None of them were above intimidating reporters if they could get away with it.

House Speaker Divine was the worst of the manipulators. His reputation as a ruthless enforcer was well-deserved. His methods were simple and classical: the ends justified the means. He'd do whatever was necessary. He'd call journalists into his office on the pretense of giving them an exclusive, then berate them and send them away, tails between their legs. He'd call their bosses to complain if he disliked coverage.

Because Divine ruled the House with an iron fist, the contributions to his campaign coffers were monumental. Fat checks floated through Divine's office, written by lobbyists and anyone else who wanted to influence legislation under the pay-to-play rule that greased the gears of Congress.

Kyle had little stomach for covering the Congress, the White House, or the rest of Washington. Most of the reporting came from quick and easy press conferences and was little more than information gleaned from press releases, expanded with quotes from a couple of phone interviews with the opposition and/or the friendlies. It was what passed for balanced journalism. Editors were part of the problem because they assigned reporters to press conferences out of fear they'd miss what a politician might say if it was controversial and therefore newsworthy. They rarely did. Now the old formulas for news had been eviscerated by the Internet, which gave a platform to anyone with an opinion or idea, no matter how twisted, biased, or baseless.

Kyle took satisfaction in the rumors that Divine was under investigation and would soon be indicted. The rumors were spoken softly at first, then repeated often enough that they had become believable. Divine's power had grown such that it was making a lot of people anxious, particularly people like President Harris.

For the better part of Harris's term in office, any proposal that arrived in Congress came with Harris's finger prints was immediately dismissed. Dead on arrival, is what Divine called the president's agenda, and he said it with a smile. Over in the Senate, Blount was no different. He'd say that Harris's proposals did not reflect the will of the people. It was an absurd statement, of course, because Harris had been elected by a substantial majority of the popular vote and nearly a two-to-one majority of the electoral votes. Blount's agenda didn't reflect the will of the American people because in reality he only spoke for "his people," the ones who were his biggest contributors.

The rumored investigation by the Justice Department was into Speaker Divine's use of campaign funds. As the top man in the US House of Representatives, Divine received so much money in contributions that he'd been forced to establish a congressional re-election fund as a separate organization from his own re-election fund. The congressional fund allowed Divine to hand out campaign money to the people he wanted to put or keep in Congress, the ones who'd do his bidding, vote the way he wanted. If they followed Divine's dictates, they were appointed as chairmen and chairwomen of key committees and became Divine's gatekeepers and henchmen. Divine could pass a bill or kill it with a phone call.

Kyle suspected that Divine was at this retreat only as a show, to make it appear as if he wanted to work with President Harris. Publically and privately Divine ridiculed and belittled Harris. Kyle sensed Divine was headed for a fall, and therefore was at this retreat to give himself a soft landing, the appearance of being cooperative. He could always then claim, "I tried."

If Divine was caught in a political corruption scandal, the ripple effects would spread far and wide. A scandal among the conservative opposition could sabotage hopes they had of retaking the White House in the next election. That's why Blount and Divine were there, Kyle believed, and was why they also stood at the edge of the trout pond casting their fishing lines.

At the end of this weekend retreat, Blount and Divine were to fly back to Washington with the outlines of a compromise legislative agenda. If they didn't, Kyle believed, the stalemate in Washington would be solidified in the public mind. Blount and Divine hoped to show that they and their party could lead the country and get things done.

The more he thought about it, the more Kyle's stomach soured. He shook his head to refocus. No, he wasn't going to write anything about a staged trout fishing event. He'd write his story about being inside the Atlas Global Security operations. Hank Benedict had impressed him with the scope and reach of his organization. Atlas Global was a prototype of private and public security forces in the future, Benedict had said. Future wars would be limited, fought by highly trained, well equipped, very mobile fighters. The kind you found in private security forces.

Kyle couldn't argue with that. But who controlled the private security companies? Governments? Corporations? His stomach sank at the thought. Private security companies had been used extensively in Iraq to supplement regular forces. They'd been an unregulated band of modern mercenaries. They hated to be called that, but that's what they were. Hired guns.

They were hailed as the new wave in modern warfare by the likes of former defense secretaries and vice-presidents. Outsourcing war. The policy had given rise to other private security companies run by former American, British, or South African, or Australian Special

Forces soldiers, all in the mold of Hank Benedict. Kyle had seen these private security forces buzz over Baghdad in their compact helicopters, gunners hanging out the oval doors clutching their weaponry. They monitored and managed the movement of US embassy and support personnel in and around the city. If they saw a threat, it was neutralized.

Then the inevitable happened. Private security guards shot and killed seventeen civilians in one of Baghdad's busiest intersections. Kyle had raced to the scene, smelled the death, seen the riddled vehicles, the bodies on the streets stained with blood. Iraqis were duly outraged. Kyle shuddered at the memory. Iraqis were already fed up with the Americans by then and this was the final straw. In the end, charges were filed against the company and personnel who'd done the killing were convicted and sentenced to lengthy jail terms. But it meant nothing to most Iraqis. The victims were dead and buried. Nothing was going to bring them back. Nothing was going to repair the damage or to sweeten the bitter taste of what had happened on that day.

It had been Hank Benedict's company back then and was called Redstone. He'd renamed it to shed the company's trigger-happy reputation. Now all security companies like Atlas Global demanded they be exempt from prosecution if they were to work in war zones. They didn't want to be held accountable. Kyle understood. How can you expect a soldier, private or otherwise, to work in a war zone and be liable for each and every person who might be shot and killed? But, and exemption from prosecution was effectively a license to kill.

Kyle drew a deep breath, pulled the memory card from his camera, and inserted it into his laptop. He scrolled through the photos of Benedict and the training activities he'd seen earlier in the day. He had some good ones. The editors would be happy. He began to write.

A couple of hours later, he looked up. The sun streamed in through his west-facing window as he looked over the story one last time.

VISTA VERDE RANCH, N.M.—While President Barry Harris huddles here behind closed doors with congressional leaders, he does so not only under the watchful eye of the Secret Service, but of Atlas Global, one of the world's largest and most secretive private security firms in the world.

Atlas Global is one of the US government's top providers of embassy security. The firm is led by Harry "Hank" Benedict, the son of billionaire real estate mogul David Benedict, who is personally hosting this unprecedented political retreat at his high desert ranch retreat.

Kyle sat back, satisfied. A knock on the door made him jump, his nerves on edge. The door swung open, revealing Ariel's smiling face. "You okay?" she asked.

Kyle nodded. "Ah, yeah." He glanced at his watch. 5:10. He'd been at his desk for nearly three hours. "I guess I lost track of time."

"You coming to dinner?"

"It's time?"

"You're not hungry?"

"I could use a drink. Who's at the table?"

"Same as last night," she said. "You, Hank, Raoul, and me." Ariel entered the bungalow, then swung an arm from behind her back. She held a bottle of the rare French wine. "Though you might like this."

Kyle smiled. "You bet. Thanks. But do we have time?"

"I got it from the wine steward," Ariel said. "It's for later."

"Good thinking," Kyle said, then tilted his head from side to side, his neck cartilage cracking.

Ariel stepped behind him and massaged his shoulders. "My God," she said. "These neck muscles feel like piano wires."

She worked the tension from his shoulders and neck, her skilled hands relaxing his knotted muscles, tight for so long Kyle considered the pain normal. "Ohh, that's feels soooo good," he groaned. Her skilled hands spread warmth from his neck down to his shoulders and to his back. When she stopped, he stood, took her in his arms, and kissed her, her body melting against his, her arms hugging him.

As Kyle held her he thought about how Ariel had come back into his life after more than twenty years. He felt like he'd been given a gift. The nagging ache suddenly returned to his left knee and so did his memories of how it had been injured.

"Are you okay?" Ariel asked, pulling away.

Kyle snapped back. "Yeah, sure. Was just remembering something."

Ariel nodded. "C'mon. You need to eat some food, get grounded."

They crossed the open field from the bungalow to the main lodge, scaled the steps, passed through a brief security pat down, and entered the dining hall, which again was filled with noisy conversation.

Hank Benedict and Raoul were pouring wine as Ariel and Kyle took their seats. "Sorry," Kyle said, "but I had to finish the story. Took longer than I expected."

"Problems?" Benedict asked.

"Not at all," Kyle said, sensing that Benedict was worried about the story. "I just wanted to get it right."

Benedict knew not to ask to see the story before it was printed, Kyle suspected, but Benedict looked at him expectantly, as if he should talk about what he'd written. I'll let Benedict dangle for a while, Kyle thought, and reached for the wine bottle, filling his and Ariel's wine glasses. "Don't worry," Kyle said after a pause. "I wouldn't be surprised if you didn't get a few more contracts after people read it."

Kyle glanced at Raoul, who nodded, and then at Benedict, who couldn't stop a small smile from crawling across his face. Kyle had handled the story carefully, fighting off the temptation to cast Benedict as a gun-crazed, paranoid ex-Special Forces operative with a super-sized sense of superiority and entitlement that gave him permission to kill anyone anywhere who he viewed as bad. That included about 95 percent of humanity. Benedict had private army at his disposal. But portraying Benedict as completely crazed would only cause trouble for Raoul and himself, if not Ariel.

Kyle had played the story down the middle and quoted Benedict at length about the virtues of private enterprise meeting the global need for security in this age of terror and the rise of ISIS. All wars of the future would all be asymmetrical, Benedict claimed. No more front lines with one army facing another. Battles would be short, sporadic, and extremely violent. They would happen anywhere, anytime. In homes, in streets, in neighborhoods, in remote territories. No place was safe, no place was immune. No longer was the enemy affiliated with recognized countries or organized states. The enemy was scattered, fractured, loosely affiliated individuals and small groups sharing a vaguely common belief—a belief for which they would gladly die and take countless others with them.

The counter to the madness, Benedict argued, private security forces were necessary because they could operate outside of traditional government structures. But they needed sophisticated intelligence and attack capabilities. Organized armies were useful only as occupiers, peace keepers, and would move into an area once the threat was neutralized.

To flesh out the story, Kyle had contacted a couple of security analysts, and after some prodding, got them to answer the question: Who controls such groups? The experts said it was obvious: whoever is paying the bill. If Benedict didn't like what they said, that was his problem.

"The story is being edited now," Kyle said. "I'm expecting calls on it anytime now. It'll be available online at the *Herald's* website after midnight, ten o'clock our time. You can read it then."

Personally, Kyle doubted Benedict's claim that his Atlas Global was the wave of future. Kyle also knew that if he thought about it too much about it, he'd tie himself up in knots. *Time will tell.* Kyle took solace in the adage that if you gave someone like Benedict enough rope, they'd hang themselves. Until then, he needed access to Benedict and all that he could provide.

CHAPTER 15

After a dinner that included another platter of grilled bison, elk, and wild turkey, along with more than enough rare wine, Kyle and Ariel walked from the main lodge across the darkened field toward Kyle's cabin.

"You're the last person I expected to find here," Kyle said. "When I left New Mexico twenty years ago, I never thought I'd see you again."

Ariel turned to him in the darkness, her face barely visible, and smiled. "Our paths have crossed once again."

"Remember the Ojo Caliente hot springs?" he asked.

"Of course. How could I forget?"

"It was a good time," Kyle said with a sigh. "You never know how good something is until it's gone."

"You were covering a big story then."

"The land grant protests."

"I remember the nights at the hot springs hotel," Ariel said, but her smile dropped into a frown and her face clouded. "What happened to us?"

Kyle's stomach sank as a wave of guilt swept over him. The affair had run its course—or so he thought. He'd grown tired of Ariel's new age notions of the cosmos, of fate, and her view of the world as a magical, mystical place swirling with unseen forces. He saw the world in more concrete terms. Cause and effect. Actions and reactions. Something happened or didn't happen because someone did something or didn't do something. There wasn't much magical about it.

She'd been a committed "vegan," even though he told her heaven had no special place for people who ate only vegetables. Ariel was never preachy about it, but Kyle hadn't stuck around for that eventuality. Those days felt like a foggy dream now. But they'd been real, very real, and though she'd faded from his life, she was not forgotten. Ariel was different now, as was he--far different from two decades earlier.

Kyle knew now she'd helped him land on his feet. He'd spent a few days with the land grant protesters and the nights with here soaking in the hot springs and making love. He'd come through it all with a stronger sense of himself as a journalist, having found a calling he believed made live worth living. Now back in northern New Mexico, he again felt her strong presence, just as he had then, perhaps more so now. Although they'd led separate lives, they both had let go of what didn't work in their lives, or had fallen away, like an overloaded truck bouncing down a rough road, the excess baggage falling out.

Ariel seemed focused and settled, comfortable in herself. Maybe it was a Zen-like acceptance of reality that put her at peace with her life. *What about me?* Kyle remembered the Buddhists talked about surrender. He understood, because at some point, you realize you have next to no control. Like the Serenity Prayer. Accept the things you cannot change, have the courage to change the things you can, and the wisdom to know the difference. Kyle preferred acceptance over surrender. Surrender meant giving up. An appealing thought sometimes, because it meant the end of struggle. But he wasn't ready for that. Not yet.

"I'm glad we met again," Ariel said. "I've changed. You've changed."

"Life will do that to a person," Kyle said, looking at her for a long moment, thinking of how neither of their marriages had turned out the way they'd wanted. "I'm sorry about your husband."

"We all need to move on."

"Hank was vague last night about what happened to him," Kyle said. "His name was Jerome, right?"

Ariel paused, her face lighted by the distant lights of the lodge, and frowned at the memory of her late husband. "Hank has always been vague about it. I don't know why. There was something strange about it."

"What do you mean?"

"Jerome and I talked almost every night by phone, you know, just to touch base. Jerome was angry about something in the days before he died. I never knew exactly what. It had to do with what Benedict was doing with security in Benghazi."

"Benghazi? As in Libya?"

Ariel nodded. "Yes. How many Benghazis are there?"

Kyle shrugged.

"He was one of the security people there."

"Jerome was there?" Kyle's mind raced. *Atlas Global. Of course! It made sense, perfect sense.*

"Yes. He was there," Ariel said.

"I went to Benghazi right after the security fiasco there when the ambassador was killed. I can tell you what I know probably happened. But I don't know exactly how Jerome may have been involved."

She looked at him skeptically, then nodded. "I'd like to know."

Ariel and Kyle walked in the cool darkness of the night, Kyle wondering where to begin.

"There's supposed to be a partial eclipse of the moon tonight," she said. "They call it a blood moon. I want to see it. But first you need to tell me about Benghazi."

Kyle paused at the bungalow door, inserted the key, and the door clicked open. "This could require a glass or two of that wine you brought earlier."

Ariel smiled and nodded. "That's why I brought it."

Minutes later, they sat on the bungalow steps, each with a wine glass in hand. Kyle took a deep drink. "There was a lot going at Benghazi that no one wants to talk about."

"Like what?"

"Benghazi was primarily a CIA operation, not a diplomatic mission. The State Department functions there were secondary. They were a cover."

"I didn't know that."

"Libya was in chaos at the time. Complete lawlessness. It's what happens when a maniacal dictator like Muammar Gaddafi is removed. There's a mad scramble for power."

Ariel nodded. "I remember seeing those awful scenes on TV when they caught him."

Ariel shuddered. "It made me sick."

"It was pretty ugly." Kyle took a sip. "So much for the high and mighty."

"Benghazi didn't happen until later," Ariel said.

"That's right," Kyle said. "In the year following Gaddafi's death, a lot of people helped themselves to all of the weapons that Gaddafi had stockpiled for his security forces and his army. The CIA and the state department were nervous about it. They didn't want the weapons to fall into the wrong hands."

"Wrong hands being Islamic terrorists?" Ariel asked. "That makes sense."

"The Arab spring was quickly becoming the Arab winter," Kyle said. "Rather than the flowering of democracy, as President Harris and others at the state department tried to sell it, radical fundamentalist Muslims took advantage of the chaos."

Ariel brushed hair from her face, then turned and stared, looking east over the forested mountains. A glimmer of light from the rising full moon shone like a beacon. "Oh, my God. The moon is rising now."

Kyle stared for a moment, then continued.

"In the lead-up to Benghazi, the dictators who had controlled the Arab world were falling, one after another. Hosni Mubarak of Egypt was one of the first. Then the uprising in Syria happened. Bashar al-Assad tried to squash it, but he couldn't. It turned into a bloody civil war. Revolution spread throughout the Arab world. Gaddafi fell in Libya followed by the government in Tunisia. The state department tried to sell it as the flowering of democracy, the so-called Arab spring."

"Okay," Ariel said, looking from Kyle back to the moon, now a white globe hovering over the mountains.

"The dictators had kept the radical Islamists under control, but once the dictators were gone, radical Islam flowered, not democracy."

Ariel sipped her wine. "So, what about Jerome?"

"Well, I'm not sure. But I know the US was worried about all of those weapons in Libya. So, The CIA contacted our friend Hank Benedict and arranged for a handful of his private security contractors to get the weapons out of Libya. They worried mostly about the portable ground-to-air missiles."

"Jesus. What the hell are they?"

"They're very useful in downing all sorts of aircraft like helicopters and commercial airliners," Kyle said. "They can be carried by one man.

Ariel shook her head, "Hmm. Not good."

"The CIA contractors, that being Benedict and his men, including Jerome, rounded up most of the weapons. But then they had another problem."

"Which was?"

"What to do with them."

"Okay."

"The civil war in Syria was getting bad at the time," Kyle continued. "It had been going on for two years by then, and the rebels were being pounded by the Assad regime. The rebels needed arms."

"Like the ones in Libya."

"Exactly. But at the time, President Harris was running for re-election. He had pulled the US out of Iraq and was trying to do the same in Afghanistan. The last thing he wanted was to drag the US into another messy war in the Middle East. And, he'd already said the US was not going to arm to the Syrian rebels. Instead, he said he was going to pressure the Assad regime to play nice. That was the official word, anyway."

"Why Harris didn't want to arm the Syrian rebels?" Ariel sipped from her wineglass, looking at him curiously. "They were fighting for democracy, after all."

"Harris wanted the civil war to burn itself out. He wanted the US to set an example by staying out and hoped the Russians would do the same. But the Russians stepped in and helped Assad. So the US had no choice but to help the rebels."

"How do you know this?"

"It's what I do. The proof is buried in Benghazi investigation. Ambassador Arnold was the US liaison with the Libyan rebels for more than a year. He'd been working with a man named Abdel Hakim Malik."

"Who?"

"One of the Libyan rebel leaders. Malik was head of the Libyan military council trying to impose some order on the country. He agreed to help the CIA ship the weapons to Syria. This was not a small project. It was 400 tons worth of arms."

"Are you really with the CIA?"

Kyle smiled and shook his head. "Me? CIA? Hardly." He drank some wine. "On the day of the Benghazi attack, Ambassador Arnold met with Turkey's Consul General in Libya."

"About the arms shipment?" Ariel asked.

"Yes. They weren't talking about the weather."

"And?"

"He explained to Malik that the CIA was using a private contractor, specifically Benedict's Atlas Global, to ship the weapons. That way the US could say that it wasn't involved."

"No wonder Jerome couldn't talk about it," Ariel said.

"The plan was to load the weapons onto a cargo ship in Tripoli and move them across the Mediterranean to southern Turkey where they'd be unloaded and trucked into rebel-held territory in Syria."

"What happened?"

"Benghazi happened. Word got out that the US had all of Gaddafi's weapons. The Islamic jihadists wanted them and figured they were being stored at the US consulate office in Benghazi."

"Oh, my God."

"An angry mob of Libyan *jihadis* attacked the consulate the night of September 11. But most of the consulate security was at the CIA annex building about a mile away. It took time for reinforcements to get from the CIA annex to the consulate. When they arrived, they fought off the attack and pulled Arnold and the others into a safe room. By the way, there were more than 30 people there at the CIA annex. Almost all were CIA and contractors, not State Department personnel. The annex was under attacked for another couple of hours."

"Sounds awful."

"It was. The CIA guys in the annex called their buddies in Tripoli who were loading the arms shipment. But, they couldn't help from Tripoli because they were several hours away. But six or seven of the Atlas Global guys in Tripoli bribed a pilot to fly them to Benghazi. When they arrived at the CIA annex about 5 a.m., it was quiet. They figured the fighting was all over."

"Let me guess. It wasn't."

"A few minutes after the early morning prayers, mortars began to rain down on the CIA annex. That's when some of the Atlas contractors were killed."

Ariel looked into her wine glass, then out to the moonlit field. "So, that's where Jerome died? He was trying to save the other Americans?"

"I'm not sure. But yes."

"That's important for my son to know. He needs to know that his father died a hero."

"Because of what the security guys did, almost all of the Americans were rescued and taken to safety. Like I said, most were CIA personnel."

She held her glass in both hands, her tears glistening in the light from the fully risen moon. She brushed the tears away. "I'm sorry," she said. "I can't help it."

"Don't be sorry," Kyle said, putting an arm around her and pulling her close.

Ariel rested her head against his shoulder and sobbed. After a few moments, she drew a halting breath and slowly exhaled, using a finger to brush away tears.

"You loved him," Kyle said.

"Yes," she said, sitting up and clearing her throat. "A part of me always will."

They sat in silence gazing at the moon, now poised, large and full over the mountains, looking twice normal size. The cool night air smelled of pine. "My God, the moon is bright," Ariel said, sighing deeply.

"When is the blood moon supposed to begin?" Kyle asked. "It might be nice to see."

"It won't come until about three in the morning."

"In that case, I'll pass," he said. "I'm exhausted."

"Me, too. I gave several massages today."

"Are you headed home?"

Ariel shook her head. "I'd prefer not be alone tonight."

"What about your son?"

"He's spending the weekend at his best friend's house. It's summer, you know." She looked into Kyle's face as she slipped her arms around his neck and kissed him.

CHAPTER 16

Tariq moved carefully, his footsteps quietly treading the high mountain trail. Crickets chirped and a couple of coyotes howled in the distant darkness. The full moon, now bright in the high mountains, lighted the forested slopes, throwing mottled shadows across the trail.

Tariq followed Carlito, who seemed devout enough, he thought, and was enthusiastic in his new-found beliefs. Tariq had insisted Carlito be given an Islamic name and had called him Omar al-Amriki, Omar the American. Like himself when he was younger, Carlito had embraced the tenets of *jihad* like few others. But, how strong was Carlito's commitment to Islamic *jihad*? Would young Omar al-Amriki die for Islam? Would he reject the pleasures of this world, embrace martyrdom, and take his reward in heaven?

Carlito wasn't the only former *kafir* with them. There was the woman Jennifer, who'd taken the name of Halima. She had come to the mosque in Abiquiu with her friends. There as the Iranian woman Aliyah, a woman whose beauty made him ache. But she was a Shia, which made her no better than her *kafir* boyfriend, the one named Miguel. They had visited the mosque and listened to his lectures on Islam and the need for *jihad*. But unlike Omar al-Amriki and his woman, now Halima, the two others had rejected his teaching and stopped attending the mosque.

It was good, Tariq thought, because he didn't trust the one they called Miguel. The young man was quiet and seemed curious about Islam, but rarely asked questions. When Tariq had faced the Americans in the mosque, he sometimes doubted his abilities to awaken their passion for Islam. They simply sat and listened. But his men disagreed, telling Tariq he inspired them much like their hero, the Imam Anwar Al-Awlaki. No one spoke as eloquently as Al-Awlaki, the emir of the Internet, or with such clarity and passion, certainly in English, about the virtues of Islam. The Americans had killed Al-Awlaki in a drone strike. *The cowards!* Tariq felt anger clutch his chest again. Yes. It was another reason why he would fulfill this mission. He would sever the head of the Great Satan.

Tariq had closely followed the teachings of Al-Awlaki, who preached one should not focus on pleasure and wealth, but on the spiritual rewards of the next life. Like Al-Awlaki, he told his men not to worry about *rizq*, their daily bread. But *rizq* meant more than just food, he explained, it meant all the material wealth the world has to offer. Attachment to the material world was the greatest evil. To crave and seek worldly pleasures did not bring true happiness, Tariq said often. Competing for material wealth was a waste of life.

It was ironic, Tariq explained, because the only inevitability of life was death. A life well lived was one in which each person prepared for the next. That meant rejecting the material world and those who were infected with a love of it. And who, he asked, drew people away from love of Allah and to the world of material pleasures? The whole of the western world! The Christian crusaders who were now led by the biggest evil of all, the United States!

Tariq had told the American students that if they practiced Islam, they should never trust their government because its army was killing Muslims every day. Of the Americans, only Carlito, now Omar, had smiled and nodded. And soon, the young woman Halima had come around as well.

Now, as they walked quietly in the cool the mountain night, Tariq pushed his lingering doubts about Carlito to the back of his mind. It had frustrated Tariq that the other two Americans had not become part of this mission. He could have used them. But still, Allah had given him the two young converts. It was enough. So far, both had done well, extremely well, and quickly learned to handle the AK-47 pistol and to shoot it. More importantly, Carlito/ Omar knew the mountain trails, and as he had promised, was taking Tariq's men undetected to the lodge at the Vista Verde Ranch. Tariq's heart pounded at the thought of what he and the others were about to do, even as fatigue clouded his mind.

Tariq tapped Carlito on the shoulder. "We need to stop here for a few minutes," he said, and raised his hand to stop the single-file column. The night forest fell silent. Carlito turned to Tariq. With his head wrapped in a black and white patterned scarf, that left only his eyes exposed, Carlito nodded silently and pointed through the trees.

Tariq saw the spacious valley below and the full moon's pale gray light reflected from the roofs of the lodge and outbuildings. He strained to see the guards posted around the lodge, shadowy figures outlined by the glow of the interior's yellow lights.

Another coyote howled in the distance.

Tariq lifted his gaze to the moon shining through the trees and noticed a slight change in its glow, a weakening of the brightness. A small shadow had fallen across a corner of the orb, as if a piece of the moon had been bruised and bitten away.

Tariq glanced from the moon to Carlito, whose dark eyes glistened, filled with a mixture of fear and joy. Carlito was handy with a weapon, but he had never been on a mission like this. Carlito could become a liability. Tariq knew he would soon find out enough. Now that he and his men were at the lodge, Carlito's job was complete. He'd done what

Tariq needed, which was bring him and his men to within striking distance. Tariq thought he should kill the young Hispanic now to get him out of the way. But he resisted the impulse, knowing that he need all of the men now. If Carlito killed just one of the infidels, it was worth keeping him alive. Tariq had known others like Carlito, Americans who had come to the Islamic State to join ISIS. No one trusted them. The Amrikis were soft. They had lived in luxury all their lives and did not know what it meant to suffer and sacrifice. That's why the caliphate sent the Amrikis on suicide missions, turning them into suicide bombers to demonstrate their dedication to *jihad*.

Tariq remembered the one they called Abusalha, the Florida boy who became the first American suicide bomber in Syria. He had lived in a gated community, Tariq learned, and no one could understand why he would leave that life to come to Syria and die. He had taken the war name of Abu Huraira, after a friend of the Prophet. It meant father of the kitten, because both Abusalha and the Prophet loved cats. Privately, Tariq was disgusted by the name, but said nothing about its silliness because the other fighters had respected it.

Now, Tariq thought, Abusalha was with the Prophet in Heaven. He'd made a video of his final testament and it ended with a scene of his explosive-filled truck detonating, sending a fiery cloud roiling skyward. In the video, Abusalha had smiled and held a cat. Tariq remembered it well. "We are coming for you," Abusalha had said, speaking directly to President Harris. "Listen to my words, you big *kafir*," Abusalha had said. "You think, oh, because you killed Osama bin Laden, that you did something. You did nothing. You think you have won? You will never defeat Islam."

Tariq appreciated the way Abusalha had spoken because he had spoken directly to Harris, telling all Americans neither he nor the rest of ISIS were afraid of the Great Satan.

Still, Tariq wondered, would Carlito die for Islam? What about the rest of his men? Tariq dismissed his doubts. He was confident his men were dedicated *jihadis*. They had been with him at the beheadings. They had been with him as ISIS surged across Syria and into Iraq for the taking of Mosul. He had no doubts about what they could and would do for Islamic *jihad* and the Islamic State. There was no turning back now. Next stop, heaven.

Tariq looked again at the girl Jennifer, now Halima. She, too, was beautiful, but not like Aliya. He needed to protect Halima because she was his bargaining chip. She was the reason they had been able to secure the device—the device that would make their dreams come true. She would do whatever Carlito wanted. He had never seen such dedication from an American woman. She embraced the teachings that required a woman to be modest, subdued, and attentive to the needs and desires of her husband. Tariq was jealous. He himself had wanted a woman like Halima, but knew it was not to be. She would not be a problem. She was part of the plan, an integral part, though she didn't yet know it.

Tariq had come to respect Halima, who wasn't like her Iranian friend, Aliyah, the apostate. Unlike women from the Islamic world who quickly lose their dedication once they get a taste of the western world, Halima had done the opposite. She was neither arrogant nor demanding. She didn't criticize her Muslim brothers. She was unattached to material pleasures and maintained her modesty. Yes, that was Halima.

Tariq refocused his mind on the buildings in the distant valley, then gazed at the moon, now burnished. The coyotes had begun to howl, giving a foreboding voice to things yet to come. No, the coyotes were not afraid of the darkness. They embraced it. This was their song, their communion with the night. In full-throated intensity, their howls echoed in the forests as the moon was colored rust red.

It was time.

Tariq turned to his men, telling them to cover themselves with their black head scarves, like the one he'd worn for the on-camera beheadings. He went from man to man, quietly whispering the instructions. They'd gone over the plan many times, but it never hurt to repeat and reinforce. This was the worst time, the moment before battle when his stomach was tight and felt like a heavily knotted rope. His breath came short and fast, his palms were moist. *Just do it!*

They would emerge from the forest shadows like creatures of the night, he told them. Move silently, swiftly, and do not fire your weapons until the very last moment. Surprise was on their side. No one would ever suspect what was about to happened. And if it was Allah's will, Tariq said, they soon would hold their blades to the necks of the Great Satan and his minions.

Moments later and lighted only by the muted moonlight, Tariq's face remained hidden by the shadows as he surveyed the distant lodge, now quiet. He signaled to his men, each armed with pistols, assault rifles, and grenades pinned to their jackets, to get ready. He nodded to Carlito, motioning for him to lead.

They moved through the forest, and after twenty minutes, paused in the shadows where the forest ended, giving way to the open and grassy field that extended to the looming main lodge of the Vista Verde Ranch. Tariq scanned the open valley eagerly, gauging the distance between the cottages and bungalows scattered in the tree line on each side of the lodge. Like the lodge, the outbuildings were quiet. Most of the government and military vehicles were clustered in the circular drive fronting the lodge. Only a few lights glowed from the lodge's interior. A handful of Atlas Global and Secret Service agents stood guard in various locations around the perimeter. All was eerily silent. The earth's extended shadow had mostly crossed the moon, and it now was quickly becoming full again. They needed to move now before the moon's blue-white light would again flood the valley and surrounding mountains.

Tariq drew a slow, deep breath and motioned his men forward. They became dark figures scurrying noiselessly from the edge of the forest across the 100 yards of the grassy field. Bent at the waist, holding their weapons close to their chest, half of the men dropped noiselessly to the ground, between the lodge and the trout pond, and waited for the other to advance.

Tariq crouched in the shadow at the base of a pine tree to gauge the progress, speaking softly into a microphone, part of his lightweight headset. "Is everyone in position?" he whispered. He paused and listened, then said, "Praise be to Allah." Tariq looked up to the moon, still half red, as it was becoming bright again. "Our target is President Harris," he whispered. "Alive. He must be captured alive."

Tariq held the AK-47 sniper rifle against his shoulder and sighted down the barrel, past the noise and flash suppressor. He fitted his eye against the scope. Through the night vision scope, the valley, lodge and environs looked light green. The scope's crosshairs settled on one of the guards posted about twenty yards from the corner of the lodge. "Does everyone have a man in their sights?" Tariq waited for a moment, then said, "Allah be praised. On the count of three. One ... two... three."

Tariq squeezed the trigger. The muffled shot thunked softly, the rifle jerking slightly in his hands, as the eight other rifles, similarly muffled, popped and emitted small flashes from the barrels. Tariq watched and waited, then counted at least six of the guards at the lodge who had crumpled to the ground.

Tariq shifted his night scope to one of the two agents on the porch near the front doors of the lodge. The man had drawn his pistol and was now prone on the porch, minimizing himself as a target after seeing his fellow agents fall. The agent scanned the surrounding forest in search of the source of the gunfire, then his shots rang out, breaking the night stillness.

Tariq squeezed the trigger again and felt the rifle's recoil against his shoulder. Through the sight, he saw the agent's body jerk, then writhe. The man struggled to his knees, gripped his pistol with both hands, and fired successive rounds into the darkness of the surrounding forest.

At the sound of the firing from the porch, the black-clad *jihadis* scrambled to their feet, and hunched, they dashed toward the lodge. Tariq trailed their rush to the porch, his AK-47 pistol at his side and firing sporadically as they charged into the return fire coming from other agents who had burst from inside the lodge to meet the onslaught.

Tariq and his *jihadis* dropped to the grass, rolled sideways, and again came up firing, just as they had been trained. The agents' bodies jerked wildly from the barrage of bullets and crumpled to the porch.

Tariq sprang to his feet and trailing several of the others, scaled the steps to the porch. They paused at the lodge's main doors where the interior lights now blazed. Tariq shouted in Arabic, telling his men to flatten themselves against the exterior wall as they broke the porch window and tossed smoke grenades into the lobby, spewing dark smoke.

As the canisters hissed and smoke filled the lodge interior, Tariq kicked open the front doors, dove to the floor and rolled, expecting more gunfire. There was none. His men followed his lead, moving through the thick smoke, guns at the ready.

Weapons fire again erupted from the interior and a couple of his men fell, the barrage coming from the top of the broad stairs that curved to the upper floor, the shooters barely visible through the swirling smoke. A couple of the *jihadis* crawled past their fallen comrades and rolled, avoiding the high-caliber bullets.

Tariq clutched his AK-47 pistol, and through the thick smoke, fired blindly toward the top of the stair case. The shooting from above paused. Through the drifting smoke,

Tariq discerned movement at the top of the stairs, then the thunk and tumble of a falling body.

In the next moment, the lodge fell silent as the hiss of the smoke grenades ended. Tariq listened as sporadic shooting erupted from outside the lodge and crept closer from the surrounding bungalows. "We are in! We have the lodge! *Allah akbar*," he shouted.

Then Tariq heard a voice at the top of the stairs.

"Fucking bastards!"

Through the floating smoke, Tariq saw the man he would later learn was Troy Divine. The man's belly hung over his boxer shorts, the only piece of clothing he wore other than cowboy boots and a hat, and he stood at the top of the stairs with a revolver in each hand. The pistols blazed as Divine fired alternately at the *jihadis* crouched at the base of the stairs, hitting two of Tariq's men who twisted and crumpled to the floor.

Tariq and another *jihadi* swung their weapons to the top of the stairs and fired, making Divine's body jerk spasmodically as bullets found their mark. Divine's eyes opened wide and his shooting stopped. The man staggered, his eyes glazed with shock, his mouth open, his jaw slack. Divine teetered, the revolvers falling from his hands and clattering down the steps. His lifeless body fell forward, thumping and rumbling noisily down the stairs.

***

Dressed in his black cargo pants, t-shirt, and flip-flops, Raoul crouched low at the corner outside the bungalow. He held his Heckler & Koch 223 assault rifle tightly against his side, then lifted it toward the main lodge where the gunfire had just fallen silent and the lights had just gone completely dark. His heart pounded in his ears, his mind racing as he imagined scenarios as to what had just happened in the lodge.

Whoever was inside had found the power box and shut it down. He raised his rifle to his shoulder and sighted along the barrel. Shoot? But at what? Raoul tried to see something, anything, as he feared the worst of all possibilities.

Kyle stepped out from the bungalow door, pulling up his pants and stepping into his shoes. Ariel was right behind.

"Get down! Get down!" Raoul shouted, waving his hand.

Kyle sank to his haunches, as did Ariel, then slowly edged along the outside wall, straining to see into the darkness, his eyes still adjusting.

Raoul squinted across the one hundred yards between him and the lodge, a futile effort to see what was going on, despite the now bright moonlight in the valley. The firing in the lodge had stopped, at least for the moment. Raoul struggled with what he feared was increasingly evident: unknown attackers now controlled the building that housed the President, the Speaker, and the Senate leader.

Then a new burst of rifle fire flashed from the lodge windows, the shots sparking in the night. Raoul lifted his weapon again to his shoulder, but didn't fire, not knowing who was inside the lodge and who was outside. Then the communications device clipped to Raoul's ear and crackled.

"What the hell is going on?" asked the voice of Hank Benedict. "What the hell is all of that shooting?"

His back against the outside wall of the log cabin-styled bungalow where he'd been waiting and watching, Raoul spoke calmly. "Ahhh, Hank. We got ourselves a friggin' nightmare. It looks to me like someone…I don't know who yet … has taken over the lodge."

"You're freakin' kidding me!" Benedict shouted. "There's no way! That's impossible."

"Yeah, that's what I thought. Where are you?"

"Where I always am. At the HQ."

"You'd better get over here, quick," Raoul said.

"What the fuck? How could they? We had that place surrounded with some of our best men. They and the Secret Service. There's no way!"

"What can I say?" Raoul said. "Someone, we don't know who, is in control of the damned lodge now, best I can tell."

"But how?"

Raoul exhaled, his stomach tight as he ran through a myriad of possibilities. He scanned the grounds. In the moonlight now, he could see about eight men lying on the ground, their bodies sprawled like logs. "I can count at least eight bodies on the ground outside the lodge," he continued. "It looks like they're some of our men and the rest Secret Service."

Raoul wondered how many others were dead that he couldn't see. He assumed they'd been killed by the attackers, but couldn't be sure. Some may have died from friendly fire in the chaos. "It was a precision strike," Raoul said after a pause. "It looks like they came out of the forests. They picked off the security perimeter with their first shots." He paused again, his mind in high gear. "It came fast, Hank. They rushed the place. Broke through the doors. Once inside, well, I can only guess. They took us by surprise."

"Jesus H. Christ," Benedict said. "What about the guys inside?"

"Don't know," Raoul said. "There was shooting inside, and I figure the guys protecting the president and the others fought back. Don't know if they made it."

"We need to find out," Benedict said.

"I'm going to recon the lodge," Raoul said. "Try to figure out what happened."

"Shit," Benedict muttered, and clicked off. Again, the night fell silent.

From inside one of the darkened lodge windows, Raoul saw movement, the moonlight glinting as a window was thrown open. A voice shouted to no one in particular.

"We now control the lodge," a man's voice shouted into the night.

Raoul listened closely. It had a strangely cultured-sounding accent.

"Stay back or we will kill the president," the voice shouted.

Raoul turned to Kyle. "Hear that? The guy sounds kinda British."

Kyle looked at him and nodded. "Yes. Yes it does. But …."

Raoul clicked on his com device again. "Hank. Do you read me?"

"Copy that," Benedict said.

"They're shouting from inside. They claim they have the president. They're threatening to kill him if we attack."

"Fuck that," Benedict said. "Let's rush the place. Overwhelming force."

Raoul swallowed, looked at Kyle, and shook his head.

Kyle shook his head as well.

"We don't have enough men to do that Hank," Raoul said. "Besides, they have the damned president!" Raoul said. "Not a good idea, Hank."

"What about the others?" Benedict asked. "Speaker Divine and Senator Blount?"

"Status unknown," Raoul said.

Benedict was silent on the other end, then said, "What do you recommend?"

"Before we do anything, we need to know what kind of weapons they have and what how many are there. They may have booby trapped the place. We can't risk an assault. Not yet, anyway. We need to know what we're up against."

"The longer we wait, the harder it will be," Benedict said. Silence filled the next few moments. "Okay, Raoul. Order all of our Global men to stand down. I'll contact the Secret Service. We need to coordinate this now."

"Roger that," Raoul said, clicking off. He turned a dial and changed the frequency of the com device. Raoul rose from his crouched position. "All Global personnel. This is commander Garcia. Stand down. I repeat. Stand down. They have the president."

Raoul stepped from beside the cabin and scanned the lodge grounds. The valley remained silent as lights came on in various upper rooms in the main lodge, including the upper corner where Raoul knew the president was housed. Lights now shone from inside the surrounding cottages and bungalows, where political aides and the news media huddled and waited.

Ten minutes later, the stillness of the night was broken as a couple of Black Hawk helicopters thudded overhead, circled the lodge, low at first, then, in larger circles, rising higher and higher, then circled away from the lodge.

CHAPTER 17

Several hours later, the sun hanging over the nearby mountains, Kyle, Ariel, Raoul, and Hank Benedict huddled inside the Global Atlas training center office. Kyle glanced through the office window where helicopters thundered overhead. On the ground, a dozen military Humvees, gray Secret Service sedans, and a half dozen New Mexico state police cruisers crowded the drive and runway.

"They have the president and there's not a damned thing we can do about it," Benedict said glumly. "We should have just stormed the place when we had a chance."

"And risk them killing the president?" Raoul asked.

"They'd love that," Kyle said. "They're all willing to die. They can't wait to become martyrs."

"We need to give them that opportunity and the sooner the better," Benedict said.

"And if they kill the president?" Kyle said. "They'd die as the heroes who killed the Great Satan."

Benedict shook his head in disgust. "Between Atlas Global and the Secret Service, we've got eight people dead that we know of," Benedict said, unable to hide his anger, his face crimson, his ice-blue eyes ringed with red. "Four of the dead were Secret Service. We lost four of our own men. Maybe more of are inside."

Kyle nodded. "Some of the lodge staff were probably killed, along with White House and congressional staffers."

Benedict grimaced.

"Who would have thought that northern New Mexico could be a war zone?" Ariel asked.

They looked at her, thinking much the same thing.

"How are you going to free the president, except by force?" she asked, her eyes searching Kyle and Raoul's faces.

Benedict nodded. "That's what I'd like to know. If these guys are who we think they are, they're not going to give up and walk away. They're going to die so they can get their fifty-seven virgins, or whatever. They'll take as many people with them as they can. Including the president."

Kyle looked at Benedict and then at Raoul, and knew Benedict was right.

Benedict glanced at his watch. "The commander of the Secret Service contingent is due here any minute. We're all going to be part of a video conference with the president's Security Council in Washington. The head of the Secret Service, the director of the FBI, Justice department, homeland security, and the National Security Agency."

"Look!" Raoul said, pointing to one of several television screens on the wall. "The news media is all over this."

"Of course," Kyle said.

The Wolfe News Network's cartoonish logo of a snarling wolf, its gleaming eyes staring at the camera, filled one of the screens. An anchor came on.

"It's a nightmare scenario that no one thought possible," the gray-haired, blue-eyed anchor said. "Today America suffered a devastating blow from which it will be difficult to recover, if ever. *Jihadi* terrorists now hold the president of the United States hostage. Yes, that's right. The president of the United States is in the hands of terrorists! What's even more outrageous is that he's being held in what was considered a completely secure location in the remote mountains in northern New Mexico. For a live report, we now go our correspondent who has been with the president at the Vista Verde Ranch."

The screen cut to a reporter standing at the edge of a graveled road in the forest. "It's too bizarre to believe, but it's true," the reporter said. He had sandy hair, brown eyes, and wore a western-cut shirt and jeans. "In the early morning hours, not far up this road, a force of heavily armed *jihadi* terrorists swept down from the surrounding mountains, killing at least eight security agents protecting the president. The dead include Secret Service agents, whose job it is to protect the president, and private security personnel who are part of Atlas Global Security. As best we can tell, the surprise attack came so swiftly the president's security detail was unable to mount effective resistance."

"Do we know the condition of the president?" the anchor asked.

The reporter nodded. "We know that the president was staying in one of the secure rooms in the upper floor. Also on the floor, but in separate rooms, were Senator Michael Blount, the Senate Majority Leader, and Troy Divine, the Speaker of the House. We've learned that Divine and an unknown number of the security agents inside the lodge may have been killed in the assault."

"Where did these terrorists come from and how do we get the president free?" the anchor asked.

"Sources tell Wolfe News that the terrorists may have entered the US by crossing along a remote and unguarded section of the US-Mexico border. Officials believe the terrorists may be the people responsible for the shooting deaths of multiple Border Patrol agents a couple of months ago."

"What's the status of the president?" the anchor asked.

"We're not really sure. All we know is that the president was in one of the upper rooms and that the terrorists now control the building."

"Have the terrorists made any demands?" the anchor asked.

"Not yet. For the moment, it's a waiting game. Intelligence officials are frantically trying to figure out who's responsible for this and what they want."

"Incredible," the anchor said with a disgusted shake of his head. "This is a day that Americans never thought they would ever see."

***

With a subtle nod, Raoul signaled to Kyle that he'd be briefed about the teleconference later, then Raoul sat back and watched as Kyle and Ariel were ushered from the Atlas Global conference room where a large wall screen showed the members of the Security Council taking their seats around an oval table.

Benedict and Raoul, along with a handful of Secret Service agents, CIA agents, and four other Atlas Global agents remained in the headquarters briefing room. Raoul returned his gaze to the large screen where US Vice-President James Peavey Marvin, along with key members of the White House staff and President Harris's cabinet filed into the Security Council room. They included the Secretary of State Helen Carter; Defense Secretary, Philip Morgan; Homeland Security Secretary Harold Schmidt; and Don Prescott, Director of National Intelligence. They were joined by of the head of the Secret Service John Dempsey; CIA Director Homer Sidow; and FBI Director Frank Huntington. Each waited glumly for the conference to begin.

Marvin, a tall and aristocratic looking man with white hair and a beaked nose, yanked back his chair, and sat down with a heavy sigh. Raoul knew little about the man except that he was from a wealthy and well-known family New England family with a Mayflower pedigree of the early English settlers to the original colonies. A former two-term Democratic senator from New Hampshire, Marvin was widely thought of as moderate to conservative on the political spectrum. He'd been selected as Harris's running mate to provide balance to Harris's decidedly liberal views on the government and society.

"Thank you all for coming," Marvin intoned, raking his fingers through his thick white mane, looking perturbed, but in control. "With our president at the mercy of terrorists, this is certainly America's darkest hour." He scanned the room slowly, pausing only briefly to glance at each cabinet member. "As you all know, since you've all been consulted and have given your assent, I have been forced by these dire circumstances to assume the duties of the president. He's clearly been incapacitated. This is all being done in accordance with the 25th Amendment to the Constitution, which provides for the smooth transition of power in such a situation. I want to assure you all that I will guide the ship of state with a firm and confident hand. I will be going on national television immediately following this meeting to reassure the American people about that as well."

"But before I do," Marvin continued, "we need to know the latest. So, what can I tell the American people is being done to free the president?" Marvin cast his eyes to the man to his right. "We'll start with the Secret Service. Dempsey, what do you have?"

A frazzled, bespectacled, and balding man in a dark suit, Dempsey looked at Marvin and cleared his throat. "Four of our agents died protecting the president. Several others have been wounded severely."

"We're here to talk about the status of the president of the United States, not your department's failure to protect him!" Marvin barked. "So, tell us. What is his situation?"

"President Harris is alive and well," Dempsey said.

"What? Are you saying the terrorists don't have the president?" Marvin asked.

"Well, they do, but not exactly," Dempsey said.

"What the hell, man?" Marvin said. "Speak plainly."

"No. They don't HAVE him," Dempsey said, making quote marks in the air with his fingers. "President Harris is barricaded in his upstairs room."

"The president is not in the hands of terrorists?"

"No. He's not. He's with one of our agents."

"You're saying he's trapped!" Marvin said, sounding exasperated. "But he's alive and well? And the only thing between him and these *jihadis* is a Secret Service agent?"

"Yes, one of our best men," Dempsey said. "That's the situation."

Marvin scowled as he processed the information. "How did you manage that?"

"When this political summit was in the planning stages, we studied the sleeping arrangements," Dempsey said. "The suites on the upper floors have special security protections. The suites are reinforced and are virtually impenetrable. The doors are bullet proof and fire proof."

"So, you're saying that for the moment, anyway, President Harris is safe."

Dempsey nodded and said, "Yes, as safe as he can be in this situation."

Marvin scowled, deep in thought. "What about an explosion or fire? I mean, what if these maniacs have a bomb? What if they try to blow the place up?"

"I can't guarantee that the president would survive."

"My God, man," Marvin said as he scanned the faces of the people seated around the table. His eyes settled on the national intelligence director. "You have a lot of explaining to do, Prescott. Who are these people? How did they get in the country? How were they able to do what they did? And, why didn't we know about it beforehand so we could stop it?"

"Let's start with where we are now," Prescott said, clearing his throat and arranging his papers. "For the moment, the terrorists seem satisfied with the present situation since the president can't go anywhere. It's effectively a stalemate.

We can't go in, and they can't come out." A somber and elderly man with a long oval face, and thinning gray hair, Prescott silently scanned the faces around the table. "The only conceivable way out now would be to jump from the third floor window."

"Jump out the window?" Marvin shouted. "Is that your idea of a rescue?"

"No, it's not," Prescott said. "Not at all."

"How long can Harris hold out?" Marvin asked, looking again at Dempsey.

"There's snack food and bottled water in the room," Dempsey said. "I'm guessing that could sustain them for a few days, probably." He paused, then added, "We've been in touch with the president, actually. He's holding up well."

Marvin's eyes opened wide. "You're in touch with the president! Why aren't we talking to him now? I know for a fact that he carries a collection of secure communication devices. I also know for a fact that you guys stripped his phones of all the fancy gizmos so that it all could be more secure."

Dempsey nodded. "You're right. But at this moment, we're not sure of the capabilities of the people who have him."

"What does that mean?" Marvin asked. "Speak plainly, man."

"We need to keep any communications with the president at a minimum," said the CIA's Sidow, interrupting Prescott.

Marvin glared at Sidow, an intense man with closely cropped blond hair, and narrow, steel gray eyes.

"We can't risk the chance the terrorists might be able to intercept those phone messages," Sidow said. "We don't want to let them have any idea of what we may or may not do to diffuse this situation."

"Of course not," Marvin said with a nod.

"What we need to know we get via the encrypted messages from the agent who's there with the president now," Sidow said.

Marvin shook his head. "What about the terrorist's phones? Can we monitor them?"

Sidow nodded. "Yes, of course. We've got our ears on them now."

"Anything worthwhile?" Marvin asked.

Sidow slowly shook his head. "They've been silent, so far, anyway."

"Does that tell us anything?" Marvin asked.

"It tells us that this operation was planned well in advance," Prescott said, jumping back into the conversation. "They're not waiting for instructions. They already know what they're going to do next."

"Which is what?" Marvin asked. "We don't even know what we're going to do!"

Prescott loosened the knot to his paisley tie and cleared his throat. "Only time will tell. But, we are expecting demands, sooner rather than later."

Marvin nodded, continued to gaze at Prescott, then asked, "Do we know who these bastards are?"

"Yes," Sidow barked before Prescott could respond. "The core of the group is from the Islamic State in Syria. Torture and beheading are their trademarks."

"We know about the Islamic State," Marvin blurted. "We all watch TV."

Sidow pointed a remote control device at the large wall screen. He clicked and the screen slowly filled with a photo of Tariq, dressed from head to toe in black, holding his knife at the throat of Nate Kennard on his knees and dressed in orange.

"Well then, as a reminder, I thought I'd show this to everyone here." Sidow turned to the camera with which Raoul, Benedict and the others at Atlas Global were watching. "Can you see that?" he asked them.

"Yes," Benedict shouted. "We can see it fine."

Sidow nodded and cleared his throat. "Our best information is this group of *jihadis* is led by a British national, a man who goes by the name of Tariq. You may recognize him as the same man who has beheaded three American citizens, two journalists and one aide worker. It was done on camera, recorded and posted on the internet."

"They're the ones who have the president?" Marvin asked.

"I'm afraid so," Sidow said.

"That's the man they call Jihadi John," Prescott said, after a couple of moments as he silently took in the video.

"Yes, the very same," Sidow said.

"What do we know about this man?" Marvin asked. "Who the hell is he?"

"As best we can tell," Prescott said loudly, interrupting Sidow, "his name is Tariq Abdullah Karim. He speaks perfect English."

"He almost sounds like he was DJ or radio guy," Secretary of State Helen Carter said.

"Yeah, well, you're not far off," Prescott said. "He was born in Yemen. His parents emigrated to England after the first Gulf war."

"Back in 1991," Sidow said.

"Yes," Prescott said with a nod. "Tariq is a Yemeni citizen. Grew up in England and also speaks Arabic fluently because his family spoke it at home. He seems to have been a handful. He had aspirations to be a rapper. He and a few of his Muslim buddies formed a hip-hop band and produced an album."

"That would be interesting to hear," Marvin said, his voice dripping with disgust.

"Yeah, it is," Prescott said. "Tariq picked up the gangsta rap style. His rhymes are pretty violent stuff. He calls for the execution of the *kafirs* and oppressors."

"My God," Marvin said.

"Yeah," Sidow said. "His songs call for *jihad* against the West. The songs are what put him on the watch list of the British security, both MI5 and MI6. He was radicalized at one of the mosques there in London and became involved with underground Islamic groups."

"That's what happens when you're soft on extremists," Marvin said, his voice choked with disgust.

Carter cleared her throat and interrupted. "Muslims have a hard time in England, despite their numbers," she said. "It's not that easy to assimilate."

"You'd think that maybe they'd appreciate what they have," Marvin said.

"So, what pushed him over the edge?" Carter asked.

"You ever hear of an Islamic group called al-Muhajiroun?" Sidow asked.

"No, but it sounds like, *muhajideen*, the word for fighter," Carter said.

"You're close," Sidow said. "Along with another Muslim cleric, the group was founded by a man named Ahmed Gaffari. He was highly critical of British involvement in the Iraq war. When ISIS appeared, Gaffari urged his followers to support the Islamic State."

"So, Gaffari and Tariq already were on the watch list in England?" Marvin asked.

"Yes," Sidow said. "But it gets better. Before that, he was praising the al-Qaeda operatives who pulled off the 9/11 attack on the Twin Towers and the 2005 subway attacks in London."

"More than 50 dead in London and hundreds more wounded, as I recall," Carter said. "They call it the 7/7 in England."

"Gaffari has called for the imposition of Sharia law throughout the UK and the western world," Sidow said.

"So, where is our friend Gaffari now?" Marvin asked, calm returning to his voice.

"In jail," Prescott said. "But it seems Tariq has done what his mentor, Gaffari, could only dream about. Tariq went to Syria and joined ISIS."

"Not directly," Sidow said. "The intelligence is that he was supposed to go to Yemen to meet with his bride, through an arranged marriage."

"Probably would have helped the guy to have a woman around, if you know what I mean," Marvin said.

"Maybe," Sidow said. "But when the bride's family found out that Tariq was on the watch list by the British government, they called off the marriage."

"That girl dodged a bullet," Carter said with a disgusted shake of her head.

"Tariq never made it back to England," Sidow continued. "The next time we see him he's working his way up the ISIS command structure with a several other radicalized British Muslims."

"They were the ones who took care of the westerners ISIS kidnapped, because they spoke English," Prescott said. "They were called the Beatles. John, Paul, George and Ringo."

"So, Tariq proved to ISIS that he was a real-deal *jihadi* by executing a couple of journalists," Marvin said.

"That's the size of it," Sidow said with a nod.

"And now he's there at Vista Verde Ranch," Marvin said.

The room fell silent as the grim implications became clear.

"How in the hell did they get into the US?" Marvin asked, breaking the silence.

Sidow turned to FBI director Huntington, who also wore a gray suit with a red tie, and had cropped white hair. Huntington adjusted his rimless glasses and looked to Marvin.

"Our best guess," Huntington said, "is that they walked across the border. Like everyone else, they paid the drug cartels to guide them across."

"Jesus," Marvin said.

"There's speculation they're the ones who killed those border guards a few months ago," Huntington continued.

"Why didn't we catch them?" Marvin asked.

"We almost did. The group was apprehended after they crossed the border in southern Arizona and entered a federal wildlife refuge. A handful of our best Border Patrol agents thought they were dealing with another large group of migrant workers. They didn't expect a fire fight with a group of armed *jihadis*. After killing the border agents, the *jihadis* made their getaway in the Border Patrol vehicles," Huntington said. "They were able to slip through a check point dressed as the border agents they'd killed. They drove away and into the night."

"And why haven't we found them?"

Huntington again adjusted his glasses. "Well, they appear to have made contact with an Islamic underground. You could call it a cell, I supposed."

"What? Like a sleeper cell?"

Huntington nodded. "Yes."

"Why haven't we been on top of this?"

"They've been very careful. They went underground. There's been no communication that we can find. But we know they communicate, but not by the typical internet providers or messaging services."

"Can't we do anything right?" Marvin asked, becoming more irritate. "Does anyone know what the hell they want?"

Prescott shook his head. "As was mentioned earlier," he said, "we've had no communications from them yet, but we expect it soon."

CHAPTER 18

Sitting comfortably cross-legged in the middle of the wide, dark leather couch, Tariq gazed at the cold stone fireplace that rose to the pitched ceiling of the lodge. His men sat near him, also sitting cross-legged, but on the Middle Eastern woven carpets that covered portions of the polished stone floor. Tariq turned and looked through the double-paned glass of the wide windows to the broad, stone patio on the south side of the lodge. It was there that they'd dragged the bodies of the infidel agents, and the nearly naked congressman.

The fat congressman had looked foolish, Tariq thought, as the corners of the man's mouth were fixed in a permanent smile, the man's laughing desk mask. It was a good thing the man was a bad shot, Tariq mused. They'd taken the bodies to the patio for the *kafirs* to see and contemplate. It was a message: You will be next. Prepare to die.

Tariq nodded to himself knowing many more would die before his mission was complete. Beyond the bodies, he saw where the grassy field ended at the deep green of the pine forest that rose along the slopes to the high mountains, shadowy in the distance. Yes, he thought, many will die.

Tariq glanced up and to the wide stairs leading to the top floor and to where the American president had barricaded himself inside the room with another of the American security agents. He drew a deep breath and slowly exhaled. He and his men could storm the room, demolish the door, and take President Harris into their hands. But that would come later. There was more to be gained now as America and the world awoke to the fact that the Islamic State had its grip on the throat of the Great Satan. The grip would tighten. Tariq smiled, his eyes unfocused as he let the coming glories flood his mind. After a long moment, he looked up to the bearskin hanging on the varnished log wall between the windows and double doors, and above it the mounted heads of three elk jutting from the wall, looking like they'd pushed their antlers, head, and necks through to get a better look.

From the kitchen, Tariq heard the sounds of banging pots and pans where he'd told Halima and a couple of his men to prepare food for them all with whatever they could find. He could smell the aromas of grilled meat and cooking rice. His hunger stirred and he motioned one of him fighters close, whispering to the man to tell those in the kitchen to hurry. He wanted to eat while they had a chance. "Tell them leave the cooking pots on the stoves. We will take plates and serve ourselves. Come, let us eat in the rich men's dining room."

An hour later, sated with a meal of meats and mounds of fresh, white rice sweetened with raisins and sliced carrots, Tariq called for a fresh pot of tea to be brought to the lodge's library where he, Carlito, and his two top lieutenants were going to meet.

The room was spacious, almost as large as the stone-floored great room and foyer, and its walls were lined with book cases. Light filtered through the tall windows falling on a piano at one end and three French-style couches covered with blue silk fabric. Tariq clenched his jaw, disgusted at the decadent opulence of the lodge.

A surge of righteous anger filled him, renewing his focus on the mission. Tariq and his men shoved the piano and couches against the stone and varnished log walls, then settled onto the Persian styled carpet that covered much of the floor, placing the tea pot in the center of their small circle. He became excited as he realized how far they'd come in this most bold of missions. *Allah akhbar!* When his leader al-Bakar first had proposed the plan, Tariq thought the man had lost his mind. Now he knew better.

Tariq had believed al-Bakar was setting a trap for him, that he was being sent on a suicide mission. But he soon realized he'd been chosen for a glorious martyr's death. All missions were suicide missions! If a soldier of God cared nothing for this life on earth, and only the afterlife, then nothing on earth could stop him. Tariq smiled again, unable to hide his joy. They had already succeeded! God willing, the victories would continue.

Tariq considered his two best men, his two sub-commanders: Abdulla and Hamid. He trusted each implicitly. Abdulla was tall and rangy, with a light beard and round eyes. Hamid was shorter and stout with a round face and dark eyes, ever enthusiastic. And there was Carlito. Yes. Carlito, the one who had been integral to the success of his mission. Carlito was part of them, now and forever.

"We must devise a statement," Tariq said. "We need to contact the White House and issue our demands. Then we will contact the news media."

Abdulla jerked upright, his eyes wide, and shook his head. "Demands? We can't negotiate with the infidels. Even if they comply with some or all of the demands, it means nothing. We have their president. We will never give him up. Alive."

Tariq nodded. "I know this, Abdulla. Please be patient. We are going to play with their minds. We are going to make this victory last as long as possible."

Abdulla nodded in silent ascent, dropping his eyes to his tea, the corners of his mouth curling into a smile.

Tariq knew Abdulla might not agree with him, but would go along with the plan. Abdulla had also been taken from Tariq's homeland of Yemen, and like Tariq's spiritual mentor, al-Awalaki, had been raised among the *kafirs*. He and Abdulla had grown up in Manchester, England, and were both educated for a time at the University of Manchester.

They had shared their journey and had grown very close, talking long into the nights. Like Tariq, Abdullah had been stung by the alienation he had felt growing up in England, insulated and isolated from all the English boys, rejected by the English girls.

During those long, late nights, when they talked about their sadness and fears and how they had wished they'd never been born, they had cried in each other's arms. Then, as if they'd been handed a gift from God, they'd visited the mosque where the each had been inspired. Like Tariq, Abdulla found purpose and meaning in life by taking up the cause of their Islamic brothers and sisters in Syria. Both had said good-bye to their families and in Syria they'd become true brothers.

"Even if our demands are ignored, think of how many people we will reach by placing our demands before the world," Tariq said to Abdulla, unable to hide his growing excitement. "Think of this, my brother. How many men will we bring to the cause? Hundreds if not thousands! Think of that, my brother! Of course we don't expect the *kafirs* to comply, but, we must take advantage of this moment. The world is watching."

Tariq shifted his gaze to Carlito. "I know you are strong with Islam. But many of your concerns are not ours. I am grateful for what you have done for us. You must help us put our message out to the world."

Carlito looked on silently, then nodded.

Tariq sipped his tea, growing more confident. Yes, Tariq thought, his inspiration, the cleric al-Awalaki, had been called the emir of the Internet. But now that al-Awalaki had become a martyr, I will take his place, he thought. *I will be the new emir of the Internet.*

Carlito nodded, seemingly eager to become involved again. "You should know that my journey began very near here." He circled his finger in the air. "Near this place."

Tariq raised his eyebrows.

"This is the heart of the land grant I told you about. This land was given to my ancestors 150 years ago." Carlito drew a breath, then quietly exhaled, gauging Tariq's reaction.

Tariq nodded ever so slightly, signaling for Carlito to continue.

"This land grant was stolen from my family and neighbors."

Tariq sipped his tea.

"This was once part of Mexico. The Americans took it after the Mexican-American war. But the Americans refused to accept that Mexico had given it to my ancestors through official grants and deeds."

Tariq nodded. "It is the same thing that happened to the Palestinians. The Zionists stole the land from the Palestinians after the Six Day War in 1967."

"Yes. Exactly," Carlito said. "That's what drew me to Islam. One day I visited an event hosted by the Palestinian students seeking justice for themselves. I realized that the people of northern New Mexico and the people of Palestine had much in common. We share the same fate. That is why I became a Muslim and have joined the *jihad.*"

Tariq nodded again, knowingly. "We fight for justice and for Islam."

"They killed my grandfather," Carlito continued, "because he was grazing his sheep on his own land," Carlito said. "They also killed my father because he fought to get this land returned to the rightful owners." Carlito sucked in a halting breath, his eyes glistening. He brushed a finger against his eyes, then cleared his throat, collecting himself. "This is where the journey of my ancestors began and this is where I am willing to die, if it is God's will."

"You speak well, Omar al-Amriki," Tariq said. "But we can speak about death later. Today we talk of justice and freedom." He sipped his tea and looked at the others. "We must craft a message for the Christian crusaders. It is the will of Allah that the oppressors be destroyed. In the Quran, the Prophet wrote, 'will any be destroyed but the unjust people?'" Tariq smiled at the passage, pleased with his recollection. "The only way the Americans want to deal with Muslims is by force. So, now we give them a taste of their own medicine."

Carlito lifted a hand and Tariq nodded. "I know of a journalist who might help us," Carlito said.

Tariq frowned. "I do not think we need such a person. We have the Internet. Besides, I have killed some western journalists. They know who I am. They hate me. They will not help us."

"Perhaps," Carlito said. "But this man tried to help my father once. He understands the oppression we suffer. We need a person we can trust to deliver the correct information," Carlito said.

Tariq scratched his thin beard, tugging at his chin hairs with a thumb and forefinger, lost in thought. After a moment, he nodded to Carlito. "There may be some wisdom to what you say. The Americans will not negotiate with Muslims. That is why the western journalists were killed. Their deaths sent a message to President Harris. In truth, it was not us who killed the journalists. It was President Harris and his refusal to negotiate." Tariq fell silent as he gazed at Carlito, then Abdulla, and Hamid. "What is this man's name?"

"Kyle," Carlito said. "Kyle Dawson."

CHAPTER 19

Kyle stared at his laptop screen, trying to form the next sentence. What he thought would be a routine political story over a weekend had morphed into a monster. The world was now riveted to the events unfolding in this luxurious retreat in the mountains of northern New Mexico. He groped for the right words to describe not only what had happen, but the dramatic and lasting implications of it all.

By any measure, it was a monumental victory for the Islamic State and the forces of radical Islam. It was a global humiliation for the United States and its vaunted security services protecting the US president. And, it was a monumental embarrassment for Hank Benedict's testosterone-fueled Atlas Global security company. With both public and private organizations protecting the president in a remote and distant location in the Rocky Mountains, it was absurd that such a thing could have happened. But it had.

Kyle had gotten no further than the first sentence as he tried to answer the question on everyone's mind: What went wrong? He leaned back and stretched his aching shoulders, then twisted his stiff neck, the cartilage crackling, as if it might loosen the flow of words. It didn't. He wanted badly to talk to Raoul to get his take on it all. But Raoul was still with Benedict, as he should be, trying to salvage what they could of this disaster by getting President Harris and Blount out alive.

The assault on the lodge and the cornering of the president in his room had been fast and furious. But how was it possible that a random group of heavily *jihadis* had stumbled across a high-level meeting between the president and the two top leaders of Congress? It was hardly an accident. Kyle smiled at the absurdity. Now that the shock was over—an attack that left the nation and the world stunned—the reality began to dawn on him.

Kyle went back to the beginning. Frankel had called and asked him to cover the story. But there had been no prior public notice about the meeting, which was common practice. Only those with a "need to know" were informed. And since news organization were critical to the success of the event for both political parties as well as the legacy of President Harris, Senator Blount, and Speaker Divine, a select group of main-stream journalists had been invited. Kyle was among them.

Whenever the president moved, Kyle knew advanced preparation and planning was extensive and complicated. When the president visited foreign countries and their leaders, security arrangements demanded all the relevant agencies—the Secret Service, the FBI, the CIA, and the State Department—be on the same page, coordinating with the security agencies of the host countries. But this was in the continental US. So, who knew about this event? And why Vista Verde Ranch?

Kyle was convinced the selection of the Vista Verde Ranch for the meeting was not a random choice. The ranch was a prize holding of David Benedict and his son Hank. David Benedict's influence on the conservatives in the country was notorious, but had been largely unexplained. Kyle wondered if David Benedict had pressured Blount and Divine to select Vista Verde? *Of course!* The two congressmen would have gladly agreed to the offer, not only to please the elder Benedict, but because it was such an obviously secure location. *Or was it?* Now Troy Divine, one of David Benedict's champions, was dead, his corpse lying on the exterior flagstone patio of the lodge.

Kyle's advance story had explained why both parties were anxious for the Vista Verde meeting to produce an agreement. Both sides wanted to claim a political victory. Certainly, President Harris could come out the meeting with bragging rights. But so could the conservatives. Most of all David Benedict and his Wolfe News Network could claim they'd instigated the meeting and ushered in a new era of leadership by the conservative wing and led by the Liberty League, the true believers of the far right. Wolfe News commentators would note the weak leadership by Harris and the strength of the conservative agenda promoted by Blount and Divine.

But the *jihadis*? How had they known? Had the Islamic State broken encrypted communications? The Russians had the capability, Kyle suspected, as did the Chinese. Had the Russians or the Chinese cooperated with ISIS? Why would they? There was no obvious benefit for either country, except to expose the inherent weakness of the world's oldest and strongest democracy.

A move like that by Russia or China made no sense. It was extremely dangerous for both. It only would give strength and credibility to maniacal *jihadis* and radical Islamists who had launched wars in Russian enclaves in Chechnya and Dagestan. The Russians destroyed Grozny, the Chechen capital, to put down the Islamists.

In China's western province of Xinjiang, the population was half Uighurs, a Muslim ethnic minority. The Chinese had made it illegal for women to wear veils, the men to grow long beards, and parents to give their children Islamic names. The Chinese had sent an overwhelming force to quell rising violence there.

Kyle's phone rattled on his desk. He didn't recognize the number, but answered anyway, after letting it ring a couple more times. "Hello?"

"Is this Kyle Dawson?" the voice asked.

"Yes, it is," Kyle said. "Who's asking?"

After a pause, the voice said, "This is Carlito."

Kyle swallowed and said nothing, wracking his brain to remember when he'd ever met or knew someone named Carlito. He flashed on the movie, Carlito's Way. That had been decades ago and starred Al Pacino, but this wasn't him. "Carlito? Do I know you?"

"Yeah, you do," Carlito said. "You probably remember my father, Carlos Miranda."

The name hit Kyle like a gut punch. His drew a breath. Yes, he remembered Carlos Miranda, the man who'd led the land grant protest in northern New Mexico. He'd been gunned down after he'd held his wife, Antonia, and his son, Carlito, hostage. He'd been killed by a sniper as he ran to the waiting helicopter he had demanded to end the hostage situation and whisk him away to Mexico. Carlito had been in the middle of it. He had seen his father's head explode with a bullet from a sniper's high-powered rifle.

"Carlito Miranda?" Kyle asked.

"Yes."

"Why are you calling me?"

After a long pause, Carlito said, "I need you to relay a message to the government."

"What are you talking about?" Kyle asked.

"If you want President Harris to remain alive, I advise you to cooperate."

Kyle's mind raced. "What are you saying? What do you mean, if I want President Harris to remain alive? Is this a joke?"

The phone line was silent for a moment. "Not at all," Carlito said finally. "I am talking to you from the lodge at Vista Verde. I can see your cottage."

A jolt pulsed though Kyle's body as he realized where Carlito was. But Kyle wasn't in the cottage anymore. The press, the aides, and all non-combatants had fled, scrambling up the forested slopes that surrounded the lodge, leaving a small army of agents and Atlas Global personnel surrounding lodge, but hidden in the trees and shadows. Carlito didn't need to know that. "You're with the *jihadis* who have the president?" Kyle asked.

"Yes."

"How…?" Kyle stammered. "What are you…? Why?"

"I'm a Muslim now. I've accepted Islam to fight for justice for all who are oppressed by the Christian crusaders. This includes my own people in northern New Mexico."

Kyle swallowed again as he found the situation incredulous. "Are you serious, Carlito?"

Carlito paused. "I don't like the tone of your voice."

"Do you know what you've gotten yourself into?" Kyle asked.

"If Allah desires, I will die here. It will be a martyr's death. I will join my grandfather and my father who were murdered by the oppressors. I continue the struggle of my ancestors and my family."

"This is not the way to do it, Carlito," Kyle said. "You're making a big mistake."

Carlito was silent.

"So why are you calling me?" Kyle asked.

After another pause, Carlito said, "You once helped my father."

"Yes, I remember. I was there when your father died."

"I thought you might be able to help again."

Kyle's stomach soured as he was overwhelmed with a sense of déjà vu. Carlito was duplicating the situation when Kyle had been with Carlito's father. Then as now, Kyle had jumped at the chance for an in-depth, exclusive story. But the story and the land grant protest had ended tragically.

"You need me to help you?" Kyle asked, skeptically. But he thought again. Carlito was with the *jihadis* inside the lodge! It gave Kyle access—exclusive access! His mind reeled with the possibilities of what this could mean for him and the *Washington Herald*. Kyle drew a breath, his heart pounding. "It all depends, Carlito. You've got the president of the United States held hostage there, along with Senator Blount. I can't be part of that."

"You don't need to be," Carlito said. "You just need to pass along some information. After you give it to the government, you can share it with everyone."

Kyle thought for a moment. "Okay, Carlito. On one condition. Everything is on the record. I can and will use it all in my stories."

Carlito groaned. "That's why I called you and not someone else. I never forgot how you tried to help my father."

Guilt again gurgled up inside Kyle. *I didn't help your father!* Sure, he'd stayed at the land grant protest camp for three days. The long hours of sitting and waiting had meant long conversations with Carlito's father and the others, some of whom joined for no other reason than they had little else to do. They were friends and neighbors who survived by cutting and selling firewood, raising sheep, and working on their cars and trucks. Carlito's father, Carlos, was the great grandson Lupe Miranda, the man who was part of the original 1830's communal land grant that was now the Vista Verde Ranch. Carlito and his mother had been regulars at the protest camp, coming and going as they pleased, passing through the state police barricade with food and fresh water for the camp.

By the time Kyle had joined the camp, the protest had been going on for nearly two weeks. He'd gotten the story, in depth. But on the third day, Carlos became despondent and began to issue demands to the state police surrounding the camp. It was the beginning of the end. Kyle had gotten out of the camp alive, just barely. *Shit!* His stomach churned at the memories. Still, he couldn't turn down this chance to have access to the *jihadis*. If he could help keep President Harris alive, he'd do it. Then he would write about it.

"Okay," Kyle said finally. "What information do you have?"

"If the government wants President Harris returned alive, they must comply with our demands."

Kyle opened a blank page on the laptop screen and began to type. "Okay," he said. "What are they?" Listening intently, Kyle's fingers flew across the keys, taking down Carlito's every word.

CHAPTER 20

They worked methodically, Kyle reading back to Carlito each of the demands, word for word, getting it right. Kyle's head pounded, his shoulders pinched with tension. The demands were what he expected from a group of *jihadis* on a suicide mission—except for the final one. It had nothing to do with Islam. Still, Kyle knew all about it because it had put Carlito's father to the grave.

"Are you sure you want to do this?" Kyle asked, making one final effort to dissuade Carlito. "Those people you are with don't care about you. They will use anybody to further their aims. Once they're done with you, they'll throw you away like garbage."

Carlito exhaled into the phone. "You're wrong. You're a non-believer and don't understand. I have found my true brothers. These men stand up for what they believe. And they are willing to die for it."

"You got the dying part right, Carlito," Kyle said. "These men will kill anyone and do anything to get what they want. They're psychopaths. They use religion to get what they want, which is power and money. God and glory have nothing to do with it."

Carlito exhaled noisily, sounding irritated at Kyle's warning. "Just do what you agreed to do. Or we will never talk again."

"Can I talk to Tariq, the leader of the group?"

"How do you know that?" Carlito asked, sounding anxious.

Kyle smiled. Raoul had briefed him after the Security Council meeting about the *jihadis* and what was being done to free President Harris, which was not much. "I know a lot about the people there with you."

After a long pause, Carlito said, "You'll be in contact with him soon enough."

Kyle's heart leapt at the thought. When Raoul told him the *jihadis* were led by Tariq, otherwise known as Jihadi John, Kyle felt nothing but hatred for the man. Tariq had murdered his photographer friend and colleague, Nate, and others in a spasm of blood and sadism. Kyle had spent a lifetime pushing his emotions to the background. But no more. He was officially on leave from his job as a staff member of the *Herald* and didn't need to hold his emotions in check any more. He despised Tariq and people like him, and for a moment surprised himself at the smoldering anger that burned inside.

"Can I call you back on this number?" Kyle asked.

The line went dead. Kyle sat still for a moment, and clenching his jaw, took a breath and told himself to stay calm. Tariq needed to be taken out, granted his wish for martyrdom, before he did any more damage. How didn't matter. But even if he were dead, it would not undo the death and destruction Tariq had already committed.

Kyle thumbed the screen to check the phone number. Yes, it was there. He had a direct line inside the lodge and to the men who held the country's two top political leaders hostage. Now, what was he going to do with the demands? His impulse was to call his boss, Frankel, and tell him what had happened. He'd do that, but later.

Kyle jumped up from the desk where he'd been sitting, walked down the hall and found Raoul sitting in a conference with several other Atlas Global agents. "Raoul," Kyle blurted, wagging a finger. "We need to talk."

Raoul twisted around and glared, irritated at the interruption, as the others stared. "Kyle," he said. "This better be important, 'cuz I'm up to my ass in alligators."

"You need to hear this."

With a sigh, Raoul rose from the table and followed Kyle out to the hallway. "What is it?"

"I just got a call from the *jihadis*."

Raoul was silent, looking stunned as he mulled the implications of the call. "You're shitting me."

"No. I'm not. The call came from Carlito."

"You're shit'n me. Carlito? He's really waded into the shit now."

"He gave me a list of demands the *jihadis* want met before they'll release President Harris."

Raoul blinked and said, "Release the president? You don't really believe those assholes would do that, do you?"

"I don't know what to believe," Kyle said. "But, no, I'm not so naïve as to believe they'll let the president go."

"Good. Because I was beginning to doubt your—"

"Jesus, Raoul," Kyle said. "I need your help, okay? I have to get these demands to the Vice President Marvin and the Security Council. Then I'm going public with them."

"Wait!" Raoul barked, raising a hand and extracting his phone from his pants pocket. "We need to talk to Hank, first. He's at the lodge site with the Secret Service and FBI." Raoul tapped a number, then hit the button for the speaker phone and held it to his mouth. The phone rang twice before Benedict answered.

"This is Hank," he said, and listened as Kyle told him of the demands.

"You had contact with the men inside?" Benedict asked Kyle.

"Yes," Kyle said. "That's why we're calling you."

"So, that was you," Benedict said.

"What do you mean?" Kyle asked.

"We monitored the phone call, but it took us a while to figure out who it was. The call came from a throwaway."

"We need to pass the demands to Marvin," Kyle said. "That's part of the deal if we want to keep talking to them."

"The only thing those bastards are going to get is a bullet in the head, and that's being kind," Benedict said.

"Yeah, whatever," Kyle said, irritated at Benedict's bravado. "I need to deliver these to the vice president or someone close to him. Now!"

"Relax," Benedict said. "We've got a direct line into the situation room at the White House. Raoul can set up a group video call. Just patch me in."

"I have to make another call," Kyle said, nodding to Raoul. "I'll be right back."

Kyle wheeled and stepped into Raoul's private office, closed the door, and called Frankel, who answered angrily. "What do you have, Kyle? I have a news meeting in ten minutes."

"You'd better sit down for this Ed."

"What? What do you have?"

"I just got a call from the *jihadis*."

"Say that again."

"I just got a call from the *jihadis* holding the president," Kyle said, speaking slowly. "They gave me a list of demands. It's an exclusive."

"Holy shit! I don't know what is about you, Kyle, but you get yourself in the middle of the most God-awful situations." After a moment, Frankel said, "well, we know what's going on page one now. When can you have the story to me?"

"I just got their demands a few minutes ago," Kyle said. "I'm being patched into a secure connection with Vice President Marvin at the White House. I'm assuming he'll be with the Security Council."

"Why are you talking to them?"

"Because that's the deal," Kyle said. "I deliver the demands to Marvin and then I can do whatever I want with the story."

Frankel exhaled audibly. "You're being used, you know. And we're being used."

"C'mon, Frankel. We're being used every time the president or anyone else in Congress opens their mouths. We dutifully print it whether it's true or not just because they said it. How is this any different?"

"But these guys are figgin' terrorists," Frankel said. "We're playing footsie with them."

"We have exclusive access to the men who have taken the president hostage!"

"I don't like it. They're effectively holding us hostage as well."

"But there's no other way it can be done," Kyle said, becoming desperate. "Like you always preached to me, we're the news media, not the news."

Frankel was silent for a long moment, then said, "Post the basics of the story in the next thirty minutes. Someone will put a headline on it saying the terrorists have issued demands. We'll promo it as an exclusive." Frankel said. "You have two minutes to tell me what the demands are, and then get your ass in gear."

CHAPTER 21

Kyle ended his call with Frankel, then paused. Yeah, he had a story to write, but it would have to wait. He spun out of the room and back into the Atlas Global conference room where a dozen others clustered, all watching as the large wall screen lit up and the White House Situation Room came into view.

Kyle scanned the faces around the polished wooden table at the White House. Vice President Marvin sat at one end, leaning forward on his elbows, looking anxious in his black leather chair. Kyle recognized the cabinet members' now familiar faces. The table was covered with paper, file folders, three-ring binders, and a handful of electronic tablets.

"How are the visuals?" Raoul asked loudly.

"We can see you just fine," Marvin said. "It's like you're in the room with us."

"Good," Raoul said, then motioned to Kyle. "This is Kyle Dawson, the reporter with the *Herald*, the one who got the call from the terrorists."

Kyle nodded, trying to calm his quivering stomach. He took a breath to ease the tightness in his chest. "Good afternoon," he said, with all the confidence he could muster.

"I assume you're familiar with everyone around the table," Marvin said, staring directly at Kyle as he waved his hand.

"Yes, somewhat," Kyle said, "but obviously we've never met."

"We're aware of that," Marvin said. "Just let me say that we've been following your work over the past few years. It was quite an investigative story that you did on our former colleague, Senator Madsen."

After a moment Kyle said, "I just go where the facts take me."

"Understood," Marvin said, then cleared his throat. "I understand from our friend Hank Benedict there, that the men who have the president have contacted you with some demands."

"That's right," Kyle said. "I received a call from one of the group. His name is Carlito."

"That's not a *jihadi* name," Marvin said. "That sounds Mexican."

"It's a Spanish name," Kyle said. "He's a local. Carlito Miranda."

"What in God's name is someone named Carlito Miranda doing with these maniacs?"

"In short," Kyle said, "he harbors a deep hatred against the government. He converted to Islam and was radicalized at a local mosque. I suspect he sees parallels between people of northern New Mexico and other oppressed minorities."

Marvin shook his head in disbelief. "You're kidding, I hope."

"No," Kyle said. "I'm not."

"I'm curious as to why, Mister Dawson," Marvin asked, "you were contacted about these demands and not someone else."

"I have some history with Carlito and his family. Some years ago, I covered a story when Carlito's father was killed. Carlito remembered me. That's all."

"Whatever." Marvin scowled and shook his head. "We can talk more about that later. We have some ground rules you need to be aware of before we talk any further."

"Okay," Kyle said.

"First, none of what we say here today leaves this room. That includes you, Dawson."

"Okay, I understand," Kyle said. "But the specific demands themselves are public."

Marvin shook his head. "We want to keep it all quite. Demands are not a matter of public debate."

"Carlito called me," Kyle said, "a member of the news media, specifically to make the demands public."

"I know that" Marvin said. "They're using you. Do you know that?"

"Everyone uses the news media," Kyle said, his chest tightening. "Especially politicians."

Marvin let the comment hang for a moment. "You don't need to point out the obvious," he said, his disgust apparent. "I'm asking that you cooperate, as an American citizen. The life of the American president is at stake here."

Kyle clenched his jaw and inhaled through his nose. "I understand what you're saying," Kyle said. "But I made a commitment to Carlito. By doing what he asked, we can keep the lines of communication with the terrorists open."

"Dawson's right about that," said the CIA's Sidow. "It's standard protocol in hostage negotiations to go along and get along with the hostage taker. You need to establish a rapport, and hopefully some trust. It's the only way forward. Once that trust is broken, you have nothing left to do but pick up the bodies."

"We've already got bodies!" Marvin shouted. "And who around this table really thinks that they are ever going to release President Harris unharmed?" Marvin scanned the faces at the table. No one moved.

"At this point, it just doesn't matter," said Secretary of State Carter. "What the terrorists say or do simply doesn't matter. Our response has nothing to do with that. I say we let Mister Dawson do what reporters do. And, as has been pointed out, it's important to have a line of communication open to them, even if it's not our own."

Marvin scowled and stared at the table. After a moment, he nodded, then looked up, again scanning the faces. "Okay. Agreed. We need to move on." Marvin turned to the screen. "Dawson, do what you have to do. But what we discuss here now will stay here. Agreed?"

Kyle looked at his screen and saw the eyes everyone in Situation Room staring at him, waiting for his response. "Agreed."

"Let me remind you, Dawson, violating any of the agreements here today constitute a prosecutable crime," Marvin said.

Kyle swallowed.

Marvin scanned the table again. "Is there anything anyone else wants to say?"

Marvin's gaze was met with stony silence.

"Let's hear their demands," said the CIA's Sidow. "We don't have time to waste."

Marvin nodded then lifted his eyes to the room's camera and looked straight at Kyle. "Showtime, Dawson. Tell us what you've got."

Kyle cleared his throat. "The first thing they want is the immediate and complete release of all of the prisoners at Guantanamo Bay, Cuba."

Kyle glanced down at his laptop screen and tapped the keyboard, calling up the file. "They call the prisoners the 'soldiers of Islam." They say the prisoners have been illegally detained and tortured. They call the prison at Guantanamo, and I quote, an abomination in the eyes of the Prophet, end quote. They also say the illegal imprisonment will be repaid with a thousand deaths for every soldier of Islam who has died in the prison."

Marvin slapped the table, tossed his head back, and laughed. "Oh, that's rich. They say the soldiers of Islam are being held illegally? But they're not legal themselves. They don't represent any government or legitimate group. They're nothing but a bunch of terrorists. They have no right to talk about what's legal and what's not."

Kyle watched and waited until Marvin was finished. "I think what they're referring to is the fact most of the prisoners have not been charged with crimes," Kyle said. "And only a few have actually gone to trial on any charges. As I understand it, most of them have been held in there since 2001."

"That's right," said Intelligence Director Prescott, drawing the room's attention. "We have about 170 prisoners there now, but only six have been formally charged. They're being tried in a military court."

Marvin shook his head. "Guantanamo prison is a waste of time and money. If I had my way, we'd just execute them all and be done with it. They're nothing but rotten apples, human deviants. They need to be thrown on the garbage heap of human history."

The room listened in silence. Then Kyle said, "That's another thing they mentioned. They claim that a majority of the people still held at Guantanamo are civilians. They are Muslims who were unjustly arrested and detained."

Marvin laughed out loud. "My God, man! It's amazing how they can pretend to give a damn about civilians when they think nothing of killing hundreds of innocent people day after day, many of their fellow Muslims. For God's sake, look at what those ISIS bastards have done to the poor people of Syria and Iraq." Marvin shook his head in disgust. "This whole thing is absurd."

"Excuse me," said Carter. "While I agree that ISIS is shedding crocodile tears, they are getting recruiting value out of the civilians at Guantanamo. They entice people to join their cause by pointing out that America is taking Muslims and putting them in jail. They say that jailing of citizens without charges shows that the US cares nothing about human rights."

"This conversation is ridiculous," Marvin said, staring at Carter. He shifted his gaze to Kyle. "What else do they want?"

"They want the US bombing in Iraq and Syria to stop immediately, along with our support of the Iraqi army."

"Again, it ain't gonna happen," Marvin said. He stretched his arms above his head, and sat back. "As most of you around the table know, the president and I often disagree on foreign policy issues. President Harris was elected to office after promising to pull America out of Iraq and Afghanistan. But, now, well into his term, the president has come around to my point of view. It was a mistake for us to pull out of Iraq." Marvin paused to scan the group, then continued. "Look what's happened there. Now we have ISIS to deal with." Marvin shook his head in disgust. "In some ways, you could say that with the president now in the hands of *jihadis*, he's gotten what he deserved. He created this problem."

"Mister vice president!" Carter shouted, pushing herself back and suddenly standing. "Are you saying that President Harris deserves to be held hostage because he pulled US troops out of Iraq?"

The room fell silent, as Carter glared at Marvin, her eyes glistening.

Marvin motioned for Carter to sit down. "C'mon, Helen. Sit down. Don't get your panties all twisted."

"What?" she said, stunned at the remark.

"Relax!" Marvin said with a dismissive wave. "All I'm saying is if we'd stayed in Iraq, we wouldn't have ISIS on our hands and we wouldn't be in the situation we are now. That includes President Harris."

Carter continued to glare, shaking her head in disgust.

"C'mon, Helen. You and I argued for much more aggressive action in Syria way back during the so-called Arab Spring. But Harris would have none of it. You and I can agree on that."

Carter grimaced. "We're not going to get President Harris out of this mess alive by pointing fingers at who may or may not be at fault about the past decisions."

Marvin stared at Carter for a moment, then nodded. "You're right. I'm just a little frustrated, as should we all be."

"We all are," Carter said, settling again into her chair.

"Next," Kyle said, clearing his throat, "they want the United States to recognize the independent caliphate of the Islamic State. They want the Islamic State to be admitted to the United Nations with all the privileges that come with that recognition."

Marvin again shook his head in disgust. "I won't even respond to that nonsense," he said, but after a pause, added, "except to say that these butchers are completely crazy if they think they're going to get anything other than blown off the face of the earth." In the silence that followed, he glared at Kyle. "What else?"

"They want all lands that were formerly part of Mexico returned to Mexico."

"What?"

"Everything in the American Southwest from California to Texas."

"What the hell? That's a third of the country! Where in God's name did that demand come from?" Marvin scanned the room, but no one spoke up.

"I can explain," Kyle said.

All eyes were on him.

"Go ahead," Marvin said. "Enlighten us."

"It goes back to the 1800s," Kyle said. "The Mexican-American War."

"What about it?" Marvin said.

"The US declared war with Mexico over the disputed border between Texas and Mexico. The US said it was the Rio Grande River. The Mexican's wanted it further north."

"Most of us are familiar with American history," Marvin said, "but go on."

"The US invaded Mexico from the Gulf side and quickly captured Mexico City."

"Yes," Marvin said.

"So, in the 1848 treaty that ended the war, Mexico gave the US all of what is now the Southwestern US, from California to Texas."

"So what the hell does this have to do our situation here?" Marvin barked.

"When the US Senate approved the war treaty," Kyle said, "it stripped the provision that recognized all of the land grants that the Spanish and Mexican governments had given to people to encourage them to settle Mexico's northern territories. That was most of the American Southwest."

"So what?" Marvin asked.

"There was a lot of land involved. Most of it was communally owned. Under the terms of the revised treaty, the much of the communal lands were declared public lands by the US government. But some of it ended up in the hands of wealthy Americans, such as the Vista Verde Ranch, which is owned by David Benedict."

"Okay," Marvin said. "Get to the point!"

Kyle cleared his throat. "Descendants of the original land grant owners never forgot. One of those was a man named Carlos Miranda. He claimed that the heirs to the land grant still had rightful ownership of the Vista Verde Ranch, which was once the largest Mexican land grant in the Southwest."

"This is nonsense," Marvin said, increasingly agitated. "Carlos Miranda led a group of land grant heirs on an armed protest. They demanded the Vista Verde ranch be returned to them. After a standoff of about two-weeks, Miranda was shot dead by police sniper. The protest ended."

"That's a nice story," Marvin said. "But you didn't explain what this has to do with our President being held hostage."

"Miranda's son is a boy named Carlito. He was there when his father was killed. He was also with his grandfather, who was killed earlier when he was caught grazing his sheep on the Vista Verde Ranch. The shooter was never found. Carlito grew up hating the police and the government for killing his father. He recently converted to Islam and is now part of the *jihadis* who are holding the president."

Marvin scowled. "How in God's name do you know this?"

"Carlito is the one who called me."

"Why did he call you?"

"I was there when his father was shot," Kyle said.

The Situation Room was silent, as the eyes of the cabinet moved from Kyle to Marvin.

"So where do we go from here?" Carter asked.

Marvin again shook his head in disgust. "How can we even pretend to have a rational conversation with these people? They're crazy, flat out crazy. They're asking us to pull out of the Middle East, free a couple of hundred terrorists, and give a third of the country back to Mexico. Remember. We don't negotiate with terrorists. Not now, not ever."

Carter stared at the screen. "What are you going to do with these demands?" she asked Kyle.

"What any journalist would do with them," Kyle said. "I'm going to write a story about them as soon as we're finished here."

"We should craft a response," Carter said, glancing at Marvin. "We just can't tell them to go to hell."

"Yes we can," Marvin said. "As the British say, never apologize, never explain."

"Well then, what do you suggest?" Carter asked.

"As I said," Marvin replied, "It has been and continues to be our policy that we don't negotiate with terrorists."

Carter nodded. "That's something, I suppose. But, what about President Harris?"

"We demand his immediate release and the full surrender of the terrorists," Marvin said, and scanned the faces around the table. "Is everyone agreed?"

The heads around the table nodded.

"Done," Marvin said. "Now what are we going to do about rescuing Harris and Blount?"

"I think what Kyle told us about the local boy, Carlito, is instructive," Sidow said.

"Why's that?" Marvin asked.

"Because this whole thing could not have happened without some local help," Sidow said.

"Homer," Marvin said, "we've already established that."

"Look at the sequence of events," Sidow continued. "We have a group of Islamic terrorists who have infiltrated this country and were able to hide out in the remote location in northern New Mexico. They were able to conduct a surprise attack on a high-level meeting that was not widely known. Now they hold the leader of the world's most powerful country hostage."

"Okay," Marvin said. "Get to the point."

"This was not a random sequence of events," Sidow said. "This was not a bizarre and freak accident. This was a carefully planned and executed attack."

"You could be right, Homer," Marvin said. "That these terrorists were in the country is bad enough. It's likely they were a sleeper cell. They could have been planted and put in place for months, even years, and activated when an opportunity for an attack arrived."

"I also have a hard time accepting that this could be just good luck," said the FBI's Huntington, an angular man who lowered his half-lens reading glasses on his beaked nose and stared at Marvin.

Marvin scanned the group. "All this speculation is useless. President Harris is being held hostage," he said. "I'm not hearing any ideas about how we get out of this mess."

"We need to look closely at how we got into this situation," said Huntington. "That will give us a path as to how we can get out of it."

From inside the Atlas Global conference room, Hank Benedict waved his hand and barked, "Mister vice-president!"

"Who's that?" Marvin said, turning to the screen.

"Hank Benedict, sir. Here at Atlas Global at the Vista Verde Ranch."

"Oh, yes, Dave Benedict's boy," Marvin said. "How are you?"

"I've had experience negotiating with terrorists," Hank Benedict said. "I volunteer myself, my men, and my agency to lead the negotiations for the release of President Harris."

"I appreciate that, Hank. But you and your men helped get us into this mess."

"And we can get us out."

"Someone has to," Marvin said, sighing. "What do you suggest?"

"We've reached a stalemate," Benedict said. "The president is secure, for the moment anyway. This gives us some time. We need to know more about these men and what capabilities they have."

Marvin shook his head in disgust. "Well, that's good. Coordinate your intel with the people around this table. For the moment, we'll just have to leave things as they are. Dawson here seems to be our pipeline to them." Marvin scanned the room again, and when no one spoke, he continued. "So, in a few minutes, I'm going to tell the American people we don't negotiate with terrorists and that we demand the president be freed immediately, unharmed. When we meet again, we need to have a plan to end this standoff."

"We will, sir," Benedict said.

Marvin looked at his watch. "We'll reconvene in two hours. I expect to hear how each of you and your departments intend to get us out of this mess."

The screen on the wall at the Atlas Global room went blank. Kyle drew a deep breath, then stepped into the hallway, tapped his phone screen, and called Frankel's number.

Frankel picked up immediately. "So what the hell happened?"

"I'm not really sure," Kyle said.

"What? Were you on the call, or not?"

"Yes. But I can't share any details about what was discussed. That was the agreement. But I can tell you that they don't have a plan to free the president. It's a classic Mexican standoff. Each side is waiting for the other to blink."

"You're kidding!"

"No, I'm not. Marvin is going on national television in the next few minutes to tell the world that everything is under control, and that neither he nor anyone else is going to negotiate with terrorists. Marvin is going to demand the terrorists give themselves up and release the president and Senator Blount unharmed."

"That ain't gonna happen," Frankel said. "We need a story from you on the detailed demands the terrorists are making, so get to it. We'll have someone here write the story on Marvin's televised address. We don't have much time."

CHAPTER 22

Kyle closed the door to Raoul's office, put his phone down, and watched his laptop screen come to life. What would the *jihadis* do when they learned that Marvin refused to negotiate with them? Nothing. They'd accomplished what they wanted. They had President Harris. But, the *jihadis* already knew they wouldn't be negotiating with the US. The demands were their way of broadcasting their message. A recruiting tool.

With the world watching, would they commit yet another act of desperation? Would they actually kill the president? Kyle felt like he stood at rim of a deep, dark hole, and the ground beneath his feet was beginning to shake. He pushed the thought from his mind and tried to focus on the story. Once the story was finished, he knew his next move, and he couldn't do it sitting in Raoul's office at Atlas Global.

Ninety minutes later, Kyle leaned back and massaged the taut muscles in his shoulder and neck. He reread his story.

VISTA VERDE RANCH, N.M.—Islamic jihadists holding President Barry Harris hostage are demanding that the United States end all military activities in and withdraw from Syria and Iraq, the *Herald* has learned.

The group, which stormed a semi-secret summit here at the luxurious ranch owned by billionaire David Benedict, also wants the release of the nearly

170 Muslim prisoners still being held at the US prison at Guantanamo Bay, Cuba.

In addition, the group is demanding the US relinquish the Southwestern states, all of which were acquired from Mexico in 1848 as part of the treaty that ended the Mexican-American war. The demand is believed to have been crafted by an Hispanic activist and Muslim convert who has joined the jihadists.

Shortly after the jihadist demands were made available to the *Herald*, Vice-President James Marvin went on national television to say the United States, as a matter of long-standing policy, does not negotiate with terrorists.

Marvin called for the immediate release of President Harris and Senator Blount, who are being held hostage in the main residential lodge at the ranch.

The *Herald* has learned President Harris and Senator Blount have barricaded themselves in secure rooms in the lodge's upper floor. Harris and Blount are believed to be accompanied by one Secret Service agent who survived the early morning attack on the lodge about 24 hours ago.

At least eight security agents were killed in the assault. The dead include members of the Secret Service detachment sent to protect Harris, as well as members of Atlas Global security, the private international security firm based at the Vista Verde Ranch.

The contingent of congressional and White House staffs who were present at the secretive meeting have been evacuated. Meanwhile, the jihadists control the ranch's main lodge, adjoining dining hall, meeting rooms, and library, with President Harris and Senator Blount held hostage in the upper rooms.

Kyle read through the rest of the story, hit the send button, and again leaned back. He closed the lid to his laptop, pushed himself from Raoul's desk, jerked open the door, and walked down the hall to where he found Raoul sitting in the operations center of Atlas Global.

A bank of screens covered one wall, depicting the outside of the embassies that Atlas Global protected, from a rotating variety of cameras and angles. On the other walls were larger HDTV screens, several of which surveyed the grounds around the Vista Verde lodge and the inside of the lodge's lobby, dining room, and library. Kyle stood and stared, then turned to Raoul, who sat at a curving console of keyboards and mini screens.

Raoul looked up and over his shoulder, then nodded and pulled the headphones from his ears. "*Que pasa, primo?*"

"I didn't know you had cameras inside the lodge," Kyle said.

"Of course," Raoul said with a knowing smile. "We've been watching these bastards from the beginning."

Kyle scanned the screens, which showed little activity in the lobby. He glanced at Raoul and asked, "What does all of this tell you?"

"Not much," Raoul said with a sigh.

Kyle nodded. "It tells me that for the time being, neither Marvin nor the Security Council, nor your boss Hank Benedict know what's going on with these guys or how to get Harris and Blount out. They can storm the place, but that option isn't viable."

"Why not?" Raoul said, with a shake of his head. "Storming the lodge is the ONLY option."

"Is that what's being planned?"

"That's what I'm recommending," Raoul said.

"It puts the president's life at risk."

"But his life is already at risk," Raoul said. "What other choice is there?"

"There's got to be a crack in the armor," Kyle said. "We need to find it."

"What are you talking about?"

"Did you know the Navajos weave a flaw in every rug and blanket they make," Kyle said.

"They do?" Raoul said.

"Yeah. It's done so the spirit of the weaving can escape," Kyle said.

"What have you been smoking?"

"Listen to me," Kyle said. "There's a flaw in the fabric here. We just need to find the right thread, pull and it will unravel. There's got to be a way to do that."

"So, what do you have in mind?"

"Remember what the Huntington, the head of the FBI, said?"

"He said a lot of things."

"About needing to find out how all this happened," Kyle said. "It will reveal a path to free President Harris and Senator Blount."

"Okay. But Hank's working on that."

"I don't trust him, Raoul. Do you?"

"I don't have a choice," Raoul said. "He's in charge here."

"There's something strange about how all of this happened so damned quickly," Kyle said. "Wouldn't you agree?"

"Of course," Raoul said. "From the get-go. But we have to deal with the reality of what we're facing."

"I figure we have less than 24 hours before the shit hits the fan," Kyle said. "It's just enough time for us to unravel this mess. But first, we've got to take a little road trip."

"To where?" Raoul asked.

"I'll tell you when we get there."

"I don't know if I can do that," Raoul said. "Hank wants me here, with him."

"Tell him that I have some inside information from the *jihadis* and you need to go with me to verify it."

"He'll want to know what it is," Raoul said.

"Yeah, you're right. Explain to him that I won't tell you unless you come with me. Tell him if you go along, you'll be in constant contact."

Raoul paused. His mouth fell open as his eyes were glued to one of the monitoring screens.

"Raoul, what are you looking at?" Kyle asked.

Raoul pointed to the screen. "Ah, Kyle, you'd better check this out."

Kyle's stomach soured at what he saw.

The screen provided a view inside the Vista Verde lodge of the towering stone fireplace. Kyle saw the man he reviled, again dressed in black from head to toe, the one who had beheaded Nate Kennard. "That fucking bastard," Kyle said.

But now, the one he knew to be Tariq, aka Jihadi John, had Senator Blount in front of him, on his knees, his arms bound behind his back, with both men facing the camera. As with the other executions, the Tariq held what looked like the same, thick-bladed knife to Blount's face, which was red and swollen. Blount's glasses were gone and marks around his eyes showed that he'd been beaten, his glasses smashed. Blount's pale eyes were swollen and glistened with fear.

"We have your president and we have Senator Blount," said Tariq's muffled, yet still clear and forceful voice.

Kyle recognized it from the Kennard's execution video.

"But still, you continue to defy our demands," the black-clad Tariq said. "We are sending a message to all who think they can defy us. It is the will of Allah that our cause should prevail. We will cleanse the world of the *kafirs*. We will kill your leaders. We will eliminate all resistance."

The blade was at Blount's throat, pressing against the taunt skin just enough to send a trickle of blood down Blount's neck and onto his white shirt.

"This is a message for Vice President Marvin," Tariq said. "You think you can show the world how strong you are by refusing to negotiate. But we are not the terrorists. The chief terrorist is you, Vice President Marvin. You and your soldiers are the ones who terrorize the world with your guns, your bombs, and your planes. But we are not afraid. Ours is a holy cause and we will break the chains of our oppressor."

Tariq shifted, spread his feet, and extended his knife, just as he had done in the earlier videos, pointing it at the camera.

"This is a warning to all who defy our demands. It is a warning that your president, who is in our hands, will soon die. It is warning to all those who are part of the evil alliance against the Islamic State that you and your leaders will die."

Bracing his knee against Blount's back, Tariq grabbed the Blount's small chin with his right hand and jerked it up, exposing and stretching the throat.

Kyle's stomach tightened, his heart pounded, as Tariq drew the thick blade across Blount's neck, the blade cutting deeply, unleashing a torrent of dark red blood spilling over the Blount's chest.

Blount jerked and thrashed, but Tariq held the jaw tight and sawed the blade, stopping only when he struck bone. The senator's eyes, wild with fear, became unfocused and blank as his body sagged and fell to the side, thumping to the polished stone floor. Tariq the executioner stepped back, his chest heaving, his hands dripping with blood.

Tariq again pointed the bloodied blade at the camera. "You now see how we can so easily spill the blood of an American leader," he said. "This is just the beginning. We will do this again and again until you know that we are serious and comply with our demands."

Nausea gripped Kyle's stomach. He turned to Raoul, who stared back at him, his lips mashed together in disgust.

"Jesus," Kyle said, his voice choked with emotion.

"Yeah, I know," Raoul said.

They watched as Tariq wiped the knife and his hands on Blount's blood-soaked clothes, as if he'd just finished butchering an animal. A couple of Tariq's men then dragged Blount's torso out the side doors of the lodge and left it on the sprawling flagstone patio.

The air outside the lodge erupted with distant gunfire as the Secret Service and Atlas Global agents fired at the *jihadis*, who had exposed themselves on the patio. Two of the terrorists twisted and fell the stone patio beside Blount's body.

Kyle and Raoul then watched as Tariq stared out the patio doors to where his men lay sprawled beside Blount's body. Tariq turned and looked up at the wall mounted surveillance camera and again pointed his knife.

"We will destroy all of you," he said.

After a moment, his mind reeling from the murder they had just witnessed, Kyle turned to Raoul. "We need to go now if we're going to get to the bottom of this."

"Are you crazy?" Raoul said. "We're in the middle of the biggest crisis this country has ever seen and you want to go for a drive? What the fuck's wrong with you?"

"Raoul, I know what I'm doing. The *jihadis* aren't going anywhere. But we don't have to stay here in place because everyone else is. We're not at their mercy."

"Think, Kyle! They called you once," Raoul said. "You got an exclusive from them. You need to be in place when the next call comes."

"That's only IF there's a next call. We need to get out of here," Kyle said again.

Raoul only shook his head. "Okay. I sure hope you know what you're doing."

CHAPTER 23

Raoul wheeled the Atlas Global Hummer through Taos and across northern New Mexico on US 64, connecting with US 84 north. There was no easy or fast way to get to where Kyle wanted to go. But finding Carlito's mother, if she was still alive, was paramount.

Raoul's skepticism about this trip was palpable as Kyle anxiously eyed the road. He refused to admit he, like Raoul, was worried this excursion could be a wild goose chase and leave them both hopelessly gone from the ranch when the inevitable assault began.

Raoul had assured him that while such an attack was being devised, it was not imminent. Kyle was not convinced, but knew that with Raoul's help, he might unravel the method behind the madness gripping the country and now the world. Like he had done before, it meant following the threads. With a little luck, the mystery would unravel and expose the truth.

Kyle pointed to a narrow strip of crumbling asphalt leading from the main highway and into a small rural village of aging homes clustered close to the road. Raoul slowed the Hummer as it passed a simple, white-plastered adobe brick church and at Kyle's direction, pulled to a stop in front of an old, western-style building with a covered front porch. A sign over the steps to the porch read: La Tienda Lana, the Wool Shop.

Kyle and Raoul climbed out and paused. "The wool store," Kyle said. "Carlito's mother is here."

"I can read," Raoul said. "I hope you know what you're doing."

Kyle nodded, checked his shirt for a pen, and stuffed a notebook into his back pocket as they scaled the steps. Yanking the door open, a bell dinged loudly above them. The ringing died quickly and the store fell quiet. Kyle gazed at racks of handwoven wool sarapes and jackets arranged between stacks of blankets and rugs. It was all just as he remembered.

"We're closed," said a voice.

A stout woman with a full face and thick, white hair pulled into a pony tail, stood in the shadowy corner of the store.

Kyle drew a breath, forcing himself to relax. "I'm with the *Washington Herald.* I want to speak with Antonia."

The woman's left eye stared straight ahead, surrounded with scars. The eye was glass, Kyle realized, and he suddenly felt sorry for her. "I'm looking for Antonia," he said, repeating the name.

"There's no one here," the woman replied.

Neither Kyle nor Raoul moved. Kyle knew she was lying and wondered why. Who was she trying to protect?

The woman sighed after a long moment, and with a small head shake, indicated that someone was in the back room.

A much thinner, older woman appeared from the back of the shop. She had angular features, a face creased with care, dark and searching eyes, and long salt and pepper hair pulled into a tight pony tail that trailed down her back. "I'm sorry," she said. "You said you're with the *Washington Herald?*" She stared at Kyle.

"Hi, Antonia," Kyle said. "Remember me?"

The corners of Antonia's lips curled into a smile of recognition and her face seemed to crack, even soften. "You were with the Santa Fe newspaper," she said. "My God! That was years ago."

"Yes," Kyle said, feeling relieved. "The land grant protests. When Carlos and his men armed themselves and tried to take the land back."

She nodded. "I remember. Now you've returned?"

Kyle nodded as Antonia eyed Raoul suspiciously, seemingly intimidated at his quasi-military garb and the handgun in the nylon holster attached to his web belt. "Antonia, this is my cousin, Raoul Garcia. He's in private security."

Antonia nodded, remaining tight-lipped, then said, "Atlas Global," reading the embroidered log on Raoul's polo shirt.

"Are any of the men still alive?" Kyle asked.

"What men?" Antonia asked.

"The men who were part of the protest."

Antonia shook her head slowly. "They're all gone now." She paused, her eyes unfocused, as if lost in the memory, then blinked herself back to the present. "So, you're back because of the hostage situation at Vista Verde?"

"How did you know?" Kyle asked.

"It was only a matter of time," Antonia said.

"Why do you say that?"

"Harris should never have trusted the Benedicts," Antonia said.

"Why's that?"

"Because of what they've done."

"What they've done?" Kyle asked.

"The ranch is a training center for mercenaries."

"We're private security," Raoul said, "Fighting terrorism."

"Really?" Antonia replied.

"Yes," Raoul said flatly. "Really."

Antonia scowled at Raoul, shook her head in disgust, then turned to Kyle. "Those protest days are gone," she said. "Carlos was the last of his kind. It's all over, now. What do you want from me?"

"What happened to Carlito?" Kyle asked.

Antonia's eyes narrowed, as she clenched her jaw. "Carlito watched his father die, shot to death by the police." Antonia raked her hand through her hair. "We don't talk anymore."

"Why not?"

"Carlito became a Muslim," she said. "He fell in with those people over there at the Al-Salam mosque." Antonia eyes watered as she turned away, wiping her tears.

Kyle stepped forward to comfort her, but she turned away with a shrug.

"He said it was a place of peace," Antonia said, dabbing her eyes with a tissue. "At first I believed him. But then he became angry. He began to say such hateful things."

"About what?"

"Everything. America. That this country was evil. That it was the oppressor of people everywhere, especially the followers of Islam. He said he was going to join the *jihad* to cleanse the world of evil."

"When did this happen?"

"It started a few years ago. But recently it became worse. He stopped returning my calls. When I went to the mosque a month ago to find him, they said he was gone."

"Gone where?"

Antonia shrugged, her eyes watering again. "The mullah just waved to the mountains."

CHAPTER 24

Raoul gunned the Hummer along a narrow paved road toward the Al-Salam mosque, slowing as he approached the side road marked with a wooden arch decorated with the words: Al-Salam. Raoul downshifted, the knobby tires grinding through the soft soil, raising a plume of dust.

The mosque sat atop a flat knoll affording a view of the sparse landscape of grit, tufts of buffalo grass, spiky yucca cacti, and scattered *chamisa* bushes. He parked near a couple of cars at the entrance. The mosque was eerily silent as they approached the main door and knocked. They paused, waited a moment, and hearing nothing, knocked again. Silence. Kyle reached for the handle as the door swung open from the inside.

An elderly man wearing a white skull cap and sporting a trimmed white beard faced them with his hand extended. "Welcome, my friends," he said with a kindly smile. "My name is Hajji Ali Mohammed. Can I help you?"

Behind the man, the darkened mosque interior was clean and quiet.

"We're looking for the mullah," Kyle said.

"That would be me," Ali said.

"Well then, we'd like to talk to you about a young man by the name of Carlito," Kyle said.

"What about him?" Ali asked, his face becoming serious.

"Can we talk in private?"

"Yes of course," Ali said with a nod. "Please leave your shoes by the door. Come with me."

Raoul and Kyle wrestled off their shoes and followed Ali into a quiet office with white plastered walls and blond aspen wood furniture. "I've been expecting you," he said, settling in behind his small desk.

"Why?"

"Vista Verde." Ali nodded and stroked his thin beard.

"Carlito is there and is involved with the terrorists," Kyle said. "He was a devotee here. According to his mother, he converted to Islam. But she says he stopped talking to her."

"He's new to Islam," Ali said, "but was a good and faithful student."

"What about others?" Raoul asked.

Ali's eyes widened and he swallowed. "We had some foreign guests here recently. They were also very dedicated."

"The men who attacked Vista Verde Ranch?" Raoul said. "That makes you an accomplice."

Ali closed his eyes and began to rock back and forth. He stopped, opened his eyes, and waved. "There was nothing I could do! They threatened to kill everyone! And they would have."

Raoul took a folded paper from his pocket and handed it to Ali, who opened it and spread it on the desk. It was a printed photo of Tariq taken from the execution of Kennard. "Were they led by the man known as Tariq?"

"That's him," Ali said with a nod, pointing nervously.

"When did they leave?" Raoul asked.

"A week or so ago," Ali said.

"Where did the go?" Kyle asked.

Ali shrugged and waved toward the mountains. "One day they were gone. Carlito was gone as well."

"Then they knew about the meeting at Vista Verde Ranch ahead of time," Kyle said, looking at Raoul.

"How many were there?" Raoul asked.

"A dozen, I'd say, including Carlito and the woman, Halima."

"Who?"

"The woman from Los Alamos," Ali said. "She was in love with Carlito. Because of him, she became a Muslim."

"Did they have weapons?" Raoul asked.

"This is a place of peace, my friends. Weapons are not allowed."

"You said they threatened you," Raoul said.

"Tariq and his men stayed by themselves," Ali said.

"Where?" Kyle asked.

"Come," Ali said. "I'll show you."

Raoul and Kyle followed Ali along graveled paths to three canvass yurts half hidden amid the sparse piñon trees about fifty yards behind the main mosque. Ali opened the door to one. Inside were metal framed bunk beds and thin, bare mattresses. "Tariq and his men often took their meals here. They preferred to eat alone."

"What else?" Raoul asked.

"They were very strict in their practice of Islam," Ali said. "They were an inspiration to all of the people here."

"Tell me about the young woman from Los Alamos," Kyle said.

"Her father is a scientist," Ali said. "He came here several times. He wanted her leave Islam and return home."

"But she refused?" Kyle asked.

"Halima was her Muslim name," Ali said with a nod.

"What was her given name?" Kyle asked.

"Morris. Jennifer Morris," Ali said.

Kyle scribbled the name in his notebook.

They turned and looked skyward as the air shook with the sound of helicopters thundering overhead, pounding the air. They closed the canvass door to the yurt and watched as two Black Hawk helicopters swept over them, circled in the distance, and returned. Kyle glanced at Raoul. "What the hell?"

Raoul shrugged. "I believe this interview is over."

The three hurried back along the path to the mosque as the two Back Hawks hovered about 100 feet above them, gunners clinging to machine guns dangling from slings and pointed to the mosque.

Three black Chevrolet Suburbans followed by three camouflaged Humvees churned onto the mosque grounds, sliding to a stop in cloud of dust. Soldiers dressed in desert tactical clothes and wielding assault weapons leapt from the Humvees and dropped to kneeling positions, training their weapons on Raoul, Kyle, and Ali, who raised their hands.

Plain-clothed FBI agents stepped from each of the Suburbans as chalky dust floated in the air.

"Nice of you to join us," Raoul said.

The lead FBI agent sized up Raoul, who was wearing his Atlas Global shirt, camo cargo pants, and desert boots. "What are you two doing here?"

"I'm Captain Raoul Garcia. I'm with Atlas Global."

"I'm Kyle Dawson, *Washington Herald*," Kyle said, turning to the mullah. "This man is Mullah Ali. This is his mosque."

The lead FBI agent narrowed his eyes at Ali, as if looking at something odious. "We're placing you under arrest for aiding and abetting acts of terror against the United States."

"I've done nothing wrong!" Ali cried in protest. "I'm innocent!"

"Tell it to the judge," the agent said.

The FBI agents grabbed Ali's unresisting arms, twisted one behind his back, and forced him to his knees. Another agent slapped handcuffs on his wrists.

Kyle grimaced and said, "He wasn't resisting!"

"Shut up!" the lead FBI agent barked. "You never know what these bastards are going to do." He looked at Kyle and Raoul from behind his sunglasses. "Unless you're interested in being arrested as accessories, I suggest you leave."

"Gladly," Kyle said.

"Ali's got some good information," Raoul said with an advisory tone. "I suggest you go easy on him."

"Are you crazy? Those bastards with the president have a bomb! A damned tactical nuclear weapon!"

Raoul and Kyle looked at each other, stunned.

"Now get out of here before I change my mind."

CHAPTER 25

Raoul guided his Hummer around the government's Suburbans and Humvees and back down the dirt road where he bounced onto the paved road, heading to Los Alamos.

"Carlito is the key," Kyle said. "He grew up in these mountains and spent his summers with his grandfather, the shepherd. Carlito knows these mountains like the back of hands. He could have easily guided Tariq and his men through the mountains, undetected."

"So they could mount the attack?"

"Exactly."

"How does a kid like Carlito fall in with people Tariq and his men?"

"It's simple," Kyle said.

"Simple? Nothing is simple."

"Not only did Carlito see his father killed by police, he found his grandfather murdered as well."

"You told me."

"I told you that the Vista Verde Ranch was originally part of a Mexican land grant."

"Yeah?"

"Well, to keep the heirs of the land grant happy, they were allowed to graze their sheep and cattle on parts of the Vista Verde ranch."

"Peace in the valley," Raoul said.

"For a while, anyway. But when old man Benedict bought the Vista Verde Ranch, he said to hell with all of that. He put up fences. Said it was his ranch and the locals could go fuck themselves."

"Of course," Raoul said. "It was private property."

"Young Carlito had a horse and could ride fairly well, I'm told. One day he rode up there and found his grandfather dead, shot in the back, beside one of the new barbed wire fences Benedict had built. It seems the old man had been cutting it to let his sheep through."

"Poor kid."

"That's when Carlito's father, Carlos, decided to fight back. He claimed a piece of the Vista Verde Ranch as his, being heir and all, and took it by force. But Carlos was killed. "

"So, this is Carlito's revenge."

"Yes. It is. Big money killed his grandfather," Kyle said. "The government killed his father. He hates them all. That's why he's drawn to Tariq."

Raoul fell silent as he drove.

"What about Miguel?" Kyle asked.

"What about him?" Raoul said.

"He was Carlito's roommate. He must have known that Carlito was thinking."

"Maybe," Raoul said with a shrug.

"Have you asked him?"

"We talked a little about Carlito."

Kyle waited as Raoul stared at the road. "And?" he asked. "What did he say? Carlito is the one who got Miguel and his girlfriend to attend the mosque in Abiquiu. He must have had an inkling as to what Carlito was doing."

Raoul glanced at Kyle, then returned his eyes to the road. "Don't go jumping to conclusions. Yeah, Carlito got Miguel and his girlfriend, Aliyah, to go up to the mosque. They went mostly out of curiosity. I've always told Miguel to keep an open mind about everything. That it's important to decide for himself and not just accept other people's opinions as his own."

"That's good. So what about Carlito and the mosque?"

"There's not much to say. After Miguel and Aliyah visited a few times, they decided they'd had enough. As Miguel tells it, Aliyah was not as excited about the place as Carlito."

"I can see why," Kyle said. "Her family fled Iran and the Ayatollah. I can't imagine she'd sign up with another group of religious fanatics, Islamic or otherwise."

"Exactly," Raoul said. "But Carlito couldn't get enough of the place. So, after that, Miguel and Carlito drifted apart. They each went their own ways."

"But Carlito's girlfriend, Halima, stuck with him?"

"Yeah. That's the story."

"So what is Miguel doing this summer? Did you get him a job with Atlas Global?"

"Hell, no. And I'm glad I didn't. I have enough to worry about without Miguel in the mix."

"He's in a good place now."

"I know. He's working as an intern at the El Paso Times, the newspaper."

Kyle smiled and nodded.

"He wants to be a journalist, just like his uncle Kyle.

"But Miguel is not the problem here. Carlito is."

"We know that."

"So, joining with jihad and this maniac Tariq gives Carlito a way to strike back at an unjust world. But with a tactical nuclear weapon?" Raoul asked, his voice dripping with disgust. "What the fuck? Where the hell did someone like Tariq get that?"

"Maybe they brought it across the border with them," Kyle offered.

"From Mexico?" Raoul asked incredulously. "That's unlikely."

"Maybe they didn't need to," Kyle said.

"What are you saying?"

"Los Alamos National Laboratory is full of bomb makers and plenty of nuclear material."

Raoul smiled and nodded. "We need to find Jennifer Morris's father."

"Exactly."

***

An hour later, Raoul braked the Hummer to a stop in the driveway of a modest house in a quiet suburban neighborhood in Los Alamos. He and Kyle sat in the vehicle for a moment, looking around at the neighborhood. The street was empty, except for a couple of boys riding bicycles on the sidewalk. The boys rode over to the Hummer and stopped close to the vehicle.

Raoul lowered his window and smiled. "Hello boys."

"Cool car, man," one of the boys said, awkwardly straddling his trail bike, which was a bit too big for him.

"Thanks."

"Is this an army truck?" the second boy asked.

"Kind of, but not really," Raoul said. "Do you boys know if mister Morris is home?"

The boys looked each other, then shrugged. "He hasn't been around for a while," the first boy said.

"He goes to the mountains a lot," the second boy said.

"The mountains?" Raoul asked. "Does he have a cabin?"

The boys shrugged. "Maybe."

"Thanks, boys," Raoul said. "We're going to go see if mister Morris is home. We need to talk to him."

The boys nodded, climbed back onto their bicycles, and wove down the street.

Raoul and Kyle went to the front door and looked up and down the empty street before Kyle knocked. No response. Raoul took a lock pick from his pocket, inserted the two small pieces into the keyhole, and wriggled the two sticks. The lock clicked. He grabbed the door handle.

"Wait!" Kyle barked, raising a hand. "What if he has an alarm?"

Raoul shrugged, drew a breath as he turned the handle, and slowly pushed the door open. They were met with silence. The air was stuffy, as if the house hadn't been occupied for a week or more. The interior was decorated in Southwestern style, with leather couches, native weavings, and native ceremonial masks on the walls. A large rawhide and wood drum served as the coffee table.

"We need to find his cabin," Kyle whispered in the silence.

"First we need to find his computer," Raoul replied softly, surveying the interior.

Moving quickly through the house, they found the master bedroom. The bed looked like it hadn't been used recently. Raoul paused at the doorway of another adjoining room, its wall shelves crowded books, manuals, and stacks of paper. He settled into the desk chair and flicked on the desktop computer. The screen flickered awake. His fingers flew across the keyboard.

Kyle looked on. "What are you doing?"

"I'm not sure," Raoul said. "I can't sign on. I bet he's got a ton of technical files in there." He rifled a pile of papers stacked beside the keyboard. "Look at this."

Kyle bent close. The page was a printout of a complex diagram. "What the hell is it?"

Raoul stared at the paper. "Look." Raoul's finger traced what looked like an electrical diagram. One block was named "detonator," and another was marked with the letters, C4. "Could be the small nuke." Raoul Maybe this will help us figure out how to disarm the damned thing."

"Are you nuts? Cut some wires? That's Hollywood! Think, Raoul. We're not nuclear scientists. We're gonna need to find Morris."

Raoul scowled. "If he's alive."

Kyle rattled a set of keys that dangled from his fingers. "Look what I found in the kitchen."

"What the hell is that?"

"Keys to the cabin."

"How do you know?"

"The key fob here says C-A-B-I-N."

"But where the hell is it?"

CHAPTER 26

Raoul shifted the Hummer into low gear and powered it up a narrow, curving, and graveled mountain road.

"There," Kyle shouted, pointing to a small black wooden sign with silver metallic numbers nailed into a Ponderosa pine tree. He showed the key fob to Raoul, who only glanced. "The same numbers."

Raoul braked hard, then swung the Hummer onto two deep ruts that led through a stand of Ponderosa pines and to an A-frame cabin set on a concrete slab. Beside the cabin was an single-car garage converted into a workshop accessed by a wooden door. The parking area was graveled, as was a walkway connecting all three. The A-frame had a deck across the front, and the structure was protected by red metal roofing panels. The solid wood front door was flanked by a large picture window, the curtains now closed. The cabin grounds were eerily silent, save for the hush of wind moving through the tall pines. Raoul pulled out his gun, checked the ammo clip, then nodded to Kyle as he approached the workshop door.

Raoul twisted the burnished door handle. The door was locked. He holstered his gun, pulled out his lock pick, and again worked the two small pieces into the narrow key hole, wriggling them until the lock clicked softly. He carefully turned the handle and swung the door open. A shaft of sunlight angled across the concrete floor, lighting a high-tech workshop.

Kyle flicked a switch beside the door and overhead florescent lights blinked on. The long, wooden work bench ran along the left wall of the garage, from the front to the back of the workshop, and covered with an array of electrical technical devices with gleaming dials and a couple of bench-mounted machining tools. He and Raoul carefully stepped into the workshop, eyes wide and searching for trip wires. Seeing none, they paused to exhale.

Raoul glanced and nodded. "It looks like the place hasn't been used for weeks." Raoul moved slowly, eyeing the equipment, then stopped. Looking down, he saw a couple of red laser beams on the ankles of his boots. He traced the beams to their origins, where the glowing red digital screen numbers flicked off the seconds: 59...58...57.... "Oh, shit! Kyle! Get out! The place is gonna blow!"

Raoul pivoted and dashed for the open door, pushing Kyle out the door and into the sunlight where Kyle stumbled and fell. Raoul grabbed his hand and pulled him to his feet. They scrambled to the Hummer, where Kyle yanked open the door and jumped in as Raoul turned the key, revved the engine, and slammed the Hummer into reverse. With tires spinning, Raoul backed the Hummer between two trees, shifted, and gunned the vehicle down the rutted drive way.

The concussive blast slapped against Kyle's ears and sucked the air from his lungs like a punch to the gut. Kyle squeezed his eyes shut as the Hummer lurched to the side, lifting slightly. As it bounced back onto all four tires, Raoul braked it to a stop. The dust and debris from the roiling explosion fell like rain, and for a moment, Kyle flashed on the day when the Hummer he was riding was upended by an IED in Afghanistan. Kyle shook his head to clear it.

"You okay?" Raoul croaked.

Kyle grunted and swallowed. "Yeah. I think," he said hoarsely, and realized he was still so pumped full of adrenalin he couldn't feel a thing.

"You got a nasty cut," Raoul said.

Kyle could feel something wet and warm on his forehead and realized he'd been thrown forward just enough to bang his head on the dash. He touched the cut with a finger, which showed a smear of blood. "Shit."

The ensuing silence was broken by a couple of Black Hawk helicopters just above the treetops. Moments later, a familiar looking convoy of three black Suburbans came to a stop at the entrance to the narrow, rutted dirt road.

Kyle and Raoul stood outside their Hummer with their hands out to their sides as one of the Suburbans roared past and up the sloping drive to the smoldering remains of the cabin, the workshop nothing more than a charred pit in the forest floor.

After a few moments, the Suburban backed down the drive and an agent stepped out. It was the one who'd spoken to them earlier. The agent looked Kyle and Raoul up and down, then shook his head in disgust. "You're lucky to be alive."

"Your concern is touching," Raoul said.

"It was a dirty bomb," the agent said, waving a small, palm sized meter in his hand.

"This place is hot?" Kyle asked.

"We did a fly over just as you guys were inside. We were getting radiation readings. Because of you, the whole area is now contaminated with radioactivity."

"How hot are you talking about?" Raoul asked.

"Enough so you shouldn't hang around too long," the agent said.

"Shit," Kyle mumbled, squinting at Raoul and the agent. "That means the bomb was assembled here."

The agent nodded. "There were fissionable materials in there. We wanted to collect them so we can trace them, find out where the material came from. That will help us determine exactly who made the bomb."

"You mean the material didn't come from Los Alamos?" Kyle asked.

The agent drew a deep breath, pulled off his sunglasses, and squinted. "Radioactive elements have their own signature. We could have traced it. Now thanks to you, we may never know." The FBI agent flexed his jaw. "I should arrest you both for interfering with an investigation."

CHAPTER 27

Kyle sat at the dining room table in his rented Santa Fe guest house and faced his laptop computer, his right hand wriggling his mouse. He touched the bandage on his forehead with his left as Raoul sat opposite him drinking a beer and with a mescal chaser.

"How can you even work now?" Raoul asked.

"My brain works just fine," Kyle said, reaching for his own glass of amber mescal. He took a sip, then set the glass beside his computer. He lifted his left arm. "This sling is a pain in the ass." He slipped it off his shoulder, tossed it on the desk, then extended his arm, stretching it, then massaged his shoulder. "That's feels better. It's stiff, but I can deal with that."

Raoul shook his head in disgust. "So, now you're a doctor?"

Kyle shrugged. They both turned to the television screen hanging on the wall. Raoul grabbed the remote control and the sound came up as the screen filled with the faces the male and female co-anchors of Wolfe News.

"Acting President James Marvin is showing strong resolve in the face of this crisis," the male anchor said.

"Marvin is the kind of strong leader that President Harris has, unfortunately, not been," his blonde female co-anchor said with an agreeing nod. "Let's listen to the Marvin now from the White House."

The screen cut to the White House briefing room where Marvin stood at a small podium, nodding grimly to the assembled White House press corps. "These days will test the mettle of this great country. Although the terrorists have threatened to detonate a bomb if any attempt is made to rescue President Harris, I can say here and now that we cannot and will not give into their demands."

A reporter lifted his hand and waved. "Even if it means the President Harris's life is at stake?"

"I have known President Harris for a long time," Marvin said. "We have talked about our unwavering resolve to never negotiate with terrorists. I am sure he would agree with this course of action."

"You're willing to sacrifice the life of the president?" the reporter asked.

Marvin scowled and flexed his jaw. "The future of this country, if not the free world, is at stake here. If we surrender to the demands of terrorists, then what's next? Do we just turn our country over to them?"

Kyle glanced at Raoul. "Marvin is throwing Harris to the dogs!" he said, his voice rising.

"Why so quickly?" Raoul asked.

Kyle shrugged, sipped again from his mescal, and frowned, lost in thought. "He's preparing the country for the worst possible outcome."

Raoul gazed at Kyle, his eyes unfocused, then nodded in agreement. "I spent seven years in and out of Iraq and Afghanistan fighting those bastards," Raoul said. "They don't care who dies or how. To them it's all the same. It means martyrdom. An eternity in heaven."

"You think they'll kill Harris?"

"Unless they're stopped," Raoul said.

"How did this situation get so bad so quickly?" Kyle asked.

"There's only one way," Raoul said.

"Inside help?" Kyle asked.

Raoul shrugged.

"I think you're right," Kyle said. "Look at this. I've been doing a little research."

"And?"

"Benedict Enterprises is the parent company to Atlas Global and a host of other companies."

"We know that," Raoul said.

"Old man Benedict and his companies have been the major source of money for a handful of super PACs."

"Political action committees. So what?"

"Super PACs can spend as much money as they want in support of any issue or candidate," Kyle said. "They don't fall under election spending laws as long as they don't give the money directly to the candidate."

"Again, so what?"

"Benedict's super PACs have backed people like James Marvin, the late House Speaker Divine, and Senator Blount, whose body is out there on the patio at Vista Verde."

"But Marvin is a Democrat," Raoul said.

"Look at this," Kyle said, pointing to the screen to his lap. "People like Benedict are only interested in influence and control. Parties are only labels and mean nothing."

"Okay."

"James Marvin and David Benedict had similar educations," Kyle said, "first at a private academy in Massachusetts and then at the same Ivy League school."

"That doesn't prove anything."

"They were both devotees of a political science professor named Archer Brooks."

"Should I know him?" Raoul asked.

Kyle went to the kitchen, refilled his glass, and brought the mescal bottle to the table. "Brooks was a well-known political theorist. He developed a body of work based on the philosophy of Ayn Rand."

"The author?"

"Yes. She wrote Atlas Shrugged. Her most famous novel."

"So now you're an expert on Ayn Rand?" Raoul asked.

"Just listen for a minute. Rand believed that the world is governed by certain principles."

"Such as?"

"That people only do what's best for themselves, not other people."

"Sounds right to me," Raoul said.

"People love others only because they want to be loved in return."

Raoul nodded. "That's human nature. People only give if they know they'll get something back."

"Yes, well," Kyle said, "some of Ayn Rand's followers turned her ideas into a philosophy. They call it objectivism."

"And...?"

"Her philosophy is again in vogue, just as it was 50 years ago," Kyle said.

"Yes, and...?"

"Brooks believed government welfare was immoral," Kyle said. "It goes against the natural order."

"Why?"

"Because people are getting something they didn't earn," Kyle said. "It's wrong. Makes people lazy. Destroys their initiative."

"I can see that," Raoul said. "You're paying people to do nothing. After a while, they expect it. Then they demand it."

"Brooks and Rand said that if people don't work, they don't get," Kyle said. "It's each person's duty to look out for themselves, not others. There's nothing wrong with giving money to the poor. If you want to do it, fine. But it's a voluntary thing. It should never be institutionalized or automatic. Welfare only makes government bigger. It's a drag on the economy and makes society weak. Worst of all, it makes people depend on the government."

"Yeah, well, that makes sense to me," Raoul said. "But what does this have to do with Vista Verde?"

"President Harris and most other Americans believe that if you help the under classes, you help society at large. A generous society has an obligation to help its poorest members."

"Contrary to Rand's and Brooks' philosophy," Raoul said.

"And the philosophy of David Benedict and James Marvin."

"Get to the point."

"I think Benedict and Marvin are trying to get rid of Harris."

"What? You think Marvin is doing the bidding of people like Benedict?"

"Benedict and his people lost two presidential elections to Harris," Kyle said. "Time is running out."

"That's pretty extreme," Raoul said.

"Why do you think Atlas Global is the largest provider of private security to the government?"

"Connections," Raoul said. "It's pretty simple."

"Contributions is a better word."

Raoul drained his mescal glass, then grimaced. "If I didn't know you better, I'd say you're crazy."

Kyle shrugged. "It makes perfect sense."

"It's treason," Raoul said. "You can't just get rid the president of the United States because you don't like his politics and take over the country."

"People like Benedict think anything is okay if it's for the greater good. The end justifies the means."

"That's crazier still," Raoul said. "It means anything goes. There are no rules."

"I'm convinced that neither Hank Benedict, nor his old man, nor Marvin, will let President Harris get out of that lodge alive."

"And you still think Benedict is behind it?"

"What I think and what I can prove are two different things," Kyle said, falling silent again. "What do you think?"

"I think your brain is working overtime."

"Really?"

"Really." Raoul sipped from his drink, lost in thought for a moment. "If what you say is true, it means I'm working for the wrong side."

Kyle sat motionless and looked at Raoul in silence.

"We can't waste any more time here, Kyle," Raoul said with finality. "The *jihadis* have the president. Remember?"

"Going back to Vista Verde now won't help anything," Kyle said.

The silence was broken by the scrape of Raoul's chair on the brick floor as he stood to leave. "You could be right about the Benedict thing, Kyle. They're capable of anything and they have the money and influence to make it happen." He exhaled audibly. "I don't know what to do, but I can't just sit here and do nothing."

Kyle stared at his empty glass for a long moment as if transfixed, then lifted his eyes to Raoul, who was staring down at him. "The bomb!" Kyle said. "Without the bomb, they're nothing."

"You're weird, ya know. They've GOT the bomb, Kyle. They're not going to give it up. They'll detonate it first. Remember? They'll all die and supposedly go to heaven."

Kyle shook his head, no. "Morris," he said, waving a finger. "We've got to find Morris."

"We tried. Remember? They probably killed him, dumped his body someplace."

"Maybe not," Kyle said. "Maybe we haven't looked in the right places."

Raoul shook his head in disgust and rolled his eyes. "All right, mister smart guy. What do you suggest?"

"Access the Atlas Global communications? Can you do that?"

"Of course. I'm director of training, unless I've been fired. So what am I supposed to be looking for?"

"Comb the communications system for any references to Alan Morris, no matter how vague. Encrypted and unencrypted."

"You think Morris is hiding?"

"Maybe he's being hidden."

CHAPTER 28

Kyle froze as a knock sounded at his door. He looked from Raoul to the door and back to Raoul, who nodded and pulled his sidearm, holding it in front of his chest with both hands. Kyle stepped cautiously to the door, then slowly opened it.

Ariel faced him, wearing faded jeans, a denim jacket, and pink running shoes. A smile spread across Kyle's face. He took her by the hand, drew her inside, and kissed her lightly on the cheek. "We were just talking about you."

"That's why my ears were burning."

"Of course," he said, closing the door and twisting the deadbolt. "Raoul's here. We're doing some work."

Raoul nodded hello to Ariel as he slipped his pistol into his holster.

"Expecting trouble?" Ariel asked.

Raoul shook his head. "Not really."

"Liar," Ariel said, a smile curling the corners of her mouth.

"How about a drink?" Kyle asked.

Ariel shrugged, glanced around, and dropped her purse on a chair. "I'll have what you're having." Kyle stepped into his small kitchen, took a glass from the cupboard, then splashed a couple fingers worth of mescal into it.

Ariel surveyed the old adobe house, with its polished, dark brick floor, white plastered walls, carved and lightly decorated vigas supporting the split juniper that completed the ceiling. "Nice," she said with an envious roll of her eyes. "How did you find this?"

"The owner and his wife became friends of mine after they published my first book. They're letting me rent. They're in the main house."

Ariel sipped, her eyes settling on Raoul, who was now at the computer staring intently at the screen. "Checking your email, Raoul?"

Raoul glanced at her and shrugged. "*Mas o menos.*"

Kyle sat down on the long leather couch, extended his feet, and stretched his arms above his head. "He's doing research. We need to know what happened to Alan Morris."

"Who's that?"

"The guy who made the bomb," Kyle said.

"The bomb?" Ariel asked. "What bomb?"

"The terrorists holding the president have a small nuke."

"You're kidding!" Ariel said, jumping to her feet, her eyes wide.

Kyle shook his head. "I wish I was. But I'm not. They had it with them, apparently. It's not widely known yet."

"And you think the man who made the bomb is alive?"

"If he is, and IF we can find him, he might be able to help stop this madness."

"How?" she asked.

"Maybe he can diffuse it," Kyle said.

Ariel sipped her mescal, then stared as she swirled the ice cubes in her drink. She lifted her eyes and scowled. "But how? If the terrorists have the bomb, they're not going to let anyone near it, especially Morris, if he's the man who made it."

Kyle nodded and thought for a moment, dropping his eyes. "You're right. I don't know what I was thinking. But if he's alive and he made the bomb, then what he knows could help."

Ariel shrugged.

"Aw shit!" Raoul shouted.

Kyle and Ariel turned to him.

"What?" Kyle asked.

"Someone named Alpha Mike."

"That's A and M," Kyle said. "It's got to be Alan Morris."

"Hank has been asking how Alpha Mike is doing."

"What's the response?"

"Still fishing." Raoul said. "Where the eagle flies."

"What does that mean?" Kyle asked.

Raoul shook his head. "Who knows?"

Kyle turned to Ariel. "You know the Vista Verde Ranch. Where can the guests fish?"

"Anywhere they can find water!" Ariel said.

"Someplace remote," Kyle said. "Not the ponds by the lodge. Someplace hard to get to. A place where someone could hide."

"There's a fishing camp in the mountains," Ariel said. "It's a place called the Eagle's Nest."

Kyle grinned and turned to Raoul. "Did you hear that?"

"That's got to be it!" Raoul said with a nod.

"Do you know where it is?" Kyle asked Ariel.

"Of course," she said. "I used to go there with Jerome."

"To fish?"

Ariel shrugged. "He'd fish. I'd meditate."

"How long does it take?" Kyle asked.

"A few hours if you're in shape," Ariel said. "More if you're not."

"We don't have much time," Kyle said, glancing at the wall clock.

"But wait! Why would Hank Benedict be hiding Alan Morris?" Ariel asked.

Raoul looked at her and nodded. "That's what I was wondering. Kyle has a theory. He thinks that Hank and his father are somehow behind the hostage situation at Vista Verde."

Ariel narrowed her eyes as she looked at Kyle. "Seriously?"

Kyle nodded. "Yes, and the fact that Hank is asking about Alpha Mike, who we all suspect is Alan Morris, only proves it."

"But why would they do that?" she asked.

"Because Hank and his old man hate Harris and everything he stands for. They're both supporters of ultra-right wing causes."

"So, you're saying they're working with the terrorists who have the president?" she asked.

"That's exactly what I'm saying," Kyle said. "I think they set up this whole thing."

"If that's true, then …." Ariel's eyes widened as she realized the implications. "We'd better get going now. We need to be on the trail at first light."

CHAPTER 29

Tariq stared silently as the moon illuminated the valley in a gray-blue light, casting a dim glow onto the floor of the lodge's library floor where he and his men lay on the plush and padded carpeting. It was comfortable, but was still a disgusting example of excess, Tariq mused, as his anger smoldered, firming his resolve. He clenched his teeth.

Tariq pondered the American president barricaded in the upper room.. He wanted to feel the man's warm and sticky blood on his hands. He and his men could break down the barrier and get to him just as they had with the senator.

But for the moment, Tariq didn't need to worry about that. He had the bomb. He could detonate it. Yes, they would all die, along with President Harris, the lodge and its contents consumed in an orgasm of destruction. He smiled. He and those with him would be instant martyrs.

He lifted his eyes to the library ceiling. If it is the will of Allah, he thought, we have the head of the Great Satan within our grasp and soon we will sever it. Victory will be ours. "*In'shallah*," he said softly.

Unlike the men who surrounded him, Tariq had been unable to sleep, despite the aching exhaustion in his bones and his sore muscles. He pushed away the pain, refusing to think of himself. He had to draw on his reservoir of strength and resolve, even as he felt drained and empty, like a hollow man. *How can I continue?* He lay still and listened to the silence, hearing only the soft breathing of the men around him. *There is no escape now. Only death. And it will come soon.* He thought of his master, his inspiration, as he recalled the man's teachings: this life means nothing. Neither its joys nor wealth or comfort. All ends in death and destruction. True joy and happiness is in the next life. Tariq smiled and nodded to himself.

Tariq heard one of his men groan and stir, then the soft rustle of the man's scarf, which served as a blanket, not enough to ward off the chill of the evening. He heard the man turn and sit up. Tariq looked across the room, catching the man's glistening eyes.

"It is time for morning prayers," the man said.

Tariq nodded.

The man crawled across the carpet, and shook the others, whispering to each it was time to rise. In a low voice, almost a groan, the man began to sing the morning call to prayer, and one by one, the others rose and imitated the posture of their leader, Tariq, who stood with hands clasped and head bowed toward Mecca. The room soon filled with the drone of the men's appeal to Allah to forgive their failings and for help to reach the exalted life soon to come.

***

The full moon hung low in the western sky, fading in the growing light of dawn, as Kyle, Raoul, and Ariel trekked a barely visible trail through the shadowy pines. Rocky peaks of the surrounding mountains glowed faintly, streaks of the past winter's snow glistening on the face of the rock.

After walking for two hours, Kyle's left knee ached, a relentless reminder of past wounds. His right thigh also hurt with every step, but the pain was not like his left knee. It could be worse, Kyle told himself, admitting to himself he'd never be the athlete and runner he'd once been.

"This is a good place to stop," Ariel said. "The cabin's about a mile from here, a fifteen-minute walk."

"I couldn't agree more," Kyle said, letting his small daypack slip from his shoulders along with the strap to the green tube that contained his fly rod. Ariel and Raoul settled on the bed of pine needles beside the trail.

Kyle fingered his pants pocket for a packet of ibuprofen tablets, ripped it open, and popped a couple in his mouth, washing them down with gulps of water.

"Any surveillance cameras?" Raoul asked.

"None that I know of," Ariel said. "People come up here to get away. There's nothing to do but watch the trout jump."

"Are you sure?" Raoul asked. "You've seen Hank's headquarters. He's got everything on this ranch wired."

"What if Morris isn't here?" Kyle asked.

"Then we've walked a long way through the night for nothing," Raoul said.

Kyle peeled back the wrapper to a chocolate-coated bar protein bar and took a bite.

"We'll know soon enough," Raoul said, twisting the top from his water bottle and taking a swig. "If we're right, things could get nasty," he said. "This is where we should split up."

Kyle finished his bar and put the wrapper in his small backpack. They went over the plan one more time, which gave him a few more minutes for the pain killers to kick in.

Fifteen minutes later, the sky was brighter. Kyle felt a tightening in his gut, a growing anxiety about what they might find and how quickly their plan might fall apart. He looked at Ariel, who had an unexpected calm about her, her crystalline eyes like ice. "You okay?" he asked her.

Ariel narrowed her eyes and mashed her lips together with resolve, then gave him a nod.

Raoul stood, brushed his pants, and shifted his gaze from Kyle to Ariel and back. "Don't worry. You're decoys. Just be yourselves."

Kyle and Ariel got to their feet, and for a moment Kyle felt like he was standing at the edge of a cliff, staring into empty space. *Can I leap into the void?* But it's too late now, he thought. There's too much at stake to do nothing. Kyle cleared his throat and took a deep breath as Raoul pulled his pistol from the holster, released the magazine, checked it, and snapped it back into the handle. "Meet you at the cabin," he said, then disappeared down the trail.

After another fifteen minutes, the sky was now light blue, the sun painting the nearby peaks red-orange as Kyle and Ariel emerged from the forest. They paused. A narrow, but well-worn path wound gently upwards and along a rocky slope between large boulders. "You ready for this?" Kyle asked.

Ariel narrowed her eyes again. "As ready as I'll ever be."

She turned and started to walk, Kyle following her up the trail. She was truly a different woman now, he thought, watching the movement of her hips in her hiking shorts as she stepped effortlessly between the boulders. He felt like he'd known her in a different lifetime, one that he remembered like a dream. He'd traveled tens of thousands of miles since those days. But now she was there with him and she was real, as real as it gets. He smiled as confidence slowly replaced his dread of what was to come.

Kyle thought about Nate Kennard and how he himself had narrowly escaped a similar fate. He thought of the confusing photo that Nate once had sent him along with the brief note about how excited Nate had been to have tracked down the Chinese and Russian-made weapons. Were these the ones that had ended up in the hands of the Syrian rebels? *Of course!* Now it all made sense. Kyle suspected Kennard and McCovey, the London freelance writer, had received a call telling them they could meet with someone who could tell them about the source of the weapons and show them the stockpiles. That's why they'd not crossed the border into Turkey, that day, and instead had driven deep into Syria. If the weapons were what they'd thought, it would have been indisputable confirmation of the US's deep involvement in Syria and would have put the US in a face-to-face confrontation with Russia over its support of the Assad regime. But they'd been captured shortly after Kennard taken the photo. Had someone tipped off the terrorists?

Kyle's thoughts disappeared as he and Ariel paused atop a knoll overlooking the small mountain lake, the kind of photogenic scene that graced travel brochures and made people dream about mountain vacations. The lake sat at the bottom of a granite basin surrounded by jagged peaks, now lighted by the sun and set against a blue sky. The granite face sloped steeply downward to broad deltas of loose scree that tumbled into the clear blue water at far side of the lake.

To their right, the forest ended at a sloping green meadow extending to the water's edge, broken only by occasional bushes. It was a fly fisherman's paradise: a remote and isolated high mountain lake, undoubtedly teeming with trout, surrounded by a wide and grassy meadow with plenty of room to work a rod and reel for a perfect cast.

Kyle's stomached tightened as he saw the cabin, the object of their climb. A pitched red metal roof, with a stone chimney protruding above, and walls of green painted cedar shingles. A broad porch extended along the lakeside, with a table and four Adirondack chairs. It was a classic fishing cabin, and just like the rest of the ranch, had undoubtedly been renovated and furnished with the best materials and workmanship available. Kyle felt a twinge of envy. It was a place he could only dream of having, and for a moment, thought about how someday he might step out of this cabin's front door and cast a line into a private trout lake each morning and evening when the trout rose to feed.

He glanced at Ariel, who scanned the lake, her eyes settling on the cabin at the side of the lake. The cabin looked quiet, except for the wisp of smoke curling from the stone chimney. "Someone's in the cabin," she said. "There's smoke from a fire."

"Just as we thought," Kyle said, his pulse quickening.

"Wait!" Ariel said urgently. Kyle flinched, wondering what she'd seen. Ariel turned, her face inches from his, and looked into his eyes. She put cool hands on his cheeks, drew his face to hers, and kissed him, her mouth open.

"What was that?" Kyle asked softly.

"In case something bad happens," she said.

Kyle nodded grimly. "We have a plan. We can only hope it works."

She took his hand and squeezed it, gave him a peck on the cheek, then turned and led Kyle along the narrow path down the sloping meadow and toward the lake. How long would it take for the ones in the cabin to notice them? And what would they do? Shoot first and ask questions later? Until now, the forest had provided cover. Exposed and in the open, walking to the lake's edge, Kyle's dread returned, his chest tightening as they approached the water.

They were to act like a couple of innocents, just looking for a good fly-fishing lake, they would say. But Kyle knew their cover story was thin, very thin, by claiming they'd wandered off course, deep into this private ranch land. Who gets that far off course and on foot? But Ariel had insisted it happened often, that avid fly fishermen and women will go to extremes to find the perfect lake. Such fly-fishing *aficionados* were occasionally escorted from the Vista Verde Ranch, she said. Kyle could only hope their story would hold. Their excuse was that the Vista Verde Ranch, though private, was surrounded by federal Forest Service land, which was open and accessible to anyone who wanted to use it. People like me, he thought.

Now Kyle was doubtful. There was a national crisis at hand. Who in God's name would be so ignorant of the national crisis they'd be tromping blissfully around the Sangre de Cristo Mountains looking for trout at this remote, high mountain lake? If the men inside the cabin were who they suspected, they'd easily be shot on sight and never be seen or heard from again.

Still, he and Ariel ambled down the slope to the water's edge. A cool breeze gusted as they arrived, rippling the surface and distorting the flawless reflection of the surrounding peaks. At the water's edge, they paused, Kyle resisting his urge to turn and stare at the cabin. Ariel shed her small pack and settled on the ground, crossing her legs. She took her water bottle from the pack, drank, then peeled the wrapper from a protein bar.

Kyle dropped his pack to the grass and opened his fly rod case, extracting the pieces of his carbon fly rod and fitting them together. He threaded the orange line through the guides and cradled the rod in the crook of his arm as he knotted the filament taper and tugged it tight. With his other hand, he took a box of flies from his pocket and snapped it open. He found a suitably colorful and fuzzy fly and quickly tied it to the line.

Kyle walked down to the lake's edge and began to work the line back and forth in graceful arcs before letting it float out and onto the lake's rippled surface. Kyle let the line sit for several minutes, then reeled it in and repeated the cast, dropping the fly in a different spot.

Kyle felt a sudden and strong tug on his line, then just as quickly it went slack. A fish had stuck, but had not taken the fly. It was gone. "Damn," Kyle muttered, even though he didn't want to catch anything. Kyle reeled the line in, then glanced at the cabin. He saw no sign of life other than the faint wisp of smoke curling from the stone chimney. *Was anyone in the cabin? There had to be!* A fire in the fireplace or stove would not smolder that long unattended. But why hadn't anyone shown themselves? He and Ariel had fully expected to be confronted when they'd first appeared. But nothing. Was this whole gambit a deadly mistake? Anxiety gripped his stomach as he stood and cast his line again, wondering if he'd get out of there alive.

Kyle could feel two sets of eyes burning into this back, where the ache of his tense muscles burned between his shoulder blades. He imagined the pain from a couple of bullets to the back, the sharp crack of gun shots echoing off the jagged granite peaks as he crumpled to the ground, his flesh and blood blown across the water.

He shook his head to clear it. *Focus!* Whoever was in the cabin had to be wondering who in the hell had the misfortune to come across this high and remote little lake. Kyle nodded to Ariel, who rose to her feet. She joined him at the water's edge and they moved another 50 feet along the shore. After twenty minutes and two more moves, Kyle and Ariel were at the lake's edge directly below the cabin.

"No one's coming out," Ariel said. "What the hell's going on?"

"They don't want to show themselves."

"Why not?"

"Strangers like us might ask questions," Kyle said, "questions they don't want to answer."

"That means they're hiding," Ariel said. "Hiding themselves and possibly someone else."

"Exactly," Kyle said. He took a halting breath and exhaled. "I hope Raoul's in place."

"I'm sure he is," she said. "What do you want to do?"

"If the mountain won't come to Mohammed, then Mohammed will go to the mountain."

"What do you mean?"

Kyle leaned close and whispered his plan.

"Why me?" Ariel asked.

"Damsel in distress," Kyle said, narrowing his eyes. "Works every time." He glanced over Ariel's shoulder to the still quiet cabin. "It's show time."

Kyle turned back to the lake, picked up his fly rod and began to cast, when he doubled over, gripped his chest, dropped his fly rod, and collapsed to the ground.

With his eyes squinting in pain, Kyle watched Ariel jump up and run to him, falling to her knees as panic spread over her face. He felt her lift his head with her hands and shake him.

"Kyle!" she shouted. "What's wrong? What's happening to you?" Ariel shook him a couple of times, then bent close, placing her open mouth on his, and began to perform CPR by pressing on his chest and breathing into his mouth. "Kyle! Talk to me!"

Kyle lay still. Ariel rose to her feet, looked around, and waved her arms in a panic. Her steps faded as she scrambled up the slope to the cabin. He heard her heavy footfalls on broad wooden porch and the distant thump-thump as she pounded on the cabin door.

CHAPTER 30

Ariel tried to calm her quivering stomach and prayed her voice wouldn't break. Damsel in distress? *What the hell?* But she'd played this role before and she could do it again. Lives were at stake here. She stood on the porch, hearing only her own heavy breath. She bent forward, her ear close to the door, and listened. Nothing. Had this all been a mistake? She began to doubt that anyone was inside. She pounded the door again and waited. "Hello?" she shouted. "Is anyone in there?"

Again, silence. She pounded on the door with her fist. "Please help me! My husband has collapsed! He's had a heart attack. He's dying!"

She pressed her forehead against the door, then jerked back at the sound of heavy footsteps from inside approaching the door. She froze as door handle turned and clicked. The door slowly opened a crack, revealing a burly man with a thick reddish beard and blue eyes. Dressed with a black t-shirt with the Atlas global monogram, desert camo pants, and desert boots, he was clearly irritated and threatening. "What do you want?" he growled.

"Please," Ariel pleaded, doing her best to sound desperate, squeezing tears from her eyes. "My husband! He's dying!"

The door opened wider, revealing the leather strap of a shoulder holster across the man's chest.

Ariel had all she could do not to crane her neck to peer inside.

The bearded man slowly shook his head. "What are you talking about? Who are you?"

Ariel turned and pointed to where Kyle lay on the ground at the lake's edge. "It's the altitude," she said, sounding on verge of hysteria. "We're from New York. He's not used to the thin air and the exertion! I think he's had a heart attack!"

The man scowled, shook his head in disgust, then said, "I'd like to help, but there's not much I can do."

"Don't you have a radio or something?" Ariel asked anxiously.

The man scowled, as if it was none of her business.

"We need to get him out of here by helicopter or something!" Ariel said insistently. "You've got to do something!"

Another man appeared behind the first, also wearing an Atlas Global shirt, camo tactical pants, and boots. "Look, ma'am," the guard man said. "We're just up here fishing like you. There's nothing we can do. You're on your own."

"On my own?" Ariel cried. "I need help! Please! I beg you!"

The two men stared, the second one resting his hand on the pistol on his web belt. Ariel swallowed, doing her best to hide her fear, as she searched their faces and brushed away tears with a finger.

"Can you at least bring him in here where it's warm while I go for help?" she asked, forcing a sob. Ariel tilted her head to peek inside the cabin, but the Atlas men didn't budge, blocking her view. "Please help me."

Ariel suddenly sank, her knees hitting the wood porch with a thunk, then leaned forward and buried her face in her hands, sobbing, her shoulders shaking. "I don't know what to do," she said, moaning into her hands.

One of the men groaned, then mumbled to the other, "We gotta get'em outta here. We can't have search and rescue people crawling around here."

"You got that right," the other said. "What are we going to do about Alpha Mike?"

"He ain't goin' nowheres," the first one said. "Let's go check out this poor bastard. Maybe he just needs some water. Maybe they can walk out."

"Okay, ma'am," the other said. "Just relax. I've had some first aid training. Let me see if I can help."

Ariel looked up and smiled, then blinked and dried her eyes. "Oh, thank you!" she said. "Hurry! I'm afraid he's dying."

The two men were already off the porch and trotting to the lake as Ariel rose to her feet and followed them, stumbling to keep up, eyeing the spot where Kyle lay on the ground.

***

Raoul rose from behind the large boulder where he was hiding and scrambled down the slope, stepping carefully so as not to dislodge rocks. He paused at the back of the cabin, and breathing heavily, he peered into a cabin window. A man who looked to be in his mid-fifties with a trimmed and graying beard and cropped hair, lay on a the lower mattress of bunkbeds. His right arm was stretched above his head and the wrist was handcuffed to a wooden cross bar. *Morris! Who else?* The man looked like a scientist, Raoul thought, with tortoise shell glasses and thoughtful eyes, staring now at bunk above him. The man looked fit, with a barrel chest and thick arms. A good thing because they'd need to move fast when and if made their way down the mountain.

Raoul tapped on the window to get the man's attention. The man lifted his head and peered toward the window, then frowned at Raoul's face, confused as to what and who he was seeing. The man eyes opened wide, suddenly panicked, Raoul feared, at Raoul's dark silhouette. The man probably suspected the worst. Raoul tapped again and motioned for the man to open the window.

The man's face relaxed slightly as he seemed to realize he was being rescued. He sat up and pointed to his handcuffed hand and shook his head. He then turned used his free hand to point a finger to the lake. Raoul nodded, then moved quickly to his left where he crouched at the corner of the cabin and looked to the lake.

The two cabin guards were bent over Kyle. Raoul turned to the scraping sound of furniture moving across the floorboards inside the cabin as Morris dragged the bunk beds closer to the window. Raoul returned to the cabin's rear window and watched as Morris used his free hand to unlatch and open the window. Morris stepped back and sat on the edge of the bed as Raoul climbed inside. Morris's face was worn with worry.

"Alan Morris?"

"Yes," Morris said with a groan. "Who the hell are you?"

"The name's Raoul Garcia."

"What are you doing here?" Morris asked.

"Rescuing you," Raoul said.

"But why?"

"Terrorists have President Harris held hostage at Vista Verde Ranch."

"Oh, God," Morris said.

"We're gonna get you outta here," Raoul said.

"Those two men down there may have other ideas about that," Morris said.

"I know. But they're expendable. You're not."

"Is this about the bomb?"

"Of course. The men who have the President have the bomb you made."

Raoul worked on Morris's handcuffs with his lock pics, and in a moment, they clicked open.

"Thanks," Morris said, massaging his wrists.

CHAPTER 31

Kyle had kept his eyes closed as the two guards drew close, their boots swishing through the grass, the gravel crunching below their feet. He had sensed one of the men kneel beside him, then felt the guard's thick, cold fingers pressing on his neck, checking for a pulse.

"Hmmm," the man said. "His pulse is just fine."

Kyle felt the back of the guard's fingers on cheek.

"And his temperature is good."

Kyle blinked opened his eyes and stared up at the guard bent over him.

"What kind of bullshit is this?" the Atlas Global guard said, springing to his feet and yanking his pistol from his belt. "What are you trying to pull? You didn't have no heart attack!"

The second guard glanced back at the cabin. "There's someone at the cabin."

They turned to see Raoul crouched in the shadows of the porch, the barrel of his assault rifle resting on the railing, his cheek against the stock and sighting through the scope. The two guards glared Kyle and Ariel. "You fucking bastards!" the bearded one said.

Kyle rolled to his side, scrambled to his feet, and lifted his hands, palm out. "Now, don't do anything stupid," Kyle said. "No one needs to die."

"Fucking hell," the bearded Atlas guard growled, but did nothing.

It was a standoff for a moment, until the second Atlas guard grabbed Ariel by the arm, spun her around, and violently wrapped his left arm around her neck, holding it tightly in the crook of his arm. His right hand held the barrel of his automatic pistol against her temple, his right elbow straight out to the side.

Using Ariel as a shield, the guard whirled to face the cabin and Raoul, who was on the porch, his rifle held high and aimed at his fellow agent's head. "Drop it or she's dead," the guard shouted, his eyes red and glowing.

A shot cracked across the mountain side as the head of the guard beside Kyle disintegrated in an explosion of blood and bone. The guard's body flopped backwards to the ground, the shot echoing from the granite peaks.

Kyle was stunned as spots of blood and flesh peppered the side of his face. *Raoul shot one of his own men!* But Kyle immediately knew why. There was no other way. If Raoul hadn't pulled the trigger, none of them would leave the lake alive. These men were loyal to Hank Benedict and no one else. They were part of the unfolding madness and it was far from over. They were trained killers. They were traitors.

"Let her go!" Raoul shouted from the cabin porch. "Or you're next."

"Fuck you," the remaining guard shouted back. "You want this pretty woman's brains all over the ground?"

Kyle twitched, unable to move, his gaze bouncing from the dead man on the ground to Raoul on the porch, and to the Atlas guard choking Ariel, her eyes glistening with fear, her head pulled back, her chin jutting upward from the guard's arm.

"Let her go," Kyle growled, wiping the side of his face with a sleeve.

The Atlas guard glared at Kyle, then grinned. "Make a move and I'll kill her," he said, "then I'll kill you." He then turned back to the porch. "Raoul, you're a fucking idiot," the guard shouted. "Don't be stupid. She'll be dead even if you shoot me."

The crack of a gunshot sounded a moment after the bullet struck the guard's right elbow, ripping his arm out and away, sending the pistol spinning into the air. Raoul's shot echoed from the granite peaks as the guard screamed, his destroyed arm dangling limp, bloodied, and useless to his side. The man staggered backward, and using Ariel as ballast, he managed to stay on his feet, gritting his teeth through the pain and holding his still good left arm around Ariel's neck. His eyes darted from Kyle to the porch and back as he calculated his next move.

Ariel gagged from the guard's grip and turned slightly to face Kyle.

"Let her go," Kyle said again. "It's over."

"Fuck you," the guard groaned.

Desperate to free herself, Ariel stomped her boot heel on her captor's foot, making the guard howl in pain, then she ducked and twisted free. Swinging her right elbow up and backward, she slammed it into the guard's nose. The guard's head snapped backwards, his arm good arm flailing as he reached for his nose.

Ariel then dove to the ground, rolled away, and scrambled to her feet. Crouched, legs spread and balanced, she clenched her fists, prepared for an attack.

His nose and upper lip bloodied, his right arm dangling and dripping, the guard grinned with bloody teeth. "You shouldn't a done that missy." The guard's good left hand slipped behind his back and came out clutching a serrated commando knife. Emitting a groan like some hellish beast, he leapt forward and swiped the blade at Kyle, who stumbled backwards and fell to the ground. The guard then lunged at Ariel, who leapt to her right, narrowing escaping the sweeping blade.

The crack of another rifle shot sounded from the cabin porch. The knife-wielding guard's head twisted wildly as if struck by massive fist. Blood spurting, the guard spun uncontrollably to the ground, where his body fell with a resounding thump, arms splayed.

Kyle and Ariel turned to the cabin porch where Raoul slowly rose, squinted at the carnage, and lowered his rifle. Moving quickly down the steps, he trotted toward them. Reaching lake's edge, Raoul looked at Kyle and Ariel. "You both okay?"

"Hell of a shot to the elbow," Kyle said.

Raoul grunted in agreement, staring at the gore. "It's nice to have some luck every now and then." He crouched beside the two dead guards and looked closely at the bodies. Raoul took the knife from the dead guard's hand and removed the sheath from the man's belt. Slipping the knife blade into the sheath, he tossed it to Ariel. "It might come in handy."

Raoul again surveyed the dead. "Hank's not gonna be very happy about this. I shot and killed a couple of his best men." He looked up at Kyle, then shook his head in disgust.

"Why keep Morris alive up here?" Kyle asked, as little was making sense to him. "They just as easily could have killed him."

"Maybe they needed him alive for something," Raoul said with a shrug.

"For what?" Kyle asked. "The *jihadis* already have the freaking bomb and the president. Why would Benedict need to hide Morris?" he asked, his voice trailing off. "Unless … where's Morris?" he asked, urgency creeping into his voice.

Raoul stood and pointed to the porch. "Right there."

As they turned to look, Morris stepped from the dark interior behind the front door and into the morning light. He stared for a moment, then stepped off the porch and strode down the narrow path to the lake.

"We need to talk." Kyle said, as Morris came close.

"There's no time for that," Raoul said.

"Yes there is," Kyle barked. Raoul stood and narrowed his eyes at Kyle, who turned to Morris. "Why did you build it?"

Morris grimaced and shook his head. "I had no choice. They have Jennifer."

"Who's Jennifer?" Ariel asked.

Morris jerked his head toward her. "My daughter," he said. "My only child. She's all I have left." Morris clenched his jaw, his eyes glistening with hate. "They took her and brainwashed her."

"So you made a nuclear bomb for them?" Kyle asked.

Morris nodded. "One day after Jennifer had disappeared from the al-Salam mosque along with the *jihadis*, Hank Benedict and couple of his Atlas Global showed up. "They said they were in contact with the *jihadis* and had been tracking them. They said they could free Jennifer and bring her back to me. But first I had to make something to bargain for her release."

"Hank Benedict?"

Morris nodded again. "Benedict said I should make bomb for them. A nuke."

"And you did?" Kyle asked.

"It was the only way they would release her," Morris said.

"And you believed them?" Raoul said.

"I told Benedict what I needed. The C4 was the main thing. Then I got a tiny piece of enriched uranium and a BB sized piece of plutonium."

"Why didn't you go to the authorities?" Kyle asked.

"I couldn't!" Morris said, his voice rising. "Hank warned me that if I told anyone, the *jihadis* would execute her while I watched." Morris's glistening eyes searched their faces. "You have to believe me."

"We believe you," Kyle said, trying to sound sympathetic.

"The *jihadis* have already killed Congressman Divine and Senator Blount," Raoul said to Morris. "They have

President Harris and they're holding him hostage with *your* nuclear bomb!"

"I was afraid something like that might happen," Morris said.

"But you still gave them a bomb anyway?" Raoul asked, almost shouting.

Morris stared wide-eyed at the bodies of the two guards who only minutes earlier had held him captive. "It's worthless," he said softly.

"What? What do you mean?" Kyle asked. .

"The bomb," Morris said, his eyes darting from face to face. "It won't work without me."

"What are you talking about?" Raoul asked.

"A safety device. I built the bomb with a safety mechanism," Morris said, again staring at the bodies.

"What kind of safety mechanism?" Kyle asked.

"Biometrics."

"Your finger prints?" Raoul asked.

Morris shook his head, no. "Iris recognition technology. It's common technology. Easy to incorporate into a bomb. Without me, no one can initiate the detonation sequence."

"Iris scan? How does that work?" Kyle asked.

"The detonation sequence is launched by an I-phone signal. It uses a scan of my iris, which is unique to me, of course, to authenticate me as the authorized user of the phone. It's like a log-in. Once it recognizes me, then it will work. Then all I need to do is launch the sequence."

"But it's radioactive!" Raoul said. "It's got nuclear materials!"

"Nothing is failsafe," Kyle said.

"I know," Morris said. "But I built it. I know how it works and won't work."

"How in God's name did you get nuclear material out of the lab?" Kyle asked. "There's got to be cameras and radiation detectors all over the place."

Morris nodded gravely. "That's the perception," he said. "But perceptions are not reality. If you know what you're doing, it's easier than you think."

"In order to make a nuclear bomb, you need a lot of fissionable material," Kyle said.

Morris shook his head slowly. "Think of it like a dirty bomb. It has radioactive material, but it's a conventional bomb. It scatters microscopic nuclear debris around when it's detonated."

"If it's detonated," Raoul said.

"Exactly," Morris said.

The four searched each other's faces.

"Maybe we can get the president out of there after all," Kyle said.

Raoul nodded. "They think they have a bomb, but they don't."

"Well, yes and no," Ariel said. "The bomb is still there, even though it won't work without Morris, who is here with us."

"They're vulnerable and they don't know it," Raoul said, as a wry smile came to his face.

"So if the bomb won't work without him," Kyle said, "then why was Atlas Global hiding Morris up here?"

Ariel squinted and said, "Because they're part of it?"

"That's right," Morris said. "They grabbed me after I had made the bomb and handed it over to the *jihadis*. Atlas Global booby-trapped my house."

"That means Hank and the boys are the ones who nearly killed us," Kyle said to Raoul.

"Does Atlas know about the safety mechanism?" Raoul asked.

"I never told them anything about it," Morris said. "I just handed it over to them and showed them the application to launch the detonation countdown ."

"So, Hank Benedict doesn't know that the bomb is rigged for your eyes only?" Kyle asked.

Morris shook his head, no.

"The key is the *jihadis* think they have a live bomb, but don't!" Raoul said.

"But Hank Benedict must know the bomb won't work without Morris," Kyle said. "It's why he's been holding off on a rescue of the president. It's also why he's been hiding Morris up here."

"It doesn't matter, now that we've got Morris," Raoul said.

"And, the *jihadis* have your daughter," Ariel said to Morris. "That won't change, bomb or no bomb."

Morris nodded. "I want my daughter back."

"Let's go get her and the president," Raoul said.

CHAPTER 32

Hank Benedict sat at his desk and stared outside, lost in thought, as the sun baked the sprawling compound of the Atlas Global headquarters and training facility. He remembered when the land where he now sat was nothing but a field of sparse, wild grass and pale green chamisa bushes. He'd designed the Atlas headquarters like a forward operating base, with runways, landing pads, barracks, classrooms, and a gun range. State of the art. It felt impregnable. Now he and his father were on the precipice of achieving their greatest victory. Except for a couple of loose ends.

Fucking Raoul Garcia and his journalist cousin, that guy Kyle Dawson. Damned liberal media SOB. He didn't trust either one of them. Raoul was a talented man, one of the best at what he did, including Hank himself. And Hank considered himself at the top. Raoul knew Atlas Global operations well, but he didn't know everything—just enough to screw it all up. And Raoul had been out of touch for more than 24 hours. *Where the fuck is he?* No phone, no GPS. Nothing. That familiar queasy feeling returned to Hank's stomach.

Was Raoul with that Dawson bastard? That could be trouble. And where was Ariel? Jerome's ex-wife, his widow. Not that it mattered. She was beautiful, but she was a masseuse. If she was gone, that'd be all right. It meant less for him to worry about. And, she could be easily replaced.

Hank refocused on the bank of video screens covering the wall. One was filled with the scowling mug of his father, David Benedict. He had watched his father age over the years, his father's once-chiseled face sag, the cheeks becoming jowls, his forehead creased, his eyelids droop, making him look like a grizzled Shar-Pei. And the eyes, once bright and determined, were now weary and wary.

On a larger screen was Vice President Marvin in the White House situation room with the CIA's Sidow, the FBI's Huntington, and Dempsey of the Secret Service. Hank knew these men could be trusted—as long as they were kept in check.

"This has to be quick," Marvin said, his voice breaking over the speakers. "I don't want to get into a lot of useless talk and speculation. So, Hank, you're on ground there. What's the latest?"

"The situation has not changed substantially since the *jihadis* issued their demands yesterday," Hank said.

"We can't just sit idly by and let them detonate a bomb and kill the president," said Dempsey, waving his hands, his voice anxious and irate.

"What would you have us do?" Marvin shouted, lifting his hands high. "Storm the place? We've already ruled that out. They'd certainly kill Harris then."

"It's better than sitting on our hands," injected Huntington. "Inaction is disgraceful."

Sidow cleared his throat. "Since when do we grant situational control to a private security company, especially when it comes to the American president?"

"Since they're the ones who are on the ground and they're the ones who know what they're doing," Marvin said. "That's worth a hell of a lot more than all of your damned satellite surveillance and drones and your boys in gray suits."

"President Harris is the one who got himself in this mess," intoned David Benedict, his baritone voice booming. "It was none of our doing."

"Okay, gentlemen," said Marvin, clearing his throat, placing his hands on the table. "Let's keep looking for a solution. It's going on nine a.m. here. We still have time today. Let's meet again in two hours with the full security council."

As the video screens went blank, Hank Benedict's phone rang. He looked at it, tapped the screen, and answered, "What's up?" The phone screen showed an Atlas Global agent in a tight t-shirt who moved leaned in close, his face filling it. "Eagle's Nest has gone dark."

"What are you talking about?"

"Dark," the agent said. "Lights out. No response."

"Shit," Hank said. "Where's Morris?"

"We don't know," the agent said. "It could just be a technical problem."

"Or worse," Hank said. "Send a drone up there. We need to know what happened."

"You got it," the agent said. "I'll get back to you as soon as I know something."

The screen went blank. Hank slammed the table and the knot in his guts tightened. He didn't need this. God-damned Raoul. Was it was him? Did he have Morris? If so, then what? "Damn!" he shouted, slamming the table again. He closed his eyes for a moment to focus. Tariq still had the bomb and President Harris. Nothing had changed that. And nothing would. He clenched his jaw and ground his teeth, his stomach burning, his breath short, sweat beading on his forehead.

Hank picked up his phone, flicked a finger to scroll through the screen, then tapped the screen to dial another number.

"What is it?" his father asked as he immediately answered his phone.

"Morris is missing," Hank said.

"How did that happen?"

"I don't know yet."

"He can disrupt everything," his father said, stating the obvious.

"I have a drone in the air now," Hank said. "If Morris is alive, we'll find him."

"You must. We can't hold off these government agencies much longer."

"Maybe we can get Tariq to move sooner than later," Hank said.

"It might be too obvious," the elder Benedict said. "Just find Morris, Hank. Kill him if we have to. We're almost there."

The screen went blank.

***

Raoul hustled down the mountain and along the winding trail through the forest, almost at a trot, passing through the mottled shadows cast by the warming sun, now high in the eastern sky. He was trailed by Morris, Ariel, and Kyle, each ten feet behind the other. Raoul stopped suddenly and held up a fist. "Wait. Do you hear that?"

They stumbled to a stop and paused to listen, the sound of their heavy breath mingling with the soft hush of the wind in the pines. Overhead was the faint buzz of a drone.

"Drone!" Raoul said." Quick! Scatter! Hide behind a tree. It will block the infra-red sensor from detecting your body heat."

They jumped off the path and scrambled through the underbrush, each crouching behind a tree. The sound of the drone drew louder as it passed overhead, following the path they had just descended down the mountain. The drone then turned and circled in a large loop, passing overhead again, floating.

"Don't move," Raoul said in a loud whisper.

The drone reversed direction again and seemed to fly away, heading up the mountain, the sound fading. Raoul exhaled slowly, sensing they'd escaped detection. But then the drone returned, flying just above the treetops, floating over the trail.

"Stay in place," Raoul ordered. "Don't move."

After a long moment, drone turned again, a silver bird of prey against the sunlit mountains, flying again over the twisting path they'd followed.

Raoul sat with his back against a tree, his breath short and shallow. "Damn!" he muttered, envisioning the wall of screens inside the Atlas Global command center. He knew what the Atlas Global agents were looking for. The drones carried high definition video lenses and infra-red cameras. They could detect the body heat of squirrels scampering up a tree and zoom in with video and watch the damned critters eat an acorn. "Damn," Raoul cursed again, sweat dripping down his forehead and into his eyes. He brushed a sleeve against his face. The drone may have detected their body heat, but unless they were standing fully upright on the path, the heat could be anything: deer, bear, skunk. Whatever. Raoul knew they'd need all the luck they had if they were to make it out alive.

They sat in place for another few minutes until Raoul felt confident the drone was gone. It had seen what it had seen. He knew the Atlas Global agents would review and analyze the data and images. But it would take time, then still more time for Atlas Global to respond. It was time they needed badly.

"Let's move," Raoul said, pushing himself up. He again checked the sky as he and the others stepped back onto the path. He heard and saw nothing. "Hopefully, they won't know if what they were seeing were animals or humans."

"If they know it's us, we're screwed," Kyle said.

"Do you think?" Ariel said, her voice heavy with sarcasm.

"We need a place to hide," Morris said. "Those things have highly calibrated heat sensors."

"I'm well aware," Raoul said.

"There's a cave further down," Ariel said, "It's only a mile or so from the ranch headquarters. It's a good place to hide."

"Exactly what we need," Raoul said. Maybe Lady Luck was on their side.

***

"Run the video again," Hank Benedict barked to the command center agent, anxiety in his voice. The screen revealed nothing obvious to the naked eye except sunlight igniting the waving bows of the pines and deep shadows.

"Damn," Hank muttered. He knew Raoul was fully aware of the command center's capabilities and knew how to evade detection. "Switch to infra-red."

The agent fingered the keyboard and the screen revealed portions of four indistinct, but ghostly figures walking along a path. The figures stopped, looked up, then disappeared behind trees.

Hank's heart leapt. His lips spread into a thin smile. "Sorry, Raoul. You can run, but you can't hide," he muttered, almost speaking to himself. He turned to one of the command center agents. "What did you find at the cabin?"

"Two bodies," the operator said. "They're already cold."

"Shit!" Hank shouted, clenching his teeth as he balled his fists. "Jones and MacIntosh. Two of my best men." He exhaled noisily through clenched teeth, and closed his eyes tightly. "Raoul, you're a dead man walking."

***

Raoul, Morris, Ariel, and Kyle crouched in the shallow cave. It was a short scramble up the side of the mountain to the cave's opening, which was apparent only when they were directly in front of it. The opening was just three feet high at its widest point, and shaped like a small, open mouth, as if the mountain were about to speak. Inside, the cave opened wide and was high enough for them to stand upright, and deep enough for them to avoid detection by a drone if they kept themselves back from the mouth of the cave.

From the cave's squat opening, they had a view across the tree tops to the valley beyond where the roof of the Vista Verde Lodge rose in the distance, a couple of the abandoned cottages visible among the trees on the sloping valley flanks.

The drone had not returned, which made Raoul worry they'd been detected. If so, Hank would send a kill team once the dead guards had been discovered at the cabin. In the dim light of the cave, Raoul scanned his companions' faces. "We'll rest here for a while," he said.

"We can't do this without help," Kyle said. "And help isn't going to come from Hank and your pals at the Atlas Global."

"I know that," Raoul said. "Any overt action by the Secret Service, the FBI, or the CIA is probably off the table. My gut tells me they'll put the whole thing in the hands of Benedict and Atlas."

"Which means we're screwed," Kyle said.

"Maybe not," Raoul said.

Kyle gave him a puzzled glance.

"I made some calls before we came up the mountain."

"And?"

"We only need a few good men," Raoul said. "A couple of my buddies from special ops in the Marines are with the Secret Service. Another is with the FBI. And a couple are CIA paramilitaries. They're all disgusted with the lack of action. They've agreed to do whatever it takes to free the president."

"It doesn't help if they're not here."

"They're here," Raoul said, "just not visible. They're not going to wait for orders from above because those orders aren't coming."

"What do you have in mind?" Kyle asked.

"They're going to be dressed like Atlas Global agents."

They all fell silent as outside they heard the buzzing of a drone. As they sat silently against the cool rock walls deep in the cave, Raoul surveyed their weaponry. They had stripped the two dead guards of their handguns, then returned to the cabin where they'd gathered up two additional Heckler & Koch assault rifle.

CHAPTER 33

Alan Morris nodded gravely, his eyes drilling into the hard-packed dirt and grit of the cave's floor. He wondered what kind of animals hid inside these sloping stone walls during storms or had made this fissure in the side of the mountain their home. Had ancients used it for ceremonies? He thought about returning to this cave someday to explore it deeper for artifacts like the others he'd collected over the years.

His mind shot back to the task at hand, the plan their *de facto* leader Raoul Garcia had just outlined. They were going to get into the Vista Verde lodge, overwhelm the *jihadis*, and rescue the president. *Yeah, right.* It was delusional at best.

Morris swallowed hard. He was the critical component to Raoul's plan. He had agreed to his role because he wanted to get Jennifer out of there. He'd do anything to make that happen. Without her, his life was nothing. Morris cleared his throat and in the dim light of the cave and leveled his gaze at Raoul. "I need to know first she's still okay," Morris said.

Raoul looked at him, thought for a moment, then said, "No problem." He turned to Kyle. "Call Carlito. Talk to him. Tell him to put Morris's daughter on the phone."

Kyle drew a deep breath, pulled his phone from his pocket, and tapped the screen. The screen came to life. "We need to go outside to get a signal," he said, and took a couple of cautious steps toward opening, then stopped and turned. "If I call, Atlas Global can get a fix on us."

Raoul shrugged. "Just make it quick!"

Kyle stepped outside the cave's opening, looking warily over the towering trees to the bright sky beyond. He tapped the number for Carlito's phone and listened to the ring.

***

Jennifer Morris, aka Halima, sat on the floor and out of sight, but close to a window in the Vista Verde lodge. She was unnerved by the silence of the morning, her fingers warmed by the tea cup she held. She sensed she was going to die. It was the only way she would leave this place now. No one would ever forgive her now. And she would never forgive herself. The way she felt, death would be a welcomed relief. She turned to Carlito, who held his cup to his lips and sipped the last of his tea. How had it turned so wrong? She knew the answer. She had committed herself to Carlito and his cause. It was good and just. Or so she'd thought. But it was all lies. Nothing mattered anymore. Not even the truth. Death hovered in the air. She could feel it.

She remembered the day she'd first laid eyes on Carlito, now Omar. It was after the death of her mother, and she'd sought solace and comfort from her father. But he had none to give as he, too, struggled with the loss of his wife, her mother, immersing himself in his work late into the night at his laboratory office.

They had first stopped by the wool shop on the way back to Los Alamos after hiking on Wheeler Peak near Taos. She'd been a sophomore at Los Alamos High School, and after other subsequent hikes, they'd visited the wool shop often. She was captivated by Carlito's eyes, the softest, brownest eyes she'd ever seen, sinking into them each time they met, responding to his flirts and smiles as he offered her the attention she craved.

She'd never forgotten Carlito, though they'd never dated. It was as if they lived in two different worlds. Then the unbelievable happened. English class on the first day of the first semester of her freshman year at the University of New Mexico. She'd not expected to see him ever again. But then he was there.

Their relationship began slowly, but quickly developed momentum. When Carlito explained his commitment to the land grant cause and the death of his grandfather and his father, she embraced his cause as her own. Then Carlito had discovered Islam. When he'd joined the mosque, so had she.

But everything was crazy now. When Tariq had held the knife to the senator's throat, the man had seemed so old and helpless. Jennifer thought Tariq was only going to threaten the man, not really kill him. But when the blade cut deep, she'd gone numb, frozen with horror. She'd wheeled and dashed into the kitchen, bent over the edge of the stainless steel sink, and wretched violently.

Visions of the killing replayed in Jennifer's mind, haunting her dreams, jolting her awake in the darkness. She now sat against the wall of the lodge, looking out a window and across the valley as the sun warmed the day. She thought about the Tariq's words as they finished breakfast together in the dining hall.

"This will be our greatest day," he'd said, without explaining why.

Jennifer knew why. Holding President Harris hostage could not continue. How long would the federal agents wait before attempting a rescue? The wait and the silence were unnerving. When the attack would come, Jennifer was certain she would not survive. But if by some miracle she did, her life was still over. She was a terrorist now. Their crime was unforgiveable. She'd spend the rest of her life in federal prison. Death was preferable. She'd become part of a terrorist group and an accomplice to multiple murders—murders recorded on video for all the world to see. There was no escape. Jennifer flinched when Carlito's cell phone rang and stared at him with fearful eyes.

Carlito pulled the phone from his pocket and checked the number. His frown melted into a puzzled look as he recognized the number and answered. "Kyle Dawson?" Carlito asked, quietly mouthing the words to her: the journalist.

Jennifer nodded and tensed, wondering why this sudden contact from the outside, the world she'd left behind. Was it coming for her? Was it a warning? She exhaled slowly.

Carlito listening intently, his eyes staring, his lips open in anticipation. After a moment, he glanced at Jennifer and nodded. "Yes, but her name is Halima now. She's fine. We're all fine." He fell silent again, listening. "Yes. She's here." Carlito handed the phone to her.

Jennifer's heart pounded and her mouth went dry as she took the phone in her hand, unable to ignore her suffocating sense of guilt for what she'd done. Jennifer cautiously held the phone to her ear. She recognized the voice. "Daddy? Why are you calling me?"

"I'm going to get you out of there," she heard her father say.

"Don't do that, Daddy. This is *jihad*. I'm with Carlito now. Whatever fate Allah has chosen for us, I must follow that."

"Jennifer, you're getting out of there," Morris said.

"I don't want to go."

"There is not going to be any more *jihad*," Morris said, calmly stating a fact.

"What do you mean?"

"The bomb doesn't work, Jennifer," Morris said. "Not without me."

Jennifer fell silent as a chill swept over her, her stomach sinking, blood draining from her face.

"You did that on purpose," Jennifer said.

"Of course," Morris said.

The implication of her father's words flashed through her mind like a lightning bolt in the night sky. "But daddy, I ..."

Jennifer stopped, her voice choked with emotion, her eyes staring blankly at the polished floor.

"Let me talk to Tariq."

"Don't do this. Please." She paused, surprising herself at the swirling emotions in her heart, a surge of concern for her father knowing what might happen to him now because of her decisions, however fatalistic she had become.

"Now!" Morris said, growling in her ear.

Jennifer flinched at the anger and resolve in her father's voice. This was about much more than just her and her father. Didn't he realize? Jennifer swallowed hard and lifted her gaze to Carlito, searching his eyes as she struggled to explain. "The bomb," she said. "It doesn't work."

Carlito's eyes widened. "That's bull shit," he said, shaking his head. "How is that possible?"

"I don't know," she said. "Maybe only he can arm it."

Carlito stared, mulling the implications. "That means...."

Jennifer nodded. "There's no reason they won't attack now."

"How many people know this?" Carlito asked.

Jennifer shrugged and shook her head slowly.

"We need to tell Tariq."

Jennifer nodded. "My father wants to talk to him right now." She handed the phone back to Carlito.

His stomach churning, Carlito held the phone to his ear and said, "I'll take the phone to him now."

"Good," Morris said. "I'm waiting."

Carlito stood, his legs feeling weak, and hustled out of the room and into the lodge's lobby where some of Tariq's men lounged on the leather couches and sprawled on the padded chairs, their eyes half open, their automatic rifles nestled in their laps, the pockets of their camo pants heavy with ammo magazines.

Carlito continued down the short hallway, pausing at the entrance to the spacious library. Tariq turned immediately from his two closest men, each sitting on the thick, blue patterned carpet, their knees nearly touching, surrounded by the piano and couches they'd pushed against the walls. A silver tray held a pot of tea and bowl of sugar sat in the center of their tight triad, each with a cup and saucer. They stopped and stared.

Seeing the look on Carlito's face and sensing the urgency, Tariq motioned for Carlito to come. Carlito dropped to his knees on the carpet beside Tariq, whose eyes opened wide.

"What is it?" Tariq asked, suddenly apprehensive.

Carlito's eyes met those of the two others, now silent. He mashed his lips together, trying to formulate his thoughts and find the right words as he held the phone against his chest, his breath short and hard. "The bomb," Carlito whispered, leaning close to Tariq. "It's no good."

Tariq scowled, as if he'd bitten into an onion, his eyes searching Carlito's face.

"The father of Halima," Carlito said, his voice hushed. "He made the bomb. He says it can't be armed except by him."

Tariq paled, his face drawn as the implications descended.

"Here," Carlito said, thrusting the phone to Tariq's face. "Morris wants to talk."

Tariq nodded, dread rearranging his face. How was this possible? Anger squeezed his chest and soured his stomach. He drew a short breath, searching Carlito's face. He had not anticipated this. But he immediately realized he should have. If the bomb was useless, he and his men were vulnerable. But wait! Who knows about this, other than the man who made the bomb, who was now on the phone? A smile returned to Tariq's lips. Perhaps Allah was giving him a gift. Tariq drew a deep breath, struggling to compose himself, and held the phone to his ear. "*Salam*, Mister Morris."

"This is what we're going to do," Morris said, his voice gruff and dictatorial. "You're going to release my daughter in exchange for me."

"I'm sorry," Tariq said calmly. "We don't need you or your bomb."

"Really?" Morris said. "If you could have, you'd have killed the president by now. But the president is in a safe room. Your only hope for martyrdom is to detonate the bomb."

"That is an assumption you should not make," Tariq replied. "Don't forget. We got into the room with Senator Blount. His body is on the patio. It is waiting for you and your friends to collect. Don't you think the senator deserves a decent burial?" Tariq listened to the silence for a moment.

"Tariq," Morris said, "I'll say it again. The only chance you have for the martyrdom you seek is with the bomb. But it doesn't work without me launching the detonation sequence."

Tariq said nothing, and listened to Morris's exasperated sigh.

"I'm willing to work with you," Morris continued. "I get something I want. You get something you want."

Tariq scratched his beard, his mind racing. "You don't expect me to fall for this trick, do you?"

Morris was silent for a moment. "No trick, Tariq. You get the bomb. I get my daughter."

Tariq swallowed, his unease with the offer growing. But Morris was right. The woman Halima was useless to him. The only reason he had let her come along on the mission was because of Carlito. "Who else knows about this?" Tariq asked.

"No one in the government, I can assure you," Morris said. "I will come alone."

Tariq sensed Morris was lying. But still, he needed the bomb to fully accomplish the mission.

"You lied to me, Morris," Tariq said. "You said the bomb worked. Now it doesn't. Why should I trust you this time?"

"But *you* lied to *me*!" Morris said. "You promised you'd release Jennifer if I gave you the bomb. But you didn't."

"That was her choice," Tariq said. "She refused to leave!"

"You could have sent her away," Morris said. "She's of no use to you."

"The hand of Allah has guided her," Tariq said. "She has chosen her fate."

Morris groaned into the phone and collected his thoughts before he spoke again. "Did she choose her fate or did you choose it for her?"

Tariq did not respond.

"Did you really think I was going to hand you the bomb and give me nothing in exchange?" Morris asked, unable to hide the cynicism in his voice.

Tariq scowled, his gut instinct screaming that Morris was setting a trap. But how? What can this old man do? He's just one man. Once he has armed the bomb, I will kill him, Tariq thought. *Yes! I will execute this crazy old man just like the senator.* He envisioned Morris's headless body beside the others on the porch for the world to see. Soon the world will tremble at the foot of Allah and fear the face of Islam! No matter what happens now, this is a great victory. Tariq clenched his jaw and inhaled, his nostrils flaring.

"Okay," Tariq said. "This is what you do."

CHAPTER 34

Alan Morris emerged from the shadowed trees on the slopes near the main lodge and stepped in the late morning sun. He paused at the tree line, squinted at the lodge porch, and exhaled slowly, his throat choked with fear. *What the hell am I doing? I'm an idiot! I'm in too deep!* He struggled to quiet his raging mind. *This is a job for a young man! Don't do this!*

But there was no one else who could initiate the launch sequence. The bomb was his baby, a unique and special device. Morris clenched his jaw and steeled his resolve, inhaling . *Yes, you can do this. This is for Jennifer, despite her misguided cause, her mangled thoughts.* He shook his head in disgust.

The bastards he was about to confront had twisted her mind, just like they had with Carlito and the others, convincing them they were joining a noble battle for the good of all mankind. They were nothing but a crazed horde of zealots who slaughtered innocent men, women, and children in the most brutal and sadistic ways possible. And they did it proudly, their hands bloodied, convinced of their own righteousness. No, Morris told himself, clenching his jaw. He was going to bring back Jennifer or die trying.

Morris's pace quickened as he strode across the grassy field, knowing that a dozen sets of eyes followed his every step. He unclenched his jaw and told himself to relax, trying to ignore the tingle in his muscles that put a spring in his every step. You're in good shape, he told himself. At least you've done that right! At the age of 54, you're as strong as anytime in your life. The time to act is now.

Morris paused at the base of the steps to the lodge porch, then bounded up them, stopping a yard away from the door, his heart pounding, his breath fast and hard.

One of the lodge's main double doors opened slowly inward, revealing a *jihadi* fighter, the man's figure indistinct behind the screen in the dimness of the lobby. Morris grasped the elk horn door handle, pulled the door open, and stepped inside.

The *jihadi* wore a black and white patterned scarf over his head with the corners around his neck like an Arab desert marauder. A loose black t-shirt covered his thin chest, forest green camo pants were cinched tight at his waist, and his feet were inside leather Mexican sandals. Two other fighters stood behind the first *jihadi*, each holding an AK-47 automatic pistol, barrels pointed at Morris.

The first fighter spread his arms, motioning for Morris to do the same. Morris did, spreading his legs as well. The fighter quickly frisked him, patting down his chest and waist, front and back, then his legs and arms. Satisfied, the *jihadi* fighter stepped back. The two others also retreated, lingering in the shadows, weapons at the ready.

Morris eyed them warily, then scanned the lobby to get a sense of what he faced. The towering stone fireplace dominated the room and scattered around it were leather couches and chairs. A smear of dried blood covered the polished stone floor in front of the fireplace. Morris swallowed hard, realizing it was where Senator Blount had been executed. The stale scent of death hung in the still air.

His throat tightened as Morris wondered how his daughter could have been taken in by these savages. How could she be among the men who had so willingly and wantonly killed the lodge staff and aides, then watched as Tariq took knife in hand and sliced it across the throat of a US senator? Morris flashed on how deadly brutal a human could be.

Morris snapped himself back to the moment as he became aware of the other fighters in the room. They seemed to appear out of the walls, stepping into the lobby, until he could make out six or seven *jihadis*, some standing, some squatting, each armed with an AK-47 automatic pistol, their pockets filled with the banana ammo magazines. Several fingered their weapons as they gazed warily at Morris.

Morris drew a breath as the man he recognized as Tariq stepped into the lobby light. He strode up to Morris, his face uncovered, his thin and scraggly beard decorating his cheeks, chin, and upper lip like mangy fur. Morris was surprised at how young Tariq looked, more like a teen-ager than a seasoned executioner in his mid-twenties. Tariq leaned close and stared into Morris's eyes.

Morris held Tariq's gaze, and in the depth of Tariq's eyes, he saw the abyss of a lost soul, the black hole of a lost spirit. He now felt unsure of himself as Tariq stepped even closer, nearly nose-to-nose. Morris held his ground.

"You deceived us," Tariq said, as if it was a revelation that carried grave consequences.

Morris stared at Tariq and said nothing.

"The bomb is worthless," Tariq said.

"No," Morris said. "It's operational."

"But only by you?"

Morris nodded. "Now keep your part of the bargain, or I don't make it operational. Where is my daughter?"

Tariq waved his hand. One of his men disappeared into a side room and reappeared, pushing Jennifer in front of him.

She was bent forward, her hands tied behind her, her scarf hanging around her neck. She lifted her head and looked sheepishly at her father. Her face was bruised, her nose bloodied, her eyes swollen. Morris opened his eyes in horror, his chest tight with anger, his stomach sinking at the helplessness he felt. He wanted to grab her and hold her. *Jennifer!* His eyes shot back to Tariq.

"What have you done to her?" Morris yelled, doing all he could to stop himself from knocking Tariq to the ground and choking the life out of him.

Tariq smiled, amused at Morris's reaction, his eyes dancing with laughter. "Nothing that she didn't deserve," he said, his mouth spreading into a grin.

Carlito came up behind Jennifer, stopped, and gazed at Morris, looking ashamed and embarrassed, his eyes dropping to the floor.

Morris glared at Carlito, his hatred of the young man seething. "How could you let them do this?"

After a moment, Carlito slowly lifted his head, shrugged helplessly, and stared at Morris, shaking his head. "It's *your* fault!" Carlito said with a growl. "You rigged the bomb!"

Morris considered the words. Deflecting blame was a tactic of the guilty. "They're going to kill you, the president, and everyone else," Morris said calmly. "Is that what you want?"

Carlito lifted his chin proudly and said, "Better to die a martyr than a slave!"

Morris pitied the young man and shook his head. "Who's a slave now?"

"You're all slaves!" Carlito said, his voice rising. "These men are freedom fighters."

An uneven smile twisted Morris's lips. He stared at Carlito and asked, "Freedom from what? Sanity?"

"Freedom from evil," Carlito barked.

Morris glared at Carlito and shook his head in disgust.

Carlito pointed an accusing finger, poking the space between them. "You don't understand! You're a non-believer!"

Morris let the words hang in the air, even as they echoed in his mind. He drew a breath, exhaled slowly as he fought to keep calm, then glanced around the room before his eyes resettled on Carlito. "I understand, all too well," he said in a low voice. "You're among killers, Carlito. Religion is just their excuse."

"Shut up with all of your talk," Tariq shouted, waving an arm for them to stop.

Morris, Carlito, and Jennifer turned to Tariq as his men straightened, their fingers finding triggers.

Tariq glared at Morris and pointed. "Arm the bomb and she can go free."

Morris looked at Tariq, then at Jennifer and Carlito, and nodded somberly. He followed Tariq across the lobby, trailed by a couple of *jihadi* fighters, past the dining room to where Tariq pushed open the swinging door to the lodge's sprawling stainless steel kitchen.

A compact desert camo backpack sat on a stainless steel counter top. Head bent forward, Tariq carefully opened the zippered closure. He grabbed the handle of a rigid, orange case of molded plastic about the size of a basketball, and lifted it free of the pack.

The bomb.

Morris looked at it without emotion. He knew it well. It was a Pelican case, waterproof, dust proof, and most importantly crush proof. He'd found the case online and for $100 plus shipping, it was at his door in two days. He'd chosen the orange because you can't miss it. Perfect for a bomb, he'd thought, because it looked dangerous. Morris had chuckled to himself at the irony when he read the case was NATO tested and approved for military use and was unconditionally guaranteed to last forever.

It came with a foam interior, which he had molded for his purposes. The bomb had fit inside nicely, and along with the potent battery that kept it alive. He'd made the bomb rectangular, a four-inch thick slab, using five pounds of C4, which alone was enough to destroy the lodge. In the center of plastic compound was a pellet of highly enriched uranium 235 the size of a BB, and it sat at the end a small metal tube the size of ball-point pen. The C4 explosion would drive the pea through the tube and against a tiny piece of plutonium, enough to set off a small nuclear explosion that would pulverize the Vista Verde lodge, leaving nothing more than a crater of rubble and spreading radiation throughout the valley. The valley would be uninhabitable for generations.

Morris snapped open each of the clasps and slowly lifted the hinged and padded cover. A touchpad screen sat atop the bomb, just as he'd left it, a modified I-phone he'd cannibalized months earlier. Morris tapped the screen and it came to life. He turned to Tariq, who looked on, dark eyes wide and glistening. "It won't operate until it reads the iris of my eye."

Tariq nodded. "I understand. You are smart man. If you want your daughter, then do it."

"Are you sure you want to do this?" Morris asked. "Once it starts, there's no turning back."

Tariq's eyes blazed, then narrowed as he nodded, his lips tight with intent. The look make Morris shudder. Tariq was hell bent on destruction. A skeptic and agnostic his entire life, Morris was not at all religious. But as he stared into Tariq's eyes, he felt a deep chill in his core and knew he was gazing at evil.

Morris nodded, used the fingers of his right hand to spread open his eye lids, then bent toward the phone's camera lens. He then touched the phone's camera icon, then touched the white circle, and took a photo of his eye as the click of a camera shutter sounded. He stood, blinked at Tariq, and asked, "How much time?"

Tariq's eyes sparkled like polished black agates. "Ninety minutes."

Morris shuddered again, aghast at what he'd heard. "Ninety minutes?" It was barely enough time to make his escape with Jennifer. On foot, they'd be far enough from the blast, but maybe not the radiation. "Are you sure?"

Tariq nodded. "This is our greatest day, for today we shall surely become martyrs!" his voice squeaking with delight.

Morris sighed, his stomach knotted, then tapped small screen where a calculator face appeared. He tapped in the numbers. A series of melodic noises and trills sounded and then the phone beeped. He tapped in the numbers: 00:90:00.00. His finger paused above the enter key as he looked at Tariq and shook his head, no.

Tariq scowled, then used his own index finger to tap the enter key.

The screen became a digital counter, the numbers flickering as the passing of the hundredths of a second became a blur, the timer reading: 89:59...89:58.... Morris looked up at Tariq. "You happy now?"

Tariq grinned and nodded.

"My daughter and I will need all of the ninety minutes to get away," Morris said, as he turned to step around the *jihadi* fighters, leave the kitchen, and find Jennifer.

"Stop!" Tariq shouted.

The *jihadi* fighters blocked the kitchen door, shoulder to shoulder, each with a rifle held at their chest, their eyes drilling Morris.

Morris froze, then shuttered as a jolt of fear shook him, then was quickly followed by a surge or uncontrollable anger. He spun and faced Tariq, his shoulders hunched, his fists balled.

Tariq stared, eyes wide and gleeful, a smile on his lips. "Did you really think I'd let you leave?"

Morris flexed his jaw and growled, "You ... fucking ... bastard."

Morris lunged at Tariq, and outweighing him by forty pounds, knocked the young *jihadi* leader backwards.

Tariq stumbled and clung to the kitchen counter to keep from falling as Morris grabbed Tariq's AK-47 pistol and tried to yank it away. But the strap was looped across Tariq's back and shoulders and he yanked the weapon back. In the see-saw struggle, the two men staggered to the side and tumbled to the floor, Morris's using his strength and weight to fall onto Tariq's lithe torso, Tariq's weapon between them, the barrel pointing to the wall.

Morris rolled to his right, grasping the pistol, but Tariq kept his hands tight on it as well, and twisted the barrel upward, hoping to wrench it free. But Morris was equally as strong, and though his arms ached, his anger raged, his body pumped with adrenaline.

Morris let go with his right hand and slammed his fist into Tariq's face, striking just below the cheek bone, jerking Tariq's face sideways and jolting Tariq enough to loosen his grip.

With his left hand, Morris's yanked the pistol upward and with his right, squeezed the trigger. The weapon erupted, spewing a barrage of bullets that clanged noisily against the hanging pots and pans, striking the walls.

Tariq's *jihadis* danced around them impotently, darting and ducking to avoid being shot, waving their weapons and pointing wildly, each hesitant to shoot as Morris and Tariq wrestled on the floor.

CHAPTER 35

Crouched in the shadows of the pines a hundred yards from the lodge, Kyle twitched at the sound of shooting inside the lodge. He looked at Raoul, who rose to his feet and scowled as the muffled gunfire crackled like distant fireworks. "The shit has hit the fan," Kyle said.

"Time to move," Raoul said with a nod. He looked across the valley to the forested slopes on the far side of the lodge. He pulled a small walkie-talkie from his belt and held it to his lips. "Now!" he said with muffled urgency. "With everything we got." He clipped the radio back on his belt and turned to Kyle. He nodded again. "Here goes," he said.

"Wait!" Kyle said, holding up a hand. He swallowed hard, looked at Raoul. "I'm going with you." Kyle fought against every fiber of his being that told him not to do it. But how could he not help dismantle these *jihadis*? He wanted to be among the men who were about to free the American president from the control of terrorists. His best by-line ever. Kyle had another reason to go with Raoul: Nate Kennard. He wanted to see the man they called Jihadi John get his just reward. He wanted to see this demented killer dead.

"What?" Raoul said, incredulously.

Kyle stared at Raoul. "I'm going with you."

Raoul shook his head in disbelief. "It's not part of the plan."

Kyle shook his head. "No time to talk."

Raoul took the Sig Saur pistol from belt, clicked the magazine release, and let it drop into his palm. He checked that the magazine was loaded, slammed it back into the grip, and handed the pistol back to Kyle, handle first. "Only use it if you need to stay alive. When we cross the field, stay low and close. I'm going in first."

Kyle held the pistol in his hands. It felt like a foreign object. His tools of the trade were a voice recorder, a pen, a pad of paper, and a laptop. Thoughts and words were his weapons. Kyle slipped the Sig Saur pistol into the back of his pants, took a deep breath, and nodded.

"I'm going, too," Ariel said, her jaw clenched, her eyes determined.

Raoul scowled at her. "No way."

Ariel picked up the Heckler and Koch assault rifle they'd taken from cabin, and held it in the crook of her left arm, her right hand on the pistol grip, her finger resting on the trigger guard.

"Do you know how to use it?" Raoul asked, unable to hide his exasperation.

Ariel nodded. "Jerome taught me. We spent a lot of time at shooting ranges. He showed me how to shoot. Pistols and assault rifles." She hefted the rifle as if it was her familiar friend, then flashed a smile at Kyle.

"What other tricks do you have that I don't know about?" Kyle said.

She then patted the commando knife from the scabbard tied to her belted jeans.

Raoul shook his head. "Are you kidding me? That won't stop a bullet."

"It's good for cutting off gonads."

"That's what you're planning to do?" Kyle asked.

Ariel shrugged. "I'm not going to sit back, watch and wait while you guys play heroes."

Raoul groaned. The crackle of automatic weapons fire outside the lodge jerked his attention back to the assault.

"We've got to move. Now!" With glistening eyes, Raoul looked at them both, nodded, and said again, "Stay low and close!" Raoul took a deep breath and bolted into the sunlight, running low and fast across the grassy meadow toward the porch of the Vista Verde lodge, his weapon held close to his chest.

Kyle looked at Ariel and nodded, then they both sprinted after Raoul, who was already twenty five yards ahead. They ran side-by-side, bent at the waist, their legs churning.

***

The sharp crackle of gunfire from outside the lodge sent a surge of panic through the *jihadis* who still danced around Tariq and Morris wrestling on the kitchen floor. Suspecting that the shots from the pistol had launched the assault, Morris felt a jolt strength return to his aching arms, and with a desperate grasp, unsnapped one end of the AK-47's shoulder strap and wrenched the weapon away from Tariq.

Tariq fell back, panting heavily, outweighed by Morris, his arms splayed and suddenly helpless, looked at Morris with fear.

Morris scrambled to his feet and jacked his head around to where Tariq's men had been. But they were gone, having darted from the kitchen at the crackle of gunfire outside, the shattering of glass, and the panicked shouts of their fellow *jihadis*.

"Help me, you idiots," Tariq shouted from the kitchen floor, his pleas echoing off the stainless steel, drowned by the growing gunfire.

Morris held the AK's pistol grip with his right and slipped his left to the barrel grip as he swung the weapon toward Tariq's torso. He squeezed the trigger.

A metallic click was the only sound he heard.

Morris's jaw dropped, his eyes opened wide, and he glanced at the black metal cover of the weapon. In the struggle, the safety lever had been turned on. He thumbed the lever down, but as he did, he caught a flash of movement to his left and flinched. He feared an attack, but saw one of the *jihadis* toss a serrated combat knife to Tariq, who with knife in hand, leapt up and slashed at at Morris. But Morris stumbled backwards, his right shoulder crunching on the floor.

Morris cried out in pain, but his cry was cut short as a deep and searing pain filled his chest, his lungs wheezing. Tariq worked the knife blade, turning Morris's torso into a pit of fire. Tariq slowly pulled the knife from Morris's rib cage, and released his hand from Morris's neck. Morris gasped as Tariq pushed himself up to his feet and stood unsteadily over Morris.

Morris stared up from the floor to his executioner, Tariq, his chest heaving as he held the bloodied knife in his right hand. Morris worked his jaw, wanting to spew obscenities, but nothing would come. He raised a shaky hand and pointed his finger. Tariq's emotionless eyes were the last thing he saw before Morris's world went dark.

***

Gunfire erupted at the far side of the lodge from the handful of armed men who emerged from the tree line. A couple wore urban camo grey with black tactical gear and helmets, with others in desert camo, boots, brown t-shirts and boonies hats, all converging on the lodge.

The weapons fire from the lodge windows, however, forced the commandos to dive to the ground and roll, taking defensive positions wherever each could find minimal cover behind the scattered and stunted pines and bushes.

Gun barrels protruded from the shadowy lodge interior, the air erupting with the staccato of gunfire. The assault drew the *jihadis'* fire in multiple directions, just as Raoul had hoped, giving the impression that the lodge was under attack from all sides. It would give him and the others a sliver of a chance to mount the porch and penetrate the interior of the lodge.

Raoul dove to the ground and rolled to his right, taking cover behind the narrow trunk of a stunted piñon tree. He glanced over his shoulder, then waved Ariel and Kyle to the ground. They dove and rolled. It was a simple and effective defensive maneuver: make yourself as small a target as possible. The *jihadis* were not known for their marksmanship, after all, preferring to capture and torture their victims, killing them only after they'd grown bored by the suffering.

Raoul paused to gauge the assault. There were just enough small trees and chamisa bushes around the lodge to give the assault team the critical cover they needed to get relatively close. Raoul felt a fleeting moment of hopefulness. Their immediate objective was to reach a low stone wall fronting the lodge, a purely decorative semicircle of rocks, three feet high and eighteen inches thick that surrounded the tall flag pole.

As return fire crackled from the lodge windows, Raoul motioned the commandoes to keep moving. Raoul fired at the vague figures visible at the base of the heavy wood window frames, filled with nothing but jagged edges of shattered glass.

Raoul fired his Heckler & Koch, confident he'd hit couple of the *jihadis*, forcing the others to duck below window sills, hold their rifles over their heads, and fire blindly. Unless they had an unlimited supply of ammunition, their wild and random shots diminished their chances of survival with each squeeze of the trigger. It gave Raoul's small yet experienced and lethal assault force yet another advantage.

Raoul watched as well-placed shots went through the windows, providing cover for the advancing attackers, who reached the protective stone barrier. Hope again flickered in Raoul's heart. One small step and then another, he thought. The three commandoes behind the low wall would soon be joined by three more, including himself. But he needed cover as well.

Raoul rolled onto his back and signaled for Kyle and Ariel to get closer, then twisted back onto his stomach and fired a couple more shots at the lodge windows. He heard the gasping breath and thumps as Kyle and Ariel dove to the ground behind the protection of the piñon tree and the shadows of the low bows.

"You okay?" Raoul asked, searching their faces, their eyes wide with fear, their breath short and labored. Neither responded and this worried Raoul. Neither, he realized, had been part of action like this, and Raoul worried he'd made a mistake by acquiescing to their demands. His stomach sank at the thought he could cause the death of either one or both of them. This was a first for Ariel and because of it, she was the most vulnerable. Shooting a weapon and knowing how to load and unload it was one thing. It was quite another to use it to deadly effect. Two different animals. If she stayed with Kyle, it would be best. They could look after each other.

Raoul knew Kyle had been these situations before, had been shot at and knew the feeling of bullets snapping through the air just inches from his head. But as a journalist, not a combatant. It was different when you carried a weapon and fully expected to use it. The weapon in his hands was something new to Kyle, and Raoul wondered if Kyle would really pull the trigger. It didn't matter, Raoul told himself. He needed both of them now.

"Kyle. I'm going to that wall." Raoul pointed to the lodge. "I'm going to lead the assault into the lodge. We're going to get our man out of there."

Kyle and Ariel looked at him and nodded, not speaking. Raoul realized they were both in a deep state of stress. The chaos of combat. He'd seen it dozens of times. Raoul had been trained to function effectively in the midst of such madness. Combat was exhilarating, an almost out-of-body experience. Unknown reservoirs of energy were tapped, awareness was expanded a tenfold, thought processes were accelerated. Time slowed, gravity seemed a nuisance, and fears faded. It was addicting, and that's what worried him. He'd done it enough that now it was second nature to him. It gave life meaning.

Raoul reached out and grabbed a fistful of Kyle's shirt and pulled Kyle's face close. "Look at me!" he shouted. Raoul had seen Kyle like this before, going back to their days and nights practicing and playing high school football in El Paso. Kyle had played quarterback because he had a good arm. That arm had served him well. It had put him on the pitching mound with the baseball team and as a forward on the basketball team. But if ever the games weren't going well, if his passes were dropped, his pitches batted out of the park, or if he took a couple of body slams, he'd become despondent and distant. Raoul shook him back to reality.

Kyle's eyes cleared. "What?" he said, clutching Raoul's wrist in his hand.

"I need you here," Raoul shouted. "You wanted this, so here it is. Stay focused!"

"I am!" Kyle yelled angrily.

Raoul glared

"What do you want?" Kyle asked, suddenly calm.

"First, I need you to take care of Ariel."

Kyle looked over his shoulder to Ariel, her hand clutching the back of his shirt back. "Okay," he said with a nod.

They flinched as new gunfire erupted from the lodge windows, the *jihadis* trying to drive back the assault. Raoul had to move quickly. "I'm going to those men at the wall," he said again. "From there we're going in."

"Okay. Got it," Kyle said.

"You need to help lay down a cover of fire." Raoul glanced at them. "Both of you. Fire short bursts into the windows where and when you see a gun barrel."

He waited while Kyle took the Sig Saur from the back of waistband, and looked at for a moment, as if it were something strange in his hands. Raoul had warned Kyle to make his shots count. Kyle held it with both hands and steadied his forearm against the side of the tree trunk as Ariel took up a position beside him. Kyle squeezed the trigger once, then twice, the pistol jerking each time. Ariel then also squeezed off a burst. Pop-pop-pop. And again. Pop-pop-pop. Kyle waited a beat.

Raoul looked at them again, then nodded. "Wish me luck," he said. Bent low to the ground, Raoul humped toward the wall, covering the fifty yards of exposure in just a few seconds. He leapt into the air as if diving into the end zone, hit ground, rolled behind the wall, and came up looking into the face of a another commando.

"Having fun yet?" the commando asked.

Raoul smiled. "You bet."

CHAPTER 36

Tariq crouched in the corner of a room inside the Vista Verde lodge, wedged in a space below the wide curving wooden stairs to the upper floor. A good command post, he thought, protected and affording him a view of the chaos. His stomach clenched at what he saw. His men had been hit, knocked back from the windows by the well-placed fire of the attackers—attackers he did not expect and who should not be there.

Who were these people? *Kafirs! They will die! All of them!* He'd been told there would be no resistance, or at most, resistance he could remove easily. He'd done that. Tariq was tempted to make a call, but that would violate the blackout. If the call was tracked, which it most certainly would be, it would take the probing eyes and ears of the infidels directly to his leader.

Tariq scratched the thin hair on his cheek, then massaged the ache in his stomach. His arms felt weak from the struggle with the old man, the scientist named Morris. He'd not expected the man to fight or be as strong. Tariq was half the old man's age, but it had mattered little. The man was dead now, Tariq relishing the feel of the blade sinking deep into the man's heaving chest and slicing into his beating heart.

Tariq scanned the room. A couple of his men lay sprawled on the varnished stone floor, having suffered head shots, their skulls broken and exposed, their arms splayed, , legs bent oddly. Others had chest wounds and were slumped against the wall, their breaths coming in gasps, their eyes searching Tariq's face for help, for any sign of relief. But there was none to give. One had been shot in the throat and lay in a pool of his own blood, the eyes open and staring blankly at the ceiling.

Anger smoldered in Tariq's belly, then flared in his chest, and finally exploded in his head. *It was not supposed to be like this!* There was not supposed to be an assault. He had been told it would never come. They would wait for him to make a move on the president. On camera. For all the world to see how the noble and fearless soldiers of Islam had broken the back and severed the head of the Great Satan.

As Tariq surveyed his dead and dying men, a smile curled the corners of his mouth. He still had the bomb, the numbers flashing steadily on the screen in the kitchen. The time for martyrdom has come. *The kafirs are defeated. Allah akhbar!*

Bullets continued to pop the air inside the lodge, a couple of his last men resisting the assault, looking lost as they sat below the shattered windows, their backs to the walls, holding their weapons high, shooting blindly to the outside.

Tariq turned to sudden movement to his right. It was Carlito, the one he knew as Omar al-Amriki. He had done his job well, leading them from the remote mosque to the lodge, but Omar was now useless. Tariq clenched his jaw and watched as Omar crouched, dragging the body of a fighter into the great room. Boots scraping along the floor, Omar pulled the body closer and lay it gently on the floor beside him.

Tariq looked at the face, and seeing the fair skin and pale blue eyes, knew it was not a fighter, but the woman Halima. She was alive, breathing slowly, the rise and fall of her chest barely noticeable. Tariq raised his eyes to Omar and saw the lips twitching, struggling to form words.

"You have to do something!" Omar said. "She's dying."

Tariq's anger flared. Still clutching the handle of the combat knife he'd used on Halima's father, Tariq contemplated sinking it into Omar's slender torso, giving the fearful boy immediate martyrdom. But he didn't. Tariq shook his head slowly, stared at Omar, and spoke calmly, as if her fate had been decided. "There is nothing that I can do."

"She's dying," Omar cried. "She's been hit! It's bad."

"Be joyful, my American friend," Tariq said. "Today she will join her father and our father Allah and live in everlasting peace and beauty. Allah be praised."

Omar glared at Tariq, confusion clouding his eyes, then he turned to the few remaining fighters at the windows where the crackle of gunfire piercing the room.

"Take her to her father," Tariq said, with a wave, toward the kitchen. "That way they can be together in death." He watched anger contort Omar's face.

Stunned at Tariq's command, Carlito, who never accepted his Arabic name, twitched with indecision, nearly paralyzed with fear. He glanced around the room, the air peppered with gunfire. He sat on his knees beside Jennifer and put his hand on her cheek.

Her eyes fluttered open, searching for help, her lips moving but emitting no sound. Carlito swallowed hard and stared at the blood now spreading across her stomach, soaking into her clothes. His eyes blurred with tears as he realized there was nothing he could do. She would die. And it was his fault.

Carlito wiped his eyes and looked again at Tariq, his heart sinking. Tariq shook his head in disgust and waved again toward the kitchen.

When Carlito did nothing, Tariq crawled over Jennifer and scrambled across the floor on all fours to join a couple of his men near a window.

Carlito looked again to Jennifer. He moved behind her, and lifting her shoulder with one hand, he slipped a hand below her right arm, and did the same with her left. Jennifer cried out in pain as he scooted backwards, dragging her into the kitchen and pulling her between the steel counter and the cooking stoves.

There he was. Jennifer's father, flat on his back, his neck arched, his chin jutting up from the floor, the entire front of his shirt wet with dark red blood. Again Carlito swallowed, staring at the dead man.

He tugged Jennifer, her eyes squeezed tight with pain, deeper into the kitchen, then turned her slightly, arranging Jennifer beside her father, not knowing what else to do. Gurgling sounds erupted from Jennifer's throat, followed by a moan and long sigh that made him shudder. He felt a chill in his bones even as sweat trickled down his temples.

Carlito crouched beside Jennifer for a moment, then turned to the crackle of unabated gun fire in the room just outside. He felt strangely safe in the kitchen, surrounded by all the stainless steel. His eyes fell on the orange plastic case sitting on the counter. He rose and stepped to it, peering onto the I-phone screen where numbers flickered. The bomb! *Fucking pendejos!* If he stayed, they all would surely die. Carlito glanced again to the sound of gunfire beyond the doorway, then turned back to Jennifer, bleeding beside her dead father. He squatted beside her.

Jennifer slowly reached out, her hand touching her father's blood soaked chest. "Daddy?" she said in a rasping whisper. "Daddy?"

She sounded surprised, Carlito thought, that the man might not be okay and could be dead, her voice carrying the expectation that Morris would lift his head, glance in her direction, and say, "What is it, baby girl?"

Jennifer drew her bloodied hand close to her face, squinting as if puzzled at the blood. "Daddy?" She stared at her palm, then looked to Carlito, her eyes searching for an answer.

He knew she wanted to hear him say everything would be okay. Carlito swallowed hard. His throat felt like sandpaper.

Jennifer turned her head sideways again to her father, and sounding like a little girl, said, "I'm sorry, Daddy. Don't leave me. Please, Daddy. Don't go." Jennifer winced, her eyes squeezing shut as a jolt of pain ripped through her. She moaned , her face ashen, her eyes unfocused.

Carlito wanted to hold her close, as if his embrace could make her well and whole, to pick her up and take her out of there. But it was useless. She needed a doctor. She needed surgery to repair the organs mangled by the random bullet that had ripped through her torso.

After the spasm of pain passed, Jennifer looked at him, her eyes refocused. "Am I going to die?"

Carlito's mind was on fire, his breath short and hard. He struggled to calm himself, to show a strong face. "You're going to be okay, Jen. Just relax. Stay calm."

He didn't believe the words even as they came out of his mouth. He was suffocating with guilt, the crushing weight of what he had done pressed down on him. She had proved her love again and again. She had clung to him from the moment she first heard the story of how his grandfather had been killed by the gringo *pendejo* David Benedict.

She had held him as he told her about his father, the heir to the vast meadows and mountains of the beautiful Vista Verde Ranch, but who was shot down by the gestapo state police when he tried to claim what was his. Jennifer had taken up his causes. She too had accepted Islam. She had joined the jihad. But this was where she would die. This was not the way it was supposed to end. Where was the victory? Carlito looked from Jennifer to her father, now only a corpse. There was nothing left of Carlito's causes. Nothing but blood and death. Nothing but defeat.

And Tariq didn't care.

Carlito clenched his jaw, grinding his teeth. He still cared. He looked out the kitchen doorway where the gunfire continued. He would find Tariq and show him what victory was. Carlito rose to his feet, darted through the kitchen entrance, and down the hall to the cavernous atrium, intending to collect a rifle from one of dead *jihadis* when a deafening blast and flash of blinding light forced Carlito to twist away and reflexively cover his face with his hands.

A moment later, a couple of canisters clunked onto the floor, spinning and hissing, filling the room with green smoke. Then another explosion rocked the room. Though the swirling air, Carlito saw armed men burst through the lodge's blown out front door and the flashes from their gun barrels. He felt three hot fists slam into his torso, one to the stomach and two to his chest, throwing him backwards against a wall where he collapsed to the floor.

The shots felt like white hot iron had been jammed into body, burning through his flesh. He gasped for breath and clutched the wounds, warm blood pumping from his body. He coughed as the green smoke enveloped him, filling the lodge. He felt the darkness come as his body grew numb. He wheezed his last breath.

CHAPTER 37

With the door to the smoke-filled atrium now in pieces, Raoul and the six other commandos charged inside. The men moved cautiously, kneeling in the roiling smoke and spraying the room with gunfire to clear it. The dining room was next, the walls splattered with high-powered bullets. But it was empty. As the smoke began to thin, Raoul quickly counted seven terrorist bodies. There had to be more! Four of the commandoes moved down the hall and through the wafting green air to the other rooms, clearing each.

Raoul waited and watched as they methodically entered each of the rooms, crouched, weapons drawn. Then silence. It made Raoul uneasy. He whirled to sudden motion behind him, and saw Kyle and Ariel through the wafting, thinning smoke. "I told you two to stay put!" he growled, his lips tight, his jaw clenched. "I almost shot you!"

Kyle jerked back, not expecting Raoul's anger. "Sorry. Didn't want to miss the action."

"Get out!" Raoul said, waving them back. "It's still not safe here."

Kyle glanced around the room, littered with bodies. "Looks pretty dead to me."

Raoul shook his head in disgust, grimaced, and pointed to the kitchen.

Kyle nodded, then crouched slightly and hurried across the room, stooped beside the kitchen door, Ariel close behind him, both with the backs flat against the wall. Raoul trailed them a few steps, then paused at the other side of the kitchen doorway where he raised a hand, signaling Kyle and Ariel to wait. He then flicked one finger, then another, and finally a third, silently mouthing the words, "one, two, three."

Raoul sprang into kitchen, crouched with his weapon leading. Silence. Nothing. Kyle slowly peeked around the corner, and then stepped inside, about five feet behind Raoul, followed by Ariel.

Raoul saw the body on the floor, the canvas desert boots, the legs clad in green camo pants, the face and neck swathed with a patterned scarf, eyes closed, seemingly dead. Raoul had been in these situations before, when the seemingly dead spring to life, and clutching a weapon, kill one more time before dying. Raoul pressed his gun barrel against the dead man's neck, kneeling to the side of the body.

"It's Carlito," Kyle said, looking over Raoul's shoulder.

Raoul pushed the scarf away from the face and gazed at Carlito's lifeless eyes, the blood already drying at the corners of his mouth, his mouth open as if he were about to speak. "Sorry, kid. But when you run with dogs, you ...." Raoul's voice trailed off. He knew the story and why the kid had a right to be angry. But this? Islamic jihad? Raoul closed Carlito's eyes with a gentle brush of his thumb and index finger. Raoul looked up at Kyle with a nod. "He paid a price for his decision."

"A heavy price," Kyle said, and drew a breath.

"Look!" Ariel shouted.

Raoul and Kyle turned and followed her pointed finger to the two partially obscured bodies on the floor near the wall. Raoul rose and held the rifle at his side as he stared at another young jihadi fighter lying beside a body—Morris's body.

"Wait!" Ariel said, brushing past Raoul's outstretched arm and dropping to her knees beside Morris.

Raoul stepped closer, thinking to pull Ariel back, fearing the bodies were booby-trapped. Then he saw the second body was a young woman, her head to the side, mouth open, skin pale, her crystalline blue eyes staring blankly.

Ariel had two fingers at the woman's neck. "She's dead."

Kyle squatted beside Ariel, then looked from the dead girl's blood soaked torso back at Raoul.

"A gut shot," Raoul said. "What the hell is she doing here?"

"It's Jennifer, Morris's daughter," Kyle said.

"Then that's Morris," Raoul said, eying Morris's bloodied body lying beside the girl. "They killed him."

"Maybe she was trying to protect him," Kyle said.

Ariel's eyes watered, her lips mashed tightly, and she turned again to the dead girl, brushing the hair from the face.

Raoul jerked back, again surveying the scattered pots and pans, the walls pocked with bullet holes. His eyes fell on the orange plastic case on the stainless steel counter, the lid open. He peered inside the case and saw the timer reeling off the seconds. It was down to 34:23 and ticking. "Fuck!" he shouted, pointing to the timer.

Raoul glanced around in panic. *Morris!* He needed Morris to stop the damned thing! But Morris was dead. On the floor. "Fuck!" he shouted again, his mind reeling. He turned to Kyle and barked, "You know anything about bombs?"

"They blow up," Kyle said, with a quick head shake.

"Okay, smart guy," Raoul said, looking back at the plastic case. "We've gotta dismantle this damned thing or were all dead. And, you're going to help me."

Kyle looked at him, lifted his hands, palms out, and shrugged. "I ...." His voice trailed off.

Raoul shook his head in disgust, then exhaled slowly as he slipped a finger under the small iPad screen and lifted it. The screen was loose, just sitting on top of a thick and tightly wrapped mound, connected by a handful of thin wires. He traced them with his finger to a series of 9-volt batteries, then to the plastic wrapped bomb, the size of a loaf of bread.

The malleable plastic explosive gave slightly as he pressed his finger into it. C4?

He looked at Kyle. "That's enough C4 to blow this place apart, us included."

Kyle stared, his eyes wide with fear.

Raoul pulled the combat knife he'd taken from Ariel and poked the tip into the wrapper, slicing through it. The pliable plastic explosive looked like bright white putty. Raoul swallowed hard. "It's supposed to be nuclear?" Raoul asked. "But this is C4. It isn't radioactive."

Sweat beaded on Raoul's his forehead as he took a deep breath and looked to Kyle for help.

Kyle shrugged. "I hope to God you know what you're doing!"

Raoul pointed to the reeling numbers on the iPad.

Kyle stepped close to Raoul, and at his side, pointed to the plastic. "That's probably a small core," Kyle said. "There's probably a small piece of plutonium in there. The bomb needs another fissionable material. Like enriched uranium, or something. When the two are jammed together, it starts an instantaneous chain reaction. Boom!"

"That doesn't help me much," Raoul said. He stared again at the slit he'd made in the wrapper, exposing the plastic explosive.

"The fissionable material might be buried inside the C4," Kyle said, pointing to the thick package. "It doesn't take much."

"Thanks, Einstein."

"When the C4 explodes, that could be what triggers the nuclear material," Kyle said. "That's my guess."

"It couldn't be that simple," Raoul said. "Even without the radioactive material, the C4 alone would destroy the lodge."

Raoul and Kyle stared again at the counter. 28:47 and counting.

"Jesus," Kyle muttered.

If Kyle was right, Raoul knew the first thing he had to do was to stop the C4 from exploding. That would prevent the second even more deadly stage of the bomb. If, not it was the end of them all.

Raoul looked the bomb over again. Maybe it was insanely simple. When the counted down, it triggered an electronic pulse to the batteries, like turning on a switch, then the batteries sent a much stronger impulse into the C4, igniting it. All he had to do was cut the wires, he guessed. Stop the process before it started. Or not.

There was only one way to find out. Raoul lifted the iPad up onto its side, then sliced the wires connecting it to the batteries. The iPad continued to flicker numbers. He threw it on the floor and stomped it repeatedly until it lay in pieces.

"I think you killed it," Kyle said.

Raoul returned to the bomb, slipped the fingers of his left hand beside the batteries sitting in tandem, then carefully worked the tip of his knife below them, and lifted them out, severing the wires that connected them to the inside of the bundled C4 explosive.

Raoul exhaled nervously and glanced at Kyle, who returned his stare.

"We're still alive, I think," Kyle said.

Raoul nodded, then closed the lid to the case and snapped it shut. He grabbed the handle and handed the case to Kyle. "I hope it's disarmed. Now get it the fuck out of here."

"What the fuck?" Kyle said, scowling. "Where?"

Raoul only pointed out the kitchen door. "Go!"

Ariel stared at them both as Kyle stood paralyzed with indecision.,

"The cave!" she yelled.

Kyle turned to her and smiled. "Of course!"

"It's a perfect place to stash the bomb," Ariel said. "If it explodes, the C4 blast will be contained by the collapse of the rock inside the cave. The mess can be cleaned up afterwards."

Raoul nodded. "The bomb guys can retrieve it later."

Kyle's eyes grew wide as he turned and bolted out the door.

CHAPTER 38

Kyle trotted across the grassy landing circle and skirted the large trout pond, retracing the path he'd taken earlier. It seemed like hours ago. The orange hard plastic case with the bomb was heavier than he expected. He strained to look through the trees, shifted the case to his left hand, and angled up and across the slope knowing he'd intersect with the path that lead up to the trout lake at Eagle's Nest. Minutes later he was on the path and moving quickly up the trail. He'd be at the cave soon.

As he trekked, occasionally shifting the case from hand to hand, Kyle felt overwhelmed with the absurdity of the situation. Why had Vice President Marvin been so hesitant to act when Raoul and a few of his men had quickly accomplished what the others suggested couldn't be done?

Now the lodge was full of dead *jihadi* fighters. Still, America's top two congressional leaders were dead, one shot, the other decapitated, their bodies on the stone patio outside. How could all of this have happened so suddenly? It seemed so random, so chaotic, so sudden. But was it? Chaos theory argued that what appeared to be chaos had an underlying pattern. The pattern was not always apparent, but if you looked hard and long enough, it could be found.

As he hurried along the path, Kyle pored over the tangle of events that brought him to this moment. It looked like Islamic *jihad*, pure and simple, but he wondered. More than two months earlier, the Border Patrol captain told him the deaths of the border agents didn't have the feel of a chance encounter with the *vajadores*, the border bandits. Why? Because nothing had been stolen. Then the killers had simply disappeared. Two months later, *jihadis* crawled out of the mountains and captured the US president and the two top congressional leaders. And the *jihadis* possessed a suspected dirty bomb made a Los Alamos scientist who'd been held hostage in exchange for his daughter, a swap that failed.

Kyle didn't like the conclusion t staring him in the face. As much as he told himself it couldn't be true, his thoughts and suspicions refused to fade.

Kyle's mind snapped back to the present as he paused to look at the narrow mouth of the cave. His arms ached, his legs felt weak, and his breath was labored. He wished he had brought water as he wiped the sweat from his face with the tails of his shirt. He exhaled slowly, then climbed into the mouth of the cave. It seemed larger now than when he, Raoul, Ariel and Morris had hidden there from predatory drone. Yes! The drones! Hank Benedict's drones. Of course! Kyle felt a surge of energy as he knew what he had to do.

Kyle made his way into the dark recesses of the cave, his eyes slowly adjusting to the diminished light, and found a crevice in the wall of the cave. It would do nicely. He looked around the cave one last time, then made his way back to the entrance, where he pulled out his phone and checked the signal. Yes! Kyle listened to the buzz of the phone call and looked out across the tree tops to the distant lodge.

"This is Frankel," the voice said.

"It's Kyle," he said.

"Where the hell have you been?" Frankel asked, almost shouting. "I've been trying to reach you for two days! Where the hell are you?"

Kyle exhaled, his stomach quivering. "Right here," he said. "Right where I've always been."

"Don't play games, Kyle. Terrorists have the president in a mountain retreat, which is where I sent you so you could write about it, and I haven't heard from you for 24 freaking hours! What the hell?"

"Calm down," Kyle said. "There's a chance the president may be freed."

"What? Are you serious? How in the hell…?"

"Just listen!" Kyle struggled to contain his impatience. "Now take some notes because I can't write a damned thing now and don't have time. I'll get you up to speed. You can attribute all of the information to me, your man on the scene."

"But, but…."

"Shut up and listen."

"Okay," Frankel said, after a long pause. "Let me clear a screen.

"I hope you can type as fast as I talk, because I don't have much time."

"Shoot."

Kyle unloaded the basics of what had happened so far—finding Alan Morris, his entry into the lodge, the successful assault on the lodge led by Raoul. "They killed Morris, though, stabbed him to death. I just removed the bomb from the lodge now."

"What about the president?" Frankel asked.

"That's next," Kyle said.

"Next?" Frankel yelled. "What do you mean?"

"The *jihadis* are dead, most of them, anyway, but the president is still in his room. Safe."

"Alive?"

"We think so. That's why I need to get back to you."

"What are you doing, Kyle?"

"I'm going to see this through, Max."

"Don't get yourself killed."

"I need something from you," Kyle said.

"What?"

Kyle briefly explained his ideas about how the president had been captured.

"If I follow what you're saying, Kyle, you're suggesting old man Benedict and his son orchestrated this whole and mess. If so, then he's guilty of high treason."

"That's what I'm saying," Kyle said.

"Oh, my God," Frankel said. "That kind of thing is not supposed to happen in our country. Who do these people think they are?"

"You been in Washington for decades," Kyle said. "Who do you know on the Security Council? Call someone you can trust who might be willing to do something."

"This is serious shit," Frankel said.

"I know."

"It'll take more than one person, though," Frankel said. "But I know a couple of people who can put things in motion."

"I gotta go." Kyle ended the call, wondering if Frankel's contacts could do any good at this point. The phone in his pocket, he turned to run back down the mountain path.

CHAPTER 39

Raoul peered around the corner of hallway. The green smoke now a thin haze hanging in the air like cigarette smoke, Raoul hurried though the foyer, paused at the fireplace, and again scanned the bodies. Five of the six men who had accompanied him on the assault were back in the main room. The sixth had been shot in the chest by a now dead *jihadi* hiding in the library. Shot through the heart, the commando died instantly. It made Raoul sick. He hated to lose anybody, ever, but one down on this mission was not bad. Still, they were far from finished.

"We need to find which one is Jihadi John," Raoul said, waving to the bodies scattered around the room.

The commandos moved quickly, tugging away each of the dead *jihadi's* facial scarves.

After all were unmasked, Raoul scanned the dead faces uneasily. "Fuck. None of them is Jihadi John."

His eyes moved from the bodies and up to the top of the stairs where the air was relatively clear. The president was there, and he feared, so was Jihadi John. Raoul motioned for the commandos to follow him up the curving stairs, wide and wooden and affixed the back wall and fanning out at the bottom.

The six men climbed one step at a time, cheeks pressed against the stocks of their assault rifles aimed high and held firmly against their shoulders, fingers on triggers. Three climbed a dozen steps, then paused while the other three moved up, wary of the creaks and groans of the aging wood.

Movement at the top of the stairs was met with the hammering staccato of automatic weapons fire from Raoul's assault team. Two *jihadis*, their heads swathed in black, snapped back, their bodies twisting awkwardly, as the fire from their AK-47s sprayed the ceiling and far wall, shattering glass.

One of the commandos was hit and fell to the side, then tumbled backwards down the steps where he was caught by another. Blood appeared on the wounded commando's arm, his chest having been protected by a Kevlar vest. The man glanced at Raoul, as if to say he was sorry, and shook his head. Raoul motioned for the man who'd stopped his tumble to take him down the steps and apply what aide he could.

The remaining commandoes paused on the stairs, each crouching. Now they were down four. Raoul pointed to the top of the stairs, and taking the steps two at a time, reached the top, then crouched again, keeping a low profile, as the others followed, weapons at the ready, unsure of the *jihadi* threat.

Raoul pointed for two of the men to go ahead. They moved quickly down the hallway, their steps the only sound, to the bedrooms where Troy Devine and Senator Blunt had stayed until they'd been killed.

Raoul motioned for the third commando to clear Blount's old room. The commando sidled carefully beside the door, his back against the wall, then glanced back at Raoul, who nodded. He disappeared inside the room, and moments later, returned, shaking his head. Nothing.

The move was repeated for Divine's room. Again, nothing.

There was only one room left, the president's.

Raoul gazed toward the secured presidential suite, where in the dim light and through the thin and drifting smoke, he saw a couple of bodies sprawled on the shadowy floor.

Raoul took a dozen stutter steps then paused at the body of the first dead *jihadi*. He yanked away the black cloth from the *jihadi's* face. The gray-green eyes were lifeless, yet even in death contrasted sharply with the face, the color of an old penny. The man had a hole in his forehead, thick with coagulated blood, his mouth frozen open.

It had been a well-placed shot, Raoul knew, and came from a pro at close range. He moved warily to the next body and knelt beside it. The *jihadi* had also taken a face shot, the nose and cheek ripped away, the scarf soaked read with blood, already drying. It had been another well placed shot. The president had been well protected and hopefully was still alive.

There was yet another, a third body, which made Raoul pause. He kept closer. This was no *jihadi*. A white shirt, dress pants, thinning blond hair. "Damn," he said, knowing the man could only have been one of the Secret Service agents protecting President Harris.

The agent's body was gouged, the wounds wide and deep. Not from a knife. An axe? Of course, he thought. The lodge had plenty of them, hanging beside fire extinguishers. And outside, there'd been heavy wedge-shaped mauls used to split fire wood.

As he gazed at the battered door to the presidential suite, he now understood. Jihadi John had used a couple of his men human shields. The Secret Service agent had resisted as best he could. He'd taken two *jihadis* with him, but not the third, the one swinging an axe.

Any confusion about weapon used disappeared as Raoul looked at mangled door. They'd used an axe and a maul to demolish the handle and deadbolts. The door's hinges had been bashed, but had held. The door was now jammed shut. Was the president behind the door and still alive?

Raoul paused, pondering what to do. He inspected the door as the commandos joined him and stood flat against the wall at each side of the door. Raoul tried the broken handle. It didn't move.

"Mister president!" Raoul shouted, holding his breath as he listened.

Nothing.

Raoul glanced at his three men and nodded, then stepped back and slammed a foot against the door just above the door handle. It didn't budge. Two of the others then joined him, as they kicked again in unison. The door gave slightly as the metal door jam twisted from the bolts holding it in the wooden frame. Another couple of joint kicks and the door finally gave way, catching a chain pulled tight.

Raoul knew he could shoot the chain apart, but feared that an errant bullet might kill the president, the man they were trying to rescue. Not an option. He turned as one of the commandos handily used the butt of his rifle to snap the door chain. The door swung halfway open.

Raoul waved his hand motioning for the others to stand clear, weapons ready. He knew the metal door provided some protection from gunfire until after they'd burst inside when all hell would break loose.

Raoul held up a hand, bent his head forward, and listened. Was President Harris already dead? That would change everything. In a loud and forceful voice, again he called out, "Mister President?"

Nothing. Raoul turned to the other commandos and nodded. He lifted his right hand, and as he'd had done earlier, flicked his fingers and silently counted, one...two... three.

Raoul burst into the plush and spacious living room of the presidential suite, but stopped suddenly, his rifle trained on the two men who stood before him: Tariq and President Harris.

They were in the middle of the living room, the crook of Tariq's left arm around President Harris's neck and chin, his combat knife at the base of the president's throat.

Raoul and the commandos froze, their guns held high and aimed at Tariq, the man they knew as Jihadi John.

Raoul sighted through the rifle's scope, knowing he had a 99 percent chance he could put a bullet in Tariq's skull and be done with it, freeing the president. But that one chance in a hundred?

"It's over, Tariq," Raoul said. "Let the president go."

Tariq flashed a wide grin. "Over? This is far from over."

"You won't get out of here alive," Raoul said. "Let the president go. Now!"

"I won't get out alive?" Tariq asked with a laugh. "Did you never think that may be the point?"

"Don't do it, Tariq."

"You stupid infidel scum," Tariq growled. "I may die, but I will die a martyr's death. And, I will not die alone."

"Listen to me," Raoul said. "Drop the knife and let the president go. Do it and I won't kill you, even though I should."

"You shut up and you listen," Tariq said.

"What do you want?" Raoul asked.

"President Harris here and I are going to take a trip."

"What the hell are you talking about?"

"Get the president's helicopter ready," Tariq said. "We're going to a location I will tell you when we are both safely on board."

"You're insane, Tariq," Raoul said. "You'll never get away with this."

Tariq tightened his grip, jerking the president's head higher, and pressed the knife blade against the president's neck where a trickle of blood showed.

"Do as he says," Harris groaned, his voice tight.

Raoul shook his head, held his gunstock against his cheek, his eye at the scope, and the barrel aimed at Tariq's head, the crosshairs on the corner of Tariq's forehead barely visible behind the president's. "Don't shoot, soldier," President Harris said. "Stand down. That's an order."

Raoul hesitated, but slowly lowered his rifle.

"Get the helicopter ready," Harris groaned. "It's our best chance."

Raoul stepped back a couple of paces, turned to his men, and said, "Stand down."

CHAPTER 40

Raoul looked at his fellow commandos, rolled his eyes, and motioned to Tariq and the president, standing 15 feet away. "Shoot him if he moves," he said.

The commandos nodded grimly, raised their rifles and drew a bead on Tariq's head as Raoul stepped out into the hallway, over the bodies, and paused at the top of the stairs. He pulled his hand-held radio phone from his belt and clicked it on. The small diode lights flickered alive as the device searched for signals. The lights froze, having found a channel. Raoul held the radio to his mouth and called out for Hank Benedict. "Hotel Bravo, this is Romeo Gulf."

He waited as static came from the small speaker, followed by a voice, "Where the fuck have you been?"

"Been takin' care of business, Hank. Over."

"What the fuck?" Hank yelled. "Who told you to lead an assault?"

"I'm outside the president's suite," Raoul said. "Three of my guys are with Harris now. If Jihadi John does anything, they'll shoot to kill."

"Jesus," Hank said, his voice calmer, but dripping with disgust. "How is that possible? The president was in a secure room. He was with a secret service agent."

"Was is correct," Raoul said. "They killed the agent. With an axe. Not a pretty sight."

"After what they did to Blount, you're not telling me anything new."

"The agent killed a couple of the *jihadis* before they got to the president," Raoul said. "They busted down the door."

"You fucked up, Raoul. Now the bastard has the president!" Hank said. "The idea was not to pressure the bastards because they'd do something stupid. That's what they've done."

"It was a risk I and a few others were willing to take," Raoul said. "They were mocking us, Hank. They're all dead now, by the way."

"Except for Jihadi John," Hank said. "You fucked up, Raoul."

The knot in Raoul's stomach tightened. "Jihadi John is making demands."

"What the fuck?" Hank shouted. "He's in no position to do that."

"Come again?" Raoul said. "He sure as hell is."

"Okay," Hank said, after a long pause. "What does he want?"

"He wants to leave on Marine One?"

"The president's helicopter?"

"You know what I'm talking about."

Hank groaned.

"Listen to me," Raoul said. "There's a way we can do this and maybe free the president and get rid of Jihadi John."

Benedict groaned at the plan, then said, "Well, maybe, but I still gotta convince Marvin and the Security Council. Maybe we can still salvage this situation, Raoul, but you stay out of the way. Hear me?"

Raoul remained silent.

"Just get the president down there and ready when the chopper lands," Hank said. "It'll be there in about 15 minutes, I'm guessing."

"Roger that." Raoul clicked off. Raoul massaged his stomach in a futile attempt to relieve the ache inside, then returned to the presidential suite where he stood behind his three men, their rifles still aimed at Tariq's head.

The situation in the room had changed, but only slightly. Tariq was now seated on a small couch, and the president sat cross-legged on the floor in front of him, Tariq's left hand cupped tightly on the president's chin, his right hand holding the blade to the throat.

Raoul drew a deep breath and nodded to Tariq and the president. "You got your wish."

CHAPTER 41

Kyle stood beside the stone fireplace, holding his phone camera. The past thirty minutes had been the longest of his life. It seemed as if time had stopped, until the thunderous pounding of helicopters circling above the lodge broke the silence.

Kyle ran out to the stone patio, still littered with bodies, and watched the choppers circle in the distance as the Marine One presidential chopper floated through the sky.

A moment later, he was joined by Ariel, who emerged from her small massage room, where she'd retreated to wait in silence and safety. Her eyes were wide with panic as they both watched the hulking chopper settle onto the grassy landing pad in front of the lodge. A half-dozen other choppers, all Black Hawk gunships, each emblazoned with the bright yellow Atlas Global logo, circled in the distance.

Then three of the Black Hawks slowed and settled on the ground a hundred yards from the Marine One. As they touched, down, heavily armed Atlas Global men spilled out the open doors, and took up kneeling positions, their weapons trained on Marine One and on the lodge's patio.

"They've got him!" Ariel blurted, turning to the lodge doors that suddenly opened nearby them.

Raoul fingered his weapon as he emerged from inside the lodge, stepped to the side of the doors, and was followed by Tariq and the president, Tariq's knife blade still against the president's throat.

Using phone as a video camera, Kyle recorded Raoul and the commandoes as they trailed Tariq and the president, who made halting steps across the stone patio. At the patio's edge, they descended the wide flagstone steps, one by one, finally reaching the grassy meadow.

The whooshing sound of the long, thick rotor blades of Marine One filled the air as the hulking chopper's door opened and the steps were lowered.

Kyle scanned the scene, capturing it all. At least two dozen of Benedict's Atlas Global men surrounded the landing site, but they were well back, crouching and aiming their rifles at Tariq and the president.

A tremor of anxiety rippled through Kyle, worried that now some trigger happy Atlas Global agent, hell bend on eliminating the *jihadi* leader would open fire, throwing this delicately choreographed event into chaos. Kyle drew a breath and waited, wondering what the madman Tariq intended to do and where he might go with the resident held hostage.

Did Tariq have a plan? Was someone or something on Marine One? Kyle hoped not. With Tariq's knife at the president's throat, the difference between life and death was the thickness of the thin skin on President Harris's neck.

Tariq and the President stood strangely still at the edge of the grass where Tariq scanned the scene. The Atlas Global rifles pointed at him did not waver. Tariq held the knife so tightly now that blood trickled steadily down the president's neck, soaking into his shirt. The two men began to move again, shuffling across the circular gravel drive, then onto the grass where they paused again, just thirty feet from the steps to the chopper door. The chopper's rotor blades churned the air.

Kyle looked at Raoul, thinking his cousin might feel a small sense of relief when the doors to Marine One would close and the polished green helicopter would rise from the landing pad and angle toward the forested slopes, knowing he'd done everything in his power to keep President Harris alive. Kyle exhaled.

Then the president's head exploded in a bloody spray as a shot cracked open the silence.

Tariq staggered backwards, his face coated with blood and brains.

President Harris' body collapsed to the ground.

"What the fuck?" Kyle shouted. He lowered his phone and stared.

Tariq stood still, the knife still in his hand, and stepped back, looking at the president's contorted body at his feet. His gaze then slowly rose from the Harris's body to the distant trees where he strained to see where the shot had had been fired.

Then Tariq's head exploded as well, his body jerking backwards and twisting to the ground.

"What the hell…!" Kyle shouted. He glanced at Raoul. Raoul eyes were not on the two corpses on the ground by Marine One, but instead on the forested slope where Tariq had been looking—the likely source of the lethal shots. Kyle looked there as well, struggling to make sense of it all. Had the first shot been a miss, intended for Tariq? Had they come from a sniper's rifle in the hands of an expert? Or a trigger happy amateur?

Benedict's Atlas Global men, who were equally stunned, froze in place, some lowering their weapons at what they'd witnessed. The steady thump-thump of the Marine One rotor blades filled the dazed silence. A handful of the Atlas Global men cautiously rose to their feet. When it seemed no more shots were forthcoming, they sprinted to where the bodies of President Harris and Tariq lay on the ground.

"Who … shot … them?" Kyle asked, hoping for some clue from Raoul. "The president was not supposed to die."

Raoul held up a hand to hush Kyle, ignoring the question as he scanned the trees. He then motioned to the three commandos at his side for them follow him. Neither hesitated, and neither did Kyle, who took off at a run, trailing the Raoul and others.

They ran across the grassy field, skirted the trout pond and quickly reached the trees where Kyle had been earlier. Kyle drew up behind the men, gasping for air, as Raoul paused and peered up the hillside for the shooter.

Kyle had no idea how, but Raoul had seen movement. He pointed through the shadows and said, "up there." As Raoul and the commandos charged up the hillside, Kyle sucked in a lungful of air and followed.

Ducking below and around pine boughs and branches of gnarly scrub oaks, Kyle heard the crackle and pop of bullets breaking through the air near his head, followed by the retort of rifle fire echoing through the trees. *Shit!* Whoever had killed Tariq and the President now wanted them dead as well! *Of course!* The man with gun had just killed the President! His life was as good as over. Unless he escaped.

Kyle ducked behind the trunk of a tree and looked up through the branches as more shots crackled through the air. One of the commandos nearby cried out in pain, spun around, and fell to the ground.

Raoul and the remaining two commandos dove to forest floor, rolled, then slowly lifted their heads, trying to determine the precise location of the shooter. Raoul pointed his rifle up the hillside, and with his eye pressed to the scope, squeezed off a burst. Then another. Silence.

Raoul pulled his head back from the scope, twisted around to the wounded commando, and then turned to Kyle and the other commandos and said, "Let's go. I think I got a hit."

They rose, and in a low crouch, continued climbing the slope, Kyle trialing, moving carefully, his chest tight, wonder now why he was again carrying a camera instead of a weapon. Kyle heard the crunch of twigs beneath his feet, his heart pounding in his ears. Further up the slope and twenty yards ahead, Raoul suddenly stopped, crouched, and raised a fist.

Kyle froze.

Raoul turned to the commando behind him, then nodded and pointed. Rising slowly, Raoul took several more steps, and holding his rifle at his waist, pointed the barrel at a body on the ground.

Kyle crept closer, then saw the target of Raoul's shot. A well-camouflaged body lay on the ground, the face smeared with green and tan face paint, the blank, blue eyes looking to the sky. Kyle glanced at Raoul, whose brow was furrowed with confusion. Kyle eyed the motionless body at their feet where the other two commandos stood, their weapons trained on it.

The body jerked suddenly and pistol shots exploded from the ground, three bullets slamming onto one of the commando's chest, his body jerking with each hit, staggering him backwards to the ground.

Raoul fired a burst from his rifle into the torso of the shooter on the ground, the man's body jerking with each shot. Then nothing. Raoul hovered, eyes on the body, and stepped around it to kneel closer. He touched their man's shoulder.

The commando looked up at Raoul and tried to smile, his chin quivering as he tried to speak, knowing that he was about to die. The quivering slowly stopped and the command wheezed, air escaping from his chest with final breath. His eyes went blank.

Raoul shook his head, and with two fingers, closed the man's eyes. Raoul pushed himself to his feet and went to the sniper on the ground who he'd just shot. He twisted the man's face upright and looked closely. He wiped away some of the face paint.

Kyle stared in disbelief. "It's Hank Benedict!"

CHAPTER 42

Its engines revved and whining, a Lear jet painted with the Atlas Industries logo sat on the paved runway, of the Atlas Global headquarters ten miles from the Vista Verde Lodge. Inside the plane, two men dressed in khaki trousers and wearing black polo shirts emblazoned with the Atlas Global logo, sat on the white leather seats and faced David Benedict.

"Where's Hank?" David Benedict asked. "We can't wait much longer."

The two men looked at the elder Benedict and shook their heads.

Benedict looked at them for a long moment, his lips in a deep frown, his chin quivering. His eyes began to water. He pinched the tears from his eyes, then waved for the men to deplane.

As the doors were closed and locked shut, the jet engines whined loudly. The jet turned sharply, nosed down the runway, and moments later, the engines screamed. The jet streaked down the runway and swooped into the blue sky, banking over the forested mountain slopes.

***

Led by their director, Frank Huntington, six FBI agents strode into the Situation Room at the White House. They were followed by an equal number of Secret Service agents and their director, John Dempsey. The dozen men took up strategic positions around the room. Two FBI agents stood at the elbows of acting president James Marvin, who sat at the head of a conference table. Marvin and the other cabinet members glanced around, confused, their eyes panicky.

"What's the meaning of this?" Marvin asked. "What are you men doing in here?"

"Mister Vice President," Madison said. "I'm placing you under arrest for treason."

Marvin looked up indignantly. "You can't arrest me!" Marvin shouted. "I'm the president now!"

The FBI agents seized Marvin and lifted him by his upper arms from his chair, then spun him around, and pulled his arms behind him as a third agent snapped handcuffs on his wrists.

Marvin struggled and shouted, "Do you want to spend the rest of your life in prison?" He fruitlessly tried to jerk his arms from their grasp. "Or maybe a firing squad is more to your liking?"

***

The five US Air Force fighter jets had scrambled from Kirtland Air Force base in Albuquerque and now surrounded David Benedict's private Lear jet as it streaked over the dry, flat prairie lands of eastern New Mexico. One jet above, one below, one jet each off the wing tips, and one behind.

The fighter pilot off the tip of the Lear jet's left wine waved a gloved hand to the pilot of the Lear jet, motioning for Benedict's Lear jet to descend. "You are instructed to land immediately," he said into the microphone embedded in his helmet.

The Lear jet pilot, earphones on and his eyes shrouded by aviator glasses, lifted both hands in exasperation and shook his head, no. "No can do, pal," the Lear jet pilot replied. "The boss says we stop at nothing."

"What is your destination?" the air force pilot asked.

"I wish I could tell you," the Lear jet pilot replied.

"We're under orders, pal," the air force pilot said. "You're going down one way or another."

The Lear jet pilot looked at the fighter pilot in horror and shook his head. "You can't shoot down an unarmed civilian aircraft."

"I strongly suggest you land the aircraft immediately," the air force pilot said. "Holoman Air Base is close. There are personnel on the ground waiting for you."

The Lear jet pilot looked back at the air force pilot and shook his head.

The air force pilot paused for a moment, then said, "You are hereby ordered to land your aircraft immediately. This is your final warning."

The Lear jet pilot again shook his head.

"Your choice," the air force pilot said.

Four of the fighter jets close to Lear jet peeled away, leaving only one air force fighter jet trailing it. A missile streaked from below the wing of the trailing fighter jet and struck the Lear jet, which exploded in a ball of fire. The flaming metal tumbled out of the sky.

***

The sun was low in the sky and a soft breeze stirred the air as Raoul, Kyle, and Ariel stood on the stone patio amidst of the scattered and sheet-covered bodies. The grounds of the Vista Verde Lodge now swarmed with FBI and Secret Service agents, all of whom had arrived from the confines of their temporary outpost at the Atlas Global headquarters ten miles away.

The president's body had been loaded onto Marine One, which had lifted off the ground and quickly risen se into the sky. It circled the lodge then disappeared over the forested mountains.

"The president's body will be flown back to Washington," Raoul said.

"What about David Benedict?" Kyle asked. "He's got to stand trial."

Raoul shook his head somberly. "His jet was just shot out of the sky."

Kyle stared at Raoul, considering the implications. "With Marvin in custody, charged with treason," Kyle said, "that leaves Secretary of State Helen Carter as president."

Raoul shrugged. "Someone's gotta do it."

"The two men most responsible for this, Hank and his father, are dead," Kyle said.

"I don't feel sorry for them," Ariel said.

"Neither do I," Raoul said.

"It would have been good to put them on trial," Kyle said.

"And let the whole world watch?" Raoul asked. "Or give you more to write about?"

Kyle smiled and shook his head. "I have plenty to write about, with or without a trial."

"What makes people do things like that?" Ariel asked.

"They're enemies of the people," Kyle said.

Raoul drew a breath, squinted and looked around. "I'm going home."

"You're a freakin' hero, Raoul."

"No," Raoul said with a shake of his head. "I wasn't able to save the president."

"You almost did," Ariel said.

***

Three weeks later, Kyle stood at the edge of Eagle's Nest Lake, his fly rod in hand, his shadow on the water's edge cast by the angular morning light of the newly-risen sun. Shadowy motions from a fisherman's cast will spook the trout, but Kyle didn't care. He just liked being there. And so did Ariel, who sat on a blanket ten yards up the slope.

They had debated returning to the lake, not wanting to stir up bad memories, but they'd decided to confront the past and replace it a new memory. Kyle rationalized that it also was a one-time chance to spend time at this rich man's lake and cabin, something he could never afford.

They had risen before dawn and driven to the Vista Verde Ranch headquarters, arriving just after dawn and had used Ariel's employee access ID card. The ranch had been closed to outsiders and would stay that way for the foreseeable future as the main building was refurbished. They had parked well away from the lodge, which was still being investigated as a crime scene. There was talk that the ranch might never again open to the public.

The jihadi corpses were long gone, having been sent back to Syria by military transport presumably to be claimed by their families.

Kyle had attended the memorial service for Carlito Miranda in the small village north of Española where his distraught mother, Antonia, had closed her wool shop indefinitely while in mourning. It was a somber event, of course, and Kyle felt badly for the woman. She'd lost three of the men in her life who'd meant the most to her.

Allan Morris and his daughter Jennifer were buried in the Los Alamos cemetery in a quiet ceremony also attended by Kyle and a few of Morris's laboratory colleagues.

President Harris' body lay in state in the rotunda of the nation's Capitol. His closed casket had been taken by horse-drawn carriage to Arlington National cemetery where he'd been buried with honors. The slow moving carriage had been followed by Harris's cabinet members and many of his former colleagues in the Senate. The bodies of Congressman Divine and Senator Blount, also lay in state at the Capitol rotunda and both men were also buried in Arlington.

Life in Washington DC ground on.

Kyle yanked the line from the water's surface with a flick of his wrist and watched the water sparkle as it fell from his luminescent green line. He checked the rod as it reached the one o'clock position, and when the line nearly reached full extension, he flicked his wrist forward sending the line out and onto the lightly rippled surface. The wet fly being the last to land, it slowly dropped a couple of inches below the surface, where it stayed.

A strong tug on his line and splash drew his attention to the water as a jolt of excitement coursed through his body. It was a strong strike, and the trout was at least a foot long, he guessed. The fly hooked in its mouth, the trout broke the water once, twice, and then a third time before Kyle finessed it to shore, and held it up as Ariel looked on. Ariel waved from the blanket spread on the grassy bank nearby.

It was his fourth catch of the day, and he kept the trout on a line in the water, fully intending to eat them later in the day. Leaving the fish in the water for the time being, Kyle carried the rod up to the blanket, placed it on the ground nearby, and sat beside Ariel.

"Nice day, huh?" he said, flashing a smile.

She nodded, then knitted her brow, concern covering her face. "Something's wrong. What's bothering you?"

Kyle looked at her for a moment, ever amazed at her ability sense his mood, even read his mind. It unnerved him sometimes, made him feel like his brain was being monitored, especially when he himself didn't always know how he felt. But today he knew. "What they're saying on talk show radio about how this all came down," he said.

Ariel nodded. "I didn't know you're a fan of talk radio."

Kyle shook his head. "I'm not. Sometimes I just like to know what they're saying."

"Which is?"

"That David Benedict is innocent of any conspiracy," Kyle said.

"And that Hank Benedict is a hero for killing Jihadi John?" Ariel said, her voice laden with sarcasm. "Is that close?"

"Yes," Kyle said, "They're saying he's a hero even though he killed President Harris first."

"Well, they're wrong," she said.

"I know. But the problem is a whole lot of people out there hated Harris and are glad to see him gone," Kyle said. "They're already spinning the story as conspiracy by the liberals to undermine the conservatives."

"Like the people at Wolfe news?"

Kyle nodded and stared out at the lake.

Ariel gazed at the lake as well, then back at Kyle. "There's not a lot you can do about it," she said. "People are going to believe what they want to believe, regardless of the truth."

"That's what bothers me," Kyle said, "because it's going to be tough to prove the truth in this case."

"Why?" Ariel said. "It's pretty obvious."

Kyle shook his head. "Not really. Raoul and I have already been doing some research. Hank and his old man did a really good job of covering their tracks. There's virtually no electronic trail that proves anything they did was part of conspiracy."

"Seriously?"

Kyle nodded. "The best sources, of course, are Hank and his father."

"But they're dead," she said.

"And people like Jihadi John."

"Who's also dead."

"And the head of the ISIS, al-Bakar ," Kyle said, "was just killed by a drone strike."

Ariel slumped and sighed, then sat upright. "Wait! What happens now to Marvin?"

"A lot of congressional hearings, of course," Kyle said. "He'll be put on trial. But he can always plead the fifth."

"The Fifth Amendment?" she asked.

Kyle nodded. "The right not to incriminate yourself."

"Even if he's guilty?"

"You only need to plead the fifth if you're guilty," Kyle said. He looked at the lake and back to Ariel. "Those in Benedict's inner circle have been arrested and interrogated, of course. They're going to be tried. But I don't have my hopes up that any conspiracy will be proved."

"Are you going back to Washington?" Ariel asked.

"Not if I can help it."

"You don't want to cover the trials?"

"And sit in a courtroom day after day?" Kyle asked. "No thanks. Others can do that."

"To think that they almost got away with it," Ariel said.

"Yeah," Kyle said. "The problem was that Marvin figured the cabinet would fall in line, no matter what. But they were loyal to Harris, even after his death."

"Marvin was wrong," Ariel said.

"Dead wrong," Kyle said.

They both looked at the lake for a moment, then Ariel opened her day pack and pulled out a bottle of wine and a corkscrew, which she waved at Kyle.

"Well, look at that," he said, a smile coming to his face.

"I liberated it from the wine cellar in the lodge," Ariel said.

Kyle examined the bottle and furrowed his brow. "Another bottle of the good French stuff. You sure can pick 'em," he said. Kyle peeled the foil away, pulled the cork from the bottle, and poured wine into two plastic cups. He gave a cup to Ariel, then raised his in a toast.

"What are we drinking to?" she asked.

Kyle frowned as if in deep thought, then smiled. "To us!"

Ariel drank, then putting her cup down, reached out, pulled him close, and kissed him as they rolled back onto the blanket.

THE END

For More News About Peter Eichstaedt,
Signup For Our Newsletter:

http://wbp.bz/newsletter

Word-of-mouth is critical to an author's long-term success. If you appreciated this book please leave a review on the Amazon sales page:

http://wbp.bz/eotpa

Prologue

Muffled shots broke the late morning stillness in the Northern California vineyard. Chao Ling dove to the ground, scrambled through a row of vines, leapt to his feet, and kept running.

A man with a pistol fixed with a silencer trotted after him, barrel held high.

Ling dove through another row of vines, and another, then crouched behind a post, his lungs aching.

Holding the weapon at arm's length, the gunman's eyes narrowed and he fired again, the bullet ripping through a cluster of the ripening grapes, splattering Ling's face with juice. He humped up the hillside vineyard, his chest heaving, and peered again through the leaves.

The gunman was nearly parallel to him, separated by four rows, aiming at him.

Ling ducked to his left as another *thunk* sounded. He cried out as his right thigh exploded with searing pain. He clutched his leg and tumbled to the ground, rolling onto his back. *The bastard is crazy! Why did I get involved with this idiot?* He looked up the row, searching for an escape. *Keep moving!* His leg on fire, he struggled to his feet and hobbled, blood soaking his pant leg. His left leg quivering with every step, he pulled out his cell phone. With shaky hands he tapped 9-1-1 and listened to the phone's buzzing ring.

"What's your emergency?" a dispatcher asked calmly.

"Someone's trying to kill me!" Ling shouted.

"Are you okay?" the dispatcher asked.

"I've been shot!"

"Tell me who and where you are, and what's going on."

"My name is Chao Ling," he yelled. "I'm at Morrison Creek Winery. It's Bernie Morrison. He's got a gun! He's trying to kill me!" Ling sucked in one breath after another, his body shaking.

"Can you get to a safe place?"

"What the fuck? That's what I'm trying to do!"

"Hold on." The line went silent for what seemed an eternity.

Ling peered across leafy vines as Morrison crawled through a row, rose, and took aim, firing again, the muffled shot ripping through the leaves. "Aw shit!"

The dispatcher came back on. "We have a unit in the area. I'm sending it now. You'll see it soon. Stay on the line and tell me what's happening."

Keeping his head low, Ling hobbled back down the slope and toward the winery, hoping the cops would get there before he'd be cut down. The phone slipped from his hand and fell to the dirt. He kept going.

Three rows separated him from Morrison, who kept moving, staying parallel to him. Blinding pain filled his head as two muffled shots sounded. Ling stumbled to the ground. He touched the side of his head and felt the wet warmth flowing from a gash in his scalp. His hand was bright red. He struggled to his feet at the edge of the vineyard, breathing heavily. His eyes stinging from sweat, his head on fire, he scanned the highway in front of the winery. A black-and-white cruiser, lights flashing, headed toward the vineyard.

Ling heard footsteps behind him and twisted around, his leg wobbly, and fell to the ground. His vision blurred, he wiped his eyes with bloody fingers, and squinted up at Morrison, standing over him, pistol pointed at his chest. "Don't!" Ling cried, staring at Morrison's bloodshot blue eyes, arms reaching up in appeal.

Morrison glanced to the winery entrance where the sheriff's cruiser swerved into the graveled parking lot and slid to a stop.

Ling saw two officers leap out and draw their weapons, crouching slightly. They shouted for Morrison to drop his gun.

Breathing heavily, Morrison returned his eyes to Ling and glared.

"No, no, don't!" Ling yelled. Three muffled shots slammed into his chest like iron fists. He wheezed a breath as the air crackled with the deputies' gunfire. Morrison's body shuddered, bullets staggering him backward and to the ground. Ling's world went dark.

Chapter 1

Dante Rath massaged the ache in his stomach. Heartburn flared from the black coffee he sipped, having devoured a foil-wrapped breakfast burrito at his desk. He leaned against the fraying pad of the low-backed office chair and re-read the memo from management. Consultants were reorganizing the newsroom. Early retirements and buyouts were coming, along with new beat assignments. He had been down this road before. He drew a deep breath and tossed the memo on one of the piles atop his desk. He yanked open a drawer, shook a couple of antacid tablets into his hand, and chewed them.

Dante crossed the newsroom to the drinking fountain and emptied his coffee mug, refilling it with cold water. He drank it down, refilled it, and looked out at the newsroom, empty but for a clerk with his feet up, reading the morning edition, and couple of section editors. Most reporters were on their beats. Dante wondered if he could survive another downsizing, or if he wanted to. He took a breath and returned to his desk.

At forty-four, he'd collected state and regional journalism awards. Three times his work had been submitted for the Pulitzer Prize as part of a team of investigative reporters at the *San Francisco Chronicle*. They won once for exposing a web of corruption around government contracts for private prisons. The stories had sparked a federal criminal investigation resulting in jail time for a state senator and the prisons' director. He ached to return to investigative reporting, but after reading the memo he knew his odds of doing it for his current employer, the *Santa Rosa Sun,* were in the negative numbers.

A call on a police scanner near the city desk caught his attention. A female voice called out a "ten-seventy-one" at the Morrison Creek Winery. Sirens wailed in the background. Then a "ten-forty-nine." Dante hurried over to the bank of scanners next to TV screens tuned soundlessly to local channels and listened closely to the calls. A ten-seventy-one was shots fired. *What the hell?* A ten-forty-nine meant a unit was proceeding to the scene. He sipped more water, his heart pounding.

The lights flickered on the Napa County Sheriff's Department band as more calls came. Another sheriff's unit was responding. The next transmissions were a ten-fifty-three and a ten-fifty-four. Person down, possible body.

Dante yanked the narrow notebook from his back pocket and jotted down the time, date, and ten-code numbers. It was nearly 11 a.m. and the crime beat reporter was out. Dante smiled as a shot of adrenaline pulsed through him. The story could be his and his alone. A shooting at the Morrison Creek Winery could salvage his sputtering career. It might even lead to … what? He didn't have time to think about it, or the personal problems he had with the winery owner. He hustled back to his desk, pulled on his corduroy sport coat and slipped the notebook into the outside pocket. Looking again at the management memo, he wadded it and tossed it into the wastebasket.

Dante wove among the desks in the crowded newsroom to the glass-walled office of his managing editor, Seth Jones. A veteran reporter and editor in his late sixties, he'd grown a little soft around the middle, but carried the extra pounds well. Jones wore hippie-styled wire-rimmed glasses, had bushy white hair, and loved murder stories even more than corruption scandals. "Did you hear that?" Dante asked, standing in the open door.

Jones looked up from his desk. "Yeah. What is it?"

"Shots fired at Morrison Creek Winery. Possible body. I'm going."

"The hell you are!" Jones barked, holding up a hand. "You're the wine editor. Let Hansen cover it."

Dante clenched his jaw, exhaled, and shook his head. "She's not here." Cathy Hansen was the newspaper's young cops, crime, and district court reporter. She'd been hired out of journalism grad school at UC Berkeley, his alma mater. She was the kind of person they wanted these days, tech savvy and a social media maven willing to work long hours for entry-level pay and who didn't talk back to her bosses. Nice girl, a good writer, but she was overly confident and naïve. She reminded him of himself at that age.

"I wrote about Morrison Creek a few weeks ago," Dante said. "Remember?"

"Yeah, I remember. What'd you call the wine? Horse piss or something?"

Dante swallowed and felt his face flush. "Not in those words. The guy who owns the place, Bernie Morrison, deserved it. He's selling box wine in bottles."

"He threatened to kill you if he ever saw you again."

"C'mon, Seth. Threats come with the territory."

"There's been a possible homicide at the winery of a man who said he hates you and the ground you walk on. Now you want to run over there and poke around? It probably has nothing to do with the wine."

"But maybe it does."

Jones leaned back in his chair behind the large oak desk, pulled off his glasses, and massaged the bridge of his nose. Dante knew Jones felt lucky to have his job. The *San Francisco Chronicle* had summarily dumped him years earlier after disbanding the investigative team Jones ran when the newspaper was sold and deflated to a husk of what it once was. Dante had worked for him then and had followed him to the *Santa Rosa Sun*.

"When are you going to accept the fact this newspaper can't afford a full-time investigative reporter?" Jones asked.

"I went to bat for you, Dante. It's how you got the wine editor's job."

Dante looked out across the empty newsroom, waiting for the lecture to end. His job was to keep tabs on Northern California's billion-dollar wine industry. Spread a thick layer of happy talk over the endless acres of vines and proliferating wineries. Exposés were a thing of the past, a fact he refused to accept.

"Did you read the reorganization memo?" Jones asked, his voice low and conspiratorial.

"Of course," Dante said.

Jones glanced out into the newsroom and motioned for him to close the door.

After quietly closing the door, Dante settled into one of the straight-backed chairs facing Jones's desk. The burn flared again in his stomach. Closed door chats were never good.

"I want to give you a head's up," Jones said, mashing his lips together, struggling to find the words. "They're eliminating your job."

Dante swallowed hard. Not long after joining the *Sun*, he'd launched a wine column called "The Grapes of Rath," replacing a blandly named column, "Wine Country Week," telling Jones the column needed personality if anyone was going to read it.

"My wine column has been well-received," Dante said. "Wineries are calling us for a change, asking for their ads to be placed on the same page."

"I know," Jones said, holding his hands up defensively.

"I've put my heart into the wine beat," Dante said, his voice rising. "Earlier this year I helped organize the annual Symposium for Professional Wine Writers here in the Napa Valley. I read every wine book and magazine I can get my hands on. They're on my desk now, under all those winery press releases I get every freakin' day. I read all the wine blogs. The newspaper is even paying for me to get a wine certificate at the UC Davis! Now they want to cut the position?"

"Calm down."

"It's not like I needed to do any of this crap, you know," he continued. "I grew up right here in wine country. I helped my grandpa make what they used to call Dago red. Barrels of it, year after year. Long before anyone took California wine seriously."

"I know."

"I've been a good boy, you know," Dante said, not letting up. "When all those free cases of wine began showing up at my doorstep, I didn't keep them, did I? No. I donated them to charity auctions."

Jones shook his head and leaned back in his chair as Dante fell silent. "Done yet?"

He exhaled. "So, what the hell are they going to do with the job?"

"Slice 'n' dice. The wine business news will be handled by Thompson in the business section. The food and wine reviews will go to Donatello in the lifestyle section. Wine reviews will be freelanced by several of the self-styled wine critics who populate this region."

Dante's heart sank. He looked at the floor, then at Jones. "So now what?"

"Do I look like an employment agency?" Jones said.

"What about putting me on general assignment?" Dante said. "I've covered every kind of story there is, from obits to exposés."

Jones was unmoved.

"We won the Pulitzer, remember?" Dante said, trying to eke out a sympathetic smile.

"That's history," Jones said. "You know how the news business is these days. The only thing publishers want to know is what you've done for them today. Even if someone else quits in the next few weeks, you're not getting the job. According to the consultants, the staff is bloated." Jones exhaled noisily. "For what it's worth, you're not alone. After this reorganization, they're giving me a bonus and pushing me out the door."

The knot in Dante's stomach tightened, the heartburn smoldered. He felt his world slipping away—again. "So, how long do I have?"

"The consultant's report is due in a couple of week. It goes into effect a month or so later. So you have about six weeks."

"What the hell am I supposed to do?"

"You're one of the best investigative reporters around. Start looking. What's going on with your buddies at that nonprofit journalism outfit at UC Berkeley?"

Dante shook his head. "No openings. They've got problems, too. Nonprofits depend on grants. The grants come from rich people who don't like reporters writing about how they and their friends make all their damned money."

"The rich just get richer," Jones said with a groan.

Dante sat up and crossed his arms as a wry smile crossed his lips. "It's all the more reason for me to go out to the Morrison Creek Winery."

"It is?"

"There's more to this story than a dead body or two."

"How do you know?"

"I just know."

"I told you, Hansen is covering the story," Jones said.

"When you find her, tell her she can do the main crime story," Dante said. "I'll write a color sidebar with some history of the winery. It'll also give me something dramatic for my next column."

Jones sighed. "Okay. She and a photographer will meet you there. Help them out, will you?"

"Glad to be of service." Dante turned from the office and burst out of the newsroom and into the warmth of the late morning sun on the loading dock. He hurried down the steps, his mind reeling. In the parking lot, he pulled open the door of his aging dark green Mustang, a retro fastback coupe. Heat roiled from inside. The V-6 engine roared to life, settling into a soft rumble, enhanced by a hole in the muffler. He loved the sound. Much better than the putter of the mufflers punks installed on their rice rockets.

Dante swerved out of the parking lot, his tires squealing. He slammed through four of his five gears and merged into traffic, quickly hitting 70 mph as he headed south out of Santa Rosa on Highway 101, and found fifth gear. He avoided the two-lane State Route 12, knowing it would be clogged with SUVs, vans, and limousines loaded with wine drinkers in the hunt for their next winery amid the rolling hills of Sonoma County.

Yeah, the winery owner Bernie Morrison had threatened him all right. He'd expected nothing less from Morrison and knew he deserved it. Still, he had dismissed Morrison's death threats. If anything, Morrison should have been the one worried about him, after how Morrison had carried on with his late wife. Dante's stomach knotted and his heartburn returned. He was going 85 mph now, swallowed hard as he checked his rear view mirror for cops, and backed off the accelerator.

After Morrison's threats, he'd done what the newspaper management wanted. He talked to the police. The cops told him to take the threats seriously. He didn't. They also told him to consider buying a weapon. He didn't do that either.

If it were Morrison on the ground at the winery, Dante knew he'd have a hell of a story. Everything about Morrison was phony, even the name of his winery—"Morrison Creek." There was no such creek. Morrison made it up to sound rustic. Dante decided if he had only six more weeks as a *Sun* reporter, it was going to be six weeks no one would forget. He checked his rear view mirror for cops again and stepped on the accelerator.

Chapter 2

Dante wheeled onto the exit to State Route 116, and thirty minutes later turned off the Carneros Highway before reaching Napa and saw the sign he was looking for. He slowed and took the narrow paved road to the Morrison Creek Winery, a renovated barn nestled in a grove of trees just off the road. His pulse quickened at the sight of the emergency vehicles, police, and sheriff's units crowding the winery parking lot, lights flashing in the sunlight. He pulled over to the side of the road, stopped, and climbed out while checking for his notebook and pen. He drew a deep breath and told himself to calm down.

Yellow crime scene tape stretched across the parking lot entrance, but no cops guarded it. A few uniformed investigators clustered around a small table near the adjoining vineyard. Dante squinted at what looked like plastic baggies on the table. Evidence. His eyes fell on two bodies covered with sheets on the sparse grass near the vineyard. A couple of officers walked between the leafy vines, eyes to the ground.

A female voice called out his name. He wheeled to the sight of a woman in heels showing remarkable balance as she hurried toward him. She was Carmen Carelli, an attorney whose clientele included some of the best winemakers in the Napa and Sonoma Valleys and beyond. They'd had lunch not long ago, but nothing had come of it. Dante had wanted her to talk about a client, one of California's biggest winemakers. She'd been agreeable and polite, but had revealed little he didn't already know.

As she strode toward him, her dark hair fell over the shoulders of a gray pinstriped suit jacket. The plunging neckline of her ivory silk blouse revealed a glimpse of cleavage. She looked at him with dark, piercing eyes and knitted her brows, as if annoyed he was there.

"Chasing ambulances these days?" he asked.

"Hardly. One of the bodies over there was my client."

Dante caught his breath. "Who? Morrison?"

She shook her head. "No, the other one."

Dante glanced again to the vineyard and back. "So, one of the dead is Morrison?"

Carmen pressed her lips together. "It's what I've been told."

"By whom?"

"I have my sources, just like you do."

"So, what happened?"

"Ask the cops, Dante."

"You're not being helpful."

"What are you doing here?" she asked. "Crime isn't your thing, is it?"

"Some of the wine around here is criminal. Like Morrison's."

Carmen smiled. "That's funny."

"I mean it."

"I know you do. I read your column. You did a real number on him. Morrison was extremely upset. So was my client."

Dante didn't feel like going into it, not here anyway, and pulled the notebook from his pocket. He wanted to get a comment from Carmen before she disappeared into the crime scene.

"Who was your client?" he asked.

"Is this for the newspaper?"

"No, Carmen. It's for a comedy skit."

"That's why what you write makes me laugh."

"I'm glad you're amused." He held his pen, poised on his notebook. "So, if your client was upset about what I wrote, he must have been involved with the winery."

Carmen squinted at him in the sunlight, saying nothing.

"So, who was he?"

"You asked me already."

"You didn't answer."

Carmen exhaled, looked to the parking lot, and back at Dante. "You didn't get this from me," she said. "His name was Chao Ling."

"C-h-a-o…L-i-n-g," he said, jotting the name as he spelled it out. "What was Mr. Ling doing here?"

Carmen crossed her arms. "You *are* full of questions."

"Was Ling an investor in the winery? Or was he a customer?"

She tilted her head to the side. "Maybe he was both."

"Everyone dreams of owning a winery, don't they?"

"Not everyone."

"What else can you tell me about Ling?"

"Nothing. Attorney-client privilege."

"Carmen, the man's dead."

"Doesn't matter."

"You're being ridiculous."

"It's the rules. I follow them. He has assets. They need to be protected."

Dante waited for more, but she said nothing. He scratched his temple with his pen and looked off to the distant table where investigators were huddled. "If Ling had a financial interest in the winery, why would Morrison want to kill him?"

"We'd all like to know, wouldn't we?"

"It might be useful for you to talk to me about this, sooner rather than later."

"Useful to you, maybe."

"Rath!"

He turned as Cathy Hansen jogged toward him, with Nate Segura, the chief photographer, trailing, his camera bag bouncing on his hip. Two television station SUVs topped with broadcast dishes wheeled into the parking lot, spilling reporters and cameramen.

"What are you doing here?" Hansen asked. "This is my story."

Dante smiled calmly. "Glad you could make it."

Hansen wore her blond hair in bangs with the sides trimmed at her jawline. She wore a burgundy T-shirt tucked into her designer jeans under her tweedy sport coat. She scowled. "I'm serious."

"So am I," Dante said.

"So what the hell happened?" Segura asked.

Dante pointed toward the investigators and the bodies on the ground. "Two people dead."

"Can we get in there?"

He shook his head. "You'd better use a long lens, Nate."

With the arrival of Hansen and Segura, along with the television vehicles, a couple of deputies hurried to the crime scene tape, waving their hands for them to stay back.

"You're Ms. Carelli?" one of the deputies asked Carmen.

She glanced at her watch, the gold links of the wristband glittering against her light olive skin, and looked at Dante. "I gotta go. Call me sometime."

"Count on it," he said.

A deputy handed her a clipboard. "Here. Sign in."

She scribbled her signature, and the deputies lifted the tape for her.

"Why do you get to go in?" Dante asked.

She turned. "They called me. They want to talk to me about Ling."

Dante watched the sway of her hips as she strode into the winery, thinking about how he'd like to get to know her a lot better. He wondered why he hadn't done so already.

"Not fair," Hansen said with a whine.

Dante squinted at her. "She knows one of the dead. She's his attorney. And, she's part of the Carelli family, one of the oldest names in the California wine business."

"I know who the Carelli family is," Hansen said. "Who can I talk to here?"

"Hold on," Dante said, pulling out his phone and stepping away to talk. He came back and looked at Hansen. "I called a friend who's on the force. He's up there now. He's agreed to talk to us, but it has to be off the record."

"Okay," Hansen said. They watched Segura screw a monopod into the bottom of his camera, attach a 400 mm lens, and focus. He snapped a few frames and moved along the tape to get better angles.

A Napa County special investigator came down from the crime scene and paused on the other side of the tape. "Jake," Dante said, reaching out to shake his hand.

Jake Henshaw was a fortyish, muscled man with closely cropped hair. He wore a black fleece vest with "SHERIFF" emblazoned in yellow block letters across the back, an automatic pistol holstered at his waist. His jeans fell on tan desert boots. "Since when are you covering homicides?" Henshaw asked.

"People keep asking me that."

"And what do you say?"

"Not much. What happened here?"

"I'm really busy, in case you hadn't noticed."

Dante turned to Hansen. "Cathy Hansen, this is Investigator Jake Henshaw. She's the one who's covering this story for the *Sun*. Our photographer is Nate Segura."

Henshaw flexed his jaw muscle and looked around the crime scene, as if worried, and back at Hansen. "You can't quote me, okay?"

"No problem," she said with a smile. "Background. The sheriff's going to have a press conference in another thirty minutes."

"The man who owns the winery—" Henshaw began.

"Bernie Morrison," Dante blurted.

Henshaw scowled. "Apparently had some issues with the victim—"

"Chao Ling."

Henshaw scowled again. "We haven't released the names of the suspect or the victim."

"I just talked with the victim's attorney," Dante said. "Carmen Carelli. She's inside the winery now. I also know Morrison. I interviewed him a few weeks ago."

Henshaw looked irritated. "The victim, Chao Ling, was chased from the winery, into the vineyard, and shot. Five times. Once in the leg, once in the head, three in the chest."

"What about Morrison?" Dante asked.

Henshaw sighed. "When officers arrived, they found Morrison standing over Ling, who was still alive. Officers ordered Morrison to drop his weapon. He didn't. Instead, he fired three rounds into Ling."

Henshaw watched Hansen take notes.

"The deputies shot Morrison?" Hansen asked.

"They had no choice," Henshaw said.

"Two men gunned down in a vineyard," Dante said with a smile. "Can't make this stuff up." He watched Hansen finish her notes and look up.

"Do you think it was premeditated?" she asked.

"Hard to tell," Henshaw said. "But, yeah."

"Why?" Hansen asked.

"There was a silencer on the murder weapon," Henshaw said.

"What was the weapon?" she asked.

"A .22 caliber."

"It's what people use to hunt rabbits, I thought," Dante said.

"Pistols like the Walther are popular among a certain crowd," Henshaw said. "They're light and easy to use." He tilted his head from side to side, bones crackling in his thick neck. "Sorry. Gotta go."

"Thanks," Hansen said. She turned to Dante, her face sinking into a frown. "It's my story."

Dante lifted his hands and waved her off. "I know. I know."

Chapter 3

Three days later, the Napa County sheriff said the investigation was continuing, despite the fact both the suspect and victim were dead. No one was talking about a motive, which made Dante wonder. Two people shot dead in a vineyard and no one wants to know why?

The Napa Valley Vintners Association was unwilling to weigh in on the deaths, which did not surprise him. Bodies riddled with bullets and lying around vineyards were not what winemakers wanted to discuss in public. Nor was it what they wanted to read about, and to comment would only provoke more questions, the kind of questions Dante intended to answer—in print.

He had helped Hansen as much as he could, and her stories dominated the front page for the past few days. But the hard news edge of the story was gone, and Hansen was back to covering the routine stories of her beat: car accidents, burglaries, and assaults. It was time to dig a little deeper. Carmen Carelli was the best place to start. She'd sounded apprehensive on the phone, but agreed to meet him for dinner.

Arriving early, Dante elbowed his way to the restaurant bar, ordered a glass of wine, and took a swallow while keeping an eye on the parking lot. He recognized Carmen's Porsche when she wheeled into the parking lot. He greeted her near the door, guiding her through the noisy, upbeat crowd as they were shown to a glass-topped table on the outside patio. Whatever scent she wore was enticing. Dante reminded himself to stay focused. The pretext for this dinner was not romance, but information. His job was to get it.

The hostess dropped two menus on the table, flashed a fake smile, and disappeared. A busboy appeared and asked if they wanted water. "Because of the drought, we only serve water on demand."

"Please," Dante said, scanning the multi-page wine list. "This place has very good wines."

"Some are from my clients," Carmen said.

"Provided here, I'm sure, at a deeply discounted price," he said.

"Of course."

He pointed to one on the list. "What about this Italian Brunello? It's quite reasonably priced."

"It's a good one," Carmen said.

"You know it?"

"It's one of Ricardo's wineries. He gave me a case for my birthday this year."

"Ricardo, as in Ricardo Santos?" Dante asked, lifting his eyes from the wine list.

"Yes, of course," she said, perusing her menu.

In little more than a decade, Santos had become one of the major wine producers in the state. From the Santos Wine Company headquarters in the San Joaquin Valley, he lorded over tens of thousands of acres of vines and owned a handful of boutique wineries as well. But the bulk of his business was mass-produced, low-cost box wines called Santos Select. He'd once been fined for mislabeling wine, and the case put him on Carmen's client list. Dante had wanted to talk to her about Santos the time they'd met for lunch. Now she might talk.

"So, you're on a first-name basis?"

She looked up from her menu. "We have a professional relationship."

A waiter appeared at the table. "Good evening. My name is Brad. I'll be your server this evening. Can I get you started with some drinks?"

"We'll start with a bottle of wine."

"Certainly. Do you know what you'd like?"

Dante looked at Carmen. "Should we go right for the good stuff and get the Brunello favored by your good buddy, Ricardo?"

She shook her head. "Let's start with something lighter. He's not my buddy, by the way. He's my client."

"Okay." Dante scanned the wine list again. "How about we start with a bottle of this Rossese Di Albenga." He pointed to the item on the wine list.

"Good choice." The waiter spun and left.

"It's from Liguria, on the northern Italian coast," he said, returning to Carmen.

"You know Italian wines?" she asked.

"I spent some time with my mother's family in Italy. Near Spoleto, in central Italy."

"Lucky you."

"They own a winery. In Montefalco. I stayed for a season and learned the business."

"Italian style."

"I took the opportunity to travel. Northern Italy, Southern France, the Rhone Valley, Burgundy, Bordeaux, and the Loire."

"So you became a wine critic by drinking your way across Italy and France?"

"I'm not a wine critic. I'm a journalist who enjoys wine. I started writing my wine column out of necessity. I try to keep it about the business, not the nonsense usually written about wine. But sometimes I stray."

"Like what you wrote about Morrison Creek?"

"Yeah, well. There's more to the story. Anyway, the column has attracted a following."

He thought about his conversation with Jones at the office and was about to say the column would soon end, when Carmen said, "Ricardo reads it."

"He does?" Dante said, curious Santos would follow a local wine column.

"Yes. He told me so. I think you'd like him."

Dante straightened at the thought. "Do you think you could arrange an interview?"

She narrowed her eyes. "I suppose I could try."

"He's a recluse," Dante said.

"He's been burned by the press a few times," she said. "It would be a stretch to get him to talk."

"All the more reason for him to come out of his shell. Set the record straight, so to speak."

She shook her head. "He's a busy man. He's got affiliated offices in Rome, Madrid, and Mexico City."

"He's probably got Mexican business partners, maybe the Italian mafia, too."

"Why do you say that?"

"Anyone with money in Mexico is involved with the drug cartels. Same in Italy."

Her face flushed in annoyance. She drew a breath and exhaled. "It's a myth and you know it."

"Do I? The drug cartels make billions of dollars a year. What do they do with the money?"

"How would I know?" she said.

"Besides buying more drugs and paying their men to hunt and kill rival cartels, some of the money is washed through legitimate businesses," he said. "So why not wine?"

She shook her head in disgust.

"So where did Santos get all the money to make himself a leading player in the California wine business in such a short time?" he asked.

"Not all of his wineries are in the US. Some are in Italy, some in Spain. He's also in the olive oil business. He has olive presses in Spain and Italy, along with his wineries. Mexico, as you may or may not know, is starting to produce some very good wines now."

"Good-bye, tequila."

Carmen shook her head in annoyance. "The point is, Santos is an international businessman. Any number of international banks would loan him money. How does that make him a criminal?"

"He's rumored to be linked to the Aragon cartel."

"Carlos Aragon and his brother Miguel have businesses in the US. So what? It's not a crime."

Her response piqued Dante's curiosity.

The waiter brought their bottle of wine, showed it to them with a flourish, and pulled the cork. As he poured, Dante wondered why Carmen so readily defended Santos. Putting the thought aside, he lifted his glass for a toast. "*Centi anni!*"

"May you live a hundred years as well."

He rolled the wine around his mouth before swallowing. "Good. Very good." He looked at the glass thoughtfully. "Hints of *frutti di bosco,* but still dry."

She sipped. "I like it." She set the glass down.

After they ordered, he took another drink and leaned back. "Thanks for meeting with me."

"It's mostly because I'm afraid of what you might write about my clients."

"The live ones or the dead ones?"

"This conversation has to be off the record."

"What are you so worried about?"

Carmen wrinkled her nose, as if the question smelled badly. "What do you think? I'm taking a risk just meeting with you here."

"A risk? I don't think of myself as a risk."

"Meeting with a journalist? Are you serious?"

Dante dismissed the comment with a shake of his head. "I did a little research at the courthouse. You sued Morrison on behalf of Ling. Tried to take the winery from Morrison. What prompted the suit?"

She sipped from her wine, slowly putting her glass on the table. "Before I answer, I want to ask you something."

"Okay."

"You said there was more to the review you wrote about Morrison. What was it?"

He winced, reluctant to go into it.

She shifted in her seat. "Quid pro quo."

He sighed and returned her gaze. "You drive a hard bargain."

"I'm a lawyer."

"There's a rehab facility north of here, near Calistoga," he said.

"I'm familiar with it."

"My late wife, Nicole, was driving there one night to check herself in. She never made it."

She raised her eyebrows. "An accident?"

He drank from his wine, the memories of that agonizing night roiling in his head.

Carmen looked sympathetic, yet curious.

Dante cleared his throat, shifted in his chair, and continued. "It was about a year ago. She'd been visiting friends, or so I thought. She'd been drinking. It was raining. The car left the road at high speed." He drew a halting breath. "She was found by a driver who saw the car lights in the field, the car upside down. She was brought to the emergency room here in Santa Rosa."

"That's awful," Carmen said.

The bright glow of the red block-letter "Emergency" sign on the hospital wall, the glare of the blue-green fluorescent light in the ER, and the confusion and helplessness he'd felt that night were as strong as if it had just happened. It was 1 a.m. by the time they'd tracked him down and called. The emergency room was quiet. Too quiet. He'd asked to see Nicole immediately. Instead of showing him to Nicole, the nurse told him to wait. A doctor would talk to him.

"She died on the operating table," Dante said, his throat tight as he struggled to tamp down his roiling emotions. "Internal injuries, they said."

Carmen's eyes opened wide. "I'm so sorry."

"The emergency room doctor told me she was pregnant."

Dante's words hung in the air.

"You didn't know?"

He shook his head. "She never told me. That's why she was driving to the rehab facility, I think. She wanted to clean herself up to have the baby." He looked across the restaurant and back at Carmen. "I found her phone when I retrieved her effects from the wreck." He cleared his throat again. "It was filled with text messages."

She frowned, struggling to understand, and quietly asked, "An affair?"

His mind lost in the memories, Dante didn't answer.

"Did you know who?"

Dante swallowed hard. He could barely form the words. "Bernie Morrison."

Carmen sat back and looked at her wine glass, pondering the implications.

"He was texting her things like he couldn't wait until he held her in his arms again. It was such a bunch of bullshit." Dante swirled the wine in his glass and took another swallow, exhaling slowly. "Morrison had used her to worm his way into Napa wine society."

"How?"

"Nicole and her first husband once owned the Shady Oaks winery."

"I know the place," Carmen said. "The wine's pretty good. Small batches, high quality."

"Nicole's husband was stashing money in off-shore accounts rather than paying creditors."

Carmen shook her head in disgust.

"The banks eventually called in their loans, and when he couldn't pay, they threatened to foreclose on the winery. So he ran off to Mexico with one of the girls who worked there. The winery went on the market as part of the divorce settlement."

"It happens more than people like to admit," she said.

"So Bernie Morrison shows up, and with the help of some investors, he bought it."

"That's how they met?"

"That's how we met, too. I wrote a story about the sale. It was my first as the new wine editor."

"And you married her?"

"Nicole was waiting for the sale to become final. We had lunch. One thing led to another."

"Wait. I don't get it. So she was involved with Morrison as well?"

He shook his head. "Not initially. They knew each other because he was the managing partner for the new owners. She was very sociable and did a lot of volunteer work, like for the Napa Valley Arts Council. It hosts wine tastings for fundraisers. The wineries donate their wines, raffle off their best stuff—you know the drill."

"Yes. Good community relations," Carmen said. "My family has donated millions to the arts."

"Morrison was a charmer, you know, and professed a profound interest in the arts and that kind of thing."

Carmen smiled, recalling the man's good looks. "Tanned, thick white mane, trimmed goatee. Contagious smile. But still...."

"I blame myself. It's a hazard of the news business. Long hours, low pay. Nicole got lonely."

"So why do you do it?"

"I've been asking myself that a lot lately." He glanced at his wine and back at Carmen.

"So you and Morrison had some history," she said. "Interesting."

Dante sipped his wine. "After Nicole died, I lost track of Morrison until he resurfaced with his Morrison Creek Winery."

She narrowed her eyes again. "So you trashed Morrison's wines in your column out of revenge?"

Dante drew a deep breath. Yeah, he thought, and it had felt good, damned good. If revenge is a dish best served cold, this one had been delicious. But Nicole was dead. Had been for a while now and nothing would ever bring her back. Dante shook his head and tried to push down the feelings of regret. "The wine deserved to be trashed. Comparing them to Santos's box wines was accurate. Morrison's wines are very similar. I wouldn't be surprised if it was the same wine. Putting it in a bottle with a nice label does not make it good."

http://wbp.bz/napanoira

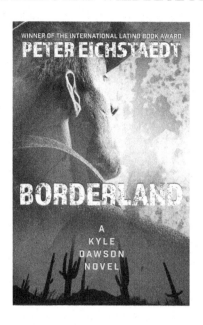
Prologue

Doña Ana County, New Mexico

Sam Dawson dreaded being on his knees.
Always had. They hurt. Badly.
And now it was worse than ever.

Pain radiated from his kneecaps to his ankles and up his thighs as he struggled to balance on the floor of the panel van. His hands had swelled from the duct tape that tightly bound his wrists. The tape encircling his head tore the skin near his eyes and ripped out his thin hair.

Bent forward, his back and neck ached. Blood dripped from his throbbing nose and split, puffy lips. His heart pounded in his ears as he drew a breath. He had thought he was being kidnapped and would be held for ransom. They did that. But now he realized. *These bastards are going to kill me!*

"You got this all wrong," Sam said in a wavering voice. "Listen to me. I didn't tell them anything, I swear."

He fell silent, waiting for a response. Nothing. Only the whine of the truck tires.

"Killing me will make problems for you," he said.

He listened for a response as the truck tore along the desert highway. Nothing.

Sam tried again. "People will find me. And when they do, they'll come after you." He paused. "It's not a threat. It's a fact." He took a breath, licked his lips, and tasted his own warm blood. He coughed, then caught his breath.

Sam felt the truck slow, then swerve off the pavement and bounce onto rutted dirt. Brush scraped the sides of the van. The truck slid to a stop. Sam cried out in pain as his shoulder hit the metal floor. *So now it comes. This is how I die. Like a dog in the desert.* The engine died, pinging in the silence. The front doors creaked open, then slammed shut as footsteps pounded to the back of the truck. The panel doors banged open. Sam felt the rush of cool night air.

Terrified, he curled into the fetal position, unable to stop his body from shaking.

"No! No!" Sam cried. Two men lifted him by the arms and tossed him out. His face mashed into the dirt, his shoulder crackled with pain. He groaned, gulping in air. Sensing that death was imminent, he began to pray aloud. "The Lord is my shepherd, I shall not want. He maketh me to lie down in green pastures..."

He was hoisted again and set on his knees. "Yea, though I walk through the valley of the shadow of death..." Sam heard only the heavy breathing of his captors. "I will fear no ev—"

The sharp crack of a gunshot pierced the stillness, and everything went black.

Chapter 1

Washington, D.C.

Kyle Dawson staked out a position in the Dirksen Senate Office Building corridor, just outside the Homeland Security and Governmental Affairs Committee room. He took a deep breath, hitched up his jeans, and straightened his rumpled corduroy jacket. He raked his fingers through his gray-flecked hair. He hated this. Ambush journalism. But he had no choice.

In moments his target, Senator Micah Madsen, emerged from the elevator and strode toward him, looking confident in his gray suit and red power tie. In good shape for his mid-fifties, he had thick salt-and-pepper hair and a rugged face. His press aide, Jodie Serna, a harried, middle-aged woman wearing a beige silk blouse and gray pin-striped skirt, trailed him, her heels clacking on the floor. She looked exasperated, loaded down with files. Both stared straight ahead, on a mission.

Dawson stepped forward. "Senator!" he barked, holding up his hand.

Madsen paused, looking irritated at the intrusion. "What is it?"

"That shootout at the border crossing yesterday."

"What about it?"

"One of the three men killed was a staff member of your Las Cruces office."

Madsen jerked his head in surprise. "Where did you get that information?"

"Why was he carrying $500,000 in U.S. currency?"

Madsen snorted as his face scrunched into a frown, his jaw muscle flexing. "No comment," he said loudly enough for others to hear.

Dawson's stomach tightened as nearby heads turned and conversations quieted. He wanted this conversation kept private.

"I have a committee meeting to chair, and you're in my way," Madsen said, again so others could hear. "So, if you'll excuse me."

Dawson didn't move. "You didn't answer my question."

A couple of television cameramen moved in, flicking on lights.

Madsen grimaced at the cameras, his lips taut, his face reddening. He turned back to Dawson. "We're looking into it. Now get out of my way before I call security."

Jodie Serna jumped between them, motioning for Madsen to go into the hearing room. Madsen pulled the door open and disappeared inside. Serna shook her head disgustedly at Dawson, then went through, slamming the door behind her.

Dawson squinted in the glare of the camera lights.

"What the hell was that about?" one cameraman asked.

Dawson slipped his notebook into his jacket pocket. "Read about in tomorrow's *Herald*."

His stomach churning, Dawson hustled back down the hall and into the committee room's public entrance, then stood in the rear. Madsen, the senior senator from New Mexico, sat in the center of the committee desk. Having composed himself, he banged his gavel down, cleared his throat, and scanned the crowd.

"Drug war violence is a deadly plague along the U.S.-Mexico border. Of particular concern is the recent gun battle at the Rancho la Peña border crossing in southern New Mexico. Because of this, I am going to conduct an emergency field hearing in El Paso to assess the state of our border security. I urge all committee members to attend. With that, I call our first witness."

After handing the gavel to his vice-chair, Madsen stood and left the hearing room, shaking a few hands on his way out.

Dawson sucked in a breath and left for the newsroom. He hadn't expected Madsen to say a damned thing. Yet he was satisfied. Madsen now knew that he was watching him. That alone was worth it.

* * *

Dawson jaywalked across the street and quickly scaled the steps to the *Washington Herald*, his employer for the past eight of his more than twenty years in journalism. The story about Madsen's staffer could make this re-election race between the sitting president, liberal Democrat Barry Montgomery Harris, and Madsen, his conservative challenger, very interesting. Three people shot dead in their vehicles by drug cartel henchmen as they waited in line to cross the border into Mexico. Two were Mexicans. The third was a U.S. citizen—Madsen's staffer—who had no apparent reason to be there. It was the kind of thing that unraveled campaigns. Just find a loose thread and pull. His pulse quickened at the thought. *Game on.*

He pushed through the glass and brass-handled doors, then waved his ID card at the guard as he hustled across the lobby to the elevator, sandwiching himself inside as the door dinged shut.

Dawson stepped from the elevator and balked at the sea of fluorescent-lit desks and waist-high dividers that filled the newsroom. He hated the fake light and felt a headache coming on. This was a far cry from Iraq and Afghanistan, where each day was a damned miracle. When you went out on a story, you might not come back. If you did, you might not have all your body parts. *I'm back. I'm back now*, he kept telling himself. It had been a way of life that he would never forget. Ever.

Dawson tried to be grateful for the assignment to cover Senator Madsen's run for the White House. Everyone said it was a reward. Help him take the next step up the ladder. *Ladder to what?* Covering this campaign was suffocating. The predictable quotes, poll-driven speeches, minutiae magnified to ridiculous proportions. An exposé on this border shootout could put him back in the field, where he belonged, where he could breathe, where things really mattered. But first he needed one man's approval.

Dawson stood at the open office door of his boss, Ed Frankel. The managing editor was as tough as they come. The glory days of big newsroom travel budgets were gone. The campaign was a priority. Dawson knew his pitch had to be a damned good one. He took a breath and rapped his knuckles on the frame.

Frankel swiveled from his computer screen and frowned, looking irritated at the interruption. A stocky man in his late sixties, Frankel was on the verge of retirement. His habitual paisley tie hung loosely at the neck, frayed around the knot. The chest pocket of his white shirt was spotted from pens he'd forgotten to cap. Matching his cropped white hair was a drooping white mustache, accenting a face creased from forty years in the news business.

"What did Madsen say?" Frankel asked.

"He wanted to know where we got the information."

"And?"

"He said they're looking into it. They're scrambling, trying to figure out how to spin it."

"Couldn't happen to a nicer guy," Frankel said. "But we still need to explain the connection. Can we quote your buddy Garcia?"

"His name stays out of it," Dawson said. "Deep background. That's the deal."

"Of course. Deep Throat's back. So what can we print?"

"The U.S. citizen who was killed—Madsen's staffer from the Las Cruces office—was just a kid, twenty-one, a student at New Mexico State."

"What about the money he was carrying?"

Dawson shrugged. "It had to be drug money."

"The staffer was dealing drugs?"

"No one carries that much money by accident."

"You're right."

"Obviously, the Mexicans knew money was coming across the border. The shooters on the Mexican side riddled the vehicle. Tried to take the money. The Border Patrol fired back. It got pretty nasty. Three U.S. border guards are in critical condition."

Frankel paused. "All that at a border crossing? Incredible. Remind me not to go. Anything else?"

"Not so far."

"We have a few more hours till deadline. Keep pushing."

Dawson cleared his throat. "Madsen's called an emergency committee meeting in El Paso to look into the shooting. I want to go cover it."

"El Paso is home for you, right?"

"My parents live near there."

"Are you missing them or something?"

"Madsen is milking the border issue all he can. He hopes to ride the issue into the White House. There's a war happening along the border. I'd like to take a serious look at it. This shooting is just the tip of the iceberg."

Frankel groaned. "This is not a good time to pull you off the campaign and send you to El Paso on what could be a wild goose chase."

"No one is writing about what's behind the violence. That's the real story."

"Causes are not news. Leave that thumb-sucking stuff to the columnists."

"Drugs and migrants flow north, and guns and money flow south. They just step over the dead bodies and keep shooting."

"Jesus, Dawson. You don't give up, do you?"

"We need a story with meat."

Frankel leaned back, locking his fingers behind his head. "This newspaper's on freakin' life support. We need another Watergate or we're all going to be on the street. Where the hell's Richard Nixon when you need him?"

"This story has potential. I swear."

Frankel gazed out his window at the Washington skyline. Dawson had heard all of his stories. Like how he had interviewed rebel commanders no one else could find, once with a gun to his head, held by a fidgety fighter who needed only a nod from his boss to pull the trigger. Frankel had always gotten the story, but never the prize. So he had settled for shepherding prize-winning stories by Dawson and other reporters. Dawson held his breath. He'd dangled the bait. Now he'd see if Frankel would bite.

Frankel sucked in a breath. "Put it in writing. I'll see what I can do."

Chapter 2

Doña Ana County, New Mexico

Special Agent Raoul Garcia surveyed the crime scene, his eyes shaded by iridescent sunglasses, his lips pressed together. Garcia scuffed his suede desert boots on the grit, then tugged up his cargo pants and smoothed his black DEA T-shirt inside the waistband. The blazing sun heated the Special Forces boonie hat covering his shaved head. Garcia clenched his jaw as he stroked his closely cut goatee. The more he thought about the dead man on the ground nearby, the angrier he got. "Friggin' bastards," he said.

The Dona Ana County sheriff had called him a couple of hours earlier, saying that his deputies had found a body. Despite the head wound, the sheriff said they were confident it was Sam Dawson. Garcia had left immediately.

By the time he arrived, crime scene tape fluttered everywhere, bouncing in the hot wind that blew across the desert scrub. A couple of county sheriff deputies stood by their vehicles as blue and red emergency lights pierced the sunlight. State Police investigators milled about. Green and white Border Patrol trucks were parked nearby. Flies buzzed angrily.

Garcia nodded to the deputies as he lifted the tape and stepped closer to get a good look. The victim's head was held together by the duct tape, the jaw mangled, upper teeth and bone exposed. Yeah, it was Sam Dawson. As if Sam was hard to miss. The jowly face, no neck, barrel chest, and medicine-ball belly covered by a bloodstained polo shirt monogrammed with the country club logo.

Garcia had known Kyle Dawson's dad since forever. "Shee-it," Garcia said with a sigh. Times were different back then. Innocent. Where had it all gone wrong?

The gun battle at the border crossing two days earlier was bad enough. Now this. Sam Dawson was dead, executed to be precise. A high-profile land developer with strong political connections. And the father of his cousin and best friend. That black cloud that he felt hovering over Juárez was growing. Now Kyle was involved.

Two medical technicians from the Las Cruces hospital unfolded a black body bag, placed it on the ground, and zipped it open. They pulled on latex gloves.

"Help me here," one said, swatting at swarming flies.

The other brushed away crawling ants and used a pocket blade to cut the tape that bound Sam's wrists, freeing the arms beset by rigor mortis.

Garcia remembered Sam's hands, big enough to palm a basketball. Sam used them to pat the backs of friends and prospective land buyers. The technicians stooped to lift the body, then worked the legs into the bag.

He gazed at the wire fence that marked the U.S.-Mexico border, stretching into the horizon, fading into the sand and sparse brush. Just five strands of barbed wire that marked the dividing line between two countries tied together in more ways than most people wanted to admit. The sun felt heavy on his shoulders. Garcia had already made one call. He dreaded the next.

A white Chevy Tahoe bounced over the gravel and skidded to a stop. The doors were emblazoned with a blue "7 News" inside a circle. El Paso television reporter Anita Alvarez stepped out, her dark hair cascading to her shoulders. She wore a turquoise blouse with a deep neckline, a linen jacket, designer jeans, and running shoes. Damn, Garcia thought. She always looked good. Hadn't aged a day from high school. He took a deep breath and slowly exhaled.

She hurried toward him, holding a reporter's notebook to shade her eyes. "Thanks for the call, Raoul. I can't believe someone would kill—" She caught her breath as she saw the body, then turned away, wincing. "Oh, Jesus."

The medical technicians noisily zipped the bag shut. They groaned as they heaved it onto a gurney, which they shoved into the back of the ambulance and slammed the doors shut. They climbed into the cab, revved the engine, and drove off. Garcia watched the vehicle disappear in the scrub before bouncing onto the paved road.

"Did the Borrego cartel do this?" Anita asked, squinting in the sunlight.

Garcia lifted his hat and ran a hand over his head stubble. "A lot people in Juárez could do this."

"Why Sam Dawson? Everybody loved him."

"Not everybody."

"Ten years of covering the drug wars. Thousands dead. This one hits close to home."

"Yeah, it does." Garcia walked to his unmarked black SUV, opened the door, and climbed in. He lowered the tinted glass window.

"Hey, I need to talk to you," Anita said.

"Go talk to those guys," Garcia said, pointing a thumb at the Dona Ana County Sheriff's Department truck. "They got jurisdiction here."

"The sheriff doesn't know crap."

Garcia shrugged.

"Does Kyle know about this?"

"I'm calling him now." Garcia showed her his phone.

Anita looked at him. "Raoul?"

"What?"

"Thanks for making the call."

Garcia nodded again and waited until she returned to her vehicle, where she slid into the front seat and made a call. Her cameraman stood nearby, panning the scene.

Garcia tapped the speed dial and held the phone to his ear.

Chapter 3

Washington, D.C.

Dawson sat at his cluttered desk, wondering when Frankel would have an answer to his request. He needed a break from the campaign. Badly. His junked-up desk was a hazard of the business, he told himself, due to the endless blizzard of press releases, studies, and reports, each spiral-bound, stapled, or glued. Much of it he refused to toss. Reference material. Someday it would come in handy. He subscribed to the bumper sticker philosophy another reporter had pasted on the side of his computer: "A clean desk is the sign of a sick mind." And this? Healthy chaos.

He leaned back in his chair, switched on the computer, and thought about the story he was about to write. It was short on details, but the link to Madsen, now in the throes of a presidential election, gave it strong news value.

Madsen's dead staffer had only come on board six months earlier. A third-year student majoring in political science. Madsen's office said the kid had been vetted, but apparently not well enough. The staffer had no apparent involvement in the drug trade or a criminal record. Jobs like the one this student had were political payoffs to friends and donors. That a twenty-one-year-old was walking around with half a million dollars was no accident. Nor was the fact that he was with those Mexicans. But Madsen's office wouldn't comment, which was why he had tracked down the man himself.

They were "looking into it," Madsen had said. It was a weak response. Dawson chuckled to himself. He'd found out that the kid was the nephew of Jodie Serna's husband, Trini. That set off alarm bells. Trini Serna was Madsen's right-hand man and had been for years. He was officially listed as a senior advisor. Maybe that's why they'd missed something in the kid's background. They weren't really looking.

His cell phone buzzed. He picked it up, read the number, and held it to his ear. "Raoul. What's up?"

"Uhhh," Garcia said slowly. "Got a second?"

"You don't sound happy."

"The police just found a body."

"Where are you?"

"State Road Nine. West of Rancho la Peña."

"Okay."

"It's your father, Kyle."

Dawson's blood went cold, his mouth dry. He swallowed hard. "My...father?" He took a deep, halting breath and exhaled.

"I'm sorry to be the one to tell you, Kyle. They just collected his body and took it to the morgue."

"Jesus." Dawson stared at his desk as visions of the desert filled his head. "What...what happened?"

"He was shot."

Dawson sucked in another deep breath as his stomach knotted.

"Back of the head."

"An execution?" Dawson said softly. "This is... Who would... I don't...understand. Why would..." He leaned forward in his chair, elbows on his knees, and stared at the floor.

"He was kidnapped after leaving the country club. We think there were several of them. It was clean. Very professional, though I use the word loosely."

Dawson straightened up and massaged a temple slowly as he looked across the newsroom. "Well...uhh...I need to get out there."

"Yeah. You do."

"Does Jacquelyn know yet?"

"I doubt it."

"She'll be a wreck. What about my mother?"

"I haven't called anyone except you."

"I'll call them." Dawson sighed deeply. "After all these years, my mother still loved him."

"She still has you."

"Yeah. She does."

Chapter 4

Washington, D.C.

Dawson put the phone down, staring at it as he struggled to accept what he'd just been told. He opened his desk drawer and fished through a sea of clutter until he found what he was looking for—an old leather baseball. He turned it a few times, his thoughts going back to a day with his father when he was eight years old.

They were living in Florida at the time. He and his father had climbed into Sam's Cadillac Coupe de Ville and headed for the baseball park. The Coupe de Ville was a yellow two-door, and the back quarter-panel of the roof was white vinyl. Kyle thought it was the fanciest car he'd ever seen. He relished each and every ride, even though he had to stretch up to see out from the deep back seat.

But that day, Kyle rode in the front. The day was hot and humid, and, like always, the back of his legs stuck to the hot leather seat. They drove to Fort Meyers, where they walked into the biggest stadium he'd ever seen. He clung to his father's hand as they passed through the turnstiles. Amid shouts and echoes careening inside the cavernous structure, they made their way through the crowd to buy hot dogs and sodas. His mind racing, his pulse throbbing, he rode the roar of the crowd and the thunderous applause and cheers like a roller coaster.

Their seats were close behind first base, where he could feel the force of every pitch and the smack of the ball in the catcher's glove rippling through his thin body. As the innings wore on and his excitement waned, the sharp crack of a bat turned his head to home plate. The ball sailed high. But rather than going into the outfield, it curved toward him, falling fast. He panicked for a moment. Sam stood, whipped off his cap, and reached out over his head. Whup! The ball was in Sam's hat.

Kyle looked up, blinking into the harsh sun as his dad shouted and danced, waving the ball to the cheering crowd. Sam reached down, grabbed Kyle's hand, and slapped the ball into it. "Here ya go, son. Don't say I never gave ya nothin'." Sam laughed and squeezed his shoulder. Kyle grinned, his momentary fright replaced by the heart-pounding thrill of a prized baseball in his hand.

Later, his stomach bloated by the ballpark hotdogs and sodas, Kyle's face, arms, and legs began to burn on the way home. He remembered his mother yelling at Sam, saying it was his fault as she sprayed him with Solarcaine to soothe his seared skin. He lay in his bed that night, heat radiating from his sunburned body as he traced the red stitching of the baseball and inhaled the scent of the smooth, white leather.

The ball was stained brown now, the threads frayed. Dawson hefted it a couple of times. Leaning back in his chair, he pulled off his glasses, squeezed his eyes shut, and massaged the bridge of his nose. He shook his head, trying to clear his thoughts and keep a headache at bay. He slowly swiped his hand down his face. *Jesus. Now what?* Still gripping the baseball, he stood. Feeling off-balance, he caught himself, then trudged through the maze of desks back to Frankel's office where he put a heavy hand on the door frame and leaned in.

Frankel again swiveled from his computer screen. "Change your mind?"

"Uh...I know this is a bad time," Dawson said, swallowing hard. "But I need to take some time off."

Frankel frowned. "You just said you wanted to go to El Paso! And we're in the middle of a presidential campaign." He lowered his voice. "What's the problem?"

"My father. He was found dead."

Frankel's face dropped. "Jesus Christ, Dawson. That's terrible." He lowered his eyes, lacing his fingers on the desktop, then looked up. "In El Paso?"

"Near." Dawson massaged the baseball. "Southern New Mexico." He debated whether to divulge the details, then decided Frankel ought to know. "He was murdered. Shot to death."

"Oh, God. That's awful." Frankel cleared his throat. "Have a seat," he said, motioning to a chair. Dawson sat stiffly. "Did it happen near the border? Was it the cartels?"

Dawson's stomach tightened as he glared at Frankel. "My father was a land developer, not a drug dealer."

"Just sayin'. Look, I'm sorry. I guess I'm not so good at talking about these things."

Frankel winced, glanced out the window, then back at Dawson. "You gonna be OK?"

Dawson twisted the ball. "It makes no sense."

"It rarely does. It's always hard when your father dies. A piece of you is missing."

Dawson stared at the baseball, his mind whirling. "I've been out of touch with him for years. Now, just like that, he's gone." He looked up at Frankel, searching for an answer. "He did some things he shouldn't have. But he paid his debt to society. He didn't deserve to die like that."

"What are you talking about?"

"It was a long time ago," Dawson said, squeezing the ball and looking down at the carpet.

"You don't have to like everything the man did."

Frankel's words hit home. He didn't like what Sam had done. No, not at all. And he had thrown up a wall between them. For far longer than he should have. Now he regretted it.

"How much time you need off?"

"A week, maybe two." As soon as he'd spoken, he wanted the words back. *How much time? Who the hell knows?* Dedication was part and parcel of the profession. The news never stopped. Only people did. Maybe it was his turn to bail out.

Frankel leaned back in his chair. "Take three. You have bereavement leave, so don't worry about it."

Dawson took a deep breath and stood. "Thanks." As he left the office and made his way back to his desk, he felt a burden had been lifted.

Chapter 5

El Paso, Texas

Dawson shoved his carry-on into the overhead bin and settled in for the plane ride back to El Paso. With a tight connection in Dallas, he'd be home before sundown. *Home? Yeah.* Despite having been gone for twenty-five years, El Paso still felt like home.

Another trip to El Paso many years earlier roiled in his memory and caught in his throat as he closed his eyes for takeoff. He'd been born in El Paso, back when Sam was selling used cars under the name of Big Sam Dawson. His father's name was in neon atop a towering sign. Sam had a mechanic, Juan Garcia, who had an instinct for auto repair that verged on mystical. He could take the worst wreck Sam could find to his shop and turn it into a serviceable vehicle with brakes that didn't squeal and a motor that purred. Sam would hire boys to clean and fix the upholstery, then he'd mount the car with retreads and put it on the lot.

Juan had a pretty young sister, Mercedes, who kept his books. Soon she and Sam, then a lean and lanky Texan, were dating. Six months later, they were married, and nine months after that, Kyle was born. Juan had three children, two boys and a girl. The oldest of the boys, Raoul, was born the same year as Kyle, and as far as he was concerned they were brothers.

But selling used cars had never been enough for Sam. He had dragged Kyle and his mother across the South, finally settling in Florida where Sam struggled to hit it big—in construction, alligator farms, demolition derbies—anything for a quick buck. The early years of Kyle's life had been spent moving from one town to another and entering one new school after another—he'd hated it. Always the new kid, wondering what it would be like to live in one place.

Not long after they'd gone to that baseball game, black squad cars had pulled up in front of their apartment building. Pounding on the door, detectives burst in. Sam left in handcuffs, collared, Kyle learned later, for his part in a fraudulent land sales scheme.

Kyle had sat with his mother in the courtroom behind Sam and his lawyer, feeling uncomfortable in the starched white shirt, the new coat and tie, his face scrubbed nearly raw, his hair neatly combed and parted. It had been for the benefit of the judge and jury: Sam the family man. It hadn't worked.

"Your father has to go away for a while," his mother told him afterwards. She had tried not to sound worried, talking as if it was a normal thing. But even then Kyle sensed her fear. It left a hollow, empty feeling inside him that only grew as he rode in the wide back seat when Sam drove his Cadillac to Fort Myers to begin serving his time. They climbed out of the long, yellow car and stood on the curving brick walkway, his father's face contorted with regret.

Kyle's eyes welled with tears and his chin quivered uncontrollably as he reached out for his father, hugging him tightly around the waist. They stood like that for an interminable time, it seemed, until Sam finally let go and stepped back. Sam's strong hand gripped Kyle's shoulder.

"Now I don't want the two of you to go worryin' about me," Sam said. "I'm gonna be fine. The time's gonna go by faster'n you think. Y'all can come visit me most any time ya want, and I hope to God you see fit to do that. Kyle, I want you to be a strong young man for your mother. Ya hear me? Got that?" He squeezed Kyle's shoulder again. "You mind what she says."

Sam took Mercedes in his arms. "It'll be all right. It'll be all right." He held her close, patting her back. "I'll call you as soon as I can. I'll let you know where they're gonna put me. Now git on home before we make a spectacle of ourselves." His father turned and walked into the police station, leaving Kyle and his mother to wipe away their tears in the midday sun.

With Sam gone, Mercedes worked multiple jobs. When she cleaned hotel rooms, Kyle collected the dirty towels and helped her tuck in the crisp, white sheets. When she waited tables at a local diner, he filled salt-and-pepper shakers, wrapped napkins around the silverware, and cleared dishes when things got busy. When things were slow, she made him sit at the back of the restaurant, where he did his homework. Mostly, he just tried to be a good kid.

Dawson gritted his teeth at the memory. *Eight years old. Left alone to be the man of the house. Helpless to do a damned thing about it. Too young to work, too old to be a child. Yeah. You were a bastard, Sam. A damned bastard.*

His chest tightened as Dawson drew a deep, halting breath, remembering the morning after Sam was released. Mercedes couldn't contain her excitement. She cleaned the apartment several times and prepared a fancy meal. That was even more emotional for Kyle and his mother than when Sam had gone to prison because now they believed they could breathe a sigh of relief. The two long years of struggle were over. Or so they thought.

The next day, Sam cast a restless eye around the sparse apartment. He began talking about going back to El Paso.

People were flocking to the Sun Belt, he said, fleeing the closed factories in the Midwest Rust Belt. There was money to be made—big money.

Two days later, Kyle again fought back tears as his father backed the yellow Cadillac out of the parking lot and drove away. "It won't be long," Sam promised. "Y'all just wait till I call, and take care of yerselves."

It was too much for Mercedes. She lasted only six more months, then quit her jobs. She stuffed what little they had into two large suitcases, and they climbed into a Greyhound bus back to El Paso. Kyle stared out the bus window, his resentment of Sam smoldering with every passing mile. The lush, green landscapes of Alabama, Mississippi, and Louisiana ultimately gave way to the brown of West Texas.

Back in El Paso, Sam wanted nothing to do with Mercedes. He'd hit it big, he said, with some desert land deal along the southern New Mexico border, just west of El Paso. Some big money people were behind it, and Sam was in the middle. He'd finally found what he was looking for, and that included a new woman, Jacquelyn. Rejected and disgusted, Mercedes went back across the border and lived in Juárez with her parents. Despite Kyle's objections, after the divorce she took him back to Texas to live with Sam and his new wife. It was a better life for him, she had insisted, as tears streamed down her cheeks. Kyle had gone, but he had not forgotten.

* * *

The flight attendant's voice blared from the speaker overhead: "Please ensure that your seat is in the upright and locked position and that your tray table is securely stowed."

Dawson stirred, looked around the crowded cabin, then out the window to the familiar, scruffy land. Golden sunlight flashed throughout the passenger compartment as the plane circled and bounced onto the baked concrete.

When the seat-belt light dinged off, Dawson pulled his bag from the overhead bin and stood in the crowded aisle, impatient to get off the plane. The other passengers seemed to move in slow motion, taking their sweet time to collect their bags and empty down the aisle. He smiled weakly as the stewardess and copilot lingered by the exit door, thanking him for choosing their airline. *As if there's much choice?*

A ripple of excitement propelled him along the concourse and to the baggage claim. It felt good to be back in El Paso. Like he was in another country, free again to move at will. Yeah, he told himself, this was about as close to a third-world country as you could get without leaving America. He felt a smile coming on.

He joined the other passengers at the rumbling baggage turnstile as bags popped out, clunking onto the conveyor. There was no crowding, no elbowing to get their bags. Yeah, Washington was a long way away. Dawson yanked his bag off the belt, turned, and banged into Raoul Garcia, who was standing behind him, his meaty arms crossed, smiling broadly.

"Welcome home, Kyle." Garcia gave him a bear hug, nearly squeezing the wind out of him.

"Hey, thanks. Good to see you. You're looking as ugly as ever."

"Still prettier'n you. C'mon. I'm parked at the curb." Garcia grabbed Dawson's bag. "The traffic cop's watchin' my ride."

Outside, Dawson took a deep breath of the warm evening air. He felt himself relaxing as he shed his jacket and tossed it on his canvas brief, then slid into the front seat. "It's good to be back," he said, as Garcia pulled out of the airport and eased the black SUV into traffic.

"I'd invite you over for dinner, but I know you got business. When you can, though…"

"Count on it," Dawson said. "No one can burn a steak quite like you."

Garcia shrugged and smiled.

Dawson glanced at the familiar sign that directed them north on Interstate 10 and to the turnoff to Rancho la Peña. The gritty landscape lay wide and open. A far cry from the concrete canyons that he roamed these days. He looked at Garcia and flashed on those years at El Paso High School, the Friday night lights on the football field, the late-night drinking parties in the desert, his pickup trucks. Anita in his arms.

Dawson swallowed hard as he remembered the reason for this trip.

"Why do you think he was killed?" he asked.

"Sam? I don't know."

"Don't know or can't say?"

"It's being thoroughly investigated. Believe me. Everyone's on the case. Local, state, feds."

Dawson shook his head and looked out the window. Not what he wanted to hear. The whole thing stunk. He felt helpless once again, like when he was a kid and Sam had gone to prison, like when his ex-wife had told him she wanted a trial separation. *Shit. There was nothing "trial" about it.* He fought back the growing sense of loss and desperation.

"So what are you going to do?" Garcia asked.

"Find out what happened."

"I told you, the police and feds got this one covered."

"I don't trust them. They'll find out what happened. But I need to know why."

"Kyle Dawson, investigative reporter."

He looked at Garcia for a long moment. "Not for a story, but for me."

"It's not like D.C."

"Jesus, Raoul. I worked in Iraq and Afghanistan. Give me a break."

"Have you talked to Anita yet?"

"Why should I?"

"You two were something else in the day."

"In the day, Raoul. In the day. Times change. People change."

"That's what they say."

At Rancho la Peña, the sun still burned hot as it balanced on the horizon, spreading thick orange across the desert, throwing angular, sharp-edged shadows.

"Are you sure you want to stay with Jacquelyn?"

Dawson nodded. "Yeah. It'll be best. Mom has a small place there in Juárez. And she's always got relatives staying with her."

"Yeah," Garcia said with a sigh. "She does. But—"

"I'll see her tomorrow or the next day," Dawson said sharply. "I've got enough to deal with right now."

"Don't get cranky." Garcia guided his vehicle down curving paved streets that seemed more crowded with houses than before. Each was coated with stucco, topped with tile roofs, and fronted by yards of pea gravel, crushed red lava rock, and spiky cactus. The house that Dawson knew all too well sat on a cul-de-sac, a two-story, stucco-and-tile McMansion. For a moment he felt like a college kid coming home from a spring break. But the feeling faded as he thought about his stepmother inside and how distraught she must be.

Garcia turned into the wide driveway and eased to a stop. "We need to catch up."

"I'll be around."

http://wbp.bz/borderlanda

DARK VISIONS by JAMES BYRON HUGGINS

Joe Mac was a legendary homicide detective until his vision was lost in the line of duty and he was forced into retirement. Now he lives a life of darkness, his only friend being a huge Raven that Joe Mac names "Poe."

But when Joe Mac's grandson is murdered by an unknown killer, Joe emerges from his self-imposed solitude to resurrect the skills of the detective he once was. And, although he is blind, Joe Mac begins to hunt down his tiny grandson's murderer.

Led in some dark way by Poe, Joe Mac relentlessly tracks a force that literally owns the darkness, uses the darkness, and belongs to the darkness. For the force he is tracking has fed upon this world for thousands of years, and has never known defeat. It kills like demons, disappears like ghosts, and leaves nothing alive. But Joe Mac is determined to follow this road to Hell no matter the cost. He will find whoever it was that so mercilessly killed his young grandson, and he will deliver justice ... even if it costs him his life.

Fearlessly following the clues, he tracks the murderers of his grandson into the deepest, most dangerous heart of ancient nightmares. And with each haunting step into that darkness, Joe Mac realizes that he has somehow challenged a power that has destroyed nations and conquered continents. And the death they have delivered to the Earth reaches back to the beginning of the world ...

It is a battle that will take Joe Mac to the edge of sanity and beyond ...

http://wbp.bz/darkvisionsa

Thrillers You'll Love From WildBlue Press

HARD DOG TO KILL by Craig Holt

Stan Mullens is an American mercenary in the Congo who is sent into the jungle to track and kill a former colleague. Stan discovers that his victim hasn't done anything wrong. And as he struggles to survive, he is increasingly drawn in by the man he is supposed to kill. Ultimately Stan has to choose between old loyalties and new friends.

wbp.bz/hdtka

HUNTER by James Byron Huggins

In yet another experiment to extend human life, scientists accidentally unleash a force that might well be a terrible curse. Now an infected creature is loose in the Alaskan wilderness, and the America military is forced to ask the world's greatest tracker, Nathaniel Hunter, to locate the beast and destroy it before it reaches a populated area. **wbp.bz/huntera**

16 SOULS by John Nance

On takeoff from Denver during a winter blizzard, an airliner piloted by veteran Captain Marty Mitchell overruns a commuter plane from behind. Bizarrely, the fuselage of the smaller aircraft is tenuously wedged onto the huge right wing of his Boeing 757, leading Mitchell to an impossible life-or-death choice.

wbp.bz/16soulsa

BORDERLAND by Peter Eichstaedt

When a prominent land developer is brutally murdered on the U.S.-Mexico border, it's not just another cartel killing to journalist Kyle Dawson. The dead man is his father. Dawson, a veteran war correspondent, vows to uncover the truth.

wbp.bz/borderlanda